Also by Olga Bicos:

RISKY GAMES

WRAPPED IN WISHES

SWEETER THAN DREAMS

MORE THAN MAGIC

SANTANA ROSE

WHITE TIGER

BY MY HEART BETRAYED

PERFECT TIMING

Olga Bicos

Zebra Books
Kensington Publishing Corp.
http://www.zebrabooks.com

ZEBRA BOOKS are published by

Kensington Publishing Corp.
850 Third Avenue
New York, NY 10022

First Printing: August, 1998
10 9 8 7 6 5 4 3 2

Printed in the United States of America

For Andrew, who gave me wings.
Here's to earth below
sky above, straight and
level flying.

Acknowledgments

When my husband earned his pilot's license, I was his first solo. With Andrew as a still-wet-behind-the-ears pilot at the controls and nothing but air between me and mother earth, I earned a healthy respect for flying that day. Over the years, it has been my pleasure to get to know a few of the men and women who build and fly these babies, developing the technology that will take us into the future. A more maverick group doesn't exist. Here are the ones I leaned on hard for this book.

Mr. C. Johnson of CSA Engineering and Mr. L. P. Davis of Honeywell, John Tracy, Richard Snell, Don Edberg, Greg Smith, and Denise Matthews, of McDonnell Douglas, now Boeing, thank you for sharing your stories, knowledge, and theories—thank you for the inspiration. Russ and Lynn, thanks for having a great sense of humor.

I am incredibly grateful to David Weinberg and Anne Toulouse. I couldn't have done it without you guys. The brilliance was yours, the mistakes, all mine.

Lynn Brown, Carin Ritter, and Rob Cohen, friends and partners in the great publishing odyssey, your support and encouragement over the years have been invaluable. And, of course, Barbara Benedict, who just knows things. Amazing how you do that, girl.

Donna Scheffer, Shelly Zimmerman, Barbara Bennett, April Carlson, and Leila Gonzalez, a special thanks for the hand-holding as well as the expertise.

And finally, Andrew, who let me be his first solo. Thank you for all the adventures, my love. It's been a wonderful ride.

CRASH AND BURN

Countdown: 30 days; 22 hours; 15 minutes

Chapter One

She was talking to Eric, again.

He was seated across the aisle from Cherish, laughing at one of his own jokes, in top form—Eric Ballas, the performer with his wild white hair and sharp eyes, the business maverick who sang opera and told corny jokes. In the window seat beside him, Henry Shanks, the representative from Reck Enterprises, listened in, making himself part of the conversation. Cherish smiled, angling into the aisle of the cargo jet, asking Eric, *Come again?* Not quite catching his gist over the engine noise, but watching his lips as he formed the words . . .

Bang! A burst like cannon fire cracked through the cabin. For an instant, Cherish floated, suspended in midair like a trapeze act.

Her seat dropped out from under her, jamming the safety harness into her chest. The energy of it seemed to suck her in, yanking her head and shoulders back, swallowing her in one big gulp. She was falling out of a skyscraper, an amusement park ride in a sheer vertical drop. *Falling, falling . . . turning, tumbling.*

Debris skidded across the cabin, ricocheting off the bulkhead. She could see the reporter from *Aviation Weekly,* his mouth wide open but silent. Bits of shrapnel smacked into her shoulder, cut her face and arms; a force like a fist crushed into her chest. *I can't breathe!* The plane bucked in wild gyrations, sucking her down to earth . . . *Oh, God! Oh, God!*—

Just before the plane hit the ground, Cherish Malone snapped awake.

Her body sprang straight up in bed, a human jack-in-the-box. "Just a dream. Not real." The words came out in a rush. "Just a dream."

She reached across the bed for Conor . . . then fell back against the headboard, trying to catch her breath, staring at the space where Conor should have been, her brain registering that the space was empty. It had been empty for some time.

She closed her eyes and whispered, "Someday, you're going to stop doing that."

The dream came rushing back. Nightmare details she wanted to forget sprang into focus. Eric smiling . . . Henry Shanks, still strapped to his seat, flying across the cabin . . . the reporter screaming . . . *all of them, dead!* . . . Conor carrying her and Alec from the inferno that had once been the guts of the cargo jet.

Cherish slumped forward, knees up against her chest, her face buried in her hands. She wasn't a woman prone to panic. Now it held her by the throat, until she knew the taste of it in her mouth, its special scent. How it made her fingers vibrate with the adrenaline rush. *Panic so pure, it could make you high.* That's how Alec described it.

She pressed the heels of her palms against her eyes, fighting the urge to hyperventilate. As always, she struggled to remember what Eric had said to her from across the aisle . . . but the memory vanished in the grisly images of the crash. The accident seemed to lay in wait for her at night, living behind her eyelids, waking her the next morning like an alarm clock. And with it came the realization that—despite long therapy sessions and relaxation exercises—Cherish Malone could not put the past behind her.

She would never fly again.

A low buzzing registered in her ears, barely audible. She pushed her bangs back, her eyes searching out the noise in the semidark until she found the source. Her pager, on the nightstand, vibrating across the polished wood like a windup toy.

It was late enough that the sun bled through the blinds. She took a moment to orient herself. *Saturday morning, another bad night. You were trying to sleep in.* She'd turned the ringer off the phone. But she'd forgotten the pager.

She didn't recognize the number as she punched it into the phone, her knees tucked up beneath her chin. Her assistant picked up before the second ring.

"Cherish? They called from Edwards. It's bad."

For an instant, she thought she might have been sucked back into her nightmare. *Wake up!* But then her training kicked in and she threw the covers off, already swinging her feet over the bed. "Who's there now?"

"Chuck called it in. He's waiting for you at the site. God, Cherish. This was supposed to be routine."

She didn't want to hear body counts. *Dear God, how many were on the crew?* She asked, "Cameras?"

"Not yet. But you won't beat them there."

"We'll see. Tell Chuck I'm on my way."

Familiar with the protocol, Cherish Malone, public relations director for Marquis Aircraft, went to do some damage control.

Another crash.

* * *

The pulsing music filled the room like a heartbeat. Whenever possible, Alec Porter listened to The Stones when he made love to a woman.

He crushed out his cigarette and glanced down at the girl huddled beside him on the rumpled cot. The threadbare sheet covered her to her waist. She looked young. She *was* young. And ballerina-thin. Her body curved around his beneath the sheets, mimicking a fetal position. Alec reached down and stroked her hair.

"Cherish," he whispered.

The girl's eyes opened, revealing the shocking laser blue color that had drawn Alec from the first. "I hate it when you call me by her name."

He only grinned, digging his fingers into the blonde curls. "Then why do you wear the wig?" he asked, pulling off the cap of false hair, watching the girl's own brown hair tumble to her shoulders.

"Because it makes you happy." When she spoke, she looked directly into his eyes, never so much as blinking, appearing so innocent, almost perplexed by his question. As if it was obvious. Alec always came first.

He sighed and tossed the wig at the foot of the bed. "Go back to sleep," he told her.

The room ignited in a camera flash of lightning, followed by a flickering beyond the shutters. Sheets of rain candy-coated the panes of glass as thunder drowned out the lyrics of "You Can't Always Get What You Want." The rain had hiked the humidity to nearly unbearable. Alec turned to get out of bed, but the butterfly touch of her hands coaxed him back.

"I want you to love me as much as you love her," she told him, her eyes showing a fierce determination.

He shook his head, saying, "Impossible," still smiling, still watching those clairvoyant eyes. He was drawn to her determination, intoxicated by it, another reason he'd fallen for her. He watched as she sat up, leaning toward him. A very desirable, very beautiful woman.

"Then again," he said, bringing his mouth to hers.

Eventually, he reached for the wig, coaxing as he whispered, "Put it on." Which she did, whimpering when he told her against her mouth, "Only you, baby. Always you." And he meant it . . . but only after she wore the wig.

This time, he waited for her soft snores, certain that she was asleep before he sat up in their bed. She usually slept after they made love, as if she'd used every ounce of strength on him. She was such a tiny little thing. A waif. A perfectly delicious waif who would do as she was told.

She rolled away, the wig slipping off. Alec picked it up, turning it in his hand. At that moment, he felt Cherish's absence with an intensity that actually surprised him. It had been more than a year.

"It doesn't do you justice," he said under his breath.

Alec rose naked from the bed, dropping the wig to the sheets. Outside, he pulled up one of the cane chairs on the veranda. The house faced the ocean. That's what he loved best about Nicaragua. Cheap ocean property. And the fact that he could be nobody here. The lease said F. Leiter, one of his many aliases. Not that he was sure they still cared. But soon. *Yes, very soon* . . . Everything depended on timing.

He stepped back into the house to the *screech, clap* of the screen door, and turned on The Stones's CD again, slipping the volume down to a purr. The storm had passed, but you could still taste it in the air. He grabbed a package of Dunhills off a table where the colored images of a music video flashed across the screen-saver of his laptop computer. He stepped out again, balancing the chair on two legs as he hummed to the music coming from inside. Lighting the cigarette, he closed his eyes, remembering Cherish.

Cherish the Strong. Cherish the Beautiful. Cherish, his Forever Love.

He inhaled the smoke deep into his lungs, then opened his eyes to the dawn breaking through the clouds, making the crashing waves curl and glow like the inside of a shell. He squinted against the smoke, thinking Cherish was like those waves. Nothing could stop them; the storm only made them stronger.

Maybe they could beat him, but not Cherish. She was too pure. His Valkyrie of Good.

He tossed the cigarette in a quick underhand into the wet sand. Inside the house, he put on trousers and made himself some coffee, the local blend, thick and hot and sweet. He'd never needed a lot of sleep.

With his coffee and the pack of Dunhills in hand, he sat down in front of the laptop, bringing up a program he'd written to route his message. He'd learned a few tricks over the last few years, enough to keep him alive.

He typed:

    Dearest Cherish,
    Someone tried to kill me today. Watch
    your back. Contact Conor. He'll know
    what to do.

He smiled, lighting another cigarette, sucking the smoke into his lungs, and exhaling through his nose. ''There you go, love.''

Behind him, the woman on the bed moaned in her sleep. He listened, waiting until she quieted down. He hated her nightmares. Creepy stuff that, at times, made her scream in her sleep. He should wake her anyway. They both had a plane to catch.

Alec turned back to the computer. On the keyboard, he finished his message, typing:

    P.S. You should have picked me, little
    girl.

Chapter Two

The horizon tilted on its axis, then vanished into a wall of searing blue sky. One weightless moment later, the earth came racing up, straight at him.

Conor Mitchell felt the g-forces nail his ass into the seat. He pulled the stick between his legs and eased the power forward, listening as the propeller hummed into new life. The next roller coaster dip punched him in the gut; the straps from the five-point safety harness bit into the muscles of his chest.

He smiled as the horizon leveled. For that single instant, Conor Mitchell didn't have a care in the world.

"Oh, God. Oh, God. Ohmigod, ohmigod, ohmigod."

The prayer crackled into his headset. Conor checked the time. Still twenty minutes to go. *She ain't gonna make it.* "You have your husband in your sights now, Elise. This is when you want to take a shot at him."

"How did I talk myself into this?" The woman seated to his right in the military trainer didn't sound hysterical, just getting there. "And that camera is pointing right at my face. Just what I wanted. A lasting memory of me throwing up."

"Concentrate on the target. Make believe you can shoot him right out of the sky." Sometimes, that worked. Distraction.

On the two heads-up displays, the iridescent green lines of a bull's-eye centered on the plane ahead. The electronic tracking system locked on target. Elise squeezed the gun trigger. "Die, David. Die!"

"That's a direct hit," he said into the headset. The "enemy" plane obligingly rolled into a vertical dive, trailing smoke, while the video camera on board caught the action, a sure hit at Elise Walden's next dinner party. "Great job, Elise. You got the kill."

Conor made the switch from hunter to hunted, easing into it. Not everybody wanted the E-ticket ride. Some, like Elise Walden, just wanted to get it over with in one piece.

"I think I'm going to be sick," she said into his headset.

Receiving you loud and clear. "Marc," he told his brother-in-law, "that's a Bravo-Alpha-Romeo-Foxtrot." To the customer, he added, "We'll be heading down, now."

"Thank . . . you . . . God."

Marc jetted past, executing a perfect series of barrel rolls in the Marchetti SF260, smoke trails spiraling behind the military trainer. Conor watched, loving the beauty of it. Marc had always been an elegant flyer. To Elise, sweating it out beside him, he said, "Your husband should be following shortly."

Fifteen minutes later, Conor had the plane down the airstrip at Chino. Elise Walden, a woman in her mid-forties, sat on a bench outside the hangar used by Dogfights Incorporated, the flying school where, for a price, you could play at flying a military trainer, *Top Gun* style.

She'd piled her parachute and flight helmet on the bench beside her and was leaning forward, her head between her knees. The flight suit she wore was all part of the show. Conor held out a paper cup of water, letting her take her time. When she came up for air, she smiled wanly.

"I feel like an idiot." She took the water, self-consciously running her fingers through curls that had somehow survived the flight helmet. What they could do with hair spray these days, Conor thought. Go figure.

"All morning you had me in class, telling me how it was going to be." She cradled the cup in both hands. "Honestly, I thought I'd die up there."

"It happens," he said, letting her know she wasn't the first to get sick on her seven-hundred-a-pop roller coaster.

"I listened to everything you said. I could *picture* myself in that cockpit. I thought, this time I won't give David any reason to lecture me. 'Why did you insist on coming, honey?' " she said, obviously mimicking her husband. " 'Tommy would have loved to be here instead.' Tommy. That's our son." She said it with a smile. "The boys usually do this sort of thing together. I guess I was starting to feel left out." She shook her head. "I thought I could do it."

Conor squinted up at the sky, used to this part as well. They always opened up afterward, whether the ride was good or bad. He had brought them close to something they had never experienced before. A brush with death or a taste of heaven, it didn't matter . . . they always wanted to talk afterward.

"Here's Marc with your husband." He watched his brother-in-law drop down to the tarmac and give a thumbs-up. Then, thinking she had a point about old David, he said, "You're going to want to watch this, Elise."

Elise Walden frowned as her husband staggered out of the cockpit, barely making it down before Marc grabbed his arm and helped him scramble to stable ground. She sat straighter, sensing something was wrong, then slowly rose to stand next to Conor. They both watched David Walden, the chief financial officer of a multinational corporation specializing in electrical fixtures, shuffle forward a few steps, then quickly turn away. He puked his guts out.

Elise's face stayed perfectly fixed in a deadpan expression.

Conor thought maybe it was shock, how she stood there, just staring. But then, she smiled.

"Please, don't take this wrong." Her voice was steady, barely above a whisper. "I've been married twenty-two years and I love my husband dearly." She handed Conor the cup of water. "You just earned a big tip."

"Always keep the customer happy," he said.

"David, you poor thing." Her voice now loud enough for her husband to hear, she jogged over to him. "Here, let me help you, sweetie."

Conor chucked the water from the cup and watched the steam mist up from the cement. Another beautiful day in Chino hell. Slipping on his aviator glasses, he headed toward the familiar skyline of palm trees and hangars surrounding the square stump of the tower. He'd let Marc finish up with the Waldens. His brother-in-law was good at this, always chumming the customers, his excitement part of the experience as he shouted commands to track and lock on the enemy, making it all more real. Not Conor's style, not the acting, anyway.

Behind him, the airfield's horizon of concrete shimmered miragelike from fumes and heat. It was one of those blinding hot days. The sky was a perfect robin's egg blue, a condition pilots called "severe clear," where there wasn't a cloud in the sky and the visibility made you think you could see forever.

On days like this, he missed it most, the utter high of pulling a few g's while you sucked oxygen from your mask, seeing how far you could push the laws of physics. He'd read once that even a gray out from the high-g maneuvers in training could get you. They likened it to a near-death experience, where you see this tunnel of light, and your life flashes by like a movie. Pilots got hooked on the euphoria just before they passed out.

Maybe that was him. Hooked. And no matter how many hours he clocked in on the Marchetti, it wasn't going to touch what he'd had before.

He heard Marc coming up behind him. His brother-in-law nodded back to Walden, who was easing into his Mercedes sports coupe, hanging on to his wife for all he was worth.

"I got to give him credit," he told Conor. "The guy lasted. Was she losing it?"

"She was okay."

Conor crushed the paper cup into a ball and lobbed it into one of the metal drums the airfield used as trash cans, scoring three points. The call letters Conor had given spelled BARF, meaning his passenger had had enough and it was time for Marc to do some fancy flying. In his experience, things just worked out better if the decision to call it quits was mutual.

Beside him, Marc gave Conor a once-over. "You know what, Conor? I do believe you're getting skinny."

Conor glanced at his brother-in-law. "Is that right." At six foot two, weighing one hundred and ninety pounds, Conor was far from skinny.

"Scrawny. Geena was just saying so this morning. Worried about you. Wants you over for dinner tomorrow night."

The two men hiked up the steps to the second floor where the school leased office space in the tower complex. Conor smiled, knowing exactly what his sister, Geena, wanted. Good old Marc.

"Dinner?" he said, playing along. "I don't know, Marc. I have a lot of paperwork to catch up on."

Which he did. Miller's doctoral thesis, *Advance Curing Techniques for Composites,* waited on the pile back home. Composite materials was Conor's specialty and it was one of his responsibilities at the university where he worked part-time to act as a reader for the engineering students, grilling them during the technical presentations that would earn them advanced degrees. But that wasn't where Marc was going with this so Conor waited, giving his brother-in-law more rope.

When Conor reached for the door, Marc stopped him. He motioned Conor aside, toward the rail and away from the office.

The sunlight hit Marc's hair like a signal fire, making Conor recall when Geena first came up with her husband's call sign, Lucky. Marc had taken offense, a little piqued that she might think his father—a retired Air Force colonel—had snagged him a spot at the prestigious academy where they'd met. But Geena had set him straight. "You look like Lucky. You know, on the Lucky Charms cereal box. The leprechaun?" All that red hair and freckles.

Conor figured Marc had fallen for her then. And though wary of Marc's good looks and overflow of charm, Geena was a smart girl. It hadn't taken long to see that Marc was putty in her hands. Which was exactly why Marc was standing here, doing Geena's dirty work.

Marc took off his aviator glasses, squinting against the sun. "You want to do me a favor and come to dinner tomorrow?"

Conor reached into the pocket of his flight suit for a cigar and lit up. Geena didn't allow smoking in the office, and he figured this might take a while. "Am I going to like her?" he asked when he had the cigar going at a slow burn.

Marc shrugged. "You know your sister. Looks like Cindy Crawford with the brains of Sandra Day O'Connor. Not to mention that winning personality."

"Absolutely." Conor stared out over the airfield to watch a Citabria practicing touch-and-go landings.

Marc said, "I'm searching my brain here to figure out how I can say 'you owe me one, buddy,' and I'm coming up blank."

Conor rolled the cigar smoke in his mouth, surprised that he was actually thinking about it—Geena was always trying to set him up.

But maybe his sister was right. More than a year had passed. Long enough for what-ifs and second-guessing.

"Lasagna?" he asked.

Marc smiled. "Your favorite."

Clipping the cigar between his teeth, Conor thumped Marc on the back. The two men strolled inside the school, immediately hit by a blast of lukewarm air from the air conditioner hissing from the window. The warranty had run out last week, two days before Marc noticed the coolant leaking.

Still, despite its many nuisances, the flight school was home. A year and a half ago Conor had come on board to sit in the cockpit of a military trainer, the E-ticket into the skies for those who could afford the ride. Marc and Geena had sunk their savings into the school and it was in trouble—they were going to lose everything. Marc had come to Conor for help. A lot of hard work and some innovative financing later, the three of them were going to make it.

Marc walked up to Geena, his wife, and gave her a long slow kiss on the mouth, still making a show of it after twelve years of marriage. Conor grinned, the cigar lodged between his teeth, thinking they made a sight. Geena, a flat-chested Sophia Loren, kissing her carrot-topped husband. Funny thing, how all three kids came out looking like Marc.

Squinting against the cigar smoke, Conor stepped over to the white board to check out the upcoming week's schedule. He found a sea of red, green, and blue marker. *Completely booked.* This was what life was all about, he thought. Saving the school—helping Geena, Marc, and the kids. By next year, Dogfights would show a profit, which was a good thing. It was going to cost a mint to put those three kids of Geena and Marc's through college.

"Take it outside, Conor."

He looked up innocently, slipping the cigar from his mouth. Before he could defend himself, Geena had the cigar in hand, was scraping the ashes on the lip of the trash can.

She handed it back to Conor, unlit. He resisted the urge to comment. Dominican. Not the best, but not bad. Pocketing the cigar, he turned back to Marc, about to ask about Monday's schedule.

That's when he saw it. The thirteen-inch television set at the back of the office. And the woman whose face dominated the screen.

One weightless moment later, the ground came racing up, straight at him.

Geena had the volume down and Conor grabbed the remote control off her desk, going on automatic, pumping it up a couple of notches so he could hear.

She was seated at a table in a small auditorium jammed with reporters, looking as always like the complete professional. She preferred suits, the kind with skirts that fell properly to just below the knees. She thought it made people take her more seriously.

"Cher," he said, pronouncing it like the French word, *chère*, meaning dear.

"It is her, isn't it?" Geena said, coming up behind him.

"The love of my life," he answered.

Marc let out a low whistle, stepping up beside Geena.

She looked the same, but not the same. The hair was different. Shorter, so that she could barely tuck it behind her ears. The cherub face looked thinner, too. Not gaunt, not like those models with the cheekbones. But she'd lost the baby fat he'd always teased her about.

He remembered he'd thought she had a nice face. Cute. The girl next door. With eyes a "severe clear" blue. Conor had his Italian mother's coloring and a five-inch scar that cut straight across his left brow to his cheek. He could imagine how they'd looked together. The Big Bad Wolf dating Little Bo Peep.

It had been a year and a half since they'd seen each other.

"At the moment, we don't have the facts to report." Cherish Malone spoke directly into the camera, her voice metered and firm, promising she would never lie or withhold the truth. Her trust-me tone had always been her greatest asset in public relations. "While we are deeply distressed by today's events, we are committed to discovering the exact cause of the tragedy.

We are taking every step to ensure that this valuable program will move forward.''

"Was there any transmission from the crew before the crash?''

"How many were on board?''

The questions were directed at Cher, but she handed the microphone to the guy at the middle of the table, to her right— Chuck Odell, the program manager and a senior vice president at Marquis Aircraft where she worked. Conor had caught the tail end of the press conference.

In the camera flash of lights, she didn't even blink. Like the good little PR person she was, she let Chuck do the talking. It was about legitimacy. No one trusted spin doctors like her to tell the whole truth.

"The pilot and copilot were on board, along with the flight engineer, and the test engineer,'' Chuck finished solemnly.

"Did anyone survive?''

Chuck glanced at Cher, catching her eye. He shook his head.

What followed was a frenzy of questions fired from every direction. Conor caught the quick flash of panic on Chuck Odell's face, watched Cher, on cue, take the mike.

"When we recover the XC-23 WingMaster, we will have an exact picture of what happened. At this point, we won't speculate on how or why the plane crashed.''

"My ass,'' Conor said, hearing it in her voice. She was scared.

Conor turned away, cutting off the buzz of words continuing from the television. "I'll be in my office.''

"Sure,'' Geena called after him. "No big deal. Why watch the woman you almost married on television—''

He shut the door with the back of his foot.

He tried to pretend she was a ghost, some television personality that had never touched his life. An actress he'd fantasized about enough that the dreams he'd come up with had a sense of the familiar . . . until a little voice inside his head butted in with the truth. Cher wasn't the ghost.

A familiar tightness filled his chest. He forced his mind blank, shutting off those images from the past. Cher, the accident . . .

He sat down, trying to regain his earlier mood—losing it in a flash of anger when he thought about her letters. Those damn letters. She sent one every week. They came in Thursday's mail. Cherish was nothing if not punctual. And always, always, he read them, convincing himself that the fact that he hadn't answered a one had cut the ties.

Only, there was the ever-present background noise from the NASA channel on the television while he worked in his office here at Dogfights—the portable at the university set to the same channel. He told himself he wasn't listening for her name, hoping to get a glimpse of her as he had today.

Right.

Compulsion. Obsession. Cherish Malone.

He thought about one letter in particular. His all-time personal favorite. The one that began:

Dearest Asshole,
Just to let you know how truly pathetic I am—to give you that satisfaction—I waited until dawn. You, of course, never showed up.

For their wedding. A year and a half ago, he'd left Cherish Malone waiting at the altar.

He knew everything there was to know about her. That she practiced those casual gestures for the television in front of the mirror . . . that she played billiards and had a love-hate relationship with her father. That she'd dreamed of getting her doctorate in engineering, but settled for peddling Marquis's image to the customer. The information came in letters he read and reread, not because he wanted to, but because he deserved it, letting her have her say.

And he knew the things she regretted most since the accident. Her deathly fear of flying, a serious handicap for the director of public relations at an aircraft company.

And, of course, Conor, the man whose character she'd synopsized in the last line of the letter that had started it all.

Conor, you idiot. You broke my heart.

Chapter Three

The lights in the auditorium made it unbearably hot.

"Pour me another glass, will you, Chuck?" Cherish waited for the next rapid-fire question from the reporters that flanked them on all sides. She nodded, giving the go-ahead to the new guy at *Aviation Weekly,* hoping against hope for something she could use to turn this thing around.

"Wouldn't you call this a serious setback?"

No, Cherish thought irritably. *We want all our planes to crash. It keeps my job interesting.* But she cut off the sarcasm and concentrated on her answer. Normally, she would have let Chuck Odell, Marquis's senior vice president, steer the course. But while Chuck was good on the technical end, things were getting personal.

"Let's not lose sight of the fact that this stage of the XC-23 WingMaster prototype has safely flown twenty-one missions," she said, trying to get them back on track. There was nothing worse than leaving the press with unanswered questions, breeding speculation. But until they recovered the plane, there wasn't much she could give them.

"The XC-23 stands to revolutionize air travel by significantly improving the lift-to-drag ratio. Its new airfoil design results in a wing that is thirty percent lighter."

She felt Lori, her best friend and the media specialist for Marquis, kick her under the table. Unlike Cherish, who was herself an engineer, Lori Sweeny was straight PR, no technical background and their safety valve against engineering lingo. If it didn't make it past Lori, it sure as heck wasn't going to make the front page.

"The goal of our wing design is to make aircraft more energy efficient," Cherish said, choosing her words carefully. Try to get some positive press for aerospace in Southern California and you might as well wait for the Second Coming—but the minute there's a crash, you're the lead story, top of the hour. "Understand, the WingMaster uses a third less fuel," she said using the cargo jet's name without its designation. "Not only is this an environmental consideration, but it will greatly reduce the cost of air travel. Our wing design stands to keep the United States exactly where it deserves to be, at the top of a highly competitive field. Keeping jobs here, giving us a technical edge."

The passion in her voice wasn't a sell job. The last three years, she had given her life's blood to the XC-23 program . . . had almost given it her life. A year and a half ago, she'd been on board the first-phase prototype when it crashed during a simple demonstration flight. It was the Challenger all over again. Three people died that day and it was a miracle of God that she hadn't been one of them.

The subsequent inquiry determined the crash was a result of pilot error—the only reason the program hadn't been canceled. Her company had worked hard to get the second-phase prototype up and flying, working with Reck Enterprises, the prime contractor for the WingMaster, pushing themselves to deliver a top-notch product to the Air Force. Until today, she'd always thought they'd done just that.

Cherish took another drink of water, buying herself a few seconds. Maybe Reck Enterprises, a twenty-billion-dollar company, could withstand the hit if the XC-23 lost its funding, but not Marquis Aircraft. Right now, more than two thousand Marquis employees depended on her keeping the headlines from pushing the Pentagon into shutting them down.

"As for today's setback," she said, trying to sound both calm and professional. "Until we know exactly what went wrong, it's hard to know the effects—"

There was a flurry of movement near the entry doors, bringing on a groundswell of chatter that drowned out her words. Cherish could see a ripple of bodies moving like a current through the auditorium where they were holding the makeshift press conference at Edwards Air Force Base. The wave dissipated at the edge of the crowd; the front line shifted. Like Moses parting the Red Sea, a man stepped through.

"What the hell is he doing here?" Chuck whispered, his hand covering the microphone. "I thought they wanted us to handle this?"

Russell Reck, the president and CEO of Reck Enterprises, made his way up to the dais, the famous hawkish nose prominently at the lead, the full, almost petulant mouth balanced by sage brown eyes. She'd seen those same features on the cover of *Time* and *Newsweek* . . . had him pointed out across a crowded room.

Russell Reck was one of life's little ironies. Those hunched shoulders, that slight build, the styled-but-mousy gray hair, you wouldn't think much to look at him . . . then you remembered he was worth a few billion.

Someone pulled up a chair beside Cherish. She scooted closer to Lori, making room.

"Holy moly," Lori whispered. " 'The Wrecker' himself."

Using one hand to unbutton his tan cashmere jacket, no doubt custom-made in Milan, Reck took his seat front and center. He nodded to Cherish and maneuvered the microphone closer.

"For those of you who don't know me, let me introduce myself." He folded his perfectly manicured hands on the table, the picture of confidence. She saw it then, the aura of power that quieted the room, emanating from him despite his average appearance.

"My name is Russell Reck. I am the president and chief executive officer of Reck Enterprises, a company that, in conjunction with the government and Marquis Aircraft, is responsible for the design and development of the XC-23." As he spoke, he removed a piece of paper from the inside pocket of his jacket. Unfolded the single sheet. "I have a few recent facts about the crash of our experimental craft that, if my colleagues here will permit, I would like to pass on to you, the men and women of the press."

He turned to look at Cherish, as if waiting for permission to continue . . . while she sat there at a complete loss for words.

Aerospace companies often teamed on projects, like Lockheed Martin and Boeing working on the F-22 Raptor, LockMart being the prime contractor. But teamwork in aerospace was a tricky business. It was like being in an *Indiana Jones* movie, you had to choose the right stones to step on or hazard a poisoned spear zinging at your head. The idea was, if anything went wrong, you wanted to hang together, put up a united front. It was usually in everyone's best interest. Usually.

She kept glancing at that little piece of paper flattened out in front of Reck, fighting the sensation that she was staring down some deep, dark precipice, waiting for a little nudge.

She didn't have long to wait.

"At 7:15 this morning"—Reck spoke in a quiet, self-assured voice—"the pilot of the XC-23 radioed the tower that they heard a loud noise, upon which they immediately lost control and went into a downward spiral. That was the last transmission the tower received. The pilot never regained control."

Cherish's light wool-blend felt as if it were shrinking on her body, becoming a straightjacket. That morning, the head of PR at Reck Enterprises, her counterpart, had called to ask if Marquis could handle the press conference for both companies. Highly irregular, but she'd called Chuck and set it up. Now, Russell Reck shows up with a prepared speech?

"We continued to receive flight data," Reck said in the hushed room. "Our initial analysis of that data confirm that the plane suddenly yawed to the right and pitched downward, we believe due to some sort of structural failure, causing the plane to fall into an unrecoverable spin."

Beside her, Cherish felt Chuck stiffen. Sudden yaw. Downward pitch. Structural failure.

The wing. He was talking about the wing. The wing Marquis had designed.

"Working together with our partners on the XC-23 team," Reck continued, "we hope to learn the exact nature of the failure as soon as is technologically possible. We have the government's complete support in this effort. As I speak to you, two helicopters are scouring the area of the crash and a recovery team is on its way to secure the site."

Cherish's mouth did a fair imitation of the Sahara. Before heading out to the base, she'd called the Air Force. They hadn't mentioned any rescue operation, only that they needed to convene the investigative board.

Russell Reck scanned the crowd of reporters, seeing that, indeed, each man and woman was hanging on his every word— while Cherish sat dumbstruck, unable to voice the fears running through her head. *He's going to blame Marquis. And he has the government's support. They're going to drop this on our lap, the subcontractor. The little guy.*

"Now, if there is anything further I or Chuck here can answer?"

Instantly, the buzz of questions swarmed to life, the pitch and volume of voices rising in a swell. From the corner of her eye, Cherish watched Russell Reck point to a woman in a yellow suit at the front of the pack. Almost in slow motion, she saw the CNN reporter glance down at her notes, open her mouth. "Then you suspect the cause of the crash—"

"I just wanted to add"—Cherish interrupted the CNN reporter, formulating her defense as she went along—"that Marquis and Reck Enterprises have worked closely together to create the innovative design for the XC-23." *Rambling, rambling. Think. Think!* "It has been our great privilege to work hand in hand with Reck, a company that has overseen every single aspect of our efforts in the current wing design and with whom we share all of our accomplishments."

As well as any blame they want to shovel our way.

She reached for Reck's hand, giving it a squeeze as if the two were pals, working through a difficult time together. "I am certain Russ here would agree that, despite today's setback, the current team, brought together by our country's Air Force, will affect military, and commercial, aviation in the most positive way possible."

Beside her, Lori scribbled on her yellow pad: *Should I break into "God Bless America" now?*

Cherish gave a tight smile. No one was going to ambush Marquis. No way.

Staring out over the crowd, she made eye contact where she could. "We are building X-planes, ladies and gentlemen. Certainly, we have moved beyond the days when they were falling out of the sky, as they did in the fifties—safety is our prime consideration. But there are risks."

"Risks worth a human life?" the CNN reporter asked.

"We take every safety precaution imaginable," she said, because it was true or she couldn't have been part of the project. "The WingMaster is a plane that will put the United States at an incredible advantage . . . but never at the expense of a test pilot's life. The final phase of the project will be on hold until we discover the exact nature of the failure. But I think Russ, here, would agree." She smiled winningly at Reck, a man with whom she hadn't so much as exchanged a word before this moment. "It would be irresponsible to speak about the cause of today's glitch"— *Oh, please Lord. I didn't really say glitch? Did I say glitch?*—"without first allowing that same team of experts to analyze the data and the investigative board to convene. Russell?"

Reck took the microphone Cherish passed off to him. For the first time, she noticed his eyes were almost too perfectly almond shaped, the lower and upper lid of near equal proportions.

Lizard eyes, she decided, the image somehow making her feel better. More than a billion in personal wealth and he couldn't do anything about those lizard eyes.

"To answer any questions on a specific cause of the crash would at this point appear premature." Reck spoke in the same self-assured tones, doing some fancy backpedaling. "Let me just say that the matter is being dealt with using the consideration and care it deserves."

"As you know, the investigative board is made up of a group of independent experts." Cherish ended on what she thought was a more positive note for Marquis. "We hope to have something more by this afternoon's press conference. Thank you, ladies and gentlemen. I think that's all—"

"Ms. Malone." Another reporter, an older man toward the back whom she didn't recognize, stood, shouting over the others. "When was the last time you flew?"

The question struck her as odd. She responded, "Pardon?"

As the man repeated his question, Cherish felt every eye in the room focus on her. She didn't recognize the reporter, but she knew most of the key players in the room. It was her business to get chummy with the press and she'd always thought she'd bought herself a little good will here, had insulated herself from this kind of questioning. But now she saw that the press conference had just taken a very different turn.

It wouldn't be difficult to find out. Certainly, anyone in the business could have heard the rumors: The woman heading public relations at Marquis had an irrational fear of flying. But she couldn't understand—couldn't fathom—that anyone would bother to focus on her, such a peripheral player.

"My personal experience aside—"

"Isn't it true, Ms. Malone, that you haven't flown in well over a year because you don't think the aircraft your company builds are fit to fly? Something that today's crash appears to prove. Marquis is responsible for the wing design on quite a few commercial aircraft flying today. Why don't you let us in on the inside information that's keeping you off those planes, Ms. Malone? For all our sakes?"

Beneath the table, she could feel Lori squeezing her hand, jump-starting her. "I'm not sure where you're getting your information," Cherish argued, sounding too defensive, "but in the last fifteen years, no commercial aircraft with a Marquis design has been involved in a fatality."

"Eighteen months ago, Ms. Malone, you yourself flew on . . ." He flipped through some pages. "The first incarnation of the XC-23 WingMaster. The phase-one prototype. It was during a routine demonstration flight that the jet crashed—"

"I think we're getting off track here," Chuck said, angry now. "That incident can in no way—"

"There were three fatalities that day?"

"Pilot error is hardly—"

"Ms. Malone, have you flown in one of your aircraft since?"

"I haven't flown on *any* aircraft since," she answered.

Chuck leaned forward, a dogged expression on his face. "Which isn't part of her job as director of public relations. I'm on one of our planes almost every week—"

"The flight you're referring to"—Russell Reck's voice boomed across the room without the aid of the microphone—"the first-phase prototype of the current experimental craft *never* suffered from a technical problem. Not even so much as a backed-up toilet."

Nervous laughter skipped across the room, changing the highly charged atmosphere. Reck gave Cherish a significant look, telling her clearly, this time, she wouldn't interrupt.

"It was determined by the investigative board," he said, "that the crash resulted not because of any design failure. Pilot error was the complete and sole cause."

He folded his hands and leaned forward, his earnest body language translating to the audience, once again, holding their attention. "That day, Ms. Malone nearly lost her life; she and the copilot were dragged from a blazing inferno by the plane's pilot. She saw three people die—one of them, my partner, the late Henry Shanks." His voice held, echoing his partner's name in the taut silence. "Ms. Malone has an engineering background. She knows the science behind these planes; statistically, they *are* the safest means of travel. But after the trauma of that day, I wouldn't blame her if she hesitates to fly."

The implication being clear. No one in their right mind could.

"Thank you very much, ladies and gentlemen," Cherish said, standing, stopping the next flurry of questions. "That ends our press conference for now. There will be a follow-up in three hours. We'll let you know if we hear anything sooner than that."

She turned immediately to Russell Reck, now standing beside her. Doing her damnedest to keep her smile in place, she said pleasantly, "I'm sure our team will be contacting you for a copy of the telemetry," she said, referring to the experimental data radioed to the ground during the test flight. "Working together, we're certain to resolve the current crisis in the best possible manner for both our companies."

Before Reck could respond, she spoke to Chuck behind her. "I was just telling Russell that you would be going over the flight data with his people."

Chuck Odell had on his bulldog face. Though in his late fifties—his hair white, his eyes a paler blue these days—he'd once been an Olympic contender. Greco-Roman wrestling.

Middleweight class. He kept in shape. Right now, he looked as if he could still go a few rounds. "It doesn't help anyone to go public with information unknown to all the team members."

The Wrecker's lips thinned into a smile. "My mistake, Chuck."

Before Chuck could get into it with Reck, putting on a nice show for the crowd of reporters closing in, Cherish grabbed his arm and nodded to Lori. Her assistant ran interference, her solid five foot, two inch frame breaking their way through the crowd like a fullback. Cherish had never seen anyone so agile in three-inch spiked heels. If you valued your toes, you moved.

Cherish smiled her response to the men and women of the press, promising more information at the next session—praying they'd have better answers by then. She kept her eyes on Lori's for-god's-sake-why-didn't-they-tell-me-it-was-purple? "aubergine" highlighted hair, the moussed curls bobbing ahead like a lighthouse. Only when they reached the exit, did Cherish turn around, searching the crowd for Russell Reck.

They stood six deep around him, microphones and recorders raised to catch every word. But those lizard eyes were focused on Cherish. Slowly, he raised his hand and gave her a short salute.

The thought struck: He could have planned it, the reporter's attack, even his very rescue of her.

"That bastard," Chuck said, catching her attention as he held the door open. "I swear to God, Cherish. They told me the telemetry was marginal."

Like all experimental craft during test flights, the XC-23 WingMaster had been instrumented with strain gauges and accelerometers. The strain gauges were glued onto the plane's structure and wired into a data acquisitions system, a computer that would take readings every tenth of a second and store the data.

Telemetry was the process by which the data was radioed to the ground. Reck Enterprises, the prime contractor, ran the flight tests and, therefore, had control over all the flight data. But they were supposed to keep Chuck informed.

"They told me the telemetry had too much noise. They wouldn't know shit until they cleaned up the data." Chuck shook his head, looking like a disgruntled bear. "Useless garbage, they told me."

Useless garbage Russell Reck had just tried to use against Marquis.

"Interesting how all of Reck's people were either out of reach or too busy to show for the press conference," Cherish said.

"My thoughts exactly," Lori answered, sending one finely tweezed brow up like a flare.

"I still can't believe they sent us here blind," Chuck said, shaking his head. "By the way. Good save back there. Nicely done."

Cherish frowned, still watching The Wrecker, wondering about her sudden bout of paranoia. But in this business, one woman's paranoia was another's parachute.

She turned to follow Chuck, exiting, stage right, behind Lori. "We need to find out what went wrong with the plane," Cherish said. "Then it will be nicely done."

Late that night, Cherish sat at her desk, her head in her hands. It always came afterward, the collapse.

There was a time when she could raid the mini bar in her hotel room to get through it, those cute little bottles going a long way toward easing the shakes and the occasional bout of tears. But Lori did all their air travel now.

After the accident, there were times when, if she thought too hard about it, she couldn't breathe. It was as if her body forgot how the thing was done. She would have to concentrate, convince herself that, yes indeed, her air passages were clear and working. Taking another breath was a simple matter of pulling the oxygen into her lungs. In, out. In, out. That's it. *You got it, girl.*

She looked up, fighting that sensation now. It had been a long night. She'd managed three press conferences, the others going smoother after Reck's people started to cooperate, admitting the data needed more analysis before going public with any theories about the cause of the crash. *Please, God. Not the wing.* Now, nearing midnight, they'd called it a day, though she'd left Lori behind to do some follow-up.

Cherish closed her eyes, drained. She kept thinking about the crew; those final seconds . . . their poor families.

After a moment, she held her hands out, parallel to her desk. They were still shaking.

Stress. That's what the doctor had diagnosed, which fell in line nicely with her panic over flying. All that expensive therapy, and she couldn't even get through the visualization exercises. *Imagine yourself calmly walking up the stairwell toward the plane's door. . . .*

Yeah. Right. And two seconds later . . . she couldn't breathe.

Cherish fisted her hands, standing. "When all else fails. There's always work."

At the bank of file cabinets lining her wall, she opened a drawer and flipped through the folders inside, stopping when she came across one file in particular. Her fingers pushed back the tab labeled *Ballas.* She closed her eyes, picturing Eric Ballas, that charmer's face and its crown of white hair as he sat across the aisle from her on the cargo jet, the image still fresh in her mind from her nightmare that morning.

Before his death, Eric Ballas had been part of the team working on the XC-23 WingMaster. His company, Joystick, had been responsible for the jet's special composite, a graphite epoxy material used to reinforce the prototype's structure. Cherish pulled out the Ballas file and scanned the pages of text and calculations. The folder contained Cherish's last work as an engineer, a small but exciting program between Eric's company and Marquis involving research into "synthetic metals," the newest and hottest theory on composite materials. Eric had always thought synthetic metals represented the future of aerospace, and Cherish had agreed.

She sighed, closing the file folder. Unlike Marquis, Eric wouldn't have been caught between Reck and a hard place. Not Eric. He'd found a way around the dilemma of private enterprise hemmed in by government regulations, never relying on government contracts as a major source of revenue. His company depended on an innovative use of cheap Russian think tanks. The setup had helped both Eric and the Russian scientists: Eric got his research at bargain basement prices while keeping food on the table for men and women who—disenfranchised by the fall of the Soviet Empire—might otherwise be tempted to work for the bad guys. Saddam, for example, could use a few of those nuclear physicists now driving cabs in Moscow.

"We miss you, Eric," she said softly, slipping the file back into place. "We needed more guys like you."

Cherish snagged the press release Lori wanted and shut the file drawer with her hip, suddenly more depressed than ever. Enough that, when she passed her desk, she stopped to look at the familiar face smiling up at her.

She put down the folder containing the press release and hitched her hip onto the desk. She picked up the photograph.

Displayed in a ceramic Mickey Mouse frame they had bought together at Disneyland, the photograph showed a man posing with Pocahontas, his eyes not on the camera, but on the woman in the sexy character's outfit beside him. The grin on his face said he appreciated the view.

That's the way she'd always remember Alec, frozen in her memory with his black hair swept back, the brown eyes slightly crinkled at the corners with his smile, the spray of freckles on his nose. In the photograph, he looked a good ten years younger than his thirty-two years.

Cherish touched the face covered by the glass, wondering if he'd changed much over the last year.

Alec Porter. One of the good ones. The kind of guy who would listen to a woman talk about deep dark secrets—a man who would never dismiss her fears or try to fix them. But how he could make her laugh. Until her sides hurt.

"I hope they're treating you right in"—she thought back to the last postcard she'd received—"Honduras."

Putting down the photograph, she stood to walk slowly around her desk. She eased into her chair, then picked up her pen, tapping it against her palm. She peeked down at the desk. The drawer, to her right.

Don't open it; don't take that first step.

The warning sounded in her head even as she pushed the chair back on its rollers and reached for the handle. She pulled the drawer open and stared at the photograph she kept facedown at the bottom. She didn't stop to think, just picked it up.

He wore his sandy brown hair short, though for him, the style would be long compared to his days in the military. He was really an ordinary looking guy. Nothing special, just brown hair and hazel eyes with a crooked smile. But nature had a way of making the nondescript features handsome—like Harrison Ford or Dennis Quaid. An ordinary guy that could turn heads.

And then, of course, there was The Scar. Nothing puckered or distorted. It was just a thin line that split his left eyebrow, then tapered off at his cheek as if drawn there by a fine pen.

After the crash, she'd been so frozen with fear, she couldn't even feel the heat burning through her clothes, the fumes and smoke making her crazy. She had looked up then, into those hazel eyes as he'd held out his hand to her and smiled. To this day, she didn't think she would have been able to move if he hadn't smiled.

She had fallen in love with him at that very instant.

Conor Mitchell. Her own personal crash and burn.

In one angry motion, she dumped the photograph in the

drawer and slammed it shut. She waited for the pain in her chest that she'd labeled "Conor" to slowly subside.

Cherish swiveled her chair around to face her computer, all business now. Alec's photograph she left where it was, next to a frozen orange juice can Lori's son had converted into a penholder at his preschool. She wondered what perversity had made her fall for Conor, when Alec had been the one who wore his heart on his sleeve for her. Alec, the guy who would have thrown his body over a puddle and let her walk on him rather than allow her to get her dainty feet wet.

Alec who had told her that he loved her.

"Someday, you're going to figure that one out, Cherish," she said, punching on the computer keys.

The screen flared to life, bringing with it the icon that said she had mail. She tried to push out the noise in her head and focus on any message that might relate to the crash. Scanning through her e-mail, she told herself she should page Lori, see how it was going over at the base. Thank goodness that Lori's ex-husband had the kids on weekends. She hated imposing on her assistant, a divorced mother of two, but at Marquis, public relations amounted to her and Lori against the world.

She was reading quickly, skimming, making a mental note on a few of the messages—until she reached the one that stopped her, cold.

Dearest Cherish,
    Someone tried to kill me today. Watch your back. Contact Conor. He'll know what to do.
    P.S. You should have picked me, little girl.

She pushed away from her desk, sending her chair rolling back, away from the terminal. The back of her chair hit the wall.

"Alec?"

The last year and a half, he'd sent chatty postcards once or twice a month, the kind that pictured famous cities from around the world. There was never a return address—never any way to get in touch. Like the e-mail, the postcards were unsigned. But there was only one person in the world who called her "little girl."

Someone tried to kill me . . . contact Conor.

Cherish jumped to her feet and bent over the keyboard. Her fingers flew over the keys, mistyping every other word, forcing her to backtrack. When she finished, she clicked on the return mail icon.

The message flashed onto the screen: Connection refused. Address had permanent fatal errors.

Twenty minutes later, she still couldn't get a message through.

"Damn you, Alec," she said, hearing the fear in her voice.

She didn't know where he was; she had no way of contacting him. And judging from his postcards the last year—always from a different country, never signed, never showing a return address—that's exactly the way Alec Porter wanted it.

She logged off, then carefully put away the files she wouldn't need until tomorrow. She packed away the papers for home in her briefcase, lining up the edges before laying them flat, putting her three-colored pen in its special slot. She picked up her jacket and turned off the lights, as if everything were fine. Just another ordinary day in chaos.

She didn't have a clue what she was going to do.

Walking down the empty hall, she thought about Conor and Alec, two men who had changed her life. They'd shared six tumultuous weeks. Six weeks that had started with one disaster and ended with another.

She wasn't sure why the men in her life disappeared. Correction, she knew precisely why Conor had gone out of her life.

And quite unfortunately, she knew exactly where to find him.

TOUCH-AND-GO

Countdown: 29 days; 19 hours; 55 minutes

Chapter Four

If there were justice in this world, Conor Mitchell would be bald.

Cherish crossed her legs, making little circles with her ankle to try and get the circulation back in her foot as she held on to that thought. She'd had a restless night worrying about Alec—the crash yesterday—trying to decide what she should do.

This morning, she'd woken Lori to ask if she could trace Alec's e-mail, somehow get a message to him. As it turned out, Lori hadn't been able to pull a rabbit out of the hat . . . which was why Cherish was sitting in the cramped front office of Dogfights Incorporated, waiting to speak to a man she hadn't seen or spoken to since the day he'd left her waiting at the altar.

Picking up her compact, she made a vain attempt to fix her makeup in the tiny mirror as the air conditioner lodged in the window basted her with warm air. She thought she might get lucky on the bald thing. Conor was of a certain age, seven years older than her own thirty-one years. Wasn't that about the time baldness kicked in?

Seated behind a gray metal desk, Geena Lloyd popped her gum as she flipped through the pages of *Air & Space* as if it were *Cosmo*. Conor's little sister. A graduate of the Air Force Academy where she'd earned top honors. A major in the Air Force and one of the first women to qualify for flight school, training for a combat role in an F-15 Eagle.

And through the facade of the magazine and the gum chewing, Cherish could feel every one of those ample brain cells focused on her. The Big Bad Brother Stealer.

Cherish snapped the compact closed, giving up on looking half decent. She'd never begrudged Geena her feelings. She had walked into their lives like a tornado, taking Geena by surprise. They'd all been ambushed by events after the first prototype crashed more than a year ago. And in those days, Conor and Cherish hadn't had time for anyone else, not even the little sister who had been the center of Conor's existence for her thirty-two years.

"You know, this will only take a minute." She stood, speaking to Geena. "Why don't I just peek my head in and—"

"He'll be right out." Geena didn't so much as bother to look up.

"I do have other appointments," Cherish said, tapping her watch, trying a change in tactics.

Geena flipped to the next page. "I'll be happy to check his schedule to see what's opening up next month." Her gaze shifted, her eyes now on Cherish, telling her there wouldn't be a second chance. "Between the engineering courses he's teaching this semester and his flying, he keeps real busy."

I'll bet. Cherish dropped back into the chair. "I guess I'll wait then." She winked. "Now that I'm here and all."

"Suit yourself," Geena said, popping her gum.

In the echo of the gum blast, Cherish heard the distinctive *click* of a door opening. Even though he didn't speak a word

or make a sound, she knew Conor had stepped into the room
. . . was absolutely sure he was standing directly behind her.

It was like radar, what she had for that man. Conor Mitchell
sonar.

She stood. She had taken great care dressing this morning,
wearing a tailored suit in a salmon pink, one of the more daring
colors in her wardrobe and one that suited her. She'd even
done her nails in Lancôme's Illusion, a minimalist frost that
screamed career woman. She'd wanted to appear the professional, a woman who had her life together.

Unfortunately, the air conditioning in her Volkswagen Rabbit
was out and though she'd lasted valiantly on the drive over,
there'd been an accident on the 91. Makeup meltdown had
commenced. She'd cracked the window, trying for a little air,
then cranked it all the way down.

Eventually, traffic had let up. Eventually, she'd looked like
she'd taken an eggbeater to her hair.

She and her eggbeater hair turned slowly.

He hadn't changed. No receding hairline, not a gray hair,
not even an ounce gained. Just all gorgeous six feet, two inches
of hard body standing there with the same dreamy hazel eyes.

"Cher," he said.

She felt frozen in place, standing there like an idiot, remembering everything. That out of uniform, he never wore anything
more formal than chinos. That he smelled like Old Spice
aftershave and the sun. That he worked out and had that gorgeous olive skin of his Italian heritage all over his body.

And she remembered how much she loved his kisses. She'd
never loved anyone's kisses like Conor's.

"Conor," she said, too brightly, reminding herself why she
was here. "As I was just telling Geena, this should only take
a minute. I know how awkward my coming here must be, and
I just . . ." *Talking too much. Shut up. Shut up now.*

She thrust out her hand, keeping it professional.

He peeled himself from his pose leaning against the wall.

He shook her hand with nothing more than a squeeze, then motioned to the door behind him, his office . . . while she stood riveted to the spot, thinking that it had been more than a year since he'd touched her, bringing back all the longing, drowning her in waves of it.

"Through there?" she asked, waking up, pointing to the door as if she'd never lapsed into a coma of nostalgia. She stepped forward at his nod, then turned back to Geena. "We'll just be a minute," she said. As if she needed Geena's permission.

Brother and sister exchanged a look.

"Ohhhkay," she said, escaping to his office.

Inside the cubicle-size room, she closed the door and sat in a chair perched directly in front of another metal desk. The room was practically the width of the desk, leaving enough room for only a couple of folding chairs, a large white board on the wall, and a credenza with a television and a VCR balanced on top, like maybe he might want to pop in a video of *Top Gun.*

She adjusted her skirt and placed her briefcase at her feet. She didn't need the case, but she felt safe with it. Armor. A symbol that, at least in her career, she'd succeeded. Now, if she could just trot out a husband and a baby that would just about say it all. *I don't need you, Conor. You didn't hurt me. I went on with my life, an executive at an established company. I didn't just fold up and die when you left.*

Of course, the letters were her biggest problem. She'd sent one every week for the last year. Very long, very revealing. At first, she'd sent them out of anger, needing somehow to hurt Conor, just as he'd hurt her. *Why should he have the last word?* A mental letter bomb.

But slowly, her letters to Conor had changed. They became her therapy, taking on a "Dear Diary" tone. She told herself she was working through her nightmares with the only man who could understand them. And she'd felt insulated writing them each week. Because Conor had never answered.

Now, those letters were a huge burden she'd carried into this room. *I didn't mean anything by all that—I wasn't reaching out.*

If only.

The door opened. She waited as Conor walked across the room. Conor never hurried; he was never slow. He was steady. Steadfast Conor. Someone you could rely on ... unless, of course, you wanted to marry him. Then it was time to duck and cover.

She watched as he sat down behind his desk, leaning into the chair with a creak of leather and springs. "Would you—"

She held up her hand, silencing him. "First off, let me say that I'm not here to rehash the past."

She'd been in public relations long enough to have prepared for this meeting. She'd given today's strategy a lot of thought, remembering that, in the end, Alec had told her Conor and he had parted on bad terms. She couldn't just slap the printout of Alec's e-mail on Conor's desk and walk away. Which was probably why Alec had used her as his intermediary.

Therefore, a plan. Conor would, of course, launch into some lame apology. The day after he'd failed to show up for their wedding, he'd had the audacity to call her, as if he could somehow explain, *over the phone,* why he'd changed his mind about marrying her. She'd hung up on him, unwilling to listen to the painful explanations she'd imagined. *Would you please forgive me, baby? I didn't mean to tear your guts out and barbecue them for lunch.* And she wasn't about to listen to him now.

"I want you to know I don't resent you, Conor. I'm not bitter," she said, sounding very reasonable. "It was something powerful what we went through. Out of control. The crash, your discharge from the Air Force. That's the kind of thing that can change a person. We were in a great moment of flux, you and I. And we just got caught up in it—I most of all.''

Conor leaned back, the scar making him look suddenly fierce, as if he didn't like what he was hearing. *Well, that's just too bad, bucko.*

''It's like that line from the movie *Speed*,'' she continued, getting a sudden burst of inspiration. ''What Sandra tells Keanu at the end. Relationships based on extreme circumstances never work out. That was us, Conor. Too much, too fast.''

She crossed her legs, leaning back. *Look how relaxed I am. Totally in control.*

She managed a small laugh. ''Really, the idea that we could get married and live happily ever after, knowing each other only six weeks . . . well. You were right. What were the odds that it would have worked? No. The way you left it was better. Nice and clean.'' She slashed her hand through the air. ''Just cut it off before we made a bigger mistake.''

She waited, wanting to fill in the silence he allowed to stretch between them as his eyes met hers. Fighting the desire to do just that.

After what seemed the definition of infinity, he said, ''I was going to ask if you would like a cup of coffee before you launched into that one. But I can see you don't need the caffeine.''

Cherish felt herself flush. Coffee. She did a fast rewind in her head of the last thirty seconds. *Coffee!*

She smoothed her skirt over her knees and cleared her throat. ''How about I settle for a dull knife to cut out your evil little heart instead?''

For the first time, he smiled.

''Or is there even one beating in there?'' she added, heating up, jumping to her feet. ''You stood me up on our wedding day, you . . . you . . . bastard. You never even answered one of my letters, when I *needed* you. You were the only one left, the only person who lived through that nightmare with me, who had a hope of understanding—No.''

She backed away, realizing what was happening. She shook her head, disbelieving, holding her hands out as if to ward off an attack.

''No, no, no. I am not doing this. I've been in therapy. I'm over all this. I am over you.'' She jabbed her finger at him, as if there might be some other candidate in the room responsible for her broken heart. ''I am so *over* you.''

Conor waited, his arms crossed over his chest . . . watching her make an enormous ass of herself.

Cherish snapped her mouth shut. She returned to the chair and picked up her briefcase. In her most dignified manner, she popped it open, *click, click.* She whipped out a copy of Alec's e-mail, realizing she should have just slapped it on his desk, after all.

She watched him pick up the single sheet, waited as he read the message.

''I received it last night,'' she said. Then, clarifying, ''It's from Alec.''

She saw the first flicker of emotion. She knew his history with Alec. But still it hurt that for Alec, he could at least show some emotion.

He dropped the page on his desk, then crossed his arms, waiting.

''He usually sends postcards,'' she told him. ''At least once or twice a month for the last year. Eastern Europe, Asia, South America. Chatty postcards talking about the normal things.'' That he missed her. That he loved her. All the things Conor had always failed to tell her . . . all the things she thought she could live without if she could just have Conor.

Stupid, stupid woman!

She watched Conor look down at those final prophetic words at the bottom, going over them in her head as he read: *You should have picked me, little girl.*

"No information on where to reach him or how to help him." She pointed to the paper when he glanced up, using the visual aid to ride roughshod over the moment when their eyes met, communicating the obvious. *You should have picked Alec; we both know it.* "Only that I should contact you." She crossed her arms, stepping back. "So here I am. For Alec's sake." And when he didn't volunteer anything, she simply asked, "What should I do, Conor?"

"I haven't a clue."

She closed her eyes. She thought about Chuck and his team of engineers, still red-eyed from working through the night . . . Lori going solo with the press . . . while she wasted her time here. She'd dropped everything, swallowed her pride and raced over to face him. Because she thought Alec might need them.

She turned and snapped shut her briefcase, realizing that she was on her own. When she finished, she held out her hand. "It's been lovely, Conor. Call me when you get a pulse."

"Sit down."

"It might be interesting to know why I would have any inclination to do that?"

"Is this the first time you've had this kind of message from Alec?"

"Of course, it is." As if Conor wasn't the first person she would contact if Alec were in trouble.

He kept his gaze steady. "Well, this isn't a first for me."

"So what are you saying?" she asked, not surprised that he would take this tact. "You think this is some kind of game Alec is playing?"

"Alec knows how to get into trouble. I don't see what either you or I are supposed to do about it."

She nodded, going with it. But inside, she was comparing the stoic man seated before her to the Conor who had actually clung to her, had made love to her with this incredible heat and unbelievable passion. The man she'd fallen in love with. The man she'd lost.

"Contact Conor," she said, reciting the message. "He'll know what to do." She shrugged. "Guess he made a mistake. Guess we both did."

At the door, she heard him say, "I never had all the answers, Cher."

She stared at her fingers on the doorknob, not turning around. "Wouldn't it have been nice if you had?" Without waiting for a reply, she slipped through and closed the door behind her.

Geena, the bulldog, had switched her position from her desk to casually standing near the door to Conor's office. Ready to pounce. Cherish made a quick survey for the handy water glass. Luckily, she knew Geena wouldn't waste her breath on Cherish. It was her brother she'd be gunning for, GI Jane.

Cherish popped her sunglasses on her nose and smiled her darnedest at Geena. "Have a nice day."

Outside, the sun was hot and blinding. She almost ran into Geena's husband, Marc, who with his quick Tom Cruise reflexes stepped aside just in time to avoid a collision. He didn't say a word, just watched her from behind the mirrored lenses of his sunglasses.

She was so tired of their silence. Their secret society. They had one another, Conor, Marc, and Geena. The dynamic trio didn't need anyone to disrupt their cozy little group. She and Alec had been shut out years ago.

She gave Marc a smart salute and walked around him, then managed to stumble in her heels, almost landing nose first into the dirt, ruining her exit. Straightening, she hobbled to her car, favoring the ankle she'd turned. She didn't stop until she reached the car in the parking lot.

Waves of energy radiated off the cement, the heat, almost draining. Cherish fished around her purse for her keys, thinking it was odd, how Alec had never been like them. The wall that Conor and his sister had built around themselves as orphans, and later, Air Force officers, was completely absent in Alec, a man who had grown up beside them like a brother.

The night Conor had left her waiting, never showing for their wedding, it was Alec who'd made excuses for him—Alec, whose shoulder she'd cried on . . . and Alec who'd asked to take Conor's place.

But she hadn't loved Alec. Not like that.

Inside the car, she dropped the briefcase on the seat beside her and jabbed the keys into the ignition. "Always pick the wrong one." The engine turned over on the first try. "My motto in life."

Leaving the dust of the airfield behind, heading for the freeway, she wondered now if there hadn't been more to those letters she'd sent than the therapy she'd branded them. What if they had been some pathetic attempt to get Conor back? To reveal to him how interesting and irresistible she had become. *When you walked away, Conor, you just didn't know me. Given a little time, a little heartfelt information . . .*

It hurt, to think she could have been that stupid. Because, as things turned out, she hadn't been nearly interesting enough.

And now, he knew more about her than anyone alive. While for Cherish, Conor Mitchell remained a perfect blank.

Conor watched the door open and Geena walk in. She dropped into the chair in front of his desk, one trousered leg hanging over the armrest.

"I called Kathy," she said, her familiar brown eyes watching him. Geena had this thing with her eyes where she didn't blink. "I told her dinner is off tonight."

He waited. He knew Geena. She was just warming up.

"Because why would you want to meet a perfectly wonderful woman?" Her voice was changing pitch, growing higher, louder. "Someone you could settle down with, someone with whom you could raise a family? Why do that when you have Barbie coming to pay a visit?"

Conor leaned back in his chair, giving Geena the chance to

let off a little steam. His sister had always put such energy into hating Cherish . . . when the two women seemed a lot alike. Dogged. Smart. Cherish Malone had a mind like a steel trap, an engineer who'd specialized in stress analysis before Marquis tried putting someone who wasn't a white male in front of the cameras.

"You know? I don't understand you, Conor. You took so long to fall for someone. I thought it was because you were being choosy. What is it with you and that I-could-be-a-weather-girl blonde?"

He had to smile at that one. "Cher was just dropping something off."

"And a piranha just wants a little taste. And that's exactly what I'm talking about. Cher? Like the name Cherish isn't precious enough? You have to come up with a cute nickname?"

His sister stood, leaning over his desk, hands balanced to either side. She was tall for a woman, almost six feet. "Listen to me. You are absolutely, without a doubt, the most sensible man I know. I was too young when Mom and Dad died to remember them. You pratically raised me—then took in Alec and his problems, to boot. And always, always, you seemed to have this grand plan, getting us out of that state facility, seeing us through the Academy. And it was only after we were taken care of that you took your turn. You had such goals, Conor. You were so . . . steady. Then one day, you walk through the door with a woman you'd known, what? A month, maybe?"

"Is this going to take long?" He glanced at his watch. He didn't want to hear any of this. "Because, if dinner's off tonight, I have a few things I could get done instead."

But Geena was already pacing in front of his desk. A woman on a mission. "I'm getting married tonight, you tell me. Just like that. As if it was nothing. I didn't even know you could do that in California. Like we have a Las Vegas chapel down the street? To make things worse, there's this complete deadness in your eyes when you say it . . . while that silly little thing next to you is beaming, looking so utterly . . . blonde.''

"And guess what, Geena?'' he said, crossing his arms, getting ornery himself. ''It's natural, too.''

That stopped her. His sister whipped around, facing him, getting his meaning. Which was why he'd said it. Because, for a moment there, the double team of Cher followed by Geena was getting to be too much.

She leaned up against the credenza, those brown eyes very lucid, catching on. ''Ass,'' she said, immediately lightening up.

"Chicken legs.''

"Penis breath—''

"Down, Geena,'' Marc said, walking in the room. He hooked an arm around her, landing his wife on his lap as he sat down. Geena was taller than Marc, something Marc took great pride in. ''Someday, I'm going to make a video of the two of you going at it. Geena yapping around you like some rabid poodle while you lounge back with your arms crossed over your chest, nodding your head, egging her on. So what did Cinderella want, anyway?''

Geena slapped Marc's hands away, but stayed on his lap. The two faced Conor, waiting.

They thought Cher was the enemy. Because, one day, Conor Mitchell had a break in character, doing something they couldn't explain. *Good old dependable Conor.* And Cher had been standing beside him when he'd done it . . . and they hadn't known how to blame him. But it wasn't Cherish Malone they needed to worry about.

Conor rubbed the scar over his eye, then, catching the gesture, jerked his hand away. He picked up the paper Cherish had left on his desk.

"Trouble,'' he said, lifting Alec's e-mail. ''Alec is back.''

Chapter Five

Sydney Shanks Reck adjusted the strap of her peignoir, prepared to make her entrance.

She padded barefoot across the carpet, the yellow brick road to Russell's office, stopping only when she heard it. Shouting. *Russell's still on the phone?*

She hesitated, her hand suspended, standing guard over the doorknob. It was almost eleven o'clock. If she waited much longer . . .

She would fall asleep looking over floor plan sketches and swatches of fabric samples, just as she did almost every night. It was a pattern they had fallen into. She would sit in bed, waiting, always waiting . . . while Russell worked in the office he kept here in their Harbor Island home, coming to bed only when she was dead to the world.

Tonight, Sydney had vowed to change that.

She eased the door open and slipped her bared leg past, giving Russell a view of her thigh exposed by the slit in the peignoir. Getting no response, she walked inside, taking her time, keeping her walk sultry across the rare Aubusson carpet, doing a silent bump and grind to a rhythm in her head as Russell barked into the mouthpiece of the phone.

When she eased her strap off her shoulder, Russ held up his hand, mouthing a silent, "hold that thought." Sydney ignored him, pushing aside papers to slink across the colossal mahogany desk, catlike.

Russell kept talking into the phone, flashing her an irritated look. "Washington," he mouthed. Kinnard again.

She tried to keep a grip on *her* irritation. She knew it must be particularly important for Russell to be talking with Joseph Kinnard at this hour. The undersecretary of defense for research and acquisition was Russell's most important contact at the Department of Defense. But before she let herself feel one bit guilty, she reminded herself that, with Russell, there would always be something. By definition, his job was consuming. Reck Enterprises was a multibillion-dollar business with interests in communications and aerospace. If she let it, the company would take everything, leaving nothing for her.

When he hung up the phone, it started. The excuses.

"Come on, Sydney. You know I have my hands full with the damn crash."

"Don't you want to make love to me anymore?"

"What an asinine thing to say. Excuse me for being a little distracted, but two days ago a plane I poured half-a-billion dollars into fell out of the sky. I can't give you my full attention right now, Sydney. That's not what you want, is it?"

He'd taken off his tie. The Armani lay draped over the wing chair in front of his desk. He'd opened the top two buttons of his silk shirt. At fifty-seven, he still looked in his early forties, keeping fit by playing squash. But men like Russell weren't judged by their appearance.

Sydney reached down to work on the next button. "Just about now, I'll settle for what I can get. This won't take long, I promise," she whispered, kissing his chest.

"That's enough, Sydney."

She licked his nipple, reaching for his belt buckle.

He grabbed both her wrists and yanked her hands away. "I said, that's enough."

They both stared at the other, each startled by the harshness in his voice. She saw it then. She wasn't enough anymore. He didn't love her.

Sydney pushed herself free. She rushed out of the room, Russell calling her name as she ran, telling her he was sorry. But she kept going, down the hall, up the stairs, stopping only when she reached their bedroom suite.

She slammed the door and collapsed against it, her arms clutching her stomach. For the first time, she was truly frightened. She had given up everything to be with Russell. She'd cheated on her first husband, Russell's partner, living all those years with the lies, then bearing the guilt of being Henry's widow, mourning not the man, but how she'd treated him those last years he'd been alive. She'd given everything to become the third Mrs. Russell Reck.

There was a soft knocking on the door behind her. "Open the door."

"Fuck you, Russell." Then, thinking better of that, "Go away, Russell. I'm very angry with you right now."

"Yes. I can see that." Silence, then, "I'll make it up to you, Sydney. I will. We can go away, maybe back to Acapulco." His voice dropped as he softly added, "Do you remember Acapulco?"

Of course, she remembered. Because they had been so very happy there.

"I love you, Syd. You know that. But Kinnard is riding me hard on this one. He practically promised his left kidney to the Senate Arms Services Committee to get us this far and they're aching for an excuse to shut us down on the Hill."

She let her head fall back against the door, knowing her

anger was useless. As always, she would give in. What choice did she have, really?

Standing, she opened the door to lean there as she said, "But it hurts, Russ. It still hurts."

He took her into his arms. "Forgive me?"

"No, I don't." But she returned his kiss, holding him fiercely. "Not yet."

He growled deep in his throat and pulled away. "Look, I hate this as much as you do. But until we find out what happened with that prototype, my time is not my own. The XC-23 is wrapped up with just about everything. And next month's flight schedule is critical."

"Okay." She leaned against him, holding his hands. "Okay."

"There's my Sydney." He kissed her on the forehead, then reached up to stroke her breast through the peignoir. "I just have a few more reports to go over before I call it a night. Will you wait up for me?"

She sighed. "Yes."

Propped against the door, Sydney watched Russell retreat down the hall lined with Japanese prints, then shut the door softly. Russell was a man of incredible vision . . . but he'd also created the monster that now controlled their lives. She knew what they called him, The Wrecker.

Yes, well, he was so very good at taking things apart.

She moved barefoot across the carpet, her toes curling into the deep pile. In the background, she could hear the soothing gurgle of the water feature in the gardens below, a granite and steel piece of art she'd commissioned when they'd bought the house last year. Remodeling was a far cry from her old position as assistant curator at the Norton Simon, but she took pride in the house. She'd wanted to make it the perfect home for her and Russ.

Stopping in front of the Regency-style vanity, she peered into the mirror and touched the small lines around her eyes and mouth. She was thirty-seven. Russell was twenty years older. But she was his third wife. He'd left the others long before they'd reached forty.

"Don't go feeling sorry for yourself, Sydney," she told her reflection. "You're a fighter. Russell wouldn't have wanted you otherwise."

She walked to the bed, an exquisite eighteenth-century Venetian antique she'd placed at the room's very center, the floor-to-ceiling windows and the view of the Pacific beyond providing a dramatic backdrop. In the gardens below, twin royal palms with fiber optics spiraling up each trunk created beacons that could be seen from as far away as across the peninsula. She climbed onto the bed, sinking her cheek into the silky Frett sheets.

"I *will* fight for you, Russell."

She wasn't going to allow Reck Enterprises to take another husband.

It was past one in the morning when Russell climbed the stairs, dead tired, but his mind still racing. He would have to fly his Gulfstream V jet to Washington tomorrow, help Kinnard convince those bastards on the Hill this was just a blip on the screen, not a showstopper. Jesus, Washington. He could just bet Sydney would love that.

But it couldn't be helped. Kinnard was right; they needed to turn this around. Make the crash work for them. If they played it right, it didn't have to be a minus but the opening they'd been waiting for.

He pictured that woman—Cherish Malone, Marquis's public relations person. He hoped he hadn't been wrong about her. A year and a half ago, he'd convinced Joseph Kinnard she was a zero. Not a factor. But the last couple of days, watching how she handled the press, that Mary Sunshine face addressing the national media so earnestly. Suddenly, she hadn't seemed so insignificant.

They had kept a close watch on Marquis the last year. It had cost him millions, but in the end, it would be worth every penny. And he thought Kinnard was right about the crash three days ago. It was a golden opportunity to deploy what Russell termed their "corrective action" plan. By the time the final-stage prototype got off the ground next month, Marquis Aircraft wouldn't even be an afterthought in the industry. And if they played their cards right, Cherish Malone would sink into the sunset with her company. Problem solved.

Russell strode down the hall, a hot rush tingling in his blood. He still had it. The love for the kill. Russ Reck, The Wrecker.

Well, this was not a business for the squeamish. That had been Henry's problem. Always talking about teamwork and progress. As if Eric Ballas would have ever played ball— Ballas, who thought he'd found the golden goose with his damned Russians. No, Henry had missed the big picture. When the millennium came, Reck Enterprises would be top dog in a multibillion-dollar communications business. Henry hadn't seen that. He'd lacked the vision.

And hadn't it cost him plenty in the end? Henry Shanks, just another nice guy for people to run over.

Poor Henry, he thought. God, he still couldn't forgive himself about Henry, the poor sap. Henry, who hadn't hurt a flea— who'd been happy to stay behind the scenes, even naming the company they'd built together Reck Enterprises because Russell's father had a few miserable contacts in the airlines. That damned spook, Kinnard. Why couldn't he have left Henry out of it?

Jesus, they all wanted a piece of him, Kinnard, Sydney, Henry's ghost. Even Russell's head of security, siccing that idiot reporter with the finesse of a lamprey on the Malone woman when Russell had specifically asked for subtlety. If he didn't watch them every step of the way . . .

Sydney, most of all. He glanced at the Japanese prints on the walls. She was almost done with the remodeling. Pretty soon, he would have to find something else to keep her mind off that biological clock humming inside her. As if he would actually go under the knife to reverse his vasectomy. He was already paying child support for five kids, goddammit. Sydney should understand that.

Entering the bedroom, he could sense his anger shadowing him, palpable and pulsing, as he found her asleep on that monstrosity of a bed she'd insisted on buying. The green silk of her nightgown had bunched up around her thighs, making her look sexy as hell with her auburn hair spilled across the nest of pillows. Why the fuck hadn't she waited up for him? He felt like grabbing her and shaking her awake. What had that little show in his office been about?

"Shit." He had to force himself to calm down, to step back and evaluate. It *was* almost two in the morning. What had he expected?

He scrubbed his face with his hand, feeling tired and strung too tight. He didn't know what was wrong with him. Kinnard, of course. The man had him by the balls and he wasn't afraid to squeeze a little. But Russell shouldn't take it out on Sydney. He loved her. That was the incredible part. Sydney counted.

For a moment, he considered crawling into bed next to her to get some sleep. But he was so wound up. That call from Kinnard.

Turning around, Russell closed the door quietly, leaving Sydney to her sleep.

He ended up in his favorite place, the bar at the Four Seasons. Though it was almost two, no one hustled out the customer, even on a weeknight. And they knew him here. As he sat on the upholstered stool, the white-jacketed bartender had already poured two fingers of the twenty-five-year-old single malt Scotch Russell preferred.

He saw her first, sitting in a rattan chair just beyond the baby grand, staring out the atrium window at the jungle foliage lit up outside. She looked incredibly young, twenty—if that. With chestnut ringlets brushing her shoulders, hair a man could sink his fingers into.

Instantly, all the pent-up frustration of his conversation with Kinnard went in a completely different direction. She turned, looking over at him, as if sensing him there at the bar, watching her. She had these laser-blue eyes. Jesus, she was cherry, a little bit of a thing with an incredible mouth.

He signaled the waitress. She was drinking a Kir Royale and he ordered her another. He cheated on Sydney off and on; he traveled too much to be faithful. And tonight . . . well, this was just what the doctor ordered.

The brunette didn't smile or acknowledge his eyes on her. For a moment, he had an instant's misgiving. Sydney. He did love her. And he had to be careful. He'd been besotted enough with Syd that, when she'd refused to sign a prenup, he'd let it slide—against the fervent advice of counsel. Maybe it was his conscience over Henry, but he figured he wasn't leaving Syd. Not like Carla and Megan.

Hell, he couldn't afford to.

But he knew it was more than that. He couldn't imagine himself wanting to leave her. Sydney was the grand prize. Beautiful, smart. The perfect trophy. How Henry had managed to land her still mystified him. Shit, from the first day his partner had introduced his new wife, Russ knew he had to have her.

But Sydney didn't understand about a man's libido. And she had the kind of redhead's temper that she'd take it out on his hide if she ever caught him being unfaithful.

The waitress arrived with the drink, letting the woman know who was paying. She nodded, those incredible iridescent eyes meeting his across the empty cocktail lounge. Sometimes, he used the professionals, which was a hell of a lot easier. But he could tell she wasn't one of those. It made it more exciting.

He raised his drink in a silent hello.

She stood, taking her glass. As she moved toward him, walking around the plush rattan and bamboo chairs and potted palms, the recessed lighting shimmered off the fabric of the clingy dress practically riding up her ass. The dress matched her eyes, electric blue. She sat down at the bar next to him.

"The waitress said you're some really rich guy." She spoke watching his mouth, looking incredibly intense. Jesus, did she wear colored contacts? She took a sip of the champagne clouded red by the crème de cassis, her lips making him already hard as he imagined that mouth somewhere else besides on the rim of the glass.

"You build satellites or something?"

"Among other things." Reck Enterprises had several subsidiaries. But Russell had always believed the future was communication satellites.

"Like what?" She leaned forward, showing her pert breasts. She wasn't wearing a bra and the front of her dress had puckered enough to show it. An invitation if he'd ever seen one.

Right now, I'm working on a great big hard-on. He almost said it. Instead, he smiled and picked up her hand. Her nails were short and painted shiny blue, the same candy color as her dress. She couldn't be more than nineteen.

"Interesting color."

She rested her chin on her palm. "I like interesting things. What's your name?"

"Russell," he said, not bothering with his last name. "And yours?"

She smiled for the first time. "Tell me about your satellites, Russell."

He grinned, liking the game. "You don't want to tell me your name?"

"I'm trying to keep it interesting."

He took out his money clip and dropped a hundred on the table for the drinks. He watched her eyes widen a bit as she stared at the bill.

"I promise." He stood, holding out his hand for her. "I won't be boring."

She was an incredible fuck.

Hot and fast and with moves he didn't even know. He wasn't into kinky shit, but Allison—that turned out to be her name—she was something else. He'd once made love with a Japanese contortionist who could learn a few things from her.

That was the problem with Sydney. She wanted to "make love." Missionary all the way. Nothing like this.

Now, Allison lay dead to the world on the hotel's king-size bed, almost as if she'd given so much in their lovemaking, she had nothing left. But when he moved to get out of bed, she woke instantly, as if she'd never been asleep.

"Are you leaving?" she asked.

She was unbelievably beautiful. Tousled curls, incredible eyes, rosebud mouth. Suddenly, he felt apprehensive about leaving her. He knew it would be a mistake to see her again. Too risky with Sydney. *Fuck it.* Hadn't he worked his ass off his whole life, never stopping, even when it would have been enough for any other man? All so he wouldn't have to worry about the rules?

And there was something about Allison, something that made him ask, "How would you like to take a trip to Washington?"

Chapter Six

After a year of her letters, Conor knew about the nightmares.

She would wake up, the sounds and sights of that day lingering like an afterimage burned into her retinas. The dream was always the same. Eric talking to her from across the aisle, Henry Shanks seated beside him, the reporter she'd shepherded on board in the window seat next to her—the plane dropping out of the sky.

Eric Ballas's death, in particular, seemed to haunt her. Maybe because she'd admired him so much. They'd had a good working relationship, Cherish and Eric. He had even offered her a job when the joint project she'd managed for both Eric's company and Marquis had been canceled in the wake of the bigger fish, the XC-23 WingMaster. Whenever Cherish woke from her nightmare, she would try to remember what Eric had said to her from across that aisle, reminding Conor of when he'd lost his parents. For years, he kept reliving those final goodbyes, wishing for more. In the same way, Cherish kept trying to recall Eric's last words.

Conor put down the letter he'd been reading. He'd brought out a whole pile of them, so that sheets of stationery littered the coffee table, right next to the empty plate of lasagna he'd polished off, a peace offering from Geena. He slid his finger over Cher's handwriting as if it were Braille.

Conor didn't suffer from nightmares. He slept fine. Just laid his head on the pillow, and ten minutes later, the world disappeared. His particular haunts came during broad daylight. That crushing sound he couldn't forget; he'd never heard anything so loud. Screams coming from the cabin . . . hitting the ground hard . . . the tearing of metal. *We're on fire!*

"Shit."

He dropped his head back against the cushion where he'd sprawled out on the living room couch. He'd always been good at investing his money, and a couple of years ago, he'd gone in on a place with Geena and Marc. Conor had staked out this little cottage in the back while Geena and Marc lived in the Cape Cod in front, Geena's dream house. Tonight, he'd thought he would come home early, maybe grade a few blue books, then head over and shoot the breeze with Marc or play Nintendo with the kids. Instead, his haunts had been waiting for him in the night shadows, so much so that he'd dragged out Cher's letters, was watching her now on the television.

He peered out from beneath half-lowered lids, staring at the old set in front of him. He'd recorded a couple of her earlier press conferences. But when he'd set the tape to play, he'd turned off the sound. She had such an expressive face. You didn't need it.

Oh, yeah. She was a persuasive little thing, all right.

A few hours ago, Geena's oldest, Christopher, had shown up—two hard knocks sounded characteristically on the door before his ten-year-old nephew barged in. He'd brought over the lasagna and they'd talked about school, Chris's new telescope and the Hale-Bopp comet, all the good stuff that made up Conor's life these days. But after Chris left, Conor had popped in the tape of Cher just the same.

Watching her on the television, he tried to focus on the things that counted. His family, Geena, Marc, and the kids— his position at the university—Dogfights.

And there was Cher, asking him to step into that den of snakes again. Crash investigations, government hearings, safety boards assigning guilt. None of it was part of his life anymore. *Not your nightmare—not this time. Don't get involved.*

The problem was, Alec was his monster. And Cher, whether she knew it or not, was going to need help.

He picked up the key he'd brought out with the letters, let it hang from its chain on his finger, watching it swing back and forth.

"And she trusts him."

Certainly more than she trusted Conor.

He closed his hand around the key, wishing it was Alec Porter's puny neck. He wondered why, when it came to Cherish Malone, Conor just couldn't get it right.

Tunguska, Siberia

A lone figure plowed through the snow, twin funnels of white trailing, the face, a shadow within the fur-lined cowl. This time of year, the taiga was a moist forest of spruce and fir covered in snow. It was the calm after the storm, early, just dawn.

The landscape spread out flat as a dish where the comet had landed a near century ago. The figure stooped, searching the ground, brushing back the Gore-tex jacket's hood with a free hand. A woman. A subarctic wind blew a strand of black hair across her cheek as she rose again to squint at the horizon.

She tried to imagine things as they had been all those years ago. The devastation.

She'd seen pictures, of course, the trees standing out like so many toothpicks spiking up from the ground, devoid of foliage. She'd read the eyewitness accounts from 1908. *We saw the flash . . . the heat burned the shirt off my back . . . an entire herd of reindeer was charred like meat on a spit.*

She closed her eyes, imagining it, the fall point, the trees leveled, the roots looking like arthritic hands stretching out from a grave, fingers grasping to the north, the direction of the blast. More devastating than Hiroshima, they said. A chunk of space debris that, through some miracle, had landed here, in this desolate spot.

The Geiger counter needle wagged to life, catching her attention. The woman crouched down to dig through the snow with her fingers to the permafrost ground below. In the distance, a wolf howled.

"The strongest of all warriors are time and patience," she said, holding up the rock, examining the stone in the infant sunlight as she paraphrased Tolstoi.

Time and patience. Indeed, she'd had an overabundance of both the last year.

Twenty minutes later, Ekaterina Bolkonsky parked her snowmobile before a prefabricated building atop wooden pilings. Gleaming white, the laboratory resembled nothing more than a space station set on the otherworld surface that was the Siberian tundra. The synthetic material of the heavy outer wall protected the laboratory's occupants and delicate equipment from nine months of severe weather, leaving an airspace for insulation between it and a lighter inner wall. The roof steeped at a sharp angle, keeping it clear of snow, solar panels lined up in rows at the top. Climbing the steps of the modular building to the front door, she stomped her boots free of snow to enter the anteroom.

Inside, Katya hung up her jacket. The engine noise from the generators dampened to a hush, then disappeared altogether into the familiar intermittent clicks and machinelike hum from instruments as she entered the lab. But Katya heard only the baby's cries.

Katya checked on her daughter, smiling as Dimitri, the toddler's nanny, gave up the fussing child. He was Evenki, what before the revolution was referred to as a Tungus. Tired of the nomad life, he had settled here, coming to work for Katya and her husband, and was now considered part of the family. They all were, those few who remained of what was once Eric Ballas's thriving company.

After breast-feeding her daughter in the module that served as their kitchen, Katya handed the sleeping child to Dimitri to put to bed. She braced both hands at the small of her back and stretched, groaning softly. Across the room, a hot plate waited with tea and she poured herself a cup. She walked back into the lab, wondering where their houseguest had gone off to. The man bore watching.

The lab was a confusion of glowing iridescent screens crowded around a vacuum chamber, a sputter coater, and a small MTS machine—everything needed to examine the specimens she found at ground zero. Her husband, Valeri, sat at a polished steel desk the size of a refrigerator. The instrument looked like a telescope stuck upside down into the desktop, a small computer lodged beside it. A scanning electron microscope. A miracle that Valeri had managed to keep it running off one of the generators.

She came up beside her husband. "Where is he?" she asked, referring to the American.

He kept his eyes on the small video screen, the CRT, cathode ray tube, focusing on yesterday's specimen, ready to take the Polaroid. "Out."

She smiled at the single barked word and the scowl that accompanied it. Her husband had a suspicious nature.

To divert him, she produced the fragment she'd found earlier, holding up the plastic sample bag, then placing the treasure before him. "Well, Valeri, what do you think of your wife now?"

The scowl vanished, replaced by his wonderful smile. "I think, as always, that she is brilliant. And beautiful."

"And right?"

He sighed, then swiveled in his chair to face her. "Always, you are in such a hurry. We need time for careful analysis. You jump to conclusions."

She kissed him, then. On the mouth, shutting him up. "My dear Valeri, I am a woman of vision, while you"—she gave him a mock frown, shaking her head—"you are only a stodgy scientist."

He watched her with complete love in his eyes. "This is true. But still, you will listen to your stodgy scientist husband and be careful."

"But I have you to be careful for me. Now." She eased past her husband to reach the computer keyboard, typing in the commands to adjust the position of the specimen on the eight-inch, black-and-white screen. "What have you found for me?"

"Take a look."

He pushed the chair back, reaching behind him for a stack of Polaroids. He spread the photographs across the tabletop.

"Here." His thick finger pointed to one of the Polaroids. "And here," he said, pointing to another image.

Her heart pumped hard in her chest as she studied the nano-tube patterns taken by the electron microscope, the images showing delicate lines like angel's hair clumped in overlapping, bubblelike circles. It was in these samples that she hoped to find her answers. *For Eric.*

"Katya," Valeri warned. "I know this expression I see on your face. Do not be premature—"

"We're so close. I will go out again this afternoon," she said, ignoring him. "I will take Georgy with me." The last months, she and the other scientists that had once worked for Joystick Incorporated had scoured the site for pieces of extraterrestrial scraps, material that had been hurtled to earth from space a near century ago. Valeri was analyzing the specimens, graphing their findings, slowly closing in on the truth.

She heard Georgy and Misha shuffle down the steps behind her. Along with Valeri and Katya Bolkonsky, these two were all that was left of a company that had thought to ignite a revolution no less significant than man's first steps out of the Stone Age.

That was before Eric's death. Before Reck Enterprises had bought and gutted his dream. Now she and Valeri struggled to revive the fortunes of a company that had saved Katya and her family from starvation. It was what kept her here. To finish what Eric had begun.

The anteroom door opened. Katya turned, watching their houseguest step inside, feeling her heart leap to her throat. She imagined it was a reaction common from a woman, this racing pulse, the heat, when Alec Porter entered a room.

He'd left his snow gear in the anteroom and stood before them dressed in black jeans and a flannel shirt, the clothes, very American. He grinned. He was an incredibly handsome man who was fully aware of his charms. "And they say it never snows in hell."

Ekaterina smiled despite herself. "You will leave us today?" she asked.

"If the weather holds."

"With your secrets intact?" She stepped up to confront Alec Porter, face-to-face. "Without confiding in us," she said, taking in everyone in the room.

"No doubt," he answered, still smiling.

"You hatch your schemes and keep us all in ignorance. You are a trickster, Alec Porter. Why should I trust you?"

"Let me think." He tapped his index finger against his lips then held it up, as if an idea had just struck. "Maybe because you have no choice?"

She frowned, not wishing to encourage his humor. "How will I get in touch with you?"

He shook his head. "It is I who will get in touch with you, beautiful Katya."

She snorted. She'd always been a handsome woman, thirty-eight years young. But she sensed this man would ply his charms on a *babushka,* not understanding, or perhaps merely ignoring, that it made little difference to Katya.

"Ah!" He strolled over to where Valeri prepared the new sample. "Another fragment?" He picked up the sample bag, raising it high up toward the fluorescent light hanging suspended from the ceiling, admiring the treasure. It was getting more and more difficult to find these pieces to the puzzle.

"When will you have more?" he asked, his excitement over the new find reflected in his voice.

She shook her head. "It is difficult to say. There are so few these days—"

He covered her mouth with his hand, smiling, always smiling. He leaned down to whisper, "We're running out of time, Katya. Tick, tick, tick . . . Eric's killer is getting away. You have to work faster, princess."

She pulled his hand away and stared at him, at once fascinated and repelled by his charisma. "I cannot promise progress without more samples."

He held up the plastic bag again, looking at the prize. "You'll find what you need," he said with incredible confidence. He shook his head. "Imagine it landing here, in the middle of nowhere. Quite a coincidence, don't you think? That a meteor or a scrap of ice comet or whatever the hell it was, would hurdle through the atmosphere to pound the earth in this one desolate spot, where it couldn't hurt. Where it would take decades to be discovered."

These were questions others had posed, some coming up with incredible answers. That the space fragment had been guided here, precisely for the reasons he'd outlined. That it was not of a natural origin.

She thought then of Eric. His quest. "Eric believed it was a ship. A spacecraft." Eric Ballas had believed the Tunguska Blast Site was actually the remains of an alien crash landing, evidence of extraterrestrial visitations. He'd been a fanatic about such things, an enthusiasm Katya didn't share. "He said he had proof."

"Did he? How extraordinary," he said, acting now as if he hadn't intimated the same thing, coming here to dangle the possibility of finding Eric's evidence for her, the missing documents Eric had promised would prove his theories about the origins of the material Katya gathered and analyzed. Documents Eric had died before he'd produced.

Alec Porter stepped closer, then whispered conspiratorially, "Do you think little green men are watching us now?"

At that moment, he reminded her so much of Eric, she felt it like a pain in her chest. The rascal.

"It was a meteor," she said blandly. "This is what I told Eric. Always. This is what I believe."

He leaned down and kissed her, a mere brush of his lips across her cheek. But the look he gave her afterward made her blush, bringing a rush of her milk stinging into her breasts, despite the fact that she'd just fed Erika. She shook her head as Alec bounded up the stairs, taking the steps two at a time.

She turned to catch Valeri frowning at her. She shrugged helplessly, as if to say: It is Alec. What could he expect? But she walked over to her husband and wrapped her arms around his neck to reassure him.

Valeri kept his eyes on the stairs where Alec Porter had disappeared. "I do not trust him."

"That is because he flirts with me. You have such little competition these days."

Her husband was five feet, five inches tall, 170 pounds. He

was bald and wore glasses, which he needed if he wanted to see anything farther than six inches from his face.

And he had the most beautiful brown eyes, with thick long lashes, and a warm smile. She loved no other.

She sighed, holding him tighter. "I don't know if I trust him, either. But, for Eric, we must try."

FLYING BLIND

Countdown: 25 days; 12 hours; 26 minutes

Chapter Seven

It had gotten so that, even the way her father breathed, annoyed her.

Cherish sat at the dining room table, across from her father. Her two older brothers shoveled food up from their plates to either side of him, a stair-step formation of engineers . . . while Cherish picked at her chicken Kiev, waiting out the lull for her father's next salvo.

Every Thursday night, she arrived at her father's doorstep loaded down with groceries. She always knocked herself out, making something special. So what if the XC-23 WingMaster had crashed? Did it matter that Reck was holding out on them, refusing to hand over critical data that could crucify or clear Marquis's wing design? At six sharp, she'd been rolling chicken breasts in bread crumbs, checking the sauce. Like her mother, she was predisposed to take care of her father.

Her mother, who had walked out on her father last year.

"I'll tell you what, if you had listened to me three years ago, you'd be team leader on the wing by now," her father said, picking up the thread of their conversation as if it were a script on a TelePrompTer. Dad's specialty was dredging up the past. Tonight's focus was Cherish's decision to leave the wing division and manage the joint project with Eric's company three years ago. At the time, her father had vehemently opposed the career move.

Her father shook his head, took a bite of the chicken. Chewed. Shook. "I don't care if it was a manager's position Chuck offered, anybody could see the Ballas contract wasn't lasting out the year. All that Blue Sky crap. Fullerenes and nanotubes. Now, look what you got." More chewing. More head shaking.

And there, ladies and gentlemen, you have it. The punch line. Applause please.

She put down her fork and linked her fingers together, resting her chin on her hands. She'd almost skipped tonight, the first Thursday after the crash. She knew her father had a tendency to bring out the heavy artillery during times of crisis, using "why don't you ever listen to me" like worry beads. And he had no trouble going over old ground.

"You're absolutely right, Dad. I should have stayed doing stress analysis on the wing, sitting in that cubicle right next to yours. And maybe, just maybe"—she tried to rein it in, not saying it, but thinking: *If I worked really hard and didn't die of boredom at the end of thirty-five years of doing the same tired calculations, I could earn a cheap gold watch*—"none of this would have happened. The XC-23 wouldn't have crashed—"

"I'm not saying the crash was your fault." He jabbed his finger in the air, using a crust of bread like a pointer. "But you being out on your butkiss next month certainly will be." He shrugged. "But no, you wanted your work to be interesting."

The piece of bread made its rounds, soaking up sauce from the plate. He popped it in his mouth. Her father was now on safe ground. *You shouldn't have wanted more. Shouldn't have risked what you had for the possibility of something better. Bird in hand.*

Chewing around the words, "Well, now you got a whole lot of interesting, don't you, Cherish?"

Mike, the oldest, rolled his eyes. Thomas wiped his mouth quickly with his napkin and rose from the table. "Gotta go," he said, giving Cherish a peck on the cheek. "I'm meeting the guys at the Rhino Room. Great dinner."

"Thanks," she said under her breath, adding a mental, *you coward.*

She and Mike were Malones through and through, their eyes a piercing blue, both towheads—though her hair was lighter, Mike having inherited her father's ash-blond curls. Thomas took after their mother's side of the family—dark hair, green eyes—the solid build of a halfback.

And unlike Cherish and Mike, who would stick it out for a couple of hours after the table was cleared, Thomas's style had always been a quick getaway. She heard the front door slam behind him.

"Chuck didn't have your best interest at heart talking you into managing that Ballas program, Cherish. That was me. Your father. In case you missed it."

Cherish played with the food on her plate. She remembered when Chuck had offered her a shot at the project, a program geared to evaluate a hot new composite material for strutural application. Marquis was a small company—it wasn't often that they could afford to do cutting-edge research. She'd jumped at it, despite her father's misgivings.

But a year later, the program floundered, then vanished altogether in the puff of smoke of a canceled contract. Along with Reck Enterprises, Eric's company had won the XC-23 WingMaster contract. Not long after that, Reck had brought Marquis on board as a subcontractor for the wing. Suddenly, all of Marquis's resources were diverted to the lucrative new project that promised a steady inflow of cash. If she hadn't been offered her position in public relations, Cherish would have been out of a job.

Now, three years later, the prototype had crashed. Reck Enterprises was holding back on the critical telemetry, sabotaging Marquis in the media by leaking tidbits to suggest the fault lay in their flawed wing design. It had taken years, but suddenly her father's prediction looked on target. *Bad move, babe, leaving the wing division.* Now, he was going for the gold, the proverbial "I told you so."

"Come on, Dad. Ease up a little, will you?" This from Mike, coming to run interference. "You're ruining my appetite. Really, sis." He held up a forkful of chicken. "This is great. The best."

Her father was massacring his bread. "Maybe Mikey's right. I am hard on you kids. But I wouldn't love you if I didn't say what was on my mind. That's not love, that live and let live crap. I see you making a mistake, I can't just sit here with my mouth zipped like your mother."

"It's called being supportive, Dad," she said.

"It's called bullshit, is what. You could learn an important lesson here, Cherish. Okay, so maybe you weren't doing so good on the wing, but that could have changed if you'd stuck it out." He shook his head. "You gave up too soon."

Cherish felt herself flush. *And there is the point of this evening's little lecture. Circle it on the page for easy reference.* She couldn't hack it as an engineer and she'd panicked, moving on to the fluff stuff of management, then public relations.

The problem was, there was this sneaky little voice inside her that said maybe Dad was right. Secretly, she feared the worse; she'd been shaky on the technical and that's why she'd taken the manager's position. It was a good thing Dad had talked her out of pursuing that doctorate.

"If you're finished screwing with your blood pressure, Dad, maybe I could clear this away?" Mike asked, rising from the table, reaching for his father's near-empty plate.

"You leave that, Mikey. Go set up the chessboard," their father said. "Cherish will clean up."

Mike was Dad's favorite. His namesake. Tall and good-looking—intelligent and personable. He'd just made senior director, himself. Dad's heart overflowed.

He was also gay, a fact that everyone important in his life knew, with the exception of their homophobic father, from whom they had carefully hidden the truth. Mike and his lover were looking for a condo together. They were talking marriage.

Mike put down the plate, leaving the dishes for Cherish. Why upset the applecart with the little things when, between him and their mother, they were ready to nuke Dad's world?

"Make some coffee, will you, Cherish?" Her father spoke from habit, not bothering to look up as he left the table.

Cherish pursed her lips. Sometimes, she really understood why Mom had left.

In the kitchen, shoveling coffee grounds into the coffee-maker—the very act, the symbol of female subjugation in her book—she told herself she wouldn't let her father get to her. She had bigger fish to fry at the moment.

Almost a week had passed since the crash. She, Chuck, and Lori had been working the problem from both the program side and the publicity angle. But so far, Reck had just given them the runaround, claiming the telemetry had too much static to be useful, his director of PR trying to pass off the old "oops!" as an excuse for every devastating news leak.

Cherish leaned back against the counter, feeling suddenly overwhelmed by the job ahead. She thought maybe she'd go home early tonight, get some sleep. The next few days were going to be tough. Because her father was right. If Marquis survived this fiasco, they would come gunning for a scapegoat. Right now, she and Chuck were looking like prime candidates.

"I think I'll be getting on home now," she said, stepping out of the kitchen. She patted her stomach. "Maybe take a walk around the block. Work some of this off."

"But it's early, honey."

"Really, Dad. I have some things to go over and if I don't get started . . ."

"Come on, Cherish. You work too hard as it is. You need the time off. Get a fresh start in the morning."

"Maybe next week, okay?"

She saw it immediately. *All systems shutting down.* "If that's what you want." He shrugged, looking hurt. "You don't have to come here, you know. I do just fine with the boys."

She tried to figure the odds of her brothers showing up if she wasn't cooking. But she didn't say anything, just kissed the top of her father's head and rubbed the bald spot. "I'll come by for church Sunday."

"All right," he said, giving her a quick hug, mollified. But when she walked away, he added, "Pour me a cup of coffee before you go."

Cherish stopped, in the process of swinging her purse over her shoulder. She dropped the bag to the chair and headed for the kitchen. Inside, she stared at the mugs. *I know it's tricky, Dad. But really. You should try it sometime. You wait for the coffee to go through the filter. You pick up the mug, set it down on the counter, pour the coffee inside . . .*

A minute later, she came out of the kitchen with two steaming cups. She placed one in front of Mike, the other—cream, no sugar—in front of her father. She noticed only Mike thanked her. Dad, engrossed in his next move on the chessboard, only managed a grunt.

"See ya," she said, saluting from the door.

Outside, she felt as if she could finally breathe. It was a cool night. Her father lived on Davenport Island in Huntington Beach. A strip of channel cut off the island from the mainland, the only entry, a bridge so small that, if you blinked, you'd miss it. But it kept things quiet.

Dad's house was on the water. He'd bought it back when you could do that for under a hundred grand. It was his pride and joy and Cherish had come to love Huntington Harbour. The ocean breeze. The smell of salt in the air. Christmastime, the houses were all decorated with lights and the locals held a boat parade.

She'd leased a house just down the street. It belonged to a friend of her father's who'd retired to Miami. They were trying to work out a deal where she could slowly buy him out.

As she came closer and closer to her little two-bedroom, she found her steps getting faster, as if she might be running away.

She smiled. Imagine. Teenage rebellion hitting in her thirties.

Cherish thought pool might be a metaphor for life.

There were these round balls. And if you hit them dead center, they never did what you expected. No, you had to hit them a little off the mark, manipulate them into doing what you wanted.

She walked into the house, kicking off her shoes as she turned on the lights and tossed her purse on the sofa. The living room was pretty much a pool table and a forty-inch television— her two vices. Chalking the cue, she picked up the game where she'd left off, putting the draw on the cue ball so she wouldn't scratch. She watched with satisfaction as the five ball rolled home.

Incredibly, a hand reached out, grabbing the ball before it could drop into the corner pocket.

Cherish looked up, straight into Conor Mitchell's face.

She leaned on the cue shaft, trying to catch her breath, her heart pumping hard from the fright and the adrenaline rush. "Funny, I didn't hear my doorbell." She stuck her finger in her ear, jiggled it up and down a little. "I should see the doctor, really. All those Grateful Dead concerts. Geez, what we didn't know in those days, huh?"

He was tossing the ball, catching it, walking toward her. "Late night?"

"Oh, have you been waiting long?" She flashed him a look of sympathy, her heart racing. "Actually, I just got back from an evening of wild uninhibited sex with Pablo." She crossed her arms and shrugged. "Is my hair mussed up? We were making up after this big fight. Pablo was a little miffed that I wasn't wearing my engagement ring." She stepped toward him, not being one to back down. "But I told him, 'Pablo, honey. It's three perfect carats. I'm almost afraid to wear it.' "

He smiled. "Still cooking on Thursday nights for Dad?"

If anything, there was a pattern to her days.

"How did you get in?" she asked.

He pulled out a key. Hanging from a key chain with a pewter replica of an F-15, the house key she'd given him a year and a half ago sparkled in the dim light coming through the sliding glass doors behind him.

She put it together in her head. "Do you ever read *Style* magazine? They have this test for rude behavior. Rule number three. Incredibly bad form to use your key when visiting an old girlfriend."

He tossed the key at her. "And now you have it back."

She caught it one-handed, then stared at it, thinking the obvious. "You really do that jerk thing well, Conor. No, honest. Have you been working on it?"

At that moment, the expression on his face said it all. She knew what was coming. She didn't need to wait to hear the words.

She held up her hand, stopping the speech she anticipated. "Let me take a wild guess here." She leaned the cue against the table, ready for a good fight. "Is this where you launch into the you-never-really-knew-me routine?"

"As a matter of fact . . .." he said.

Cherish sat down on the sofa and crossed her legs. She leaned forward as if hanging on his every word, getting into it because, what the heck, she didn't have much to lose here. Self-respect had disappeared about . . . oh, say, eighteen months ago. "Go on, Conor. I wouldn't want to miss this."

Surprisingly, a slow smile warmed his mouth, one corner lifting higher than the other, so sexy it hurt to look at him. He picked out a pool cue from the rack on the wall. "How about a game?"

That threw her.

"With you?" she asked. The man who had crushed her heart into itty bitty pieces, never bothering to look back to see if he'd left anything intact?

But there he stood, pool cue in hand, flashing The Grin, the one that could melt the Ice Age, generating more heat inside her than a fusion reaction.

She looked down at her bare feet, breaking eye contact. He was like that pillar of salt thing or Medusa. *Stay strong, girl.*

"Let's see," she said, finally moving, getting up from the couch, "what are my choices? Death by asphyxiation, root canal, game of pool with you." She shrugged, crossing her arms. "What the heck, a little dental work never killed anyone, right?"

"You never know, Cher. I might even let you win."

She had to give him credit. He knew the right buttons to push.

Still.

"Rack them up," she said.

The truth was, she and Conor had played pool often, going over to a popular hangout nearby, the House of Brews. Along with pool tables, it specialized in microbrews. The two of them would go there for a "Hollywood Blonde" and a game. Conor had never beaten her. Not once.

Chalking her cue, she envisioned herself beating the pants off him now, wondering how much satisfaction she could get from seeing him just stand there while she worked the table. The superior player. No. The Superior Being.

"There is a point to this visit, right?" she asked.

She watched him rack the balls, then gestured for him to break. Without answering, he walked to the head of the table and positioned the cue ball. *Bam!* An explosion of balls radiated out from the center, four balls slipping into the different pockets.

His stance, the way he held the stick, the force of the break. He'd been working on his game. It brought up a few interesting possibilities.

He lined up the next shot, choosing solids. "I've been thinking about the e-mail Alec sent you."

"Right. The e-mail you told me to ignore?" Geez. Had he actually put English on that ball?

Another ball dropped into its pocket. He turned to her. "If Alec contacts you—*when* Alec contacts you . . . it's not a good idea. You be smart about this, Cher. You listen to me for once. Leave Alec the hell alone."

She nodded, nibbling on her lower lip as if she were thinking on this incredibly sage advice. He wouldn't be jealous. He couldn't be jealous. She'd picked him. They both knew it had always been Conor.

"I think I'm a little confused here. Maybe you could clear things up a bit. A few days ago, you blew me off—now you're here, using keys, playing pool, warning me away from a man I was under the impression you once considered your friend. By the way, that would be the same man who thought it might be a good idea if I told you someone was trying to kill him."

He was staring at the table, maybe figuring his next shot. But she knew better. They'd been together for six torrid weeks. That might not seem long to some, but for Cherish, it had been a lifetime.

"Stop it," she told him.

He turned, a look of surprise on his face.

"Stop . . . it." She grabbed the cue stick from him. "Stopitstopitstopit. Stop editing what you're going to say to me in your head. Talk to me. For once, just talk to me."

He was taller than she remembered. She hadn't recalled him

looming like this. But she wasn't intimidated. She was too angry for that.

And it registered. Conor was giving her one hundred and ten percent. The kind of concentration a man might use to put an F-15 into a 4-g spiral and expect to come out of it alive.

"All right." He almost whispered the words. "Why not." The smile he gave went nicely with the five-inch scar across his cheek. "Here it is, straight, without the chaser. You're in trouble here. The XC-23. Reck. I'd say the odds are you still don't have a copy of the telemetry. But every day, Marquis makes the headlines. And it's never good news, is it? Reck's holding out on your team. On the same day, out of the blue, Alec e-mails you?"

"You see a connection," she said, crossing her arms. Because she didn't want him to see they were shaking. "Care to connect the dots for me?"

His scar had always set him apart, that fine line from brow to cheek. He used it now, making himself look just a little mean, capable of anything.

"A year and a half ago, we walked away from a crash of an experimental vehicle." There was an intimate quality to his voice, almost as if he were reciting poetry. "The companies involved included Reck, Marquis, Joystick—all teamed under the umbrella of the government. Joystick disappeared in a puff of smoke after the crash, swallowed whole by Reck. Now, there's another crash on the same program. The Wrecker himself gives the sell job. Or weren't you listening? Problems with the wing. Working closely with the government."

"We work as a team—"

He shook his head. "Marquis designed the wing. Reck Enterprises has the government's ear, winning contracts when they have no business beating out the competition." He grinned, almost enjoying it. "He's going to eat you alive."

"Eric Ballas didn't walk away from that crash. It killed him," she said, pointing out the differences in the two scenarios.

"He was the life and breath of his company; everyone knew it. Marquis still has all of its top-level management in place. And what does Alec have to do with this?"

Again, that slight lift at the corner of his mouth. Not a smile. More like a warning. "He'll let us know soon enough."

He gave the table another look, then took the cue and put it down. He turned, walking away.

"That's it?" she called after him, incredibly angry now. "You have your instructions, Cherish. Don't call me, I'll call you?"

She could see only his profile when he stopped, the moonlight catching the sharp angles of his face. But he looked tired. "Look, Cher. I said what I came to say. Anything else is a bad idea."

She turned beet-red. Losing it. "You think I'm still in love with you." She actually sputtered the words, she was so upset. "Of all the conceited . . ." She walked over to him and pushed him in the middle of his chest. "Look, bucko. You may not have noticed, but I have moved on. I'm not into jet pilots in tight jeans anymore—"

He grabbed her, his reflexes so quick, she didn't see his hands move. She actually registered the pain of his fingers digging into her arm before she realized he'd even touched her.

He pulled her up flush against him, holding her there. He bent down, whispering in her ear, "So who are you into, hmm? Pablo? I don't think so. Because for the last year, you've been writing me. Once a week I get those damn letters." His words were soft, menacing. Hiding a threat. "And I read between the lines, Cher. You were begging me to come look for you. To let you know it was all some terrible mistake, my not showing up that night. And nowhere—not once—does it mention anyone else but me."

His breath was coming hard, his eyes, narrowed with anger . . . and then with something else. It was a kaleidoscope moment, what happened next: a confusion of images, then crystal-clear focus as it all came rushing back. The memories.

She knew without a doubt he wanted to kiss her. That he knew it, too.

"It's still there, isn't it?" she whispered, a little awed.

He pushed her away, looking almost startled. Giving too much away. She almost laughed at the expression on his face.

He hadn't expected it, the electric shock of their attraction.

"You made a mistake once," he said, reaching for the door. "Think about that, Cher. Bad judgment when it comes to men." He was halfway out when he gave his parting shot. "You don't know Alec any better."

Cherish stared at the door as it closed behind him. She dropped down to the carpet, shaking.

"Well," she said, holding on to her anger and the tears she'd sworn she would never again shed for Conor. "At least he still wants to have sex with me."

Chapter Eight

Conor downshifted, spraying gravel as he maneuvered the 4Runner up the driveway and parked. Taking a minute, he sat with his hands resting on the steering wheel, thinking about the last couple of days, dissecting it to figure out where it had all gone wrong.

Maybe that videotape of the press conference . . . or the newspaper, combing through it every day, reading how she was getting deeper into it with Reck.

Of all the bonehead ideas, going out to see Cherish ranked right up there.

He closed his eyes. He couldn't seem to keep it together anymore. Couldn't shut off the noise and walk into his sister's house, play with the kids or have a beer with Marc, restricting Cher to some dark corner of his mind, keeping her there, confining her *there,* so he could just go on with his life without thinking about it. The accident . . . that night.

Rapid roll to the left! Full forward yoke. Shit! Roll to the right. Left rudder deflection!

He opened his eyes. It was full dark; you could see Venus just over the top of the pines. He stared out the window at the front house. If he went over now, asked Geena about the weekend's schedule, pretending . . . she'd see through it. His sister was too good at reading him these days.

He slammed the car door behind him and walked up the drive between the two houses. The scent of night-blooming jasmine perfumed the air, its sweetness almost overpowering. Geena loved flowers with strong scents. Roses, jasmine, honeysuckle. She'd planted a jungle of the stuff around both houses.

Tonight, the smell reminded him of Cher. Her perfume or maybe something she used in her hair. He hiked up the two steps to the lanai in one long stride, letting the screen door slam shut behind him. He stopped to lean against the screen, staring out at the yard.

A week ago, life had been normal. A week ago, life had been good.

But he hadn't managed a single instant of peace since Cher walked into his office. So Conor had come up with this plan. Go over there, warn her, head on home into the sunset. Just a strategic hit-and-run.

And didn't he owe her that much? If not for him, Alec couldn't hurt her now. Alec was Conor's responsibility. That's how it had played in his head. Clear, sweet, ever-loving logic.

He curled his fingers against the screen. He just hadn't read it right, how much he'd wanted to see her again.

When he'd stood next to her at that damn pool table, so close he could feel her breath on his mouth, could taste it, only then had he seen it. What was it Proust had said? The taste of the madeleine . . . that's what it had been like. Tasting her. Remembering. Feeling it all over again, that wild ride of the heart.

It's still there, isn't it . . .

"Oh, yes," he said under his breath.

He turned, almost savagely jamming the key into the lock,

thinking about the nice bottle of Stoli he kept in the freezer for nights like these, when the air seemed almost hot with memories. He turned the key.

It gave easily, turning too quickly.

The door had been unlocked.

He frowned, having the fleeting thought that Geena had come over and used her key, maybe forgot to lock up again. But he discarded the possibility as soon as he stepped inside the room. He could sense someone was there.

He reached for the light switch. The overhead light came on like a photographer's flash, framing Alec sitting on the couch.

He'd bleached his hair a near white and cut the layers short. The color made his eyes appear an iridescent green. *Colored contacts,* Conor thought. Alec's hair was naturally dark, almost black. His eyes, a deep brown, so you could barely distinguish the pupil from the iris.

He grinned at Conor from the sofa, his arms stretched over the top of the cushions, lounging back. He'd always had the charisma of an actor. He could walk into a room and light it up with that smile.

"Long time no see," he said.

Conor tossed his keys on the shelf holding his stereo system. He leaned against the console of the television. It was one of those big pieces of furniture that was popular when television was king. Now, everybody tried to hide their sets in cabinets and armoires.

"What the hell do you want?" he asked.

Alec *tched.* "I should be the one to carry the grudge. You got the girl, didn't you?" He snapped his finger, as if remembering something. "Now wait a minute. I remember now. You *didn't* get the girl." His face changed, becoming instantly hostile. "You left her at the altar, crying her heart out."

Conor didn't encourage him by responding. Alec was the last person he was apologizing to. "That's a different look for you."

Alec shrugged, the gesture saying it all. *Nothing to it.* "They say blondes have more fun. I was there that night, you know." His voice was serious now, taking them back. "You had no right to hurt her like that."

But Conor wasn't buying his Alec-the-champion act. "What are you running from this time, Alec?" It had been more than a year since they'd last spoken—it was too much of a coincidence that Alec should show up now. Conor walked around the Barco-Lounger facing the television. "What did you bring to Geena's door?" he asked, reminding Alec that Geena and her kids lived in the front house, believing it still might matter, what happened to the people he loved.

"I was careful." Alec stood. He strolled over to the bookshelf, making himself at home. Picking up a book, he flipped through *Moby Dick,* then put it back. "Staying one step ahead of them."

"Them? As in the nebulous forces trying to kill you?"

"So you got my e-mail. How is our Cherish doing? Did the two of you have a nice chat tonight?"

Conor tried not to let anything show on his face. All day, he'd had the feeling that someone was watching him. He'd told himself he was being paranoid, jumpy because Cherish had shown up out of the blue. Now he knew better.

Alec continued milling around the small room. "You know, I did it for you." He took the top off a candy jar, rummaged around the caramels Geena had put there. "Not that I thought you'd give a shit about my sorry ass. But if I put the two of you together . . . let nature take its course." He shrugged. "I figured after you stood her up, it would probably take a death threat to get her to see you again."

"That's you, Alec. All heart."

Alec grinned at the sarcasm. Picking out a caramel from the jar, he peeled off the wrapper and popped it in his mouth. "How about it, Conman," he said, using Conor's old call sign. "Did you hear music? See any fireworks when she came looking for you?"

Alec glanced down at his shoes, pricey Ferragamos. He rubbed the toe against the back of his calf, using the linen trousers like a buff. He had always liked nice things.

When he looked up, the devil was in his smile. "Or is the field clear for me now?"

"You want Cherish?" Conor crossed his arms, standing straighter. "Is that right?"

Alec laughed. "I love it. You don't want her, but nobody else can have her?"

"Just you, Alec. You leave her the hell alone."

Alec stepped over to Conor, his chest puffed out, hostile. He was shorter than Conor, but not by much. "That's what you said eighteen months ago." He jabbed his finger into Conor's chest in a punching motion. "I stepped aside for you because, you know what? I thought you deserved to be happy. Poor Conman, all his life he busts his ass for me and his baby sister. I owed you. I thought you loved her."

Conor shoved his hand away. "I didn't see you doing a lot of stepping aside. What I saw was you every day, in her face. Pouring on the famed Porter charm."

Alec made a face, dismissing it. "We were just friends."

"You should have picked me, little girl?" he said, quoting the last line from the e-mail.

"So you were paying attention. Hey. You threw her away. After that night, it's no holds barred."

Conor grabbed him. He swung him around, pushing Alec up against the wall, almost lifting him up by his nicely pressed shirt. "You know what you are, Alec? You're poison. Only, you've dressed yourself up like candy. But I've seen the rotten inside. You can't fool me. Not anymore."

Alec took a swing at him, hitting air as Conor ducked. Almost in reflex, Conor's hand struck out, hitting Alec's jaw. His head snapped back—he stumbled, shoulder blades hitting the wall.

Alec braced himself against the wall, shook his head. He touched his lower lip where a thin streak of blood oozed from the corner of his mouth.

"You've been waiting a long time for that one." Alec reached inside his sports jacket for a handkerchief. "You never really trusted me after you found out about Geena." He dabbed at the cut. "We were just kids."

"You always have an excuse, don't you, Alec?"

"You know what the problem is, Conman? All those years, bailing my ass out of one fracas or another has pretty much set the picture for you." He folded the handkerchief neatly and put it away. "In your book, people don't change. They're not allowed to."

"I know you, Alec Porter. You will never change."

Alec's eyes narrowed into an expression that reminded Conor of a cornered rat. "But I never killed anyone, did I? When you make a mistake, you don't believe in small ones. Perfect Conor. You killed those poor people, and now, you're letting it kill you. Get a grip, Conor. Let go of the past before it destroys you."

"Get out of here."

"I was willing to fix things for you. I was willing to lie to the safety board—whatever it took to cover for you. But you wouldn't take me up on it. Saint Conor, the golden boy. You couldn't for one minute be in my debt."

"It's so easy for you, isn't it Alec? To twist things around until perjury sounds like a little favor? You know, you're right. I don't want you to see Cherish. Point of fact, if you go near her," he said it clearly, so there would be no mistake, "I will rip out your heart."

Alec started to laugh, holding on to his sides. "Right. I'm the Big Bad Wolf and you're going to save your little Cher from me."

He stood back and dropped his head, chuckling now. When he looked up, he said, "They're going to kill me." He wasn't laughing anymore, but he kept his smile. "And Cherish," he added, just in case Conor wasn't listening. "You, old man, are in the clear. You could walk away, go on your merry way playing protector to Geena and her brood and no one would care. But when the six o'clock news hits, telling the world of the unfortunate accident that took the life of Cherish Malone ... well." He shrugged, the body language saying. *What the hell. What do I know?*

Alec walked past Conor to the door, brushing past him even though there was plenty of room to step around Conor. He stopped when his hand reached for the doorknob, as if changing his mind. "Maybe I'm just being an old hen," he said. "I could be wrong. But hell, what do you care anyway? What's one more body to add to the count?"

He opened the door. From the threshold, he said, "Oh, I left some goodies for you on the table. Sweet dreams, Conman."

Conor waited until the door closed firmly behind Alec. Like a reflex, his hand came up to rub the scar on his face, as if he could scrub it off somehow. He'd always made excuses for Alec. He hadn't seen the venom brewing there. Until it was too late.

Alec Porter was in trouble. And if he had to, Alec would drag Cher down with him.

Conor looked around the room. The cottage where he lived once had its own attached garage, but the previous owner had punched out a wall and converted the space into an enormous kitchen and dining room. Conor used the dining room half as a small home laboratory.

He could see the table from where he stood. On the far end, a manila envelope waited. He stepped closer, taking the two steps down into the kitchen level, his heart pounding as he walked over to take a better look.

The envelope was stamped "Confidential." The familiar insignia for Reck Enterprises was printed across the top: a stylized image of a globe surrounded by four stars. When he opened it, a diskette and several stapled pages slid onto the table.

Conor stared down at the missing telemetry for the second-phase prototype of the XC-23 WingMaster.

Alec flipped on the high beams, punching the accelerator to sixty-five. The rented convertible flew over the deserted road, radio cranked, air whipping past, clearing his head. Talking to Conor was always a little bit of heaven and hell.

He felt the pager vibrate against his hip. Steering with his knee, he turned on the interior light and peered at the numbers on the pager while touching the cut on his mouth. Picking up the cell phone, he punched in the number, using his thumb. He spoke first. "Tell me."

"You have to say you love me first."

He smiled, feeling good now. She was always such a blast. "I love you."

There was a long-suffering sigh on the other end. "Say it so I believe it, silly."

This time, he spoke with a thick Italian accent. "I luuv you."

"Better. Guess where I am? Never mind. You haven't the slightest. I'm in a suite. In a hotel. The rate is one thousand dollars a night. I peeked at the invoice while we registered. I'm waiting for Russell Reck. He's in the next room on a business call."

He whistled, actually impressed. She had been in the country less than a week. "Fast work."

"Now tell me you love me."

"More than life itself."

There was a pause. "I almost believe you, Alec."

The phone clicked off as she disconnected the call.

He smiled, shaking his head as he put the phone down on the seat next to him. "What a woman."

Alec turned for the freeway, heading back toward the beach.

Chapter Nine

In the morning, Cherish took the long way to work—Pacific Coast Highway south, straight into Newport. Her mission: air out the cobwebs from last night.

At Jamboree, a road she knew well from furtive trips with Lori to Bloomingdale's, she made a three hundred and sixty degree turn, heading right back down PCH for Seal Beach. She flipped up the sun visor, smiling, another fifteen minutes of Karmic bliss just ahead.

She had the windows down. Peach Union blasted from her car speakers, the sound loud enough to let her feel the bass. Crossing over the salt marshes back into Huntington Beach, the silhouette of Catalina Island on the western horizon, Cherish took in the crashing surf, the swaying palms, the tower-of-Babel power plant. It was a brilliant day. She had to squint to see the brown haze over Long Beach.

Around Bolsa Chica State Beach, the idyllic beauty of the wetlands and bluffs hiked up her Karmic bliss to a new high. She loved the wetlands, would soak in the sight of those birds and marshes for as long as the powers-that-be didn't cover them with houses. The seesaw-like oil pumps bordering the ribbon of coast highway bobbed up and down with the perpetual motion of a plastic duck dipping into a water glass, the rhythm, hypnotic.

At that perfect mellifluous moment clarity struck, bringing with it the truth to ring in her ears as loud and clear as the music on the radio.

All that therapy, the letters she'd written . . . what a colossal mistake. She wasn't supposed to get over Conor. Forgive and forget. She was supposed to *brand the experience into her heart,* clutch it to her chest, forever guarding herself against a repeat performance.

The truth was, a year and a half ago, she'd been a sitting duck for Conor. They were the three sole survivors, Cherish, Conor, Alec . . . why wouldn't they band together, waiting to see how that calamity would play out in their lives?

And somehow, it hadn't seemed right just to survive. Not when someone as dynamic as Eric Ballas hadn't made it. She'd felt the need to do something life altering. Make it count.

What she hadn't expected was that, after years of focusing on her career, she would go the woman's route . . . marriage, starting a family, sniffing around for Mr. Right. But it was the only explanation that made sense now, how she'd honed in on Conor, her heart screaming, *soul mate!*

Certainly, falling in love was no voluntary act. If it were, she would never have picked the stoic jet jockey. No way. If she'd had any control, it would have been Alec. Bird in hand.

Cherish reached down to change the radio station, remembering how it had been between her and Alec, that wonderful fit. From that first night when they'd stayed at the hospital for observation, she and Alec had bonded, filling some need in each other. Cherish liked to nurture people . . . her father, her brothers. And Alec loved it, the calls to see how he was doing. Homemade cookies. Little notes in the mail just to say, ''Hope you're coping,'' progressing to messages on the machine. *Give me a call; I had a bad night.*

He even understood about her father. It wasn't so much that she let Dad bully her. Michael Malone was this perfectly ordinary guy. He liked beer. He gave up smoking when they told him it was bad for him. He bought Lotto tickets and gardened on weekends. And he didn't like to see his kids have a hard time of it, so he tended to be a little too hands-on.

After watching her maneuver through a family dinner, Alec had started calling her ''Cherish the Good.''

But Conor. The phone calls, the cookies, the considerate little notes—it didn't take a brain surgeon to see he hated it. He didn't want nurturing. He didn't seem to want anything from her. Not chocolate chips and certainly not a ''thank you for saving my life.'' By week two, she got the picture. So she stopped making the effort.

A few days later, guess who shows up on her doorstep.

Cherish eased her foot off the accelerator, experiencing it all over again, how she'd opened the door to find him standing there. Conor Mitchell. The man who had pulled her out of a barbecuing plane. He of the deltoids and the melt-me-with-a-glance hazel eyes.

He'd stepped inside and grabbed her, pulling her up hard against him to give her one of those movie-of-the-week, this is it, The Big Moment, stares. The kind that left you breathless, thinking, *Go for it, Harrison. I'm yours.*

He didn't let her say a word, just kissed her.

Within fifteen minutes, they had their clothes off, their bodies, a tangle of arms and legs on the floor of the entry.

Cherish turned off the highway, heading inland toward Marquis Aircraft, the memories zinging back into her head with the force of a migraine. That's the way it was with them. Sex first, face the consequences later. After their encounter in the entry, it seemed as if everything in her life revolved around sex. Wonderful, fulfilling, endless, orgasmic sex.

Conor was this incredible lover. *Does it feel good, baby?* How could he make it better? *What do you want, Cher? Tell me. Come for me, Cher. Again.* She had been a nice Catholic girl up until then . . . which meant she'd lost her virginity in her twenties and not her teens. She'd only slept with one other man, practically a virgin in her age group.

And she'd never had an orgasm before Conor. Suddenly, she was having them regularly, miraculously. *Again, Cher.*

Why hadn't she kept it simple? Chalked it up to hormones? It wasn't as if six-foot, two-inch, single men with those deltoids and those eyes were knocking on her door every day. Of course, she'd been susceptible.

Judging from last night, she still was.

Cherish pulled up alongside the security box to swipe her badge, feeling her Karmic bliss slipping as she waited for the gate to the executive parking lot to raise slowly. Last night, the Almost Kiss . . .

What a mistake.

She couldn't seem to keep the equation straight. Boy rescues girl from burning plane. Boy agrees to marry girl. Boy jilts girl. Girl learns valuable lesson: Boy is a jerk. She kept putting her hand back in the fire, not learning the lesson.

Driving into her slot, she grabbed her briefcase from the seat beside her. "You can't take all that heat you feel for a man who saved your butt and stamp it *love.*" She said it out loud, like it might stick better that way. "That's where you keep blowing it."

Three minutes later, she walked toward the skyline of office buildings, laboratories, and eucalyptus trees at the main entrance where a banner proclaimed, "Marquis Aircraft: Let Us Be Your Wings." She flashed her badge at the security guard in the lobby as she walked briskly into the plant, opening her case in a practiced gesture for the guard, never even slowing, trying to get Conor out of her head—deltoids or no deltoids—and focus on what she needed to get done before her meeting with Chuck. She'd left a message on Lori's machine, planning to double-team their boss. Chuck had been dead set against ham-fisted tactics, dissing anything that smacked of a confrontation with Reck, their biggest customer. But this morning, she'd make him see the light. Conor was right about one thing: They were getting killed in the press and it was time to forget gentlemanly sensibilities. Put up or shut up—

A piercing siren burst across the quad, then pulsed into a pattern. Cherish stopped, puzzled, until the significance of that pattern registered. The fire alarm?

She started walking, then broke into a run, heading for the main office building. As head of public relations, she would have been informed about any fire drills. To her knowledge, there weren't any scheduled for today.

All around her, doors were opening from the different buildings and labs arranged around a central quad. People with badges hanging from their necks and clipped to shirt pockets milled outside in a haphazard fashion, assuming it was just an exercise . . . while Cherish looked around frantically, trying to find a trail of smoke, or someone waving their arms for attention, pointing out the direction of the disaster.

"Ms. Malone!"

She turned. A man dressed in a uniform flashed a badge through security and strolled toward her. *The fire marshal,* she thought, her chest easing up a little. He was wearing mirrored sunglasses and a fireman's uniform, the brim of his cap pulled down low against the sun. As if recognizing her, the man pointed toward the building behind her. Cherish headed there, wondering what on earth was going on.

She reached the front doors only seconds after the marshal, but didn't see him inside. The corridor and adjacent cubicles were quickly emptying, a steady flow of Marquis personnel passing her. Cherish smiled at people, trying not to set off a panic until she spoke to the fire marshal. But she'd lost sight of him. The hall and offices were empty now. Not a soul around.

Someone grabbed her wrist, jerking her back, making her lose her footing. She stumbled, almost falling to the floor until an arm anchored around her waist. A large hand—a man's hand—clamped over her mouth as she was dragged back.

She tried to dig her heels into the linoleum; she kicked backward. But he kept drawing her past the door into one of the high-wall offices across from the empty cubicles.

Struggling, she kicked and thumped her briefcase against the man's legs until she lost her hold on the briefcase, her only weapon. He was pulling her away from the windows. At the last minute, she reared up, breaking his hold to push him away. But he only latched onto her shoulder, getting a better grip.

She made herself a dead weight, forcing him to carry her or fall. The two of them stumbled—the small of her back hit a sharp corner. Manuals and books tumbled to the floor as she grabbed at air to break her fall. *Thump, thump, thump.* She reached for one of the books. Grabbed it. Swung. *Thwack.*

"Shit!"

He let go. Cherish crawled back, then jumped to her feet, propelling herself at the desk to seize the phone. She punched the number for security. One ring ... the phone went dead. A hand had come around her to press down the disconnect.

"Damn, Cherish. I think you gave me a black eye."

Her scream died in her throat. She turned, looking up into the face of the fire marshal in utter disbelief. In the struggle, he'd lost his hat—he wasn't wearing the glasses anymore.

"Alec?"

"In the flesh, little girl."

She took it in, the differences. He appeared almost taller, more formidable. As if maybe the young man had grown up. But the last year hadn't done much to age that timeless freckled face.

Alec.

A very blond, very tanned, very buffed, Alec. Dressed in

what was distinctly a fireman's uniform with the name "Largo" stitched into the front pocket.

"By the way, I forgive you," he said, smiling. "For the black eye. God, I missed you."

And then he kissed her.

He'd never kissed her before. Not even when he had tried to convince her that she was making a big mistake, looking at Conor with doe eyes, her heart gunning for the wrong man. Now his lips were harsh but coaxing. A demanding kiss. He opened his mouth, and with a little disbelief, she did the same, tasting mint and Alec and all the things she'd missed the last year of working day and night, trying to pretend she didn't *need* this, a man's body next to hers, a man's mouth on hers. . . .

"You think it's him you want." He spoke against her lips, the words coming with the rhythm of his breath against hers. "But I can show you. It was never him."

It would be easy, she thought, allowing the kiss, returning it. He loved her. It was there, so clearly in his voice, his eyes glowing with it. She wouldn't be alone . . .

She wouldn't be with Conor.

He stopped, responding instantly to her freezing up in his arms. She heard his breath, the harsh pounding like a winded horse. He took a step back, releasing her, a surprised look in his eyes.

He shook his head. "I don't fucking believe it. You're still in love with him."

She turned away. She leaned both hands against the desk. "I don't believe I just did that."

"Hey," he whispered, his voice different now, gentle as he turned her around and hugged her. He kissed the top of her head. "It's okay. I'm sorry. It was too much. But I needed you. I just needed you. I won't anymore. I promise." Light, warming brushes of his mouth followed, all over her face, on her eyes, her mouth. His fingers were buried in her hair as he tipped her face up to his.

He had always been incredibly handsome. Seeing him now, after more than a year of missing him—that little boy smile, the dancing light in his eyes—he quite took her breath away.

"I'll wait," he said. "Until you're ready. I won't push, Cherish. You let me know when it's okay."

Reality came rushing back. "Alec." She pushed him, not believing he was here. In a disguise, no less—in her office, a high-security facility that was supposedly guarded against the ruse he'd just pulled off. "What is going on?"

"I had to see you." The grin turned mischievous, his old self. "I saw Conor last night. God. To think you still have the hots for that old fart. No—" He covered her mouth with his hand, playful now. "Don't answer that. I don't want to know the gory details."

She took his hand from her mouth, but didn't let go. Instead, she held it tight between both of hers. He could always do that, disarm her with just a few words and a grin.

"You're not here because you're jealous of Conor," she said, knowing it was true.

His whole face changed, the brows drawing together, his lips forming a solid line. The expression made him look uncharacteristically serious. He squeezed her hand. "It's bad. Monster stuff. And they are going to make it sound incredibly believable. I won't blame you if you believe them."

"Alec, you're scaring me."

"I know. And I'm sorry. It's just that, if I say too much . . . just this, then. You've always been an independent thinker. Not one of those minions you feed your stories to, putting your spin on it. When you hear them talk about me, about the things they say I've done or will do—"

He placed his hand just above her breast, pressing it there. The gesture struck her as incredibly bonding, his palm against her beating heart.

"—I want you to listen with your heart. Can you do that for me, little girl? Just listen with your heart?"

"Okay," she said, a little breathless.

"Let Conor believe them. Hell. He'll want to. There was some bad blood between us just after the crash." Again the disarming grin, as he leaned forward and whispered, "I don't think he trusts me anymore."

"I'm voting, not," she said, remembering Conor's warning last night, her heart feeling two sizes too big for her chest.

"But I have faith in you, little girl."

He held her for a moment, not letting her go. And she didn't want him to, falling into the old feel of him comforting her.

"I've changed, Cherish. This time, I won't play fair. That Alec is gone," he said, in a low, sweet voice. Stepping back, he tilted her face up to his. "I love you. Has he ever even said those words to you?" And when she didn't respond, "I'm not going to step aside. I'm not going to be the nice guy and let him have you. Never again."

Even as she tried to figure out what to say, he turned and left. Reaching for the doorknob, he looked back and flashed his dimples. "He had his chance. Now it's my turn."

He blew her a kiss and slipped out.

Cherish dropped into the nearest chair. She reached up and brushed her fingers over her mouth. "Holy moly," she said, repeating one of Lori's favorite phrases.

She didn't know how long she just sat there, zoning out as she stared into space, comparing Alec's kiss with The Almost Kiss, the one that wove in and out of her consciousness all night as she swatted it away, an annoyance. At some point, she had the presence of mind to get up, gather her things. When she walked into her office a few minutes later, the telephone was ringing. She stared at it for a minute, until her mind caught up with the sound. She answered it, barely whispering, "Cherish Malone."

"I'm in the lounge." It was Lori. "Get here, now!"

She'd known Lori long enough to hang up and run. The lounge was just around the corner and down the hall. When she walked in, it was jammed, people huddled around, buzzing with talk. She had to push her way to the front before she could see the screen.

A man's face stared solemnly out at his audience. A newscaster for one of the networks. She listened, unbelieving.

She hadn't realized Lori had come up behind her, didn't know she was there until Lori spoke. "Are you listening to that? Do you believe this?"

She remembered then what Alec had told her. *Monster things.* Now, she was scared.

Russell stepped out of the shower, drying his hair with a towel. He thought he heard voices coming from the bedroom and padded across the wet tiles. Over the last few days, he'd discovered that Allison tended to have nightmares. Bad ones. Last night, she'd had a doozy, waking up screaming, clawing at him, drenched in sweat.

But this time he saw it was the television and not Allison making the racket. She was awake, channel-surfing, her arms propped up by several pillows as she stared rapt at the cinema-sized screen. She was butt naked, laying on her stomach across the mussed sheets, her cute little tush, a perfectly delicious peach.

He leaned against the doorjamb, watching her. She had her legs up, heels to the ceiling and ankles crossed, looking at the same time sexy and adorable. She'd painted her toenails earlier with a polish she'd bought in the gift shop downstairs, a delicate powder blue. Her feet wove an interesting pattern in the air as she crossed and uncrossed her ankles. He stood back, enjoying the view.

An incredible heat rushed through him, making him hard against the bathrobe. His heart belonged to Sydney—she was his true love—but he couldn't seem to get enough of Allison, couldn't seem to control his desire for her. And why should he, really?

But he knew he was taking a big risk. Every night since they'd arrived in DC, he'd called Sydney, stalling. *I'll be on the Gulfstream tomorrow, honey.* Promise. He'd hang up and swear, tomorrow morning, he'd get on his private jet. He was being stupid about Allison. Too obvious. But it didn't seem to matter. Maybe, it even added to the high, that he was pushing it like this.

When morning came, somehow, he always managed to find another excuse why he needed to stay an extra day. Like now. Seeing Allison naked on the bed, he was thinking he could call Sydney. *Kinnard is riding me hard on the XC-23; it's killing me, Syd, really. But I have to stay.* Asking for one more night of heaven.

"Hey," Allison turned to look at him, all that curly hair tumbling to one side as she pushed up on the pillows to expose the plump underside of one breast. "Isn't that your company they're talking about?" Seeing what held his attention, she rolled her eyes, and pushed up the volume on the television.

"On April 25"—words blared out with near-Dolby strength from the twin speakers—"we warned Reck Enterprises." The television focused on a single individual, a man, possibly edging into his sixties, with pale blue eyes held wide and unblinking. "The day before these tragic events, we knew what would happen if Reck flew the XC-23 WingMaster. Reck's decision to ignore our plea not only cost the taxpayers of this country more than a billion dollars, but the lives of innocent men. Let us not forget, the pilot and copilot, the flight crew, who gave their lives in last Saturday's fatal crash."

Russell dropped to the bed. *What the hell . . .*

"We at the Millennium Society understand that, because of the nature of our beliefs, some have cause to doubt the accuracy of our information. But to totally disregard the possibility, we feel, showed a complete disregard for life. To think we're just

crackpots . . .'' The man shook his head, looking forlorn. "We
sent Reck Enterprises a copy of the terrorist's demands; we
invited company representatives to come to our offices and
examine the diskette we received. We provided the exact date
the bombing was to take place, and still they continued with
the scheduled test flight.''

The phone beside the bed rang. Russell ignored it, intent
now on the man whose face filled the screen, hanging on his
every word.

"Wow." Allison sat up, crawling back on the bed to kneel
beside him. "Did you know about it? That there was a bomb
on that plane?"

A bomb? It couldn't be possible. The wreckage they'd assembled in the hangar at Edwards would have shown . . .

But not if they assumed it was a design failure. They wouldn't
even be looking . . .

Jesus Christ. A bomb.

"And so now, we dare not hesitate, lest Reck Enterprises
once again ignore our plea. For that reason, we have contacted
the networks. They call themselves Marduk, referring we think
to the chief god in Babylonian religion.'' He glanced down at
a note in his hands, appearing to read from it. "If the sum of
$2,532,000 is not paid in the manner outlined below, we of
Marduk will strike down the next scheduled test flight of the
XC-23 WingMaster.'' The man looked up. "We hope that—
by informing the public—we will force Reck's hand and avoid
yet another catastrophe.''

The man's face disappeared. Two newscasters, a man and a
woman, took his place. The phone kept ringing. Russell figured
he knew who was calling. Knew they wouldn't hang up until
he answered. He picked up. "Hello."

"Are you watching this?" It was Joseph Kinnard. "Are you
fucking watching this!"

Russell thought maybe he was having a heart attack.

* * *

"Conor? Get in here, man."

Hearing Marc calling him, Conor gitty-upped into the den, carrying his three-year-old nephew, John, on his back, his twin sister Alexa trailing behind, urging the "horsey" on for her brother. Conor was supposed to be helping the twins get ready for preschool, but, as usual, they'd been waylaid by some roughhousing and now a quick game of rodeo. But when Conor saw his sister's face, he put his nephew down on the couch.

"What happened?" he asked. He didn't like Geena's expression.

His sister turned to her eldest. "Chris? Go help your brother and sister get their things together for school."

Chris stared at his mother, about to protest, but Geena just gave him the kind of look a child learns not to ignore. "Come on you guys," he said in a pained voice, guiding the twins back down the hall.

She turned to Conor. "It's the XC-23." She motioned to where Marc stood rapt, his coffee mug in hand, staring at the television. "They're saying it was a bomb."

Conor stepped forward, listening, disbelieving as the newscaster's face disappeared from the set to be replaced by a photograph of another man.

" . . . We have reason to believe that the man pictured here is responsible for planting the bomb that caused the XC-23 disaster Saturday morning. . . ."

Geena was saying something, but Conor couldn't hear her anymore. He just stared at the photograph that filled the screen. Geena's hand squeezed his shoulder. He blinked, pulling away from that mesmerizing face and the possibilities it presented.

Christopher walked in, passing his uncle and parents to stop in front of the television screen. His eyes furrowed, showing the same disbelief that held the adults in the room.

He reached out and touched the familiar face smiling at them from the television.

"Mom." He turned, facing his parents and Conor. "It's Uncle Alec. They think Uncle Alec is a terrorist."

Chapter Ten

The Wrecker sat front and center surrounded by his minions, lizard eyes at half-mast, making Cherish wonder what was behind that trancelike stare. She kept thinking about Alec. The newscasts about the bombing had played throughout the weekend.

Reck's chosen spokesman for this fine Monday morning was the head of security at Reck Enterprises, a man in a checked sports coat and too small button-down oxford that made the engineers in the room look like snazzy dressers. She figured he'd worked out once, but the bulging muscles had gone to fat years ago. He wore a rug. A bad one.

Sharps was his name, the height of irony. As far as Cherish was concerned, if they ever gave Leo Sharps an epitaph, it would read: He Was An Idiot Among Men.

"This is what we know about the Millennium Society." Sweating despite the air-conditioned room, Sharps handed out several sheets of paper stapled together.

"Any chance they're part of it?" Joseph Kinnard sat beside

Reck, the bishop to Reck's king here at the home offices of Reck Enterprises. A tall man in his early sixties, Kinnard's wardrobe showed what Sharps's lacked, a sense of style. Today, he appeared lit up by the electric color of the French blue shirt beneath a Saville Row suit, his closely shaved white hair recalling bygone years as head of covert operations for the CIA. To Cherish, it was like sitting across from a viscount, some son of an effete but long dying aristocracy, someone you might see standing with his arm around Ivana Trump on the cover of a tabloid.

And in a way, he was aristocracy. One of the few appointed positions that seemed to thrive despite changes in the administration. As undersecretary of defense for research and acquisition, he'd been involved in appropriations for the last ten years—which, interestingly enough, coincided with the rise in the fortunes of Reck Enterprises. People said when Kinnard got a cold, Russell Reck sneezed.

"Trust me, these Millennium guys are just a bunch of kooks," Sharps answered, patting the sweat from his forehead with a handkerchief as he sat down. "We're talking Heaven's Gate all over again. Who would have guessed they were actually on to something with the bomb threat?"

The conference room overlooked the picture-perfect Newport harbor. Yachts and white-sailed schooners bobbed alongside small, canopied electric boats that reminded Cherish of the Jungle Cruise ride at Disneyland. There was enough glass surrounding her to give a goldfish bowl feel to the place. Even the walls leading into the hallway were glass, so that anyone walking by could see the worker ants busily at it inside. A slew of security grunts and military types bellied up to the conference table that dominated the room, the table big enough to make a UN delegation happy. She figured it might take a compass to find the other end.

Joseph Kinnard and his troops, including an Air Force general with requisite lieutenant-colonel attaché and military police, circled the polished oak. With an interesting addition. Luis Lebredo. Special Agent Luis Lebredo. Since the telecast Friday, the FBI had formally taken over the investigation of what had befallen the XC-23 WingMaster.

Lebredo appeared to be in his late thirties—a good decade younger than most of the men in the room. With dark thick hair and Hispanic good looks, he'd dressed in a *de rigueur* conservative blue suit. He had eyes that didn't miss much and a nose that appeared to have been broken more than once. By the look of distrust he gave everyone in the room, Cherish didn't peg him for someone under Reck and Kinnard's collective thumb.

But the real surprise was the man seated at the far end of the table from Cherish. Conor Mitchell.

He wore chinos, a dark olive T-shirt that brought out the green in his hazel eyes, and an expression that said he didn't care one way or the other what Kinnard, Reck, or Cherish had to say, he just wished they'd get around to spitting it out. He had better things to do with his day. His hair was wet, as if he'd just stepped out of the shower. He'd walked into the room five minutes ago, about the time Cherish had taken her last clear breath.

Kinnard flipped through the pages of the report Sharps had handed out, then tossed the stapled sheets on the table, looking unimpressed.

Sharps cleared his throat, his gaze darting from Kinnard to Reck. "I'm sure you can see why it was unlikely that we would take these claims seriously." Not getting any response, he continued, "The Millennium Society began five years ago, founded by one Dean White."

"Dean White. He won the Nobel, right?" Looking tired, Chuck skipped to the next page, his white brows pinched over the bridge of his nose. Along with Lori, he and Cherish made up the Marquis contingent. Between the three of them, she figured they could probably clock in about ten hours of sleep over the weekend, tops.

"One and the same," Sharps answered, smiling now. "He discovered a new GUT, a grand unification theory. You know, electromagnetics, strong and weak nuclear forces, gravity. A big shot at Caltech. Then, five years ago, bam. The guy claims to have been abducted by aliens."

"No shit." This from Reck's chief engineer, the man dropping the memo to the table as if it had suddenly caught fire.

"You got it. This is fire-in-the-sky, take-me-to-your-leader, *X-Files* stuff. We're talking really woo woo. The Millennium Society started when White discovered others who'd had the same experience. Fellow abductees. Only, these guys don't beam up to the mothership and come back talking strange medical exams. It's much more . . . transcendental." His smile said he should score points for the big word. "Some kind of meeting of the minds that happens on a long walk after dinner or when you're out on the porch contemplating your navel." Sharps picked up the memo, reading now. "They describe the contact as seeing a big white light followed by an overwhelming sense of euphoria."

He shrugged, the gesture saying it all. *Bunch of crap.*

"What's this stuff about ESP?" Reck's program manager asked, flipping to the next page.

"As an added benefit," Sharps answered, "they claim to acquire a sort of extrasensory perception from the contact. A heightening of their senses—smell, hearing, sight—as well as an uncanny ability to know what others want. It's a strange kind of charisma. Their own special gift from beyond. Hell, they even have some celebrities on board."

"Marte Sims, last year at the Golden Globes," Lori said beside Cherish. She and Lori had spent a long night preparing for this morning's meeting. But unlike Cherish, whose sleepless night showed in the dark circles under her eyes and caffeine jitters, Lori had put her personal arsenal of makeup to good use, looking fresh as a daisy. Cherish reminded herself all that Lancôme wasn't doing her any good in the drawer.

"Right," Sharps said, now on solid ground. "I owe it all to . . . yada, yada, yada. According to White and his group, these aliens—they call them The Others—will come back at the turn of the century. 2001. Returning for their converts."

"Kinda like when PanAm kept a reservation list for their first flight to the moon," someone said, the comment punctuated by nervous laughter from others around the table.

The security chief smiled, seeing that maybe things would be okay. That it would look like he'd been right to disregard the group.

"Is there any proof of these special gifts?" The question came from Special Agent Lebredo. Cherish noticed he hadn't bothered to read the memo laying undisturbed on the table next to his well-manicured nails.

"Not a chance."

"And yet," Lebredo said, "they do enjoy a distinguished membership. Like Eric Ballas."

Reck frowned. "Dean White was Eric's advisor at Harvard. He hired White as a consultant when White started taking an interest in composite materials."

The last twenty years, there had been a move toward using graphite composites on planes rather than metal, though it was much more prevalent in military rather than commercial aircraft. The graphite fibers imbedded in an epoxy plastic made structural components that were stronger, stiffer, and lighter than metal. The B-2, the Stealth Bomber, was the most famous example. It used a composite with a special outer coating that absorbed radar, making the plane invisible to enemy radar. Cherish knew that Dean White had been a part of Eric's quest to develop a composite for the future.

"Even with this Millennium Society nonsense," Reck continued, "Dean managed to publish a few thoughtful pieces, buckyballs, nanotubes, synthetic metals, and such. Eric always put great stake in White and his theories. Frankly, I thought them too esoteric.''

"Rumor has it, White had access to some secret Russian papers," Sharps said as if on cue. "UFO sightings, wreckage of an alien spacecraft. It was supposed to give him a breakthrough into a new composite material, something revolutionary.''

"Don't they claim we found the technology for the Stealth Bomber and the silicon chip from Roswell?" This from Reck's chief engineer, said with a grin. Again, a ripple of laughter.

But Chuck wasn't joining in. "Maybe he was on to something," he said. "The stuff White published was out there, but plausible. And I've talked to a few of the higher-ups in the Russian Academy of Sciences. If you ask someone in the Pentagon about Roswell, they roll their eyes. Not in the Kremlin. The Russian government takes this stuff pretty seriously. Makes you kinda wonder. Like maybe they know something we don't?''

"It's true that Ballas was a card-carrying member of White's group," Lebredo said. "And he worked with the Russians. That's a connection.''

"Superficially, I would agree," Reck said. "But I happen to have known Eric for a long time. He was . . . a maverick. An idea man. He wanted to use cheap Russian think tanks." Reck shrugged. "A lot of companies did. After the fall of the Soviet Empire there were too many unemployed physicists and engineers, men and women with dangerous knowledge to share. We tried to help the situation, keep the engineers from being hired away by extremists.'' He shook his head. "It was one big headache.''

"In the Russian Academy of Sciences Institutes," Sharps chimed in, "you got a paycheck whether you were doing any work or not. Too much chaff among the wheat.''

"And yet, Ballas appeared to make it work," Lebredo said.

"So he got lucky and found a few reasonably talented engineers who were willing to work for peanuts,'' Sharps said, pulling at the tight collar of his oxford as he reached for his handkerchief again.

"It was the basis for his company—a financial consideration, not an ideological one,'' Reck said. ''You had to give Eric credit for that much. He was a charismatic person; he motivated people. And his operation was small enough that he was completely hands-on with the Russians. But the Millennium Society, that was just Eric making nice with Dean White. I'm absolutely positive.''

"When did you become aware of the terrorist's threat?'' Chuck asked, sitting back now, massaging his temples in a gesture that showed he was fighting off a migraine.

"I was never informed.'' Reck shook his head, he of the oh-so-clean hands. ''But I support my people's decision. These are lunatics. How could we possibly put off a billion dollar program on the say-so of such a fringe element?''

Lori scribbled across the Sharps's memo—*Because they said our plane was going to blow up?*—underlined it twice and turned the paper for Cherish to read.

But Lori knew enough to keep her mouth shut. They'd talked strategy with Chuck before coming here. He had opted for the wait-and-see approach. Reck had left them out of the loop before; they didn't want to be the enemy here.

"The security on that prototype was airtight,'' Sharps said, sounding defensive.

"But it blew up, just the same,'' Lebredo answered.

"It's clear we overlooked something,'' Reck said. He shook his head, the weight of that loss clearly on his shoulders as he worried his fingers through his mousy-moussed hair. ''Everyone working on the XC-23 has a high security clearance. This isn't a black program, but it's as close to one as you can get.'' He leaned forward, his eyes on Lebredo. ''I hope your people can help us find the hole in our security.''

"So if there's no connection with Ballas, why these guys? The Millennium Society?" Chuck asked.

"Who the hell knows?" Sharps said. "Maybe they thought it was cute, after the disaster in San Diego, the Heaven's Gate suicides. Maybe they knew we wouldn't take them seriously and we'd look like idiots."

"And the terrorists, this Marduk group?" Chuck asked. "What do we know about them? Or are these reports we're hearing on television correct? You know who's behind the bombing?"

Lori squeezed Cherish's hand under the table, knowing this was the moment of truth.

Kinnard nodded toward one of his people, his assistant, an attractive young woman who looked straight out of law school with her page boy hairstyle and power suit. The woman stood to pass out three folders, one to each of the executives in the room.

Cherish stared at the folder placed in front of Chuck. It was the kind where access was carefully controlled, complete with a signature block for signing out. There was a sheet stapled to the front of the folder, with SECRET stamped in red across the top and a border of red stripes slashing down at an angle. Directly below, someone had typed a name: *Alec Porter*.

"We know who did it, all right," Kinnard said, sitting back. "There's no question."

After a quick read, Chuck passed his folder to Cherish. They had all heard the television reports, CNN scooping the networks, breaking the story first.

Her hands shaking from lack of sleep and too many cups of coffee, she opened the folder. There was a photograph inside, the kind that would appear on a military identification—Alec in uniform, fresh faced and smiling.

"It looks like Porter went off the deep end after the crash of the first-phase prototype. Unfortunately, these things happen," Kinnard said.

Cherish glanced up at Conor. But Conor gave nothing away, still slumped back in his chair, appearing uninvolved and uninterested.

"We have the diskette White received." Agent Lebredo took over now. "The name Marduk hit a note with Joseph here." He nodded toward Kinnard. "He remembered Porter had been shot down in the Gulf and spent time in an Iraqi jail with some Mesopotamian scholar. Apparently, the man had been locked up for beliefs not in line with the current regime. Porter came back with an interest in Babylonian deities, even spoke a little Arabic. He was also a wire head, loved to surf the Net, into all the newest software."

"Let's face it," Kinnard said. "Alec Porter was a loose cannon. A real hot dog. The file shows several unfavorable Officer Performance Reviews. Apparently, he had a problem with authority. His chosen call sign said it all, Wildman." He flipped through the folder before him. "It says in the file they grounded him after he buzzed the Rose Bowl during a routine demonstration flight of an F-15 at half-time. He disappeared when he was FEBed," he said, referring to the Flight Evaluation Board hearing that had put an end to Alec's military career. "Who knows what he's been up to the last year."

"Luckily for us, he left several computer diskettes in his quarters. They were in storage. After Joseph"—again Lebredo nodded to Kinnard—"gave us the heads up, we were able to examine them in the Crime Lab at our facilities in Quantico over the weekend. The diskette sent to the Millennium Society had the same signature marks as those found in Porter's quarters."

"Meaning?" Cherish asked.

"Anything mechanical leaves a particular mark, a signature, even a computer disk drive. Not many people know it, but no two machines execute quite the same. So, just like a ballistics lab can match a bullet to the gun that fired it, we tested the diskette. It's not always so clear with a computer drive. But we were lucky. We found a match.''

"And of course, there was the psychological profile," Reck added, flipping to the back of the folder. "You can read the report for yourself."

Cherish turned to the personality profile and quickly scanned the information, each word digging into her heart.

Manic behavior . . . Narcissistic tendencies . . . Schizoid personality.

"The Air Force put up with Porter because he was a talented pilot. But as you can see, the evaluation states he could be perfectly capable of aberrant behavior," Kinnard said.

"I don't believe it."

She hadn't intended to say it out loud.

Kinnard gave her a small smile. "Perhaps that's where you can be helpful. You and Colonel—Dr. Mitchell, here. You knew him better than most."

The way he said it, that small gaff with Conor's old military rank, the insinuation was there. *You're here to help us find him—but we're not sure we can trust you.*

"We believe he's been in contact with you," Lebredo said. It wasn't a question.

A million scenarios flashed through her head. *Monster things—aberrant behavior—Alec knows how to get into trouble.* She knew she'd hesitated too long.

She shook her head, as if she was in the middle of a nightmare, trying to wake up. "He writes me. Postcards from all over the world."

"When was the last time you heard from him?" Lebredo asked, taking over now.

"He e-mailed my office." She hadn't erased the e-mail. In any case, her computer wasn't secure. She'd bet dollars to doughnuts they'd already gone through her stuff and had a copy.

For the first time, Cherish realized she and Conor hadn't been asked here for professional reasons. This was personal.

"And your response?" Lebredo asked.

"Nothing." She shrugged, forcing herself not to look at Conor. "When I tried to e-mail him back, I couldn't. I couldn't access the address where the message originated. I even had my assistant take a look at it," she said, nodding to Lori beside her. "Nothing."

Lebredo nodded. "He could have sent the e-mail with a fake address. Do you still have the postcards?"

"Yes," she said, not daring to hesitate this time, her mind going a mile a minute to figure out the pitfalls of anything she might say. *Listen with your heart,* he had told her. *Oh, Alec, what have you gotten yourself into?* "But it won't do you any good. There was never a return address."

"It is vital that you be on board with us on this." It was Reck who spoke, voicing what was certainly going through the minds of Lebredo and Kinnard sitting to either side of him.

"Of course," she said.

There came a long protracted silence, possibly meant to get her to reveal more. Cherish didn't move. Didn't shuffle papers. She played the good soldier awaiting instructions.

Lebredo turned to Conor. "Our files show that—"

"Alec Porter is for all intents and purposes my brother," Conor said, speaking for the first time. "We grew up together in a state-run home. I formally petitioned the court for guardianship over Alec and my sister when I turned eighteen. And no, he has not contacted me. But if he does, you'll be the first to know."

"If we can put a stop to this before the May—"

"Dear God, Russell. You can't possibly believe we're going forward with the test flight for the final-phase prototype?" Chuck asked in disbelief. "We have to straighten this out first. Find out what's going on."

"The flight is a go," Reck said without hesitation. "We're

behind schedule as it is, Chuck. You know that. It will kill our funding if that prototype doesn't fly.''

"Maybe this is all about revenge," Sharps added eagerly. "Porter was copilot on the first-phase prototype; he blames us for his career falling apart. As far as he's concerned, the WingMaster program should crash and burn, just like he did. And it wouldn't hurt your little company, now would it? You haven't sunk half a billion of your profits," Sharps said.

"We have as much riding on this as Reck Enterprises. Possibly more," Chuck said, that bulldog face going a long way to cutting Sharps off. "Those were good people you let die on the prototype with your carelessness. Don't you think it's time to start playing it safe?"

Sharps grunted, backing down.

"Of course, Russell here will take all the necessary precautions," Kinnard said, showing that he supported the decision to go forward with the next flight. "And there's little good to be gained by giving in to terrorists. We're on guard now. The final-phase prototype will be watched around the clock by the FBI. It will be completely secure."

"Why the $532,000?" Lebredo asked the question as if he was thinking out loud. "It has to mean something. Why not keep it at two million?"

"I thought the same," Kinnard said. "It's a very specific amount."

"Maybe he wants it to pay for a sick friend's operation? Or it was the pension he lost with his discharge. Who the hell cares?" Sharps said. "The point is, we get the guy. And you help us," he said, looking from Cherish to Conor.

Conor unfolded his large frame to sit up. "You're right. We should all help each other," he said. "Work as a team."

He took out another set of papers, stapled sheets that he had brought along with him. He placed them on the table so everyone could see. Cherish hadn't noticed the papers before, sitting there at his side. Now she couldn't take her eyes off them.

Stamped across the top and bottom in bold 16 point type: RECK ENTERPRISES: CONFIDENTIAL.

"How did you get that?" Sharps sputtered the words in a spray of saliva, turning a beautiful shade of eggplant. He looked as if he was going to bust a button.

"I found it in my mailbox at the university," Conor said, looking relaxed. "It's the telemetry readout for the last test flight, and perfectly readable, I might add. Apparently someone didn't like your company keeping it under wraps." He looked coolly at Reck. "I'd watch things a little more carefully at home if you plan to fly the final-phase prototype. Just a friendly warning." He said it with a smile.

Still keeping his calm, Reck said softly, "I would appreciate you handing those over."

Conor shrugged. He pushed the stapled sheets so that they slid across the slick surface of the table. Reck stopped them with his fingertips.

"And any copies you might have," he added, his eyes on Conor.

Conor smiled, lounging back in his chair. "I don't recall making any."

Knowing a good exit when he saw it, Chuck stood. "I don't know what's going on here, but make no mistake, I am appalled by the tactics your company has chosen to employ the last week. I was told there was a problem cleaning up the telemetry readout. Now it appears your company has purposefully kept the telemetry from us. It makes for a difficult relationship, gentlemen, to know that we don't trust each other," Chuck said getting one in for the good guys.

Marquis's senior vice president gathered up his folders and made for the exit. Cherish and Lori fell in behind him. From the door, Chuck scanned the room regally, adding, "I realize Reck Enterprises is the prime contractor and can do whatever the hell it pleases, but we are your major subcontractor and a member of this team. We deserve to be treated with respect and honesty. I suggest you work on regaining our trust, then we'll see how we can work together against these terrorists."

Cherish followed Chuck out, Lori bringing up the rear, giving the door a good slam behind her.

Outside, they walked briskly down the hall, moving on beyond the granite-accented entry and its sign of welcome, "Reck Enterprises: We Bring the Future." Beyond the glass doors, the Marquis trio stood at the bank of elevators pondering the fate of their small company.

Lori punched the down button a couple of times, as if that might help speed things up. "Those bastards," she said, breaking the silence.

"Yup," Chuck agreed. "I'm just wondering what would have happened if Dean White hadn't gone public."

But he didn't need to say it. Clearly, Reck had wanted Marquis to take the fall for the crash.

Just then, Cherish heard the glass doors to the offices behind her open, felt the whisper of air conditioning on the back of her neck. Before she could turn around, a hand clamped onto her elbow. She looked up into Conor's face.

"What do you think you're doing?" Chuck stepped between them, ready to intervene. Like Lori, he knew Cherish's history with Conor.

"It's okay, Chuck," she said, holding him off. Her eyes on Conor, she said, "I sincerely hope you lied when you said you didn't make any copies of the telemetry readout."

"I said I didn't recall making any." He took her arm, guiding her to the stairwell, leaving the Marquis team behind. "My memory just improved."

Allison was screaming in her sleep again.

Alec stared down at her, the book he was reading opened on his lap. Beside him, Allison seemed to calm down a bit, moaning softly. They were in bed together, in a motel room

Alec had been using as a sort of headquarters. The Blue Waves Inn had quaint little cottages just off PCH, right on the sand. You could hear the surf at night. Allison turned, her face now angled up to his. She was crying real tears, still fast asleep.

When she screamed again, he shut the book, putting it down on the nightstand. He told himself to ignore the sound. "Shit."

He glanced at his wristwatch. What the hay, it was time to get going anyway. "Get up, sweet cakes." He shook her. "Rise and shine."

She opened her eyes, laser blue pinpointed with black pupils. She stared at him silently as she woke, then sat up, the sheet pooling to her waist, revealing her young breasts.

"I told you never to wake me," she said.

He grabbed her chin, holding her face up to his. "And I said if you start screaming, I'm going to wake your ass up." He said it with a smile, *just a little joke, sweetie.* But he couldn't keep the edge out of his voice. He knew he was hurting her, holding her chin so tight that her delicate skin would be red from his fingertips digging into her. But those dreams of Allison's. They made his skin crawl.

She started shaking then, her thin arms coming around her middle, as if she was freezing cold. Her reaction was always so physical; she was trying to control the shakes by holding herself.

After a while, she lay down, curling up next to him. "It was a good dream."

Alec stroked her hair, his anger leaving as quickly as it came, wondering what could possibly have been good about it. But that was Allison.

"Tell me about Conor," she said.

That was Allison, too. She would wake from these dreams, and she would want stories, just like a child. She liked the ones about the crash best.

Alec put his arm around her, her frame almost bony, she was so thin. He'd noticed Cherish, too, had lost weight the last year. But Cherish wasn't like Allison, looking like those models in the perfume ads. No, Allison wasn't anything like his Cherish.

Last night, he'd thrown out the wig. He could still see it from the bed, slumped in the trash can, curls flopped sideways over the rim so that it looked like some unidentified roadkill. After seeing Cherish up close and personal, the wig . . . well, he just didn't have that good of an imagination.

"So you want a Conor story." He was stroking Allison's hair, thinking about Cherish. About seeing her and kissing her.

He'd never kissed her before, though he'd thought about it. A lot. It had made him incredibly angry to realize she still wanted Conor.

"Conor the good guy. Such a fucking, boring good guy. Why do women always go for the guy in the white hat?"

"I don't," she said, reaching for his hand.

"No." He smiled. "You don't."

"Tell me about the scar."

Maybe that was Conor's big draw, Alec thought. He wore his scars so well. So goddamn stoic. He just went on his way, always going forward. Never mind life's little tragedies, parents dying, Geena getting pregnant, the FEB.

"Geena and him," he said it like a bedtime story. Little Red Riding Hood. "They landed in that state-run facility after a couple of years making the rounds of foster homes. But me, I went straight there. The place of last resort for those incorrigibles like myself."

"Conor helped you," she said, knowing the story.

"There were these kids, and they were beating the shit out of me." But there wasn't anything they could do to Alec that hadn't been done before, harder and worse. "I was eight. I remember I was crying, skinny arms swinging. I'd wet my pants," he said, laughing as he remembered. It never hurt to talk about it. "Then out of nowhere, comes this kid. He towered over us. Almost a man. He actually picked up both those guys by the scruff of their shirts, so that their feet dangled off the ground. That's how I remember it, anyway.''

"One of them had a knife."

It had been incredible to watch, that knife slashing right at Conor's face. Opening his cheek. Branding him for life.

"They told him he was going to lose the eye at the hospital." He remembered that. Geena, crying her heart out. Conor had already started flying by then. Some program for the underprivileged sponsored by the local airfield. Alec had been standing there looking at Conor, waiting for him to hate him. Because, until that day, everybody in his life had hated Alec for the mere fact that he existed. As far as he could see, Conor at least had a good reason.

"He was already talking to the ROTC people. He was thinking Air Force. Flying meant everything to him. If he lost that eye . . .''

"But he didn't blame you."

He shook his head. "He told me it wasn't a big deal." He laughed. "And when he said it, God, he could make you believe it. I'm going to lose an eye. No big deal, man. Moving on."

"It was a big deal when he didn't show up for his wedding."

He thought about it, remembering. "Maybe that was the first true fuck up of his life," he said. "Anybody who knew Conor could see he didn't want to get married." He laughed. "He was scared. Nothing ever scared Conor before that."

"You made sure he wouldn't show up," she said, anticipating.

"I loved her . . . he was having second thoughts. I just helped him out a bit telling him about Geena."

He frowned, remembering. How many times had Alec pushed Conor never to see that man break? And what was the big deal, anyway? Him and Geena? Something that happened so many years ago?

But he cut off the rationalizations. Geena was everything to Conor. The only person he'd expected Alec never to hurt.

"And there was Cherish, the woman I love." He was still frowning. "I was holding her, letting her cry on my shoulder. Cherish the Good. So perfect, that moment." He had wanted her so badly. *Cherish the Good.* The woman who had brought out the good in him.

"She surprised me, she did."

"Because she didn't want to marry you?" Allison asked.

"Nah. I knew Cherish wasn't going to be easy. What surprised me was that she still wanted him. He was going to break her heart, and she knew it. And she still loved him."

Allison sat up straighter. She turned his face toward hers. "You didn't tell him about Geena just to make him disappoint Cherish. You had another reason."

He looked into Allison's eyes, listening carefully. There were times when she spoke with this incredible insight. You'd be a fool not to listen.

It was probably what drew Reck to her. What they were all drawn to, men and women alike. Allison just seemed to know things. What you needed—what you wanted. And then, she gave it to you, like a present, exactly what you needed most at the moment.

"You wanted him to hate you that night," she said. "You thought you deserved it. His hate."

Hate? Alec thought about that, wondering what she was trying to tell him. He pulled at a loose curl stuck to the corner of her mouth, frowning. Had he wanted Conor to hate him? Well, who the hell knew. Certainly, Alec had earned Conor's hate.

"Will he believe them about the bomb?" she asked.

"Undoubtedly—"

But he hesitated. He remembered that fourteen-year-old boy looking at him with his eye bandaged. *No big deal.* He wondered suddenly, if Conor would believe them.

"I don't know," he said.

On the bedside table, his wristwatch beeped. Alec jumped

out of bed and turned off the alarm, remembering why he'd set it. "Got to go, sweet cakes," he said, slapping Allison on her rear.

He grabbed the clothes he'd set out and the book off the nightstand, *Applications of Advanced Electronics*. The jumpsuit he carried was white, the logo for Beechwood Security Systems sewn on the front pocket. He wondered if he had time for a shower, then decided he could just make it.

A few minutes later, Allison stepped into the shower with him. "When will I see you again?" she asked, her arms coming up around his neck.

"You know the drill." He kissed her, laughing out loud, letting the water sluice over them as he cupped her breast. What the hell. Maybe he could be a little late.

Chapter Eleven

"Don't tell me you actually believe that bunk about Alec?" Cherish paced back and forth, barefoot on the carpet, the shoes she'd kicked off the minute she'd walked through the door slumped one against the other on the floor.

Conor lay sprawled out on her couch, making the biggest piece of furniture in the room look amazingly small. But Cherish couldn't sit still if her life depended on it. Inside her head, she felt as if she were experiencing one of those computer glitches. Like maybe she needed to push restart. She couldn't synthesize the information. Couldn't make it come into focus.

"The real question is, why don't you believe it?" Conor asked, looking a little too calm, the tennis shoes he wore propped on her coffee table. They'd come to her house, the closest and most private place near Reck's Newport office.

"Oh, sure," she told him. "Like they couldn't have fixed that profile to say whatever they wanted?"

"Are you talking government conspiracy? Because that was his Air Force record."

"Not 'the government,' " she said, wagging her fingers up to put the word in quotes. "But someone. Yes."

He shook his head, looking dead certain. "He ran away, Cher."

"The act of a guilty man?" she asked. "You're buying that dribble from Kinnard?" Because she had other theories about why Alec had disappeared.

"What about the diskette? They matched it to his laptop's drive."

She pushed her bangs from her face, having no answer for him. Instead, she turned toward the pool table, her mind automatically seeing the shot, concentrating there because she didn't want to think about Alec's guilt. *Angle it off the rail and into the corner pocket.*

After a minute, she simply said, "I don't know."

But it just didn't ring true. *Alec, a terrorist?* After the crash of the first prototype, they had spent countless hours talking about all the things that mattered in life now that they'd been given this second chance: the people they loved, what they planned to do with the rest of their lives. Blowing up planes hadn't come up as an option.

She picked up the cue ball, pushing it across the felt surface, purposely ruining a perfect setup. She wondered if she was being insightful or just plain stubborn. *What if you're wrong?* Conor had left her waiting at the altar. Maybe it was time to start questioning some of those gut feelings of hers.

"He told you someone was trying to kill him. Why?" She kept with that, giving Conor more questions rather than answers. "Man gets death threat. A week later, man is accused of a terrorist bombing? You don't smell some sort of conspiracy? Scratch that," she said, knowing he would discount any theory that made Alec out to be a hero. "Forget what we don't know. Let's talk about what we do. Alec. Do you really think he's capable of cold-blooded murder?"

She waited, watching him carefully. She almost sighed in

relief when she saw it, the change in his face. "There. You see. You don't."

"Now you're reading minds?"

Cherish shoved his legs off her coffee table and sat down, in his face. "Okay, so you measure my ability to get to know someone's character by the length of time I've spent with that person." She leaned forward, elbows on her knees. "But what if what we went through, the accident, what if that condenses it all together, making it different. Changing the rules." She put her hand on her heart, where just a few days ago, Alec had held it, asking her to believe in his innocence. "I feel as if we went through a lifetime together."

"It's an interesting theory," he said.

"So I repeat. Do you believe he's capable of murder?"

She thought he might not answer. But then she remembered Conor never talked off the top of his head. You had to show patience with him. Wait while he got the right angle on the thing so it would come into focus and give up its wisdom.

"When Alec was nine years old," he told her, "he asked me to help him kill his father."

The words came out of the nowhere. His expression said there was more. She waited for the other shoe to drop, knowing it wouldn't be good.

"It wasn't as if he didn't deserve it," Connor said, almost drawling the words. "They put Alec in that home to get him away from the bastard, in any case. But Alec wasn't acting out of passion or anger. He was real cool about it. He wanted a foolproof plan. He trusted me to come up with something brilliant. His words, not mine."

She felt her heart pound against her blouse so hard that, certainly, Conor could see it. *Ba dum. Ba dum.* "And what did you tell him?"

"That I would help him get away from the old man, protect him, though it wasn't true. I wasn't even legal yet, and I was talking about getting him and Geena out of there." Conor shook his head. "Alec told me that wasn't good enough. He said, if his father didn't die, he would. I took it to mean suicide."

It was difficult to imagine. Somehow "Alec" and "suicide" weren't two words you put together in your head.

"You read the file, Cher. Manic. Schizoid personality. An IQ off the charts. Let me expand a little. Alec's life was a living hell. You don't think that could mess him up a little?"

She'd always thought Alec was an orphan, just like Conor and Geena. That's why he'd craved those family dinners at her father's house so much, hinting around for an invitation. Because he'd never had a family. She never asked him for specifics. She thought they had enough dealing with their memories of the crash. Now she saw his smiling face, the freckles, remembered his jokes. *Suicide?*

"You and Geena turned out okay."

"No one was using us for a punching bag every time the system decided mommy and daddy had gotten their shit together and it was time to make us one big happy family again."

He leaned in so close, she could feel his breath on her cheek. "Did you ever wonder why Alec doesn't drink? He had enough of it as a kid. His parents even shot him up once, with heroine. They thought it was a hoot to see their kid high. You think about that, Cher. You see it in your head. And you imagine what kind of man comes through that."

There were some things you just didn't want to know. Pictures you didn't want in your head. She'd been dealing with quite a few of those over the last year. Conor had just added another one.

She stood, unable to think straight. She stared at Conor's scar, recalling that he'd once told her it was the result of a childhood accident. She'd imagined a bicycle or something. Now, she was beginning to wonder.

You don't want to know, Cherish, she told herself.

"Did Alec kill his father?" she asked instead.

Conor left the question suspended between them with the

finesse of an aerial maneuver. Finally, he shook his head. "As it happens, he didn't. Both his parents died of drug overdoses."

She shut her eyes. All those weeks—those long talks with Alec, and never so much as a hint of this. The stories he'd shared had always been about Conor and Geena. The Air Force. She'd assumed, she'd just assumed . . .

She considered, for a moment, that the man who had held her in his arms the other day—the man who had kissed her, telling her that he loved her—that maybe Conor was right. He could be a stranger.

But after a while, she opened her eyes and shook her head. "I won't believe it. He's not a killer. And I think you know it."

Conor stood, hovering over her, reminding her of the times he'd tried to use his height to intimidate her. He was a good foot taller. It hadn't worked then, and it sure wasn't going to work now.

"You have to tell me," she said.

He turned away, shaking his head as if she were hopeless. She knew Alec and Conor had parted badly, though neither man would discuss the details of their last meeting. But whatever they had fought over, it sure had Conor gunning for Alec, a man he'd just told a conference room filled with people he considered his brother.

But after a while, Conor sat down. "I don't know." He spoke grudgingly. "I always thought . . . I thought, if Alec was capable of murder, he would have killed his old man."

She felt an intense sense of release. It was the only endorsement she needed. "So what is going on?"

Conor gave her a hard stare, the expression somehow making his scar more pronounced. "Whatever it is, it's not good. Thursday night, Alec came to see me."

She forced herself to keep quiet. She wasn't sure she should tell Conor about her own visit from Alec. That he might be watching them now, keeping tabs on their conversation.

"When he left," Conor said, "he told me to check out a gift he'd left for me. On the table, I found these."

Conor held up a diskette and a file folder. She took the folder. Inside, she found a copy of the telemetry readout.

"Alec gave you the telemetry?" She caught her breath. And then she smiled, seeing it. "He's trying to help us."

"Maybe," Conor said, looking at her dead on. "Or maybe he's just setting us up to take the fall."

"Two million five hundred and twenty-three thousand dollars." Joseph Kinnard crossed one leg over the other, exposing an expensive loafer. He seemed to taste the words in his mouth like a fine wine. "Why does that sound so very familiar?"

"I understand," Russ answered. They were in his office, he, Kinnard, and Sharps, the pleasing black leather furniture and rare African masks lining the wall doing nothing to comfort Russell. All three men knew exactly where they'd come across that specific amount of money.

The meeting with Kinnard wasn't going well. It didn't look good, that file getting into Mitchell's hands—the bomb, the Millennium Society. Kinnard didn't like loose ends. And Alec Porter was one hell of a loose end.

"Russell," Kinnard said, his colorless eyes unreadable. "The shit has hit the fan."

"I can see that."

"And you know where I have that damned FBI agent, don't you?" Kinnard continued. "Right up my ass. Looking over every scrap of paper that crosses my desk. Now, how am I going to get business done like that, Russ?"

Russell thought about the delicate operations under Kinnard's thumb. If Lebredo started sniffing around . . .

Russell turned to his chief of security, that fuck-up Sharps, focusing his hostility there. "From now on, I want to see anything and everything that crosses your desk. Got it!"

Sharps looked shocked by the attack, his eyebrows raised comically, practically disappearing beneath the ridiculous hairpiece he wore. ''Sir, do you have any idea how many crackpots—''

''I don't really give a shit,'' Russell answered. ''What concerns me is that one of those crackpots just blew up my plane and I could have stopped it. Do you have any idea what happens if we don't fly that final prototype?''

''Of course—''

''Then get your ass moving to make sure those crackpots don't stop us from doing just that. Goddammit, Sharps. You knew he was out there.''

''I'm on it, sir,'' Sharps said, clearing his throat. He took out his handkerchief, wiping the perspiration from his upper lip and neck. Russell wondered if he'd lift the hairpiece and pat his bald head. ''How the hell did that flight jockey get those papers? There's no way.'' Sharps shook his head, looking nervous. ''There is just no way.''

Russell mulled it over, the possibility that Conor Mitchell had access to Russell's secrets here at Reck Enterprises. But he dismissed it. Conor was nothing. A nobody. A washed-up test pilot with some interesting theories on composite materials he peddled to undergraduates. That was it. He wasn't a threat.

Alec Porter was another story.

He cut Sharps off at the next breath. ''Someone handed Mitchell that file. Someone who has something to gain by throwing egg on my face,'' he told Sharps. ''You find that person and you'll find our security breach. And just maybe, you'll find Porter.''

Sharps nodded, putting away the handkerchief. ''There's a company I use sometimes for the delicate stuff.''

Russell nodded. ''I don't need the details. Just keep an eye on Mitchell and that damn Malone woman.''

The door burst open, the sound almost shocking in the silence of the room—but not as shocking as Sydney marching in, red hair blazing in loose curls to her shoulders, Russell's secretary fast on her heels.

Looking apologetic, his secretary said, "I told her you were in a meeting."

"It's all right, Dolores," Sydney said, coming to sit on the edge of Russell's desk. "These gentlemen were just leaving."

"This isn't a good time," Russell said, trying not to let his anger show in front of Kinnard. *Just what I need right now.* First that spook Kinnard has him doing a tap dance, now Sydney falls in for an encore.

Goddammit. He felt pushed to his limit, watching Sydney sitting there on his desk, looking as happy as you please. The biggest gamble of his career was slipping through his fingers. He didn't have time for Sydney and her antics!

He told himself to calm down. No sense in panicking. He'd proven over and over he had what it takes, and he'd do it again. Sure, he'd been handed a few million by his father . . . and he'd turned it into a billion-dollar company. Not that the thankless bastard had ever given him any credit for it. He was too busy kowtowing to his firstborn, the idiot who eventually bankrupted him.

Well, Russ wasn't a loser like his brother. Not The Wrecker.

"On the contrary." Sydney crossed her legs, giving a view of her beautiful gams beneath the tasteful Chanel suit. "This is the perfect time." She looked at her watch, a Cartier with a pavé diamond case he'd bought her for Christmas. "Let's see. I can give you five minutes before my next appointment."

He couldn't believe it. Her voice, her heated face. She was drunk.

He stood. "Gentlemen. If you will excuse us? Dolores"—he spoke into the intercom—"have lunch catered." To his security chief, he said, "I'm sure you have a few things you need to go over with Joseph here. We'll meet in say, twenty minutes?"

He planned to have Syd out in less than three.

Kinnard and Sharps left the room, Sharps trying to convince Kinnard everything was under control as he closed the door. When they were alone, Russell stared at his wife, taking in her red eyes, her slightly disheveled hair. "You've been drinking."

"Oh, no, darling. I have been celebrating. Drinking champagne and counting my millions. You see, Russ. I am going to be a very rich woman when you divorce me."

Alarm bells set off in his head. *Jesus.* "Syd. What's this about?" His voice, his whole demeanor—instantly, he transformed himself into the injured husband. "You want to divorce me now? In the middle of this shit, because I haven't been there for you?"

"Who is she?"

That stopped him cold. Russell had been married twice before. He knew that look. *Oh, fuck.*

But when it came to his wives, he lived by one motto: When all else fails, deny.

"Now you're going to accuse me of cheating on you? For Christ's sake, Syd. Get a grip—"

"She's young. You like them young. And blonde." She pursed her full lips as if she was thinking about it, then shook her head. She opened her purse and reached in. "Maybe not. It's been done so many times, the blonde. Megan and Carla," she said, referring to his first two wives. "But certainly she's a sweet little thing you just had to have."

"This is crazy—"

She threw a set of photographs on the desk. "Oh, my. How very indiscreet. It looks like you've been a very naughty boy."

They were pictures of Allison, standing next to him at the hotel in Washington, looking bored as he talked to Kinnard beside him. Then later, at the "21" Club, her hand in his across the table.

"What do you know. I must be psychic," Sydney said, tears in her voice. "Young, but not blonde." The tears began falling silently down her face. "Are you leaving me, Russell?"

Hearing those words, he almost sighed with relief. She didn't want a divorce. She was afraid he would leave her.

He stood and walked over to her. Dropping to one knee in front of her, he buried his face in her lap. "She doesn't mean anything to me, Syd. I love you. You're everything." He even managed a few tears himself, looking up at his wife. Jesus. If Syd left him now, in the middle of all this. "I love you, Syd."

She dropped down to the floor beside him, her arms coming around him. "You have to stop seeing her."

"It's the pressure, Syd. It got to me. I only started seeing her a week ago. It's nothing. Nothing at all."

"You'll call her today. You'll tell her it's over."

"The minute you walk out that door, baby. God, I love you."

He stood, taking her in his arms. He started kissing her, surprised that he was hard for her, that he wanted to make love to her right now. "Forgive me, baby. Forgive me."

She was kissing him back, into it as much as he was. But then she pulled away.

"You promise. Today," she said. "As soon as I walk out."

He could see she was putting a stop to it between them. There wasn't going to be hot sex on his desk like the old days when Henry was still alive. Too bad. He leaned his head against her forehead, surprised that he was breathing hard. "It won't happen again."

He could feel her shaking in his arms. But when she looked up, there was a hard glint in her eyes that he didn't like.

"See that it doesn't," she said, her voice suddenly flat.

"Syd. You're not driving?"

She seemed distracted as she thought over his question. She shook her head, stepping to the door. Her hand on the knob, she shook her head again. "No." And then she walked out.

He got his breath back, leaning against the desk. "Okay. That was close." He turned and picked up the phone, dialed for an outside line, his breath still coming hard. It was for the best. He needed to focus on the XC-23 WingMaster. No distractions.

Allison's machine picked up on the second ring. He listened and left his message. "We have to meet. Same place—the usual time. Don't make me wait this time. I have something important to tell you."

He hung up, relaxing now. Yeah, Syd had the right idea. His life was complicated enough. Kinnard, the fucking FBI. He didn't need to push it like this. Next time he saw Allison, he'd let her know. It was over.

Sydney got behind the wheel of her Mercedes sports coupe. He wasn't going to leave that woman. She knew it with a certainty that amazed her.

She punched in the cigarette lighter and waited. She fished a cigarette out of her purse, her hands shaking. When the lighter popped out, she just managed to light the cigarette and inhaled deeply. She'd quit smoking last year. Smoke gave you wrinkles.

Fuck wrinkles.

"He's not going to leave her."

And even if he did, there would be another one. Just as surely as there had been others before her.

Her marriage was a sham. And she'd given everything for Russell. Everything.

Still holding the cigarette, she crossed her hands over the steering wheel and let her head fall forward. She cried softly. She didn't know what to do.

Fifteen minutes later, she was driving the Mercedes down PCH, slow and easy, knowing she'd been drinking, though not much. Not enough. It was false courage, the champagne. Thank God, she had another bottle waiting for her in the refrigerator.

By the time she pulled into the driveway, her mascara had run and she'd smeared her lipstick. She wobbled on her heels inside, throwing the keys on the granite counter. She always kept a bottle of Cristal in the refrigerator. Now, she popped the cork, staring at the foam gurgling up like a geyser. She drank straight from the bottle.

She heard the doorbell. A little dazed, she let it ring several times before she walked to the door. Harbor Island was a private estate. You needed a key to get a car past the gate. But the island was small enough that you could park on the mainland and walk across.

She had the thought that it could be one of Russ's cronies, looking for him. The crash Saturday had sent everyone at the plant into code blue. She smiled, liking the image of Russell's trophy wife answering the door, mascara bleeding to her cheeks, house in disarray from the remodeling from hell.

But when she opened the door, she found a man in a uniform waiting. Taking her elbow, he steadied her when she lurched back a bit, losing her balance. She felt a little ashamed, realizing that she was swaying on her feet, holding a bottle of champagne in her hand.

She pushed her hair out of her face, trying to get a hold of herself. "Yes?"

He looked young, a Generation-Xer with buzzed-cut hair and long sideburns bleached a near white, his eyes, a startling green. He smiled, flashing a clipboard with forms in triplicate. He wore a badge with his photograph and name clipped onto his white coverall uniform. "I'm from your security company. You called about a glitch in the new system?"

She vaguely recalled the system going on the fritz last Thursday night. But even in her blurry state, she knew she hadn't called the company. She had enough on her plate with private investigators keeping tabs on her philandering husband.

"My husband must have called." It was the sort of thing Russ always took care of. She started shutting the door. "It's not really a convenient time right now. Perhaps you can come back another day—"

Surprisingly, he inserted the clipboard past the doorjamb, keeping her from closing the door. ''It's not a good idea to put this off, Mrs. Reck,'' she heard him say from the other side. ''Frankly, I only fix the system—I don't counsel the clientele— but common sense says a woman like you shouldn't let this go.''

She let him nudge the door open. He had a boyish smile, and he made good use of it now. The freckles, too, completed the picture of earnest young man.

''I promise. You won't even know I'm here.'' His expression said as much as the words themselves. *I hope you don't mind my stepping in. Like me. I'll do a good job.*

She smiled, despite the fact that she wasn't feeling herself this morning. All that crying. That wasn't like her. She was a woman of action. That's why she was here, married to one of the most powerful men in the world.

Losing him. *Just like Carla and Megan. Get in line . . .*

''Yes, of course,'' she said, putting a stop to the mental spiral. ''You're right.'' She looked at the plastic-coated badge. ''James. Come in, please. The control panel is—''

''I know where it is, Mrs. Reck. Don't you trouble yourself. This shouldn't take long.''

She watched him disappear, then sighed, her shoulder blades hitting the masonry work that framed the enormous custom-made doors. She stared across the entry into a gilded mirror meant to complement a marble-topped table, both expensive antiques she'd bought herself in New Orleans. She held her breath, than laughed out loud at the raccoon eyes staring back at her. ''What will become of you, you silly thing,'' she told the woman in the mirror.

She wiped the runny mascara off with a tissue from the guest bathroom, taking a breath, trying to calm down. In the front room, she dropped into a Chippendale love seat they'd delivered earlier, swigging from the bottle.

Russell was having an affair.

He'd called Sydney three times to tell her his meeting in Washington had been extended. He would be staying out of town longer than he'd expected. Always, it was just one more day. Then, the next morning, he'd call with the same story, apologizing.

As if she was an idiot. As if she couldn't figure it out.

Now it was all coming together. His lack of interest in sex. In her.

She put her face in her hands, hunching over, her mouth frozen in one of those horrible moments of pain where no sound comes out. *What did you expect, Sydney?* Russell was a rich, powerful man. A man of vision. But he'd never been faithful. *Why did you think it would be different for you?*

Now, there would be another woman taking her place—the next Mrs. Russell Reck, please step forward.

"Are you okay?"

She glanced up, foggy from the liquor and her grief, her eyes swimming with tears. The security man was standing over her. What was his name? Her eyes went to the badge. *Beechwood Security Systems. James.*

"That's not going to solve anything." Very gently, he took the bottle from her hand and put it on the round tray that rested on a tufted ottoman—the newest thing for a coffee table, the decorator had told her.

James knelt down beside her chair. "Problems at home?" he asked. "Kids in trouble?"

"I don't have any children." At least Megan and Carla had babies, children they could pour their love into. But not Sydney. *Too far down the line . . .*

"Your husband, then?"

She frowned. "I don't think that's any of your business."

"Then I guess you wouldn't be up for a cup of coffee or something? Maybe a shoulder to cry on?"

The way he said it, with that smile . . . a kid on a dare. She had a fleeting thought that this is how it happened. The bored housewife, ignored by her mogul husband. The handsome pool cleaner . . . the sweet boy fixing the security system.

And he was a boy, seriously younger than Sydney's thirty-seven years. And quite good looking, though not at all her type, of course. Sydney had always been attracted to powerful men. Men with influence. Not some muscle-bound studmuffin.

You could show Russell . . .

"Whoa," he said, standing, taking a step back. "That was a big *no* on your face. Too bad." He picked up her hand, looking at her fingers as he stroked them with his thumb. He kissed the knuckles, then let go before she could take her hand away. "But if he keeps being a jerk. Keep me in mind. You can always reach me through the company." He winked. "James. Tell them to page me."

Almost mystified by his bravura, Sydney watched him write something on the clipboard. He snapped out the form, and dropped it on the tray next to the champagne bottle. She noticed he'd circled his name.

"I'll show myself out. It was just a faulty relay in the master bedroom." He stared back at the tray with the champagne bottle, then shook his head. "Coffee and a shoulder to cry on might have been a better idea, but it's your call."

Beneath the uniform, she could see his well-honed muscles. Not bulky, as if he spent a lot of time building up, but nice to watch, giving her a warm sensation in the pit of her stomach.

He shrugged, then saluted her. "Remember. Just call me if you need anything."

After a while, she heard the front door close. She couldn't forget how he'd watched her, with such incredible energy, as if, with a look, he could convince her to have an affair.

She tried to imagine what it would be like to have all that

attention she'd seen in those eyes focused on her as he made love to her.

Like Russell, when she'd been married to another man.

She closed her eyes. The truth was, she wanted only Russell. Her husband. It was all she'd ever wanted.

Chapter Twelve

"Here." Conor moved the tip of his pen to the next line on the screen. "And here. What do you think?"

She stared at the numbers, knowing something was off, but unable to pinpoint exactly what. She pushed her hair out of her face, so tired—too tired to think clearly. And rusty. It had been a while since she'd analyzed this kind of data.

"I don't know." She shook her head. "And another cup of coffee isn't going to clear it up for me either."

"Could be anything. A little turbulence. A gust load."

But he was talking to himself, staring at the numbers with a look she'd seen before. Losing himself in finding the pattern.

Cherish stood, taking their mugs and dumping the coffee into the sink, leaving Conor to it. Seeing him there, staring at the computer so intently, it twisted something inside her, reminding her too much of the weeks after the crash. Conor had spent hours here in her kitchen, staring at the screen of his laptop as he tried to discover the cause of the crash.

A year and a half ago, he'd told the safety board the prototype he'd been testing had acted anomalously, not responding correctly to his commands. All three prototypes of the WingMaster were fly-by-wire, which meant the plane Conor had flown had a flight augmentation system using computers. Conor controlled the yoke, which in turn, told the computer what he wanted the plane to do. But it was the computer that did the actual flying.

Conor had thought the trouble might be there, with the onboard computer. But the investigation had reported that the software checked out as okay.

Conor had remained unconvinced. Every night, he would scour the Internet, looking for information on other crashes, searching for an analogous situation . . . trying to understand what had happened up there when he'd lost control.

He'd been afraid that the safety board would make a finding of pilot error, determining to convene an FEB. In the end, it had done just that, ending his career.

Cherish let the water run over the mugs as she watched Conor at the table. Such concentration, he used, staring at that screen. As if, on his own, he could figure it all out. Just one more key search away from his answer.

She turned off the water, her fingers gripping the faucet. *Don't go there, Cherish.* She wouldn't feel sorry for Conor. No way. That was all over with, the hearing . . . the crash. And Conor had done well for himself since then, a research professor at the university, part owner in his own flying school. She wasn't going to worry about him. Not anymore.

Pushing her bangs out of her face, she glanced at the clock. *I gotta get out of here.* "Look, Chuck and Lori are expecting me. Maybe with a fresh look . . ."

"Yeah," he said, standing, stretching. "Can you get a copy of the wing stress analysis report? I'll need to see the strain output. Compare it with this flight data."

"Sure. If you think it will help."

He frowned, still looking at the computer screen and the data. "Maybe. If there's anything there."

Two things made them suspect there was. Reck had been keeping the data from Marquis for a reason. And Alec, of course. He'd taken a big risk to deliver the telemetry.

Cherish leaned back against the kitchen counter. Conor was standing in profile, hovering over the laptop, scar side turned toward her, emitting a sort of energy as he focused on the laptop's screen. You could see it, that he liked the puzzle of it . . . enjoyed the process of figuring it out.

She shook her head, seeing the difference between them. While she felt tormented by doubts, staring at those numbers with one thought—*don't let me fail them!* Alec and Conor, Marquis—Conor, he only saw the possibilities the data presented.

"Why did you give Reck the telemetry today?" she asked, knowing there had to be a reason.

He hit the page up key, then scrolled up the screen. "Reck plans to fly the final-phase prototype in less than a month. I thought it might be kinda nice if he knew he wasn't impenetrable. Might make him think twice about pushing the schedule."

"He has a lot to lose if that prototype doesn't fly. Maybe even more than he's letting on," she said. Then, going with that, "Didn't it strike you as odd, how hard he's pushing to keep the flight schedule? I mean, how big can this contract be for Reck Enterprises?"

"Could be the company's profit margin isn't as good as they'd like people to believe. Maybe this contract is special."

She shook her head, wondering what was going on. Alec delivering telemetry reports—Reck trying to fly prototypes someone wanted to blast out of the sky.

She glanced at the clock again. "I really have to go." She bit her lip, thinking. But there was no way to tiptoe around it, so she just said it. "Maybe we should plan to meet later?"

Conor watched her for a moment, long enough that she could to see something was brewing in that Ph.D. brain of his. He nodded toward the living room, then walked out.

She almost didn't follow, not liking how he'd just assumed she'd be right there behind him. Almost.

In the living room, she watched him saunter down into the lower level and drop onto the couch. She could probably boil an egg in the time it took for him to strut his stuff to that couch. But then, she'd been accused of walking everywhere as if she had a train to catch.

She didn't know why, probably lack of sleep, but a memory came buzzing into her head. Conor and her going out to dinner. It had been a typical Friday night; they'd been waiting for a table, standing in a crowded lounge. Then, out of the blue, Conor had kissed her.

He'd looked so pleased with himself that an older gentleman standing nearby had commented, "You hold on tight to her, young fella." Conor had hugged her and told the man that he would. Everyone around them had laughed or smiled.

That's when she'd known that he loved her. At that very moment, smiling at her like that, Conor Mitchell had been in love for the first time in his life. She just knew he'd never shown that kind of affection to a woman before that moment. Not in public. Not Conor.

And damn him for making her feel special.

And now that I am thoroughly depressed . . .

She could see he was waiting for her to join him, apparently having something to say. She shrugged, walking down to sit on the couch beside him, but keeping quiet. This time, she'd let Conor do the talking.

"Let me tell you how this is going down," he said. She could see he was thinking about what he was going to say, choosing his words carefully. "Alec thinks you're in trouble. That's why he came to see me, to give me the heads up. So it looks like all bets are off about life as usual. For you and me. You'll have to call or page or do whatever it is you people do to let them know over at Marquis that you're out for a couple of days. And that's starting now. This very minute."

She waited, thinking she knew where he was going with this. "And you're going to be staying here?" Hoping to God she was wrong. "With me?"

He nodded. "I figure I should move in."

She sat there, just sat there. He couldn't be serious. But she could see he was.

She tried to conceive of what she might possibly say at this moment. How to present her answer so there was absolutely no discussion or ambiguity? *When hell freezes over . . . ?*

"You're saying." She kept her eyes forward, talking casually, as if there was a possibility of this moving-in thing happening. "I'll be safe as long as I have you, big bad Conor, watching over me for a few days."

"If that's the way you want to put it."

"Hey, listen. Words are my life."

She had another mental flashback. This time, she was crying her eyes out on Alec's shoulder, realizing Conor wasn't going to show up for their wedding. The complete sense of misery she'd felt, it all rushed back, smacking her in the chest.

When he'd called the next morning, she remembered cutting him off. *I don't want excuses, Conor . . . and since I didn't hear from 911 last night, I figure you don't have a good one anyway . . .*

But the fact was, she hadn't wanted to know the truth—couldn't have borne it. Conor was special. All hers, or so she'd thought. Give Alec ten minutes with a waitress over his menu, and he had her life's story. Not Conor. It wasn't that he was shy or snotty, but he was a very private person. Not many touched his life—only a few special people counted. Geena and Marc, his nephew Chris and the twins.

And he picked her. Cherish.

Then, just like that, he'd changed his mind . . . or maybe he'd just come to his senses.

"I already talked it over with Marc," he said sitting beside her, oblivious to or ignoring what had to be a look of utter disbelief on her face. "We didn't think it would be a good idea for you to move in to the house. Not with Geena and the kids living in the front. But Marc is covering for me at the flight school for as long as it takes. I'll have to check in at the university, but you can tag along for that. I thought I'd bring over a few things. For tonight that is."

He crossed his legs, ankle on knee. Oh, he was here for the duration, all right.

"So. Are you going to call?" he asked after a long silence.

"Work? Oh, yeah. Sure. I mean, if that's what you think I should do." *You, who I want to kill at this very moment, strangle with my very hands.* She shook her head. Really, she had to control those impulses.

He glanced at his watch. "You want me to call for a pizza for dinner?"

She nodded solemnly. "Yeah, great. A pizza would be nice. Ham and pineapple this time, okay?" Saying it as if they could just take off where they'd left off. Because, that's how he was acting.

Conor made a face. He didn't like ham and pineapple, Cherish's favorite. In those weeks after the accident, when they'd ordered pizza, she'd always gone with his choice. Pepperoni. Extra cheese. *Boy, what a girl could learn with a little trial and error.*

He stood, unfolding his large frame from the couch. "You want to use the phone first?"

"No, no. You go ahead."

He knew which room she used as an office and headed there. He was very familiar with the layout of her house. After the accident, he'd been living here with her.

When he left, Cherish stood. Quietly, she gathered up her handbag and put on her heels.

Some things in life needed to be experienced to be learned.

She was outside and in her car, about to shut the door, when a hand grabbed the car door, preventing her from closing it.

She took one look at his hand, those long elegant fingers wrapped around the edge of the door. It was his right hand. Conor, if she remembered correctly, was right-handed. Slamming the door wouldn't be nice.

He opened the door a little wider, crouched down there in the space between her and the car door. "It's for your own good, Cher," he said. And then, just for good measure, "I'm not any happier about it than you are."

Cherish turned on the ignition.

"Cher," he said.

She jammed the gears into reverse.

"What do you think you're—"

She punched it, forcing Conor to roll out of the way or get knocked down by the opened door.

Halfway down the drive, she hit the brakes and yelled, "Could you do me a favor? Could you lock the door when you leave? You just push the little button doohickey in and shut it behind you. Really, it's a piece of cake. Oh, by the way. You moving in. Well, frankly, I would rather be on that plane again, falling from the sky, the big earth racing up right at me. You saved my life once, Conor. Trust me. It was enough. That's not what I want from you. Not anymore."

She burned rubber, peeling out.

Russell waited for the elevator doors to open. He glanced at his Rolex. Forty-five minutes before he had to meet Sydney at The Hobbit for dinner. Given their little discussion earlier, he'd better not be late.

He tapped his foot nervously, knowing it was going to be close. Jesus, what a day. Kinnard hadn't been wrong about that FBI guy. Lebredo had come around Reck's office later that afternoon, asking a lot of questions, wanting records Reck would have felt better never handing over—purged or not. But he figured Lebredo had his hands full with the security for the upcoming flight. If they wanted to keep to the flight schedule for the final-phase prototype, the FBI had to bust its butt. Lebredo wasn't going to have a lot of free time to dig around.

Not that it didn't make Kinnard nervous. The old spook had plenty of skeletons in his closet, more than Reck Enterprises . . . though they shared a huge one with the XC-23 WingMaster. But Russell thought they'd be okay with Lebredo. Kinnard needed to keep his eye on the ball. The real problem right now was finding Alec Porter, neutralizing his threat without raising the body count.

The elevator doors opened. They'd told him at the front desk that Allison was already in the room, waiting for him. Russ hurried down the carpeted corridor, passing exotic Hawaiian flowers in Chinese vases, the arrangements, as tall as he was. He knew what would happen to him if the government canceled the contract for the WingMaster. He would lose. Everything. He'd taken a big gamble, thanks to Kinnard.

Shit, he thought, tugging at his collar. He couldn't even think about that right now.

Using the plastic card key, he opened the door and stepped inside. The lights were off, the drapes drawn. "What the . . ."

He saw her then. Allison, waiting for him.

She was on the king-size bed, posed against the headboard like a Playboy centerfold. She was perfectly naked, except for one of his ties around her neck.

He stared as she took off the tie, letting it slip across her bare breasts. He hadn't even missed the damn thing. Now, seeing the magic it was doing on Allison's body, he knew he'd never let it out of his sight.

"She thinks I want to be the next Mrs. Reck." Her voice had a hoarse quality, as if she'd been crying. "But that's not what I want."

With a sharp twist, she knotted the tie tight around her wrist, pinning her hand there to the bedpost so she couldn't lower her arm. She looked incredibly young at that moment, pouting so splendidly as she continued to tie herself to the bedpost.

"I just want to make you happy, Russell."

He walked to the bed, out of his mind with lust, mesmerized by the sight of her—Sydney and their dinner, completely forgotten.

Chapter Thirteen

Ekaterina Bolkonsky stared down at the sleeping angel in her arms. "Do you see her, Eric," she whispered of her daughter, Eric Ballas's namesake, "up there in the heavens?"

She was upstairs in a room they used as a nursery. The laboratory had three bedrooms, the rooms more like lofts than actual chambers because the ceiling pitched down to follow the steep roofline. There was only enough space for a few bits of furniture for Dimitri and Erika. But to Katya, everything about their new home seemed palatial. In Moscow, their entire apartment was practically the size of this nursery.

Humming softly, she remembered the days before Eric Ballas had found her and Valeri. She'd been working for the Russian Academy of Sciences. Hard times living off a diet of potatoes and cabbage each week. The Soviet system had failed—the government-run programs, vanished. In those days, a taxicab driver made several times more money than an engineer. They still did.

And then, at the suggestion of the United States government,

American companies began hiring scientists and engineers, afraid that terrorists would get ahold of important technology through the disenfranchised professionals. Bringing opportunity. It was a partnership profitable for both sides. A company could hire a Russian engineer for a few dollars a day. And they did things differently. It provided companies with another perspective.

When Eric hired her and the others for Joystick, Ekaterina had vowed he would never regret it.

"We had a good run, didn't we, Eric?"

At the sound of the door opening, she looked up to see Valeri, her husband, step inside. He frowned, seeing the tears in her eyes. She quickly brushed them away, careful not to wake Erika.

He came up behind her, looking down at their sleeping daughter, reaching to hold both Erika and his wife. "I miss him, too, Katya," he said.

He knew her so well, her Valeri.

"He was so happy about Erika," she said, unable to hide the emotion in her voice. "Do you remember the night we told him?"

"It was a good time for us."

They'd asked Eric over for dinner; she'd cooked his favorite, *pelmeni*, a dish of stuffed cabbage leaves she'd learned to make from her mother. He and Valeri had toasted to the future.

Ten weeks later, Eric was dead.

Gently, Valeri took the year-old infant from her, laying Erika on her crib mattress, covering her. They both stood there, arms around each other, watching their sleeping child.

"We have had a transmission from America," Valeri said after a while. "From Alec Porter."

Katya turned. "The papers." It was the first thing that came into her head, their final hope. "Eric's papers? He's found them?"

"Now, Katya. We've talked about these strange and secret

documents of Eric's." He tightened his fingers around her arms. "It is unlikely they even exist."

"Eric said they were real." But she frowned, because she too had doubted. Now, they were running out of time and she was clutching at straws. She hadn't found any samples since the day Alec Porter had left them almost a week ago.

She looked up at Valeri. Alec Porter rarely contacted them here at Joystick. Certainly this transmission from the American had to be significant. "He said he would help us."

"Now you are putting your hopes on alien spacecraft?"

In her husband's eyes, she could see her all hopes and all his fears.

He sighed. "Come, see what Mr. Alec Porter has to say."

Downstairs, her fingers shaking on the computer keys, she opened the enclosure Alec Porter had attached to his e-mail. She looked at the screen, reading:

```
Greetings from America,
  Have been unable to obtain Eric's
documents. Thought this might tide you
over.
```

Immediately, text, equations, tables of data poured across the screen.

Katya scrolled down page after page, trying to take it in and decipher its significance. Until she realized what it was Alec had sent them.

"Valeri?" She paged up to the key sections, rereading, hoping she wasn't mistaken. "Valeri! Not Eric's papers. Something much better!"

She hadn't imagined it. She told herself it wasn't possible, yet going over the pages of data, she saw that it was all there. The secrets she'd waited a lifetime to see.

"He found it," she whispered, squeezing her husband's hand.

Neither scientist could take their eyes off the screen. She wouldn't need to search for any more extraterrestrial scraps, digging into the permafrost ground for her clues. Here, at last, was the answer.

"It's incredible," Valeri said, disbelieving. "The formula."

For Eric's dream.

"Da," she said, smiling. "And now, it is up to us to see if we can make it work."

Alec logged off the computer. "Not bad for a night's work," he said to himself.

He picked up his briefcase and straightened his Mickey Mouse tie. He was wearing glasses and a wig. But he didn't think he looked good as a redhead.

It had been surprisingly easy to get inside Reck Enterprises. They'd hired him as a contract worker. In this world of computer data banks, it was a simple thing to assume another identity. Even one with a high-level security clearance.

On his way out, he flashed his badge at the security station, smiling at the guard. It was after normal work hours—the only time a computer jock might be able to tinker with the system without interfering with the day's work schedule.

"Hello, Ralph," he said to the uniformed guard.

"Hello, Mr. Drax. They said it was a bad one this time. Been hearing complaints all day."

In fact, it had been a rather nasty virus they'd hired him to eradicate from Reck's computer system . . . a bug with which Alec was infinitely familiar, given that he'd written it himself.

"That's why they bring me in." He winked at the guard. "The troubleshooter."

"Good man."

Alec left, whistling softly.

Back at his quaint cottage by the sea, he finished his shower and came out, a towel wrapped around his waist. Allison had left him a bag of oranges—she worried that he didn't eat right. He grabbed one and dropped onto the bed. After he popped in the diskette he'd smuggled out of Reck Enterprises into the drive of his laptop, he scanned through the file he'd e-mailed to Ekaterina Bolkonsky, peeling the orange.

"I bet old Valeri is shifting bricks just about now."

When he finished, he put the diskette away and opened one of the drawers from the Dutch-style bureau, digging out the uniform from the security company, the one he'd worn earlier. He reached inside the pocket of the white coveralls and found the folded piece of paper he'd shoved inside. He changed the station on the clock radio, then flopped back onto the bed.

He'd sabotaged the security system at Reck's house right after he'd left Conor last Thursday night. Today, he'd stayed in the master bedroom just long enough to reset it. That's when he'd come across Sydney's Filofax planner on the nightstand. Now, humming to ELO on the radio, he unfolded the scrap of paper where he'd jotted down her schedule.

10:00 A.M. Ryan. Gym.

He smiled, loving a challenge. "Poor, Sydney. You're just too good for him, baby."

Cherish was talking to Eric, again.

They were on the plane together, Eric seated next to Henry Shanks, the representative from Reck Enterprises for the test flight. Both men were situated across the aisle from Cherish and the reporter from *Aviation Weekly*. Eric was in top form, laughing at his own jokes.

Earlier, he'd leaned over to whisper in her ear, *Come work for me. Leave those fuddy-duddies at Marquis,* using his best pied-piper voice.

Cherish had only smiled. But later, she'd wondered, *Why don't I? I could do research . . .* Eric the maverick, who brought out the risk-taker in all of them.

She turned then, not quite catching something Eric said to her, Henry listening in as well. She smiled, asking Eric, "Come again?" liking the way he looked, a silver-haired wizard with twinkling blue eyes who sang opera.

She watched Eric's lips, listened as he said—

Bang! The sound burst through the plane, deafening as cannon fire.

Her seat dropped out from under her, the safety harness biting into her chest, pulling her with it. Falling, falling . . . *dear God in heaven* . . . Turning, tumbling.

The reporter beside her latched onto her hand, his mouth wide open but not making a sound. He looked like a child staring at an oncoming train, his foot caught in the rails. Knowing he was going to die. Not understanding why. *Please, no . . .*

They started to roll. Upside down, right-side up. Again. The cabin had become the inside of a tornado, debris flying, striking her arm, cutting her face. A tremendous force crushed into her chest, making it impossible to take a breath. *Can't breathe!* The plane was a wild beast, thrashing, sputtering in wild gyrations, howling its rage as it fell to earth. *Oh, God. Oh, God!*

Cherish covered her face and ducked out of the path of equipment careening through the cabin. With her head in her hands, she tried to make her body so small, smaller still, protecting herself against the bulletlike fragments. The seat beside her shuddered, then snapped back like a slingshot. She felt the reporter's hand go lax on her arm. She turned to help . . .

No head! Oh, God, no head! Just the body strapped to the seat!

Henry Shanks flew past, imprisoned in his chair, his arms stretched out before him. Almost in slow motion, she watched as he crashed into the bulkhead, punching a hole.

A black hole . . . sucking the oxygen . . . a spiraling vortex full of stars.

Star light, star bright, first star I see tonight . . . I think I'm going to die tonight . . .

Cherish sat bolt upright in her bed, waking just before the plane crashed to the ground.

She slumped against the headboard, breathing hard, feeling sick to her stomach. "Just a dream. Just a dream."

She didn't know how long she lay there, paralyzed, repeating those rushed words over and over. Eventually, she pushed the covers aside and swung her legs to the floor, almost stumbling when she stood.

In the kitchen, she grabbed a glass, one of her Disney anniversary glasses that spoke of how often she visited the "happiest place on earth." She stood over the kitchen sink and turned on the faucet. She drank nearly two full glasses of water, one after the other, drinking so fast that the water dripped down her mouth and slipped down her chin and neck.

Her greatest fear was that, one day, she wouldn't wake before her body hit the ground.

She collapsed against the sink, the glass still in her hand. She wondered if she could die in her sleep. If she didn't wake before that plane crashed, would her heart burst inside her chest, a heart attack? Could that death she'd cheated so long ago find her here, in her dreams?

She braced both hands against the counter. Closing her eyes, she whispered, "Go away."

Only the image of Eric lingered. She saw his face, watched his mouth, moving to the rhythm of the words he'd spoken right before the crash. She squeezed her eyes tighter. It was on the tip of her tongue what he was saying to her . . . her whole body shuddered with the effort to remember.

Nothing.

She couldn't. She had no idea what Eric might have said to her. But she was certain she'd heard the words right before the explosion rocked the cabin.

Cherish dropped into the kitchen chair, feeling drained but knowing she wouldn't get any sleep. Not tonight. On the table before her, she turned the Disney glass in her hand, frowning

as one nightmare blended with another. She could still hear
Alec telling her: *Listen with your heart.*

Those things she'd read in his file . . . what she'd learned
from Conor. *Alec, a terrorist?*

She thought she should know. The three of them—they had
this bond. Sure, they'd stretched the ties a little, running away
from one another. But here they were again, as if the rubber
band that held them together had snapped them back into place.
Even Conor was back.

"Yeah. And what are we going to do about that one?" she
asked Mickey on the glass.

Questions, questions. More questions.

And Mickey wasn't talking.

She glanced at the clock. Not at this hour anyway. "Hey,
Cherish. How about a game?" she asked herself. "Don't mind
if I do," she answered, standing to pad out of the kitchen
barefoot.

A girl's best friend at one in the morning. Her pool table.

The great oak beast dominated the living room. She smiled,
passing her hand over the felt her brothers called pink but
which was actually a beautiful shade of mauve. She'd bought
it off Lori for a hundred dollars. It had belonged to Lori's
ex-husband. Somehow, after the divorce, Lori had gotten the
impression that, "Gary isn't going to be needing this anymore."
Cherish smiled, picking up the cue to line up a shot. Poor Gary.

"Nine ball in the corner pocket," she said, feeling a little
less shaky, the focus the game required going a long way to
dissipating the nightmare images in her head.

That's when she saw it, a shadow passing in front of the
glass sliders to her right.

She froze in place. The hint of darkness appeared again, as
if someone might be searching for a way in.

She'd left the kitchen light on and was playing by the pale
glow bleeding in from there. Where she stood in the living
room, she couldn't see if the sliders were locked. She lived in

a neighborhood where she'd always felt safe. Sometimes, she didn't take the necessary precautions.

She kept thinking about what Conor had told her, implying that she was in some sort of danger.

Holding the cue stick gripped between both hands, she walked over to the phone, about to dial 911. But she hesitated.

She glanced at the sliding glass door. If it was Alec out there, the last thing he needed was the police looking around. Taking a chance, she walked toward the sliders, pool cue still in hand. If she was wrong, at a minimum, she figured she could whack whoever was out there upside the head. Do some damage.

She opened the door, careful not to make a sound. She held her breath, then leaned out to take a look.

She let out the air from her lungs. "Oh, for the love of . . . ."

Not Alec. Much worse.

Conor.

She propped the pool cue up against the wall and walked outside. The houses in the harbor had small lots. Hers sported a courtyard enclosed by decorative wrought iron. She'd always thought it would look great with a little fountain. Like she could afford one.

Barefoot, she walked to the gate where he waited. He stood on the sidewalk propped against the wrought iron, squinting against the plumes of cigar smoke weaving a lazy pattern around him. She stopped directly beside him, following his gaze. The Hale-Bopp comet had set so there was no white smudge in the sky tonight. He was looking at Jupiter.

"I thought the idea was to sleep across my doorstep," she said. "How do you expect to save me from the bad guys standing out here?"

He took the cigar out of his mouth long enough to smile. "I have my ways."

"Sure, the psychic warrior. That's you." She opened the gate, gesturing him to follow, because it was one in the morning and she was just too tired to fight him anymore. "Do you still take your coffee black? By the way, you're not smoking that nasty thing in my house."

He shook his head, following her inside. "You and Geena," he said.

Ten minutes of tense silence later, they stood in front of the refrigerator, facing each other, both with coffee mugs cupped in their hands. Conor looked tired, the lines of his scar appearing more pronounced. Unfortunately, it didn't make him look any less the hunk.

She blew into the cup, cooling the coffee. "So, Conor. Does baldness run in your family "

"Happens that it doesn't, Cher."

"Really?" She took a sip. *What a shame.*

He would keep that lovely thick hair. He wouldn't get fat. And she was kidding herself if she thought any of those things would have made a fig of difference.

"Look. Maybe I didn't handle it so well today," he said.

She almost laughed. The understatement of the year. "I don't think it was a matter of semantics. You want to park it outside my door at night? Follow me to work?" She shrugged. "All you'll get for your trouble is a nod and a wave." She raised her cup. "And the occasional cup of coffee."

"That'll do."

"You're not really going to do Kevin Costner's *The Body-guard* thing, are you?"

"I think I am."

She smiled. "This is like a Sartre story. Ever read *No Exit?*"

"Must have missed that issue of *Private Pilot.*"

She made a face. "It's a French classic on existentialism. The author's idea of hell. Three people stuck in a room with no exit, driving each other crazy."

He smiled, getting it. Because Alec was there with them, in spirit if not in body.

"How about a game of pool?" she asked, taking his coffee cup.

"Rack'em up," he said, following her into the living room.

Conor had a really bad feeling about this.

He'd known he was in trouble when she'd come outside in only a T-shirt. He knew that's what Cherish preferred. Not sexy lingerie, just T-shirts. Extra large, barely scraping the tops of her thighs. Soft, cotton, incredibly thin, T-shirts.

Point of fact, the damn thing was translucent. With the streetlight coming in at an angle, he could see everything.

Never should have gone to check out that light coming from the kitchen.

He should have stayed out here on the sidewalk, smoking his cigar, trying to convince myself Alec's warning about Cherish was just a bunch of crap and he was losing sleep over nothing.

Now, standing here, Cherish just a few feet away playing pool wearing nothing but that T-shirt and a tiny scrap of underwear . . . well. This was going to be a real test of moral conviction.

Cherish leaned over the table, going for the shot, her T-shirt riding up high to give a peek at the wonderful curve of her buttocks. Watching her, Conor began to wonder if this wasn't the point after all. Just Alec getting one last shot at him, throwing her in his face. Knowing only too well the result.

Spontaneous combustion.

He closed his eyes, telling himself he could handle this. That was the problem with Cher, too many things went into automatic around her. Too many times, he'd found himself acting without careful, objective analysis. He had to remind himself he was a pilot. He knew how to commit his course of action to memory so that, when faced with an emergency, he would know what to do without thought. He started going over it in his head now, trying to focus on what counted—*keep an eye on her, make sure there isn't any danger.*

And then he opened his eyes, taking it all in.

He remembered the last time they'd made love. Right here. In this house.

Cher moved around the table, her concentration there. While he couldn't take his eyes off her. It had been so very long . . .

Everything was always the greatest with Cherish. The greatest sex he'd ever had, the greatest moments of his life. The greatest fears.

Putting down his cue, Conor came up behind her. It was like his brain had shut down. Some voice, possibly the voice of reason, was frantically trying to rouse him back on the job. *What's the next step?* But he only turned her around, staying in the flat spin, not bothering to fight it anymore. He'd held out for as long as he was going to.

She looked up at him, those blue eyes searching his. He could never forget her eyes. They were the color that surrounded him up there in the sky.

She licked her lips, a habit she had whenever she was nervous. Or turned on. "What are you doing?"

"Shit if I know," he said, bending down to kiss her.

It all came rushing back then, the wonder of what it was like to be with her—the hell of the last year without her. He braced her up against the pool table, angling his body closer, feeling the softness of her rubbing up against him, coming home. God he'd missed her. He'd missed this. *Just a kiss—a taste. Only that.*

Her hands fluttered up around him, reaching to touch him—then holding back. But her mouth was opening under his, taking him inside.

When he finally pulled away, he waited for her reaction, searching for it. He watched her eyes open, her expression filled with wonder, as if she, too, was just waking from the magic of it.

And then he saw it dawning on her face. Where these kisses would lead.

The pain. The anger.

She slapped him. Hard across the cheek.

And then, she was all over him.

She wrapped her arms around his neck, reaching up, trying to mesh with his body. Grabbing at him, she dug her nails into him, needing to hold on. He felt it too, wanted it just as badly, to feel again, to melt the ice that had frozen him up inside the last year.

They were trying to get closer, closer than was physically possible. He pushed up her T-shirt, grabbing her bottom, cupping his hands beneath the silk of her underwear, leaning over her until he just wanted her and nothing else. His mouth was all on her, crushing against her lips, tasting everything he'd missed. He could feel hot skin under his palms, making him want more . . . until his brain registered that Cherish wasn't humming along at the same pace he was.

With her two fists against his chest, she shoved him away. She leaned up against the pool table, her chest heaving up and down, her eyes black with emotion. The only sound in the room was their labored breathing and the balls softly clicking together, rolling across the table like atoms colliding.

"I can't do this," she told him.

"Right." He tried to catch his breath, sanity coming back. Thank God one of them was going to be smart about this.

And then she grabbed him by the shirt and fell back, pulling him on top of the table with her, her kissing him.

They scooted across the table, the balls bouncing off the rail to roll against them, then shooting off in different directions. She pulled his shirt out from his pants, coming up to feel him. Her fingers spread across his stomach, her mouth on his. She reached up to the muscles of his chest and opened her legs to him as he came closer, Conor groaning against her mouth when she locked her ankles around his back.

"I can't believe I'm doing this. Oh, God. Stop me," she begged, still pressing up to feel him.

"I can't," he answered.

The two of them together were like an unfinished experiment. They'd played with fire before. Now, like a couple of kids who hadn't learned their lesson, they were coming back for more. No, he wasn't going to end this.

And then, he heard her crying.

"Okay," he said, pulling away, catching his breath. "Now, I can stop."

She shook her head, laying back on the table, arms dropped wide apart in apparent defeat. Tears slipped down her eyes to mingle with the curls of hair spread across the mauve felt. "Why did you leave me, Conor?"

He held his breath.

Because I tried so hard to take in your enthusiasm for life and make it mine. You saw the crash as a second chance instead of a giant failure. The answer came in loud and clear inside his head.

I tried to go on and make life count again, just like you. Get married, have a family. And when they told me the crash was my fault, I knew I didn't deserve it.

"It's the accident, isn't it?" she answered for him, because he couldn't say those words out loud. They were too locked up inside him. "You look at me, and you see it. Alec and I are both mixed up in it."

She sat up. She always made it so easy for him; filling in his silences. Just like that morning, when he'd called to explain why he hadn't shown up to marry her. Cherish had hung up on him, making it all so easy.

"Alec told me about the safety board," she said. "That they called earlier that day. He tried to explain. He said you weren't yourself." She shook her head, the tears just welling in her eyes. "I wanted so much to be part of the solution for you." She reached over, still filling in his silences, her hands fussing over him, smoothing the wrinkles from his shirt so it lay sleek against his skin. *Everything in order.* "I wanted to help you get over it." The moonlight coming in from the sliding glass doors behind her made her eyes luminescent. "That night, when you didn't show up. You made it clear I was part of the problem."

"You're wrong. I don't blame anyone but myself," he told her, sounding angry.

She held his face in her hands. She had such small hands. Gentle and soft against his cheeks. "I think I should hate you, Conor Mitchell."

"Hate would be good, Cher."

But she had never been any good at hate. That's what those letters he received every Thursday had taught him. That Cherish, with her big heart, would forgive him. If only he could forgive himself.

He let out a sigh and dropped his head against hers, touching his forehead to the top of her head. "I think we should go to bed," he told her.

She blushed. "Just like that," she said, pushing at him. "You think I'm going to bed with you?"

That was another thing he loved about Cher. Her translucent skin that turned the deep color of a rose when aroused. "I meant as in sleep."

"Right," she said, flushing even brighter. "That's what I meant, too. Sleep."

He just had to smile.

He slipped off the pool table, then turned for her. He picked her up and carried her past the short steps to the hall, taking her toward the bedroom. She weighed less than nothing, feeling less substantial in his arms than he remembered. It made him worry about the last year, made him think about how unhappy she might have been.

Conor set her gently on the bed. But when he tried to step away, she kept her arms locked around him.

"Don't leave." She whispered it like a secret.

He thought about it, just easing into her invitation without considering the consequences. It's what they usually did. Sex first, think later.

Instead, he leaned down, hooking a curl of blonde hair around her ear, just wanting to touch her. "It's been more than six months since I slept with a woman," he said, so that she would know what she was getting into. "One of Geena's helpful blind dates. She was a nice person; we got along. I thought it was a good idea at the time." He wanted to make sure she understood. "I called her Cher. At precisely the wrong moment. And I haven't slept with a woman since."

She closed her eyes, looking as if he'd hit her. Maybe it was a mistake, telling her. He'd meant to make it easy—*look here, Cher. Horny little devil that I am, it would be a huge mistake for me to get in that bed.*

But when she opened her eyes, he didn't see a woman ready to melt in his arms.

"I am not going to love you ever again." There was some serious conviction in her voice. "I *will not* let you hurt me ever again."

He nodded. "Smart." He tried to pull away.

But still, she didn't let go.

"I just want you to hold me," she told him. "Okay?"

Her nightmare. It was probably what woke her in the first place, why she'd gone to the kitchen, turning on the light . . . getting him to come take a closer look and see if she was all right.

He knew those dreams made her crazy. The accident was always there, waiting to follow her into sleep.

Sitting on the bed, he took off his shoes, then slipped in beside her under the sheet.

Bed, but no sex.

That was another thing about Cherish. There was always hell to pay.

Chapter Fourteen

Birds. There were always so many birds in the morning, bribed there by the bath and seed Cherish kept on the deck. Today when she woke up, the sun was beaming in through the sliders to her bedroom. The birds were singing.

And Conor was sitting on the edge of her bed.

The night came bursting back into her consciousness with the force of a hangover. Conor. The pool table. She closed her eyes and counted to ten. But when she opened them, he was still sitting there, big as life.

It was all real. Conor's kisses, her body spooned up against his on the bed, like Goldilocks making peace with Papa Bear.

She sat up, staring at his back. "I think last night clinched it. I have some sort of mental defect. This accounts for the fact that I have learned nothing from the past." She shook her head. "Imagine, making it through all those doctor visits with a clean bill of health when I actually have a serious condition."

"And that would be?" he said.

"I-am-an-ass-icitis."

He turned around, but he wasn't smiling.

"You're supposed to laugh," she said. "It's a joke. I was working on a light touch to get us through the awkward moment."

"Awkward." Their eyes met, as if they were waiting for the other to say it. *About last night . . .*

He leaned down and picked up something from the floor. His sneaker. He didn't favor the fancy kind. She'd noticed earlier the left one was starting to get a hole in the toe.

He finished tying the laces, then rested both hands on his knees. "You think the nights are the worse part. Because you miss it, that wonderful sound sleep. You used to be such a sound sleeper."

She realized he was quoting from her letters. Her heart kind of paused inside her chest, doing a little syncopated number.

"You're good with words," he told her, then nodded, as if he was agreeing. "I think that's what I liked best about the letters. How you would come up with these phrases that said more than the words themselves. Now, every night, you only sleep because you're exhausted, fighting it. Fearing it. Because you think you might not wake up. 'That Conor won't be there to pull me from that death.' " He turned around, looking at her. "You believe that, whatever it is you think is trying to find you, the death you escaped that day, it will finally catch you, there, in the dark. And I won't be able to help you this time. Because I wasn't there when you were counting on me most."

He picked up the other shoe. "I probably don't have the words right . . . I didn't memorize it. But I think that was the gist." He put on his sneaker and tied it. "Well, I'm here now, Cher. Don't push me away. It's not what you want and we both know it."

"I'm really going to regret writing those letters to you, aren't I?"

But she could see he wasn't going to answer.

She tried to think of what else to say. What could she say? Don't worry, Conor. I don't expect anything from you.

Screw that.

She gave him a kick on his butt.

He jumped off the bed. Then he smiled. "I think your aim is off."

"You were facing the wrong direction. I had to make-do."

Beside her, the alarm clock went off like a fire alarm. It was a travel clock, the old windup kind. They both stared at it until the silly thing exhausted itself. And then, for no reason at all, she started to laugh.

She rolled onto her side laughing so hard, she got a stitch. Conor just watched, but she could see he was doing his best not to join in. *The end of round one.*

She took a breath, sighed, still smiling as she stared up at the ceiling. "Now what, Chief?" she asked.

"If I can't convince you to take a few days off"—he held out his hand to her—"I guess it's my turn to make the coffee."

They were seated at the kitchen table. The morning light dappled across the water, painting it turquoise, rose, and purple. She had a great view of the channel here. A million-dollar view. What did they say in real estate? Location, location, location. She really should buy the house.

She glanced across the kitchen table at Conor. He was chewing on a piece of toast, comparing the telemetry readout on her laptop to the copy of the wing stress analysis report she'd brought home last night. Alec had once told her Conor could do the most complicated equations in his head. She figured that's what he was doing now.

He scrolled up a couple of pages, seeming to compare something in the data to the report. "You notice what the wing is doing here?"

She stood, stepping over to take a look over his shoulder.

He scrolled down again. "So why does it change here?" he asked.

It was subtle, but it got her attention. She shook her head. "It shouldn't."

He paged down, then turned the laptop so that she could read the screen. "The deflections are too great; the strains are too high."

"That's impossible. See here"—she pointed to a column of data—"for those air loads, which are what we expected, the deflections aren't consistent with our design."

"Well, then," he said, "either they changed the material or they changed the design."

She blinked at Conor. There was something there. They both knew it.

"Reck changed our wing design," she said, knowing it was the only possibility.

After the first prototype crashed and killed Eric, Reck Enterprises had—supposedly in a goodwill gesture—bought out Joystick to take over the material development subcontract for the program. The graphite composite material Reck had chosen to put on the wing wouldn't be able to handle the strains shown on the telemetry readout. In fact, no composite material available today could. That kind of advanced composite was a good decade or two away from development.

"My God," she said, working it through her head. "They changed our wing design. Then, when the plane crashed and they thought their tinkered design was at fault, they tried to lay the rap on us. Marquis. Only, this Marduk group steps up to the plate to take credit." She turned to Conor. "That's why Alec left you the diskette with the telemetry. To let us know what Reck was doing."

"Maybe." But Conor looked unconvinced. Perhaps he was having trouble trying to decide who he trusted less, Reck or Alec.

On the kitchen table beside her, her beeper went off. She

picked it up, displaying the message. She frowned as she read the words scrolling past on the tiny screen. "I have to go."

Conor grabbed her arm, his expression, uncompromising. She gave him an exasperated look. "It's Lori. She's waiting for me." She held up the pager so he could read the message. Lori wanted to go over today's press release on the XC-23. *Coffee. 8:45? Starbucks.*

"All right," he said, releasing her arm. "We'll meet up later. I have a few things to look into myself."

She shook her head. "I already have an ant problem. What am I going to do about you?"

But he was back staring at the computer screen and the stress analysis report, lost to her.

"Please, do me a favor," she said from the kitchen door. "Refrain from moving in while I'm gone."

Outside, the birds were still singing, the sun was still shining, and Cherish was getting into her car, wondering why Lori was asking her to meet for coffee. Lori was a health nut. They always met at Juice Me, the closest place to the plant that served wheat grass tea, Lori's staple of date.

Fifteen minutes later, she walked into Starbucks to find Alec waiting for her. He was sitting in plain view, reading *USA Today.*

"I was hoping he would let you out of his sight." He smiled up from the paper, most assuredly referring to Conor. He wore a tight white T-shirt tucked into equally tight jeans, the sleeves rolled up to show his biceps and a tattoo that looked like a dragon. Today, he'd accented his look with a stud earring and contacts that turned his eyes an eerie yellow. When she looked closer, she realized the contacts had a tiny happy face in black where his real eye color peeked through.

Cherish pulled up a chair and sat down. She wasn't going to bother with small talk and ask how he got her pager number. "What is going on, Alec?"

"It's going to be a nice day," he said, putting the paper down. "A high of seventy-four. Love that California weather."

"I'd get to the point if I were you. If the FBI is watching me right now, they're going to be all over you in about five seconds. You don't look that different."

"The FBI is not watching you. They are, in fact, keeping rather close tabs on Conor, who they think will be the person I'll contact." He leaned forward, lowering his voice. "They hadn't heard about our little falling out." He winked. "And, by the way, I look different enough."

"Did Reck alter Marquis's wing design?" Cherish asked. There was no other explanation for the telemetry data.

"You're focusing on the wrong thing, love. Conor won't make that mistake. That's why I gave him the diskette and not you. That man has a fucking doctorate from one of the best institutions in the world. You and I both know, if anyone can figure it out, it will be the Conman."

"But not without my help?" she said, guessing that she fit in somewhere. "Which means, he's going to need access to places where only I have clearance."

"Smart girl." Then, looking suddenly very serious. "I am not, repeat, *not* bombing planes out of the sky. It might be kind of fun to figure out who is. Just to save my ass, you understand."

"So to speak. And the cryptic death threats you e-mailed? Contact Conor. He'll know what to do."

Again, that Dennis-the-Menace smile, looking so at odds with his wolf yellow eyes and their futuristic design. "I had to get the two of you together, didn't I?"

"No one is threatening your life?"

"I didn't say that . . . just that I wouldn't necessarily tell you about it if I didn't think it was important that you and Conor work together. Despite my deepest desire against admitting it, you always were a good team."

"Okay. Someone is trying to kill you. You start looking into a few things. Now, you're getting credit for bomb blasts. And you want us to find out who's really behind it?''

''Preferably before anyone else gets killed. Like me, for example.'' He finished his expresso in a swallow and folded the paper. He tucked it under his arm. ''Conor always did underestimate you. I wouldn't have made that mistake.''

''No. Something tells me you would go for something a little more flamboyant.''

He pushed his chair back, standing. He came around the table and leaned down to whisper in her ear, ''I'll try and help you as much as I can.'' He kissed her cheek, his lips lingering there, brushing against her skin in a way that made her blush. ''I hope when this is all over, you'll show better taste in men.''

She didn't bother to stop Alec or call him back. She didn't know who might be watching, didn't want to put him in any more danger.

But the thought crossed her mind. What if Alec was the danger?

She watched him leave, saw him glance both ways before he put on his sunglasses and disappeared, walking straight ahead.

Bad taste in men. Conor had said much the same thing.

''Right,'' she said.

As if the biggest problem she faced right now was choosing a hot date.

About twenty minutes after Conor parked, he heard someone knocking on the front door.

''Come on in, Geena,'' he called out.

He knew it was his sister. Neither Marc nor the twins bothered to knock and Chris, the oldest, had his own special cadence, just a staccato warning before he too barged in. But mostly, he knew that only Geena would be aware of his absence last night. Would come here, minutes after he arrived, to discuss it. Geena was as good as any bloodhound when it came to his private life.

She sat down on the stool next to his. He'd been analyzing the flight data in the dining room where, in the corner by the window, he had a state-of-the-art Toshiba that Chris called Darth Vader.

"Did you sleep with her?" Geena asked.

Without looking up from the screen, he said, "I balled her all night. She's still a great fuck."

From the corner of his eye, he saw Geena close her eyes. Which wasn't the reaction he'd expected. Usually, she would have a quick comeback for his foul-mouthed remarks.

But what really floored him was when she started to cry.

He took his hands off the keyboard, turned on the stool to face her. She was staring at him in that unblinking way she had, tears filling her eyes.

"You slept over at her place. You stayed with her all night. But you didn't have sex with her?"

"You're making too much out of this."

"If you'd slept with her, you never would have said anything."

Which was absolutely true.

Geena shook her head and brushed off her tears. "I was hoping this was about sex. It's not sex, is it?" She closed her eyes. "Please tell me you're not in love with her. Unless I'm not making it perfectly clear, I want you to lie if you have to."

"Geena. I'm a big boy." He looked away for a minute. "I can take care of this myself."

"Okay. You're not going to ask me what I have against her. You probably don't want to know. But here goes." She looked completely earnest as she spoke. "That woman messed you up, Conor."

"You're right, I don't want to hear this." He turned back to the computer, grabbing the mouse.

Geena stood to hover over his shoulder. "She was supposed

to help you get over that crash. That's what people who love you do. Instead, you and Alec have your lives turned upside down . . . and she goes on her merry way, back to her old position, her old dreams. Nothing touched her, do you understand that? She went on.''

''And I didn't?''

She slapped her hand on his over the mouse, preventing him from changing the page on the screen. ''No, Conor. You most certainly did not.''

He didn't argue with her. Instead, he crossed his arms and leaned back, trying to get past it, Geena's undying devotion. Wondering how he could make her understand. *I fucked up. Not Cher.*

''And I bear no responsibility for what happened?''

''It wasn't your finest hour, I'll admit. But that's all part of it. If she loved you, she wouldn't have let you get away with it. You think Marc has never been a jerk? When I asked him to marry me, I thought he was going to have a heart attack. I could see him going through the options in his head. If I say no, will she still sleep with me? Will she leave me? Can I stall? But people who love each other don't give up on each other. By staying away, not confronting you, it's like she agreed you were right all along. The two of you would have been miserable together and you were just smart enough to stop it before things got official.''

He thought about Cher's letters, how she'd written so diligently every Thursday. Thought maybe he didn't want to think about that right now. Or about last night.

''If she loved you, Conor, she would have come looking for you long before she got that e-mail from Alec.''

He was trying to think how he could get his sister to shut the hell up. Because, no matter what, he and Cherish were stuck together through this thing with Alec. But he knew Geena. She would stay planted in that chair, yapping until she got her answers.

He shook his head, thinking about the week that lay ahead. He was going to have to be around Cher day and night. Trying desperately to keep sane, not to want her so badly that he screwed up again like last night.

"Look, Cher and I aren't trying to relive some moment in the past. That's over and done with." Images of the pool table flashed through his head, but he cut them off. "I was over there because . . . well, I think she's in trouble."

He'd already talked it over with Marc. But Geena. He hadn't wanted to get into it with her. Now, he didn't have a choice. "In fact, I may be spending a lot of time there. Until I figure out what's going on."

"Because of Alec? You need to protect her from him?" She was spitting the words out, she was so angry. "Maybe the two of them deserve each other. Did you ever think about that?"

"There was a bomb threat, Geena. If the XC-23 flies, some nut says he's going to blast it out of the sky. They're trying to pin it on Alec."

She held her breath. It was the first time they'd talked about it, a painful topic they had tiptoed around, each talking to Marc but not to each other.

"Do you think he did it, Conor?" she asked.

Conor sighed, his chin falling down on his chest. His sister knew there was a wildness to Alec that no one could predict. Certainly not Conor or Geena, the two people he'd hurt most.

He remembered what Kinnard had said at the meeting, bringing up Alec's call sign. Wildman.

Conor stood and walked over to the phone. He brought the portable back to Geena, then scribbled a few numbers on a sheet of paper near the computer. He handed the sheet to her, waited while she read it.

"Look at the amount the terrorists want in exchange for letting the XC-23 fly."

She stared at the numbers, taking in the strange amount. He

turned the phone over in her hand and pointed to the number pad.

"You remember his old trick?" he asked. "He used to send coded messages this way. Quick and dirty James Bond, he called it."

Geena looked at the numbers on the phone, then glanced up. 2532.

It spelled Alec.

Chapter Fifteen

Sydney fell back against the mat, panting. She was covered in sweat, her abdominal muscles screaming in release.

"That's terrific." Ryan, the personal trainer she worked with, held out his hand for her to stand. "Why don't you take a rest—"

"No. I can do more." Fingers pressed to the back of her neck, Sydney curled into another sit-up, her ribs pressing in toward the small of her back. She closed her eyes, counting softly as she released her breath. She'd been pushing all session, demanding more weight, adding reps. Ignoring the agony of pain skewering her muscles.

Her trainer merely looked away, pretending from his Viking's height not to notice—knowing her well enough not to ask. But the story was there on her tired face, her red and swollen eyes. *Aging trophy wife seeking to keep Father Time at bay.* She focused on the pain, using it.

Last night, Russell had left her waiting at the restaurant for forty-five minutes. She'd been on her second glass of a rather nice chardonnay when he'd deigned to make an appearance, the sweet smell of perfume dogging him, whispering of orange blossoms and peccadilloes. Sydney wore only one scent, Joy by Patou.

"Twenty-one, twenty-two . . ." *You let him get away with it. Coward!*

She had in fact sat there, across the table from Russell, and choked down that dinner, acting as if everything was now right with the world. One ugly scene at the office and a makeup dinner later, Mr. and Mrs. Russell Reck were a team again. All the while, that hint of orange blossoms wafted through the air between them.

He'd gone back to work afterward, leaving her to go home alone. *Another crisis at work, Syd. It can't be helped, sweetheart.*

Crisis, crisis.

She focused again on the pain in her abdominals, her back. *Relax the neck, that's it. Push. Push!* Only the physical pain managed to cut through that voice—*Coward!* Blocking out the ache inside her chest that told Sydney her heart was crumbling.

Ryan's hand pressed against her shoulder, keeping her from launching into another rep. "Come, on, Sydney. You'll hurt yourself."

Collapsing back onto the mat, she bit her lip against the white heat ripping through her lower stomach as her muscles relaxed. She wanted to curl up right there on the floor in a fetal position and cry. *My husband is going to leave me!*

"Twenty minutes on the bike and we'll call it a day, okay?"

She nodded, this time taking the hand he held out to her. Twenty minutes on the bike . . . and forty on the treadmill, she added mentally. Because what else was there for her to do? Go back to that empty house and meet with another decorator's lackey?

Almost an hour later, exhausted and muscles burning, she dropped onto the bench in the locker room and took off her shoes. They were cross trainers with special arch supports. Sydney massaged her foot, almost moaning with the relief it brought. They say the feet were the place where you could best gauge the aging process—bone spurring and other damage. Sydney's were in pretty bad shape, requiring special orthodics.

She put her face in her hands, hunching over to lean against her opened palms. Henry would never have cheated on her. Stalwart, loving Henry. He'd been so proud of her career as assistant curator and so utterly thankful for any scrap of attention she'd given. Why hadn't she known how to appreciate him?

When she finally went out the door half an hour later, she was still asking herself the same questions, wondering if there was a part of her that only wanted things the hard way. She hadn't known what to do with the simple gifts Henry had just handed to her.

She walked out blindly, almost colliding into a man standing near the entrance. He grabbed both her elbows, steadying her, smiling as if he recognized her. It didn't happen very often—people tended to recognize Russell, not her.

And then she realized who it was. "James?" The man from the security company.

"You remembered."

She took a step back, out of his arms. "You made it a little difficult to forget. You come to this gym?" But even as she asked the question, she realized that it wasn't a coincidence, finding him here. "Are you following me?"

"Hey. I'm not stalking you or anything. It's just that . . ." He looked away, pushing his fingers through that bleached hair just a fraction of an inch long in places. "Oh, hell." When he turned back, he reached over so that the tips of his fingers grazed hers. It was an incredibly sweet gesture, almost boyish. "Pretty stupid, huh? Coming here to see you."

She knew she was vulnerable. Here was this young man following her, looking at her with complete infatuation. A sweet little goody dished up for her when she was feeling rejected and unloved. *Do you want some candy, little girl?*

She crossed her arms over her chest, her gym bag swinging from her arm behind her. "How did you know I'd be here?"

"You sort of left your Filofax open on your nightstand." He shrugged. "Hey, don't be mad. I was fixing the system and I thought—I know it was wrong. Shit." He let his hands fall to his side. "Even saying it makes me sound crazy."

He smiled. Shook his head, looking suddenly very embarrassed. She thought he might even be blushing. "I'm outta here. Have a happy life, Sydney."

She let him walk away almost twenty feet before she called out, "James?"

He turned, appearing for all the world as if she'd given him the greatest prize in the world. A second chance. He jogged back.

"Would you like to go for that cup of coffee now?" she asked.

"Yeah," he said, taking her hand. "I would like that very much."

Allison sat with her legs crossed, listening like the others seated at the circle: five women, three men—and, of course, the good doctor who led the group. Allison came to this particular support group once a week.

"They call it missing time." The girl, who had introduced herself as Harriet, appeared curiously detached as she spoke. "For me, it was about three hours." She peered up, her soft green eyes taking in the group. She had brown hair she wore parted down the middle with little barrettes holding back her bangs. She was young, possibly just seventeen. "I couldn't account for three whole hours."

Allison waited. She'd heard it all before from others just

like Harriet. She could almost say what was coming next. Harriet was just warming up.

"I was spending the night over at Rachel's. We decided to go out. Rachel thought Tommy was cheating on her. That's her boyfriend, Tommy. She wanted to go to the point and spy on the couples. To see if Tommy was there with that witch, Christina. When we were driving up, that's when it happened." Her bottom lip began to tremble. "They left Rachel in the car. They only took Myra and me. But they didn't do anything to Myra." Now her voice was shaking, choking up. "It was me they did it to. Only me."

Dr. Simons seated next to Harriet reached over and placed a comforting hand on the girl's shoulder. "Go on, Harriet," she said.

Harriet nodded, brushing away her tears with the back of both hands. "When I woke up, there was all this light. I couldn't tell where it was coming from. You know, there were no lamps or anything. I could see Myra. She was on a table next to me. It was all shiny, like it was made of steel or something. She looked like she was in a coma. Maybe sleeping."

Allison shifted her gaze to the older woman seated just across the circle from her. Like everyone else, the woman listened carefully. But Allison could see by her expression that something about the story troubled her.

In her late fifties, the woman was dressed in a conservative navy blue skirt and a white cotton blouse. She had ash-blonde hair and the curvy figure of someone who wasn't concerned with dieting. Allison had been watching her through most of the session.

"They didn't look human," Harriet said. "They were really weird. Tall and skinny with these big eyes, no hair, and really gray skin. The eyes. That's what I see at night, when I can't sleep." Harriet looked at Dr. Simons, a little girl lost. "Just those eyes, floating in front of me. Round and round, in a figure eight."

"It's perfectly natural," Dr. Simons assured her.

The woman across the circle frowned.

Harriet peered down at her hands, worrying her fingers in her lap, plucking at the material of her jeans. "They did things to me. They stuck a really long needle in my belly button. I wanted to scream, to do something. I think maybe I did." She shook her head. "I don't remember everything. Even with the hypnosis. That's why I came to Dr. Simons. My mom heard about her book, *The Lost Abductee*." She smiled up at Dr. Simons, who took her hand. "She thought a group like this could help."

"You were right to come," the doctor assured her. "We all understand what you've been through, Harriet." Dr. Simons nodded to the others in the support group. "You're not alone. Not anymore."

Harriet burst into tears. "My mom. She thought I was crazy. She thought maybe I was with a boy or something and felt guilty so I had to make up some wild story." She looked up, her eyes, pools of green. "But I didn't make it up. I don't think I could make it up. I mean, I don't watch *X-Files* or anything. And Myra. She was there. She still has nightmares."

Dr. Simons nodded. "When did the dreams start?"

The woman Allison had been watching stood and excused herself quietly. No one took notice, intent on young Harriet's alien adventures. It wasn't unusual for people to leave during a session. The experiences revealed by the abductees who came to the encounter group could be extremely unsettling. As Harriet continued her story, Allison, too, stood to take her leave, following the woman outside.

She caught up to her at the elevator. They both waited for the elevator door to open, watching the floors light up as the car ascended. Allison smiled, catching the woman's eye.

"You look a little shook up," she said when the woman smiled back. Allison was a good thirty years younger. "Did Harriet's story strike a nerve?"

The woman didn't answer at first. When the elevator chimed its arrival, she whispered, "I just needed a cigarette, that's all. I thought I would go outside for a minute."

"Mind if I join you?" Allison nodded her head toward a balcony at the end of the corridor. "This way. It's real nice out there. You can watch the surfers across PCH."

Allison knew the woman would follow.

Outside on the balcony, Allison lit the woman's cigarette and watched her take a deep drag. She noticed that the woman's hands shook as she smoked.

"I'm Allison," she said, introducing herself.

"Mary," the woman answered, seeming to calm down a bit. "Mary Wescott."

Mary offered her a cigarette, but Allison shook her head. "Those things will kill you," she said. And when Mary looked confused, Allison laughed. "I just wanted to talk to you, Mary. I don't smoke. So why did you leave?"

At first, Mary didn't respond, just quietly looked out over the railing as if thinking over her answer. Across the highway, surfers bobbed along the water like black seals, awaiting their turn at the waves. Directly below, the streets hummed with bikini-clad inline skaters and boys jogging toward the beach, their wet suits peeled to their hips and surfboards tucked under their arms. A long-haired man with a nut-brown body struck a disparate chord bumming a smoke in front of the shiny new Starbucks, his presence heralding a bygone era when the area was better known for Fourth of July riots and the slam dance. At the pier's entrance, a youth wearing cutoffs played the bagpipes, his instrument case opened in front of him awaiting contributions.

"That girl's story about her abduction," Mary said after a minute. She frowned. "I came to the encounter group think- ing . . ." She shook her head and tapped her cigarette free of ashes. "Nothing. Forget it. I made a mistake coming here, that's all."

Allison nodded, because she knew what Mary wasn't saying. Allison came to Dr. Simons' group regularly looking for people just like her. They always appeared a little confused by the abduction stories they heard from those seated around the circle. Allison visited several groups, but rarely did she find what she was looking for. Today, she knew she'd found Mary.

"It started out with this incredible white light," Allison said, watching the seagulls hovering on the wind. "You don't even remember stopping the car or going outside. You were alone, and then suddenly, you weren't. This light, this wonderful white light surrounded you, making you a part of it. And it felt good. Great, actually. Like being a baby again in your mother's arms."

The woman stopped smoking. She stared at Allison open-mouthed.

"They're not little green men," Allison said, turning to Mary. "They're not tall or gray or bald. They're not men at all. It's a feeling—like having someone inside your head telling you that they love you. And suddenly you know you'll never be alone again."

The cigarette slipped through Mary's fingers, falling to the balcony floor.

"You've noticed the changes, of course." Allison leaned her elbows back against the railing. "Your skin is clearer. The lines less noticeable. Maybe your husband keeps asking you if you're using a new perfume, you smell so nice. It's like you're on some kind of drug." She laughed. "Suddenly, you're super-woman. Your hearing, your vision, your sense of smell and touch—everything is much more vivid and powerful. Intense. And you know things about people. It's not like ESP. You don't read their minds. You just know what they need to be happy at that moment."

"Yes. My God, yes."

"And you know how to give it to them, don't you, Mary? Everyone is attracted to you, as if you've suddenly developed

Take advantage of this offer to enjoy Zebra's newest line of historical romance novels....Splendor Romances (formerly Lovegrams Historical Romances)- Take our introductory shipment of 4 romance novels -Absolutely Free! (a $19.96 value)

Now you'll be able to savor today's best romance novels without even leaving your home with our convenient and inexpensive home subscription service. Here's what you get for joining:

- 4 BRAND NEW bestselling Splendor Romances delivered to your doorstep every month

- 20% off every title (or almost $4.00 off) with your home subscription

- FREE home delivery

- A FREE monthly newsletter, *Zebra/Pinnacle Romance News* filled with author interviews, member benefits, book previews and more!

- No risks or obligations...you're free to cancel whenever you wish...no questions asked

To get started with your own home subscription, simply complete and return the card provided. You'll receive your FREE introductory shipment of 4 Splendor Romances and then you'll begin to receive monthly shipments of new Zebra Splendor titles. Each shipment will be yours to examine for 10 days and then if you decide to keep the books, you'll pay the preferred home subscriber's price of just $4.00 per title. That's $16 for all 4 books with FREE home delivery! And if you want us to stop sending books, just say the word...it's that simple.

4 Free BOOKS are waiting for you!
Just mail in the certificate below!

If the certificate is missing below, write to: Splendor Romances, Zebra Home Subscription Service, Inc., P.O. Box 5214, Clifton, New Jersey 07015-5214

FREE BOOK CERTIFICATE

Yes! Please send me 4 Splendor Romances (formerly Zebra Lovegram Historical Romances), ABSOLUTELY FREE! After my introductory shipment, I will be able to preview 4 new Splendor Romances each month FREE for 10 days. Then if I decide to keep them, I will pay the money-saving preferred publisher's price of just $4.00 each... a total of $16.00. That's 20% off the regular publisher's price and there's never any additional charge for shipping and handling. I may return any shipment within 10 days and owe nothing, and I may cancel my subscription at any time. The 4 FREE books will be mine to keep in any case.

Name _____

Address _____ Apt. _____

City _____ State _____ Zip _____

Telephone ( ) _____

Signature _____ SF0998
(If under 18, parent or guardian must sign.)

Terms and prices subject to change. Orders subject to acceptance by Zebra Home Subscription Service, Inc. . Zebra Home Subscription Service, Inc. reserves the right to reject or cancel any subscription.

‖‖

SPLENDOR ROMANCES
ZEBRA HOME SUBSCRIPTION SERVICE, INC.
120 BRIGHTON ROAD
P.O. BOX 5214
CLIFTON, NEW JERSEY 07015-5214

IllIIᵢᵢIllIᵢᵢᵢᵢᵢIllIᵢIᵢIᵢIᵢIᵢIᵢIᵢIᵢIᵢIᵢIᵢIᵢIᵢIllIᵢᵢI

a case of super-pheromones. But you don't mind. Because now you know what it's like to be really loved. To have that love inside you all the time. And you have so much more to give people because of it.''

Tears came to the woman's eyes. She closed them, relief in her expression as she smiled.

"Only the dreams disturb you," Allison said. "Your husband says you cry out in your sleep. You try to explain to him that it's okay. You beg him not to wake you. That it makes things worse. You need to see the dreams through. It's almost painful to feel the intensity of how it was when they first came to you. To remember and try to be patient and wait. But the memory of it only comes to you in your sleep.''

The woman nodded. "I never want to wake up."

Allison opened her purse and reached inside. "You're right. You don't belong back there.''

She handed Mary a card. In bold letters appeared the word *Millennium*. Beneath it in small print was an address.

"This is where you need to go.'' She looped her arm through Mary's, walking her back inside, loving this part—when a new member discovers there are others just like them, witnessing their sense of relief and joy. It's how Allison had felt when she'd come looking for help.

"The next meeting is Thursday night," she told Mary. "Eight o'clock.''

"Will you be there?''

"Of course.'' Allison punched the elevator button, watching the floors light up. She squeezed Mary's hand. "I'm your sponsor now.''

They were seated at a booth together on a vinyl bench seat the color of wine. Sydney had paraded out the whole sorry story over their expresso coffees. Occasionally, James would reach over to give her fingers a squeeze on the table. *I know*

*how it must hurt, baby. The guy's a bastard to mess around
on you.*

But Sydney hadn't told him everything. She had kept her
dirty little secrets. She hadn't spoken about Henry, her first
husband. That she deserved what was happening. Tit for tat.

"He kept you waiting at the restaurant because he was too
busy banging his girlfriend." He shook his head. "You don't
deserve that. Nobody does." He turned her head toward his,
his hands lingering on her face. He used any excuse to touch
her, and she liked it. That soft, considerate stroke of his fingers.
It had been a long time since a man had touched her like that.

"It's like you're just letting him get away with all this shit.
Why?" he asked.

She picked up the stirrer encrusted with sugar and swirled
it a few times inside her cooling expresso. *Tit for tat.* "You
could never understand about Russell and me."

"Sydney." He looked so earnest, those beautiful green eyes
shining with youthful passion. "I'm going to level with you.
This is California. You own this guy. Half of everything is
yours." When she didn't answer, he turned away in the booth
and cursed softly. "You signed one of those stupid prenups."

"No."

He let out a soft whistle, lifting his brows in surprise. "Then
nail him."

There really was something about James. Something so
entirely charismatic. As if, at last, she had found someone who
understood . . .

"Why am I sitting here listening to you?" She hadn't meant
to say the words out loud.

He leaned forward, his body shielding his actions from anyone who might be watching in the darkened restaurant. He
brought his mouth close to hers. "Because I care."

He kissed her, gently. So gently. It seduced her, that kiss,
enough that for an instant, she responded, opening her mouth
beneath his. Oh, God. It was wicked. This young man holding

her, his mouth eating hers up with such excitement, making it difficult to catch her breath. How long had it been since she'd had that rushing feeling inside her, as if she was in a hurry to get where this kiss might lead?

When he pulled away, he stroked her neck, his fingers resting there so that his thumb touched the pulse point at her neck. "It's been a long time, hasn't it, Sydney?"

At first, she thought he was talking about sex. And it had been ages, too long. She felt heated up with his touch, so ready. But then she realized what he meant, remembering his earlier conversation.

It's been a long time since someone has cared about you.

How easy it would be. To go to some anonymous hotel and listen to James tell her all the ways he needed her. Suddenly, she felt as Russell might, the adrenaline rush of this younger man's attention. She imagined how his more youthful body might feel, so firm, with the kind of musculature Russell could only dream about. Now *she* was the older, richer, more powerful partner, basking in the beaming admiration of the young, sizing him up as if he was a treat. Tempted. So tempted.

She closed her eyes. "I can't."

If she left with James now, her marriage *was* a sham, some package dished up for the board of directors, letting Russell skip the formality of paying her alimony as he did his other ex-wives . . . while she carried on behind his back. *Tit for tat.*

She grabbed her purse and scooted out of the booth. "I'm sorry, but I can't do this." Perhaps Henry in his goodness had taught her something, after all.

James followed close behind. Outside, he grabbed her arm. "Don't leave. Sydney. I just want to talk. Get to know you. I want to help."

But she shook her head, coming to her senses at last. "This isn't me." When she'd cheated on Henry, she'd felt despicable. But she'd done it out of a sense of love, not desperation.

"I'm sorry. But this isn't happening," she said firmly, so

there would be no question she meant every word. "Do you understand? I don't want you following me anymore. It won't do you or me a bit of good."

Alec watched Sydney march off. She had this funny little walk, like a fast clip, as if she was rushing to some meeting. Or running away. She had a great ass, he thought with no little regret. Because she'd just blown him off big time.

He frowned, taking a cigarette out and lighting it. Yes, indeed, she had dissed him good.

He blew out a puff of smoke. "Well, that pretty much fucked up my day."

Chapter Sixteen

Cherish sat in her chair at her office, headphones on, listening to the sounds of the ocean as she imagined herself boarding the plane.

The images clicked past like a countdown. Precision clockwork. She watched herself stare up the long metal staircase, fixing on that mental snapshot of the opened door for courage, calculating the next step. *Calm, stay calm,* the words ran like a current inside her, bringing a taste of serenity within reach, making her believe, *this time, yes this time* . . . until the images began to fade, to change.

She saw her hand gripping the handrail, her fingers attempting to fuse with the metal. The ground beneath her feet quivered, then bucked, mimicking the turbulence. Their faces, she remembered those terrified faces—the reporter, Henry, and Eric—pictured each like cards in a deck shuffling past as the memories rushed in, beginning the disintegration. *Three, two, one* . . .

Cherish stripped off the headphones and dropped them on

the desk, covering her face with her hands. She slumped into her seat, the air seizing up inside her lungs so she made odd, wheezing sounds.

Imagine a white light filling you . . . Mentally, she recited the words like a mantra, trying to calm down. But it wasn't until a good fifteen minutes later that she opened her eyes again.

Her spine curled against the leather of the swivel chair, she felt the air come more easily into her lungs. Cherish sighed and peered down at the tiny wheels of the relaxation tape still turning inside the tape recorder.

She pushed eject and flipped out the cassette, holding it inches from her face. "Another fine investment."

After the crash eighteen months ago, she'd seen a therapist. Her mother's suggestion. The woman had told Cherish about these relaxation tapes and taught her the visualization exercise where she imagined herself calmly boarding a plane. If the exercise went bad, Cherish was to imagine a light entering her body through the top of her head, filling her with warmth, then coming out through her fingertips and toes. Theoretically, everywhere the light touched, she would relax. It was supposed to keep her climbing those stairs to board the plane.

Cherish let her head drop back. She remembered Conor that morning reciting from her letter, parading out her fears. *I'm here now, Cher. Don't push me away. It's not what you want and we both know it.* Reminding her that she still needed him.

She'd thought, if she could just board that plane . . .

The door to her office opened and Lori peeked in, her brown eyes framed by false lashes, her burgundy curls teased to new heights with fashionable wisps brushing her cheeks. Lori took one look at her and closed the door behind her. From Lori's expression, Cherish figured she didn't look so good.

Cherish held up the tape in her hand, giving Lori a weak smile. "It was worth a try, right?"

Lori glanced at the tape recorder on the desk. "You know. They're having a free gift with purchase at a couple of the

cosmetic counters at Bloomingdale's.'' And when Cherish hesitated, she added, ''Come on. We have to go to Newport to
pick up that report anyway. It's on the way.''

Cherish dropped the tape in the trash can, then seeing Alec's
photograph still on her desk, grabbed it as well, dumping it
next to Conor's in the drawer. She gave the drawer a good
slam shut with her foot.

''I'm there,'' she said, grabbing her purse.

Shopping. Cheap therapy.

Russell walked across the product-room floor, ignoring the
hundreds of models in glass display cases, icons set for public
worship. Each model represented a stepping-stone in Reck
Enterprises' rise to power. Today, his company and its wholly
owned subsidiaries commanded fifty-two percent of the market
for satellites and aircraft, both commercial and military, making
the product room rather crowded—The Wrecker's war prizes.
They even had the engineering test unit of a manned capsule
from the 1960s on a dais front and center.

The auditorium-size room stood empty; only the hum of the
air conditioner and Russell's footsteps disturbed the hollow
hush. It was a Tuesday, six o'clock. The public had been shooed
out nearly two hours ago. Save for the guard at the entrance and
the man waiting for Russell inside, the product room appeared
abandoned, inhabited only by its miniature planes, rockets, and
satellites.

Russell headed for the far section where satellites of all
sizes and shapes festooned the wall like oversized Christmas
ornaments. Joseph Kinnard stood in profile, his hands clasped
behind his back, face angled up like that of a true disciple at
worship. Beneath an ostentatious banner proclaiming it, ''The
Future,'' appeared a mock-up of the company's crowning glory.
The GI Joe-size figure beside it bespoke its majestic dimensions—an antenna nearing thirty meters in diameter with a

band width that could service tens of thousands of Internet users simultaneously: the Pegasus Satellite.

To Russell's knowledge—and he paid good money to make certain he had the most up-to-date information on his competitors—the Pegasus Satellite was the most powerful ever conceived, servicing all the technologies of the future, cell phones, Internet access, pagers. Its potential was unlimited. With it, Russell would become the Kublai Khan of world communications.

Only, the technology that could make the Pegasus a reality didn't exist. It cost ten-thousand dollars to send even a pound into space. The Pegasus waited for a revolutionary material: a fiber light and strong enough to send its enormous proportions reliably into earth orbit, as well as able to conduct electricity as efficiently as a superconductor, only at microscopic sizes.

"Look at it, Russell," Kinnard said in a reverent voice. "A communications empire in the making."

The threat hung in the air between them. *Your future, Russell. The future of your company.*

Kinnard pressed his fingers to his well-shaped forehead as if fighting off a migraine. "What did you find out?"

"Bad news." It was all Russell could do not to fidget. *The dog ate it.* He was the CEO of a billion-dollar organization bearing his name, dammit, not Kinnard's lackey. "I don't know how he managed it, but the telemetry readout Conor handed over, it's the real thing. A copy of the original."

For the first time, Kinnard appeared startled. He swung around, his hands braced behind his back, his eyes comically wide and nearly colorless in the lighting of the room.

The fact was, they had "fixed" the telemetry readout, changing the data to show normal stresses on the wing. That's why Russell had held out so long before releasing the flight data to the public and the subcontractor, Marquis. In a series of brilliant moves—tactics that had required all the combined muscle that Russell and Kinnard could pull together—they'd managed the feat in total secrecy. They'd been ready to hand over the doctored telemetry to Marquis when the shit had hit the fan in the form of Dean White's impromptu press conference. *We at the Millennium Society were sorry to hear our warnings ignored . . .*

"Holy Christ." Kinnard turned away, as if it was all too much.

"Mitchell doesn't have any experience with this kind of data," Russell was quick to add. All they needed was some bumpkin professor taking an interest in that flight data. "He's spent most of his time in the lab or in the stirrups of some jet rocket. For all we know, he was telling the truth; he didn't even keep a copy."

Kinnard shut his eyes. "And doesn't this all smack of the Wildman himself," he said, speaking of Alec Porter.

Russell let out the breath he'd been holding, admitting it. "Yes. I'm afraid it does."

"He's probably having himself a good laugh right now, while we have our balls in a vise."

Both men remained quiet, standing in the shadow of the Pegasus model. *Whoever has the Pegasus will have a communications empire.*

"You'll leave this in my hands now, Russell," Kinnard said, his voice, too quiet.

A chill passed through Russell. *Just like it happened to poor Henry.* "Aren't you jumping the gun, Joseph? Who's going to believe Porter anyway? With his record. What we need is—"

Kinnard turned, his eyes locked on Russell like two laser beams sighting on a target. "What we need is for you to shut the hell up and listen to me for once. I'll take the appropriate steps and you will do as I tell you. Do I need to make it any clearer?"

"I understand."

Russell pulled out a handkerchief as Kinnard walked out. He hoped to God the damned spook didn't get sloppy on him. If something happened to Mitchell or the Malone woman and they traced it back to Reck Enterprises, everything Russell had worked for would be destroyed.

He wiped the sweat from his palms, telling himself Joseph Kinnard had been the head of covert operations for the fucking CIA. He knew what he was doing. And this program was important to Joseph. To both of them.

Russell remembered when Joseph had first approached him about the Ballas problem. Eric was going to get there first, discovering the ultimate fiber, carbon nanotubes. Nanotechnology was the wave of the future. Composites using nanotubes would be virtually unbreakable. They were also good electrical conductors, characteristics that not only made the Pegasus Satellite a reality, but could lead to a revolution in computers, making them smaller and faster.

They couldn't let Ballas own such an important technology, Kinnard had said. Not Ballas, a man who complained about the government's stranglehold on research and technology in aerospace. How many times had Russ heard Eric say teaming with the government made the weak strong and the strong weak, reducing competition by handing lucrative contracts to companies based largely on political considerations? Fuck who had the best ideas.

Ballas wanted to cut the government out and Kinnard knew it. Eric thought he could get the job done with his Russians. He practically had.

But Russell, he had always been Kinnard's man. So deep in with the government these days that Kinnard practically told him when to take a shit. So Joseph had come to Russell, holding out to him the ultimate prize, the key to the future. But at a cost. *Jesus, Henry.*

Christ, they were coming at him from all sides. Kinnard threatening him; Sydney threatening him. *I'll divorce you . . . appropriate steps, Russell.*

Only Allison seemed to understand. Even now, he was living in the glow of their night together, her softly scented promises weaving through his head like visions of sugarplums. *I just want to make you happy, Russell . . .*

In his mind, he could still see her tying herself to that damn bed, completely naked. All the while, those words coming from her beautiful lush mouth.

You can't afford to divorce her—she owns everything. I don't want any part of that. Let her be Mrs. Russell Reck. But she can't have your heart, Russ. That's mine now.

And he realized it was true. That he didn't love Sydney anymore. It was Allison he wanted.

Allison and the Pegasus Satellite.

Chapter Seventeen

Cherish leaned back against the bar, watching the Japanese chef just a few feet away shape the fried rice on the grill before him into a giant penis, complete with anatomically correct molding. He added two egg shells at the base, getting a few nervous giggles from the couples seated around the grill of the Teppan-style restaurant, drinking sake. The penis pointed directly at one of the women . . . the one conveniently dressed like a Playboy centerfold wannabe, swaying, half crocked, in her seat. Crowning his masterpiece, the chef squirted a white sauce from a plastic bottle at the tip of the rice penis. His audience burst into laughter and applause.

Cherish sipped from the sugar-coated rim of her martini glass. The glass was filled to the brim with a pink concoction called a Cosmopolitan. Her oldest brother, Mike, had told her about it, a drink that tasted like punch but carried a wallop . . . which meant she was going to be nursing this baby all night.

She glanced casually at the far end of the bar where Conor stood wedged between two business sorts arguing fraternally as they popped peanuts into their mouths. Conor was drinking a beer, straight from the bottle.

She smiled, taking another drink of the Cosmopolitan. If there was anything in the world Conor hated most, it was barhopping. Which was the very reason she and Lori had come here. If he wanted to follow Cherish, the least she could do was make it interesting.

To complete the picture, Cherish had dressed in a skimpy leather miniskirt that rode daringly up her thighs. Lori had talked her into buying it. *Trust me, Cherish. It makes you look ten pounds thinner!* Music to any woman's ears. After Conor, there'd been a few chinks in the armor she'd tried to camouflage with an interest in running and makeovers at the cosmetic counter. The latter proved more addicting than the former. Nowadays, she had everything a girl needed to look "natural."

The skirt she regretted, since it made it impossible to sit comfortably on the bar stool without pondering the view. She'd never had the guts to wear it before, filing it at the back of her closet with the other rejects under "What was I thinking?"

Beside her, Lori reached down and dug acrylic nails a full inch long into Cherish's thigh, getting her attention. Cherish swallowed a yelp and turned. The guy drooling over Lori was short and stocky, in his mid-fifties with an obvious tan line where a wedding ring ought to be. He wore his shirt opened to his belt. A thick gold chain with a cross lay half buried in a tundra of chest hair.

Lori released her hold on Cherish's leg and turned to face her. "So what do you think, Cherish?" she asked, bringing Cherish into the conversation. Lori made her eyes go big and raised her hand to her forehead to form the letter *L* with her thumb and forefinger as she mouthed the word, "loser."

Getting the idea, Cherish chimed in. "I'm sorry, Lori. I wasn't paying attention. I was just watching Marco over there"—she nodded toward Conor—"wondering if what you're doing is so smart."

"Whatever do you mean?" Lori asked, all innocence as she leaned back to give the guy a better view.

Cherish swooped in, speaking directly to Mr. Disco. "See that big bruiser over there?"

"Yeah." Mr. Disco tried not to be too obvious, checking Conor out.

"That's Lori's ex." Lori's ex-husband was about three inches taller than Lori, topping off at a walloping five foot, four inches. An engineer who wouldn't hurt a flea, but hadn't made Lori happy. Particularly when he'd started boffing some woman he'd met on a business trip. Cherish thought Lori had handled things pretty well on the whole. She'd smashed Gary's five-thousand dollar IBM computer to kingdom come with his golf club and left Gary's head intact.

"He just got out . . . what would you say, Lori? Maybe a week ago?"

Lori rolled her eyes, into it now. "If that." She took a sip of her Tanqeray and tonic. "Marco can be such a pain."

"What do you mean *out?*" the guy asked, his eyes starting to look like a couple of eggs, sunny-side up. All white around the pupils.

"Prison," Cherish said. "For beating up some poor man who took an interest in Lori. Was it a felony charge, Lori? I forget."

Lori shook her head, *tching* softly. "It's like, if he can't have me, no one else can."

The guy eyed Conor, who did Cherish and Lori the favor of looking capable of murder. As an added bonus, The Scar side faced them.

"I don't know, Lori," Cherish said, putting on the finishing touches. "I think we should maybe call it a night. Before anyone else gets hurt."

Mr. Disco paid for his drink, glancing down the bar for a quick getaway. "That's probably a good idea."

"You took long enough," Lori said. jabbing her straw into

her drink. Lori had a code for men at bars. L for loser. P for player. So far, Conor had gotten rid of two losers and a player.

"I don't know why you bother with bars," Cherish said. It was Lori's theory that Mr. Right was just one happy hour away. "Why don't you try a dating service?"

"Please. Single white male into skydiving looking for fit mate. I lie; he lies. Then Tiny Tim shows up at my door and we're both disappointed. Me, I'm the lady hovering over the tomatoes at the fruit vendors. I want to pinch a few before I buy." She slurped loudly from her drink. "So how long are you going to make him stand there, watching?"

"He wants to play the macho jet pilot." She shrugged, taking a sip of her drink.

"Gee," Lori said. "It's really a shame, you know, that it didn't work out between the two of you. There's a tomato I wouldn't mind giving a squeeze."

"If you go for that sort, I suppose," she said, too casually.

"Now, I wouldn't say he's handsome in the conventional sense." Lori was focused here, finely plucked brows furrowed, tapping her lip with her finger. "Good body, though. That could be it. And that scar makes his face more interesting, you know? More macho. Or maybe it's the mouth. He has the crooked grin thing that sort of zings up a woman's spine when he smiles—"

"I get it, Lori. I get it."

"And presence. Yeah. That's it. I mean, look. The bar is crowded, and still"—she was using her hands to talk now—"there's like this space around him. Nobody crowds him."

Despite herself, Cherish glanced over, catching sight of Conor taking a drink of his Corona. Zing. That about covered it.

She frowned, looking away. "He's got the big *T.*"

"*T?*" Lori asked.

"Trouble."

"Well, darling," she said with a smile. "Looks like Trouble just lost his patience. He's coming this way."

Cherish didn't turn around. She didn't need to. She could feel the small hairs rise at the back of her neck.

She watched Lori grab for her purse. Realizing what her friend was intending, Cherish slapped her hand on Lori's before she could move.

"You promised," she said, holding on to Lori for all she was worth. "There is no abandoning ship here, remember?"

"I lied. Besides, I promised Gary I'd be home early." Lori was on surprisingly good terms with her ex given the reasons for the divorce, which Cherish thought was for the sake of their two kids. But Gary was good for about two hours of baby-sitting before absolute terror set in.

Lori leaned forward and looked directly into her eyes. "You have to do this, Cherish. You understand that, don't you? You have to conquer the beast."

"I want to assure you, Lori, that I do not have to conquer anything right now," she argued, holding fast to Lori's hand.

Lori pried Cherish's hand away, one finger at a time. "I know you don't believe this, but I'm doing this for your own good. *Ciao,* girl. Give him heck."

She watched Lori disappear into the crowd. She reached for the Cosmopolitan, draining the glass, almost choking on the lime twist at the bottom. She knew the beast was standing behind her and she wasn't going to give him the satisfaction of turning around.

"All right. Let's go," she heard him say.

She turned, looking at him with a surprised expression. "Conor?" She glanced around. "I thought you hated these kinds of places?"

He glanced at his watch. "All that's missing is the disco music."

Disco! Why didn't I think of that?

"We're getting out of here."

"Really? And where exactly would *we* be going?" she asked.

"To the hangar out at Edwards." He threw money on the bar to pay for her drink. "If we leave now, we'll just make it. I'll need a piece of the wing and I don't have clearance. Luckily for us"—he grabbed her hand, pulled—"you do."

I need a piece of the wing.

As if it was that simple. Just walk into a secured building. Ignore the guard carrying the M-16. Pluck up a piece of debris that has been meticulously catalogued to prevent anyone from spiriting it away.

Piece of cake.

The moon shone overhead, flooding the tarmac and the tower on the flight line with an iridescent light. Edwards Air Force Base was essentially a dry lake bed: miles of flat, hardened mud surrounded by Joshua trees and sagebrush. Fifty years ago, Chuck Yeagar had broken the sound barrier here in what amounted to a rocket with wings. The bright orange Bell X-1 plane, the words *Glamorous Glennis* painted on its nose, still hung in the Air and Space Museum at the Smithsonian. Today, the space shuttles used Edwards as their landing site in California. It was also a chief testing facility for experimental aircraft for both the Air Force and NASA, and where the second-phase prototype for the WingMaster had crashed.

They were in the parking lot right outside the main flight line. Ten miles back, they'd been waved through the gate courtesy of Cherish's contractor's base pass. Ahead loomed the eighty-foot hangar where the Air Force and the FBI were reassembling the wreckage found at the crash site. It was the typical course after an accident. Everything would be pored over until they could determine the exact cause of the failure.

It was eight o'clock. Conor "Mario Andretti" and his Mean Machine had sliced a good half hour off the drive through the desert, making her regret chugging that Cosmopolitan. The FBI and military investigators working at the site would have retired for the night . . . not so many prying eyes lounging about.

But there was plenty of security. It would be impossible to remove so much as a paper clip from inside that hangar.

"And yet here we are," she said.

Conor flipped through a small notebook he'd brought along, looking over what appeared to be calculations.

"I'm not exactly dressed for this," she said, tugging self-consciously at the hem of her miniskirt for the umpteenth time.

"You'll do fine."

She was having a little trouble getting her pulse to believe that. Coming here in the dead of night, flashing her pass for the guard at the entry gate, she felt as if she was in a James Bond movie. "It's like we should use a code phrase or something."

"The rooster crows at dawn," he said, pocketing the notebook and giving her a little push forward in the small of her back.

"Now he gets a sense of humor," she mumbled, moving toward the hangar but keeping to the shadows.

Across the tarmac, Conor signaled her to stop. He pulled her up close, so that his mouth was right next to her ear. "It's just a hunch, Cher. Don't take too many chances. I'll be waiting for you back at the car."

And then he disappeared.

Taking a breath, she walked forward. *Don't act guilty.* She was one of the good guys. She was supposed to be here. *Just checking up on a few things . . .*

At the entrance to the hangar, an SP waited, wearing his Security Police beret and carrying an M-16. The hangar doors were gigantic panels that could be rolled back on tracks, making it possible to park a full-size cargo jet inside. Right now, the olive green hangar doors were shut tight, but there was a normal-size door built in to the towering panel. The entrance was open but roped off.

She flashed her base badge as she walked toward the SP.

"I'm with Marquis." She kept going toward the door, as if it were nothing that she was stepping inside the hangar at eight o'clock at night wearing an outrageous miniskirt and heels. She felt like Mata Hari.

The SP stepped forward to block her path. "I'm sorry, ma'am. This is a restricted area."

She was about to argue, tell him that was her company's plane lying in itty-bitty pieces on the floor, when a voice came from inside the hangar.

"Ms. Malone?" It took a moment to place the voice as the man inside stepped into the light, walking toward the rope barring the hangar entrance. Tall, good-looking, Hispanic, he wore a got-to-take-me-serious pinstriped suit.

Luis Lebredo, the FBI agent who'd practically taken over the meeting yesterday at Reck's Newport office. Special Agent Luis Lebredo.

"I thought I recognized your voice," he said.

"Mr. Lebredo." She forced a smile. "What a surprise to see you here." *The frigging FBI!*

"Not as surprised as I am to see you." He nodded to the guard and unhitched the rope. "I'm certain Ms. Malone is on the roster. Do you want to come in and take a look?"

She was thinking about what Conor had said. *Don't take too many chances.* But instead of making an excuse and looking as if she were trying to avoid the agent, she stepped inside, waiting as he latched the rope once more.

"What exactly are you trying to pull?" she asked, improvising quickly, just in case he wanted to ask a few questions himself. "Disbanding the investigative board, taking over like this? That group was put together specifically for this type of contingency. They are all neutral experts in the field."

Like an enormous wounded bird, the superstructure of the prototype loomed over them. Engineers had attached broken pieces of the fuselage to a grid, trying to reassemble the plane and examine the wreckage pattern. The XC-23 was a prototype for a cargo jet, but it was relatively small, perhaps half the dimensions of the Boeing C-17 Globemaster. The first- and second-phase prototypes were both half-scale. The program didn't call for a full-scale model until the final phase, and that prototype was being assembled at Reck's facility in Palmdale.

The hangar was a deep cave of aluminum over steel girders. Cherish could hear her footsteps echo hollowly as she stepped across the concrete. Set on the floor to either side of the fuselage, were the puzzlelike fragments for each wing. Cherish walked directly to the wing closest to the door. Scanning the area quickly, she saw tiny scraps, pieces small enough to fit in the palm of her hand.

She had no idea how she was going to get one past Lebredo.

"This is an FBI investigation," he said, stepping up behind her. "We have our own trained personnel."

"Really?" She turned, facing him. "And what about Marquis? Why are we cut out of the loop?"

He looked almost amused. "Are you looking for material for your next press release?"

"Of course, I am. Marquis is a small company. If the public believes that we're the target of some depraved terrorist, they're going to ask questions like, 'if one Marquis plane goes down, are the others safe?' This could be devastating for our company." She took a step closer to him, thinking fast, raising her voice. "Until this thing is settled, we're at risk. Any day now, our customers could cancel ongoing contracts, claiming that public confidence in our product makes it impossible to sell planes with Marquis wing designs."

She used her hands to talk, just like Lori. She turned, as if trying to indicate the wreckage. Her purse flew out of her hand—seemingly by accident, she hoped. Enough Lancôme cosmetics to satisfy a drag queen flew in every direction.

"Darn it," she said, sounding genuinely distressed. She dropped down to gather up a lipstick case, EyeColour Duo, Lip Brio, thankful that the last year's lust for Lancôme had

come in handy. There was plenty of stuff rolling around, mingling with the wing fragments on the floor. Grabbing her Dual
Finish compact, she scooped up a nearby piece of the wing
skin approximately the same size, covering it with the compact.
She prayed Lebredo hadn't seen her.

They both stood, Lebredo handing her the few things he'd
picked up. Cherish dropped them into her bag where the piece
of wing lay hidden. She looked up at the agent, waiting for
him to sound some sort of alarm. But he was just watching her
calmly.

"Look, I didn't mean to yell," she told him. She took a
deep breath, holding her handbag to the side and pinching her
fingers at the bridge of her nose as if she might have a headache—all the while, a little voice inside her head screamed: *I
have a piece of the skin! It's in my purse. The FBI is standing
here and I have a piece of the skin!*

"I shouldn't have come. Not when I'm this upset." She
hoped he couldn't hear her heart thumping against her chest
like an atomic blast. "Just don't cut us off, all right?"

"You'll know everything you'll need to know."

"Yeah. That's what I'm afraid of," she said.

She turned and walked toward the door. She kept thinking
he was going to call her back. *Stop! Thief!* Search her purse.
Or maybe it was a trap. He wanted to see her actually step
outside the hangar before he nabbed her, catching her red-
handed.

"Ms. Malone."

She was two yards from the exit. She turned, trying to catch
her breath, to look natural.

He came right up to her and took her hand. He placed a tube
of lipstick in the center of her palm.

"I found it under the fuselage."

"Thanks," she said with a smile. "Venus," she said, giving
the name of the lipstick color. "It's a seasonal color. Heck,
this puppy might be hard to replace."

She didn't breathe again until she was back in the car. She slipped inside Conor's 4Runner and closed the door.

"Drive," she told him.

He turned on the motor and drove in silence. He didn't say a word until they were well past the gate at the perimeter and heading for the freeway. "Did you get it?" he asked.

She held up a piece of the wing skin five inches in diameter. "You bet your bottom, I got it, flyboy."

Chapter Eighteen

The wing fragment lay on the counter between them, right beside a small spiral notebook the size of Cherish's hand, the same notebook Conor had consulted during their ride out to the desert. Though new, its price sticker still gleaming white, half the pages were scribbled over with notes, diagrams, and calculations. Conor had been a busy boy.

He picked up the wing fragment, turning it in his hand. They were in his house, nestled in the cozy hills above Chino, both seated at the kitchen counter on high stools, an echo of the bar they'd left just hours before. Only, the world had turned upside down since then. It was just past ten o'clock.

"So I started to think," he said. He'd been going over his calculations with Cherish, honing in on his conclusions like a doctoral thesis. "What if they changed the material and not the design?"

He held up the piece of the wing skin. Cherish took it from him, careful not to cut herself on the edges. It looked like a thin, hard, piece of shiny fiberglass, grayish in color, tiny threads fringing the edges like a ripped hem. The paint, a dark gray, had chipped off in most places.

"There's something strange about it," she said, frowning.

Conor smiled. "Very good."

She wondered what it would be like to be one of his impressionable coeds, sitting in her first engineering course, and hear those words from Dr. Mitchell. Maybe she would be expecting a difficult semester, perhaps even a boring one regretting signing up for the course. Then, in walks Professor Hunk. *I'll be your instructor in structural analysis. . . .*

What would you be willing to do to get him to look at you with that sexy smile and say: *Very good.*

"Look at the color, Cher."

As soon as he said it, the discrepancy came into focus. "It has a slight silver sheen."

Any composite she'd ever worked with was nearly black. The graphite fibers turned the material a dark gun-metal gray in the curing process.

Again he smiled, this time making his eyes gleam with it, the excitement. "I kept looking over the flight data, the tremendous stress on the wings. What could handle those kinds of stresses?"

One side of his smile hitched up a notch. It was just as Lori said. The man had *zing.*

"I think it's buckyballs," he told her.

It took her a moment to place the name. Most engineers weren't familiar with the term. But she'd heard it, of course. Because of her work with Eric.

Advanced composite materials was a field that had grown with increasing importance the last twenty years. It started with fiberglass, a plastic reinforced with glass threads. Today's composites used graphite, like those Eric had developed for the XC-23 WingMaster and other projects. But in the future, the real cutting edge was synthetic metals. That's where buckyballs came in.

R. Buckminster Fuller was a U.S. inventor, philosopher,

author, and mathematician known for the concept "Spaceship Earth," and inventing the Geodesic dome, an architecture that resembled a gigantic soccer ball. The carbon 60 molecule, sixty carbon atoms arranged in a microscopic sphere, became know as buckyballs because of its geodesic shape. It had been hypothesized that you could cut the sphere in half and insert ten more carbon atoms, like a belt around the middle. By placing the atoms between the two pieces before you put the halves back together, you elongated the sphere into an egg shape, achieving carbon 70. If you kept adding more and more belts of ten carbon atoms, you would stretch out the shape of the sphere to make a long hollow tube, or a filament.

These had been coined nanotubes. The filaments were stronger than anything ever before discovered. Essentially they were diamond fibers. Use these nanotubes in your epoxy instead of carbon fibers and you had something popularly termed a synthetic metal, because of its silvery sheen. It was the next evolution in composite materials, a composite that was several times stronger and stiffer, and much, much lighter than the current composites using graphite.

But no one had been able to make nanotubes more than a fraction of a millimeter long. Fullerenes, another nod to Buckminster Fuller, was the general term used for nanotubes and buckyballs. Commercially viable fullerenes, fibers long enough and produced in large enough quantities for use in aerospace, weren't technologically possible. It was what engineers referred to as "unobtainium," a material that was so good, it didn't exist.

"Fullerene fibers? No way," she said.

"What exactly did Eric have you working on at Marquis?"

She frowned. "It *was* a composite using fullerenes," she told him. "But he had only whiskers." Eric and the Russians had gotten that far, making nanotubes that were fractions of a millimeter long. "They were using whisker-size pieces of the fullerenes, mixing the whiskers in with the epoxy to develop a new composite. Eric wanted us to find a way to make it useful—come up with a structural design, find out where the material was best suited on the airplane.''

She turned the piece of silvery composite over in her hand. She shook her head, remembering. ''But my research showed there wasn't enough of a benefit using the fullerene whiskers. Not enough bang for his buck. I was hoping we could go on with the program, maybe explore some other avenues, but the XC-23 came along and management canceled the project.''

He took her hand in his, holding it tight, the gesture much more significant because of its casualness.

''What if Eric got beyond the whiskers he gave you to work with? What if he and his Russians discovered a way to grow the nanotubes long enough for filaments?''

''Unobtainium,'' she whispered. And then, raising her voice, ''He'd have a viable composite for structural application on an aircraft. A synthetic metal.''

''So he works with your company, the little guy, trying to find a way to make the whiskers work for him commercially . . . only, all along, he has something better in mind. Maybe his Russians found a way to grow the nanotubes.''

She shook her head. It was incredible . . . impossible.

She remembered the first time she'd learned about nanotubes. Arthur C. Clarke once wrote a science fiction book using an elevator that could go from the ground straight into space. No more space shuttle, just push the button and, *next floor, lower earth orbit.* The elevator used a cable. It was science fiction because there wasn't a material strong enough to make the cable work. Fullerene fibers could do that.

''But what's it doing on our plane?'' she asked. ''How could Reck Enterprises change the material without letting us know about it? We *designed* the wing.''

''The prototype was manufactured at Reck's facilities. They tell you, we're using this composite; they hand you a set of properties for it. You come up with the design. You wouldn't know if they changed the material. How could you unless you tested it?''

She held up the wing skin. It appeared similar enough to a graphite composite that—unless it was tested—you would assume it was just a variation on the standard material. The investigative engineers wouldn't bother to run those types of tests, not with everything else they had to do.

Conor leaned forward, still holding her hand so there was a slight tug, bringing her closer. ''You think about it, Cher. If you created a revolutionary material, how would you make sure it stayed quiet?''

''Keep it in-house?''

He shook his head. That smile. He was enjoying this. ''Word always gets out. Corporate espionage. Leaks. Someone gets wind of what you're doing and then it's the race to market. But what if you said you weren't doing the research at all?''

''They might not come looking.'' She looked at their hands, how he held hers so lightly. Here, at last, they could put aside their differences and work together. ''But how could you hide it?''

''I've been thinking about that. How could a company like Reck Enterprises conduct completely secret research? Joseph Kinnard. A man in charge of research and acquisition for the last ten years—head of covert operations at the CIA before that. God knows what Kinnard's resources are. And he and Russell Reck go way back.''

She tried to imagine what kind of machinations that would take. Government contracts were strictly overseen—a lot of paperwork and a lot of people went into developing the XC-23 WingMaster.

But if anyone could make it happen . . .

''Joseph Kinnard gets my vote,'' she said.

''Exactly. So here you are, working with Eric on a program that smells not just of money, but also control of the hottest cutting-edge technology. Only, Eric doesn't want to tip his hand so he shows you only a hint of what he's got up his sleeve. Fullerene whiskers, not the filaments. It looks tentative and a little weak, not worth pursuing if something better comes along.''

"And it did,'' she said, still looking at that shiny piece of composite. "Joystick pulled out when Reck hired Eric's company on the XC-23. Marquis was brought on board as well. It was a nice, fat contract, so everyone was happy.''

"And who brought them together?''

"Kinnard . . . Reck.''

"Maybe they knew Eric was on to a viable nanotube composite, something better than the whiskers.''

The way he said it, his tone.

"You smell a rat,'' she said.

"I smell something.''

"So what are we going to do?''

That's when he let go of her hand. *"We* aren't going to do anything.'' Standing, he picked up the wing fragment, making it disappear into a drawer near the phone. *Abracadabra.* "Not yet, anyway. Tomorrow, I'll run some tests at my lab. We'll know soon enough what this stuff really is.''

She wasn't going to argue with him. Composites were his game; Conor was the expert. But the way he'd slipped that fragment into the drawer and what she knew about him. *My way or the highway.*

"And where exactly do I come in?'' she asked.

"I can pretty much handle things from here on.'' He leaned back against the counter, crossing his arms over his chest, the perfect picture of the Macho Jet Pilot. "It's pretty late—too late to drive out to your place. Do we flip for the bed? Or should I just be a gentleman and offer to sleep on the couch?''

"Oh, I get it,'' she said, standing, snapping her fingers as if the lightbulb just came on over her head. "I'm the Princess in Peril. I sit here twiddling my thumbs, and let *the man* handle it—while Reck Enterprises makes mincemeat out of Marquis.''

She walked around him, straight for the drawer. "On second thought, I think I'll take back my fragment now."

He grabbed her before she could reach the drawer, his arm hooking around her waist, reeling her in. "Listen to me. Something really stinks here. A bomb threat? Strange composite materials no one knows about? Don't get involved in this, Cher."

"I *am* involved." She braced her hands on his arms, pushing him away.

"Not if I can help it."

He swept her up against him. He held her there, just held her, with his eyes, with his hands. And then his gaze dropped to her mouth.

She felt her heart stop, just stop.

"Don't," she told him, knowing the heat of their argument had just taken a new direction. But despite the protest, she tipped her head back. It was completely involuntary, how she stood on her tiptoes, bringing his mouth closer. "Oh, boy."

It was the green light—all the encouragement he needed.

He kissed her, a continuation of where they'd left off on her pool table, with all the sizzle and pop of two people who knew that at least in this, they were good together. It was the final breach—the break in the dam. After that, Conor knew. All was lost.

He couldn't get enough of her.

Cher pulled away, taking a step back, catching her breath. "I'm not doing this, Conor." She shook her finger at him, *for shame,* taking several steps back. "It's like, I don't know myself anymore. Running hot and cold like this. I don't have any control around you. You're turning me into this big giant hormone. We have got to get a grip."

He kept walking toward her, a parody of a dance. But maybe this was their dance. She saw things her way; Conor, his. She wouldn't listen—didn't see the threat. If there was something going on that involved Eric against Reck, Cherish was the missing link, the only person involved in both projects. Someone who might put one and one together and come up with Reck as the villain of the story.

The most troubling part was Joseph Kinnard. He was government, all the way. If Kinnard called the shots, there wasn't anyone they could turn to for help. Not the police, not even the FBI.

And here was Cherish, acting as if there wasn't any reason for her to back off, making him come after her—*just a game, bucko*—forcing him to follow her to bars and watch her laugh and flirt and drink from that pretty pink glass, in that damned tight skirt. How long had he sat there watching her legs swinging back and forth atop that stool, making every man in that room want to see if there might be a peekaboo glimpse of what lay beneath.

Oh, the danger was there all right. Between them now, surrounding them, bringing them inextricably together, as it had since the first crash eighteen months ago. And suddenly, he knew without a doubt that, from here on out, it wasn't hot and cold. No way. Just hot. *Full throttle.*

He grabbed her hand. "Come here, Cher."

He saw her eyes widen as she realized what was happening. Hot. Vaporizing hot. 3,000 degrees hot. He needed to be with her, in a way he didn't understand. And it was Cher who had created the spell between them. Those never-ending letters. *I won't go away, Conor. I won't make it easy for you! Not this time!*

At that moment, she wrenched her hand free and took off. Grabbing his car keys off the counter, she raced for the door, slamming it in his face. But he was right behind her, catching the screen before it hit. At the car, he opened the door and grabbed her, pulling her out before she could start the engine.

"I can't stay here with you," she said, kicking him, pushing him.

"You don't have a choice."

She ducked under his arm and tossed his keys in the yard. He took off after her, chasing her in the wet blades of grass. She didn't have her shoes on, but he did, giving him the advantage.

He tackled her, bringing her to the ground with a *whoosh* of air from both of them. She kicked him, but he turned her over like a downed calf. She tried to haul him off, but she couldn't stop him. His hands came up under her blouse. She pulled it off, throwing it in his face, then wriggling out from under him to run again. He snatched her ankle, stopping her cold. She turned this time, kissing him, taking off his shirt until he was all tangled up in it, then pushing him off balance, trying to crawl out from under him. He tossed the shirt and grabbed her again.

"I hate you!"

"I know," he said, kissing her back.

She kissed him again, giving it everything she had. They were good at this. They were *A,* number one, primo, at this. They stood, the motion coming off in perfect unison, Olympic pairs precision, their mouths never parting. She jumped into his arms, her legs coming around his waist, her hands around his neck. He held her, carrying her back to the house.

He slammed the door shut with his foot. He dropped her right there on the hardwood floor in front of the couch. She unbuckled his jeans; he took off her bra, then reached for her underwear from beneath the leather mini.

"This is so crazy," she said, kissing him.

He pulled her to him so that she knelt over him, straddling him, his back up against the couch, her hands braced there, right behind him. "Do you always have to talk so much?"

He kicked off his jeans and settled her on his lap facing him. Her hands were in his hair, on his face. Her nails were digging into his shoulder as she nipped at his lower lip, nuzzling him, lowering herself to him, reaching for his underwear.

But somewhere in the depths of his sex-drugged mind, he

thought he heard a gasp. Conor opened his eyes, looking up past her shoulder.

It was his nephew, standing at the front door.

The ten-year-old boy had his telescope tucked under his arm, the one Conor had given him for Christmas last year. He turned red, then brilliantly white, his freckles standing out like soft brown dots. His little boy eyes were stuck on Cherish kneeling over Conor, naked except for her leather miniskirt.

He ran out the door.

Cherish fell back on the floor, rolling off Conor. She grabbed a pillow off the couch and hugged it to her chest, covering herself. Conor leaned up against the couch.

"You better go after him," she said.

"Yup."

He put on his jeans and went outside to hunt down his shirt. Finding it, he shoved it on and walked across the grass to his sister's house. He thought about knocking, but he figured by now, everyone would be up.

He found the three of them in the living room, Marc and Geena standing guard over Chris.

"You okay, Chris?" Conor asked his nephew.

"Sure." He looked down, then shrugged. "It was just kinda weird. I'm sorry I walked in like that. There was supposed to be a neat meteor shower tonight. I thought we could go out and take a look."

"Marc, take Chris to his room," Geena said.

Her tone more than Marc's wink told Conor what was coming next. But Geena waited until her husband and son left the room before launching her attack.

"Ever hear of locking your door?" She was shaking, she was that angry. Arms crossed before her, she paced the room. Back and forth. Back and forth. "I'm always so careful. For their sake." Back and forth. "I never thought I had to be careful about their uncle. Damn you."

"Are you mad because he saw a woman's breasts or because I was with Cherish?"

Geena stopped. She stared at him. Blinked. Good ol' Geena with that drill-through-your-skull stare. "You're right."

Without another word, she turned and walked past him, going for the door. He heard the screen slam shut.

Marc came out of the bedroom then, his eyebrows raised in question as he stared at the backdoor beyond the kitchen. "She went over there?"

Conor had his jaw locked. In his mind, he saw his sister marching through the yard, a locomotive at full steam. But he surprised himself by saying, "One way or another, Geena has to get this out of her system."

His brother-in-law patted Conor's shoulder. "Chris is fine. Geena's just being overprotective—of both of you. Hell, she just signed the papers for him to learn all about that stuff in health class." Marc flashed one of his patented smiles. "Now he can have visual aids."

"Thanks, Marc."

He kept wondering which hole in the dike to plug first. Chris? Cherish? He knew his sister—and he knew Cherish. It would be one hell of a scene.

He pushed his hand through his hair and turned for the bedroom. "I'll go talk to Chris," he said, for once in his life, letting someone else steer the course.

By the time Geena walked through the front door, Cherish had already dressed and was sitting on the couch, waiting. She hadn't expected Geena. But then, she wasn't sure what she'd expected.

Geena rounded the coffee table to stand in front of Cherish. She had the distinctive feeling that Conor's sister was checking her out . . . and finding her lacking. But then, what else was new?

"I'm sorry about what happened," Cherish said.

"Why don't you just leave him the hell alone?"

She knew immediately who "he" was. This meeting had nothing to do with Geena's son. *Just like that.* "So we're going right into it, are we?" she asked. "How refreshing." This hurt. A lot. "You never did approve of Conor and me."

"Lady, you're the biggest mistake he ever made."

"It must have been a great relief to you then, when he backed out of our wedding." And because she *was* hurting, she added, "Let's be honest, Geena. This isn't about protecting your brother. This is about your jealousy. For once in his life, you weren't the center of Conor's universe and you couldn't stand it."

Geena looked as if Cherish had struck her. She actually took a step back. It made Cherish feel a little better to see that surprised look on Geena's face. *Didn't see yourself so clearly, did you, Geena old girl?*

Score one for Cherish's side.

But Geena wasn't through with her. "If you could have made him happy, it wouldn't have mattered to me."

"I tried."

"Well, I guess you just weren't up to it, were you?"

Cherish felt an incredible anger rise up inside her, ugly and hot. But she didn't have the words to thwart Geena's attack, didn't have the weapons. "I can't believe I'm sitting here taking this," she sputtered instead. She stood, getting ready to leave.

"Sit down."

Geena had that whole military thing going. Cherish actually sat down before she realized what she was doing. It was the sort of commanding voice that got a woman through the Air Force—or maybe it was the sort of tone you adopted when you were the mother of three-year-old twins.

Conor's sister walked around the room, her eyes on Cherish. But there wasn't so much anger anymore. She looked almost tired. "You couldn't be more wrong to believe I was happy when he didn't marry you. It scared me to death. If you knew Conor, you would know he isn't capable of that kind of betrayal. That would be Alec. Never Conor."

"Funny. And here I've been blaming Conor all these months."

"I kept thinking it was the crash," she said, ignoring Cherish's sarcasm. "That's why he fell for you. You weren't his type—though to be honest, he'd never made much time for a personal life. Maybe I didn't think you were good enough for him. Or maybe I *was* jealous. That he didn't let me help him get through it, the accident. That he went to you." Geena stopped, shaking her head. "But I love my brother. I got over it. I wanted you to help him. And you didn't. And that's why I can never forgive you. He came to you, and you failed him."

It amazed Cherish how those words reached deep down inside her, twisting around her guts. As if Geena had found her worst fears, put them into words, then paraded them out, exposing too much: a sense of failure Cherish hadn't been able to wipe away with letters or accusations.

The truth was, Conor *had* needed someone after the accident. Cherish had tried to be that person. And, just as Geena said, she'd failed.

"I—" She cleared her throat when her voice broke, trying to keep composed. *Still not good enough.* "I truly gave it my all, Geena," she said, at last admitting defeat. "And I thought for a while, I could do it. If it had been Alec . . ." She shook her head. "I tried."

"Alec?" Geena looked at her in surprise. Conor's sister sat down in the beat-up Barco-Lounger parked in front of the television. "Alec?"

Geena shook her head, those unblinking eyes boring into Cherish. She leaned forward. "Oh, my God. You don't know what happened the night you *think* my brother let you down?"

"Alec told me about the phone call from the safety board—"

"Alec, Alec, Alec." Geena shook her head, looking at Cherish as if she'd grown a second head. "You say it like that means something. Like you're talking about a friend . . . a normal person."

"Look, I know about his childhood. But the Alec I knew helped me get through a living nightmare. And for the record, he was the only person waiting with me when Conor didn't show up that night. That means something to me."

"Well goody for him. Now, would you like to hear why he did it? Because, it's a pip of a story."

Cherish snapped her mouth shut, stopping her next verbal volley. Outside, she could hear a neighbor's dog begin to howl.

"It's a little long," Geena said, leaning back to cross her arms. "But it has a hell of a punch line. Alec and I were lovers."

The words fell over Cherish like a bucket of cold water. *Alec and I were lovers. Lovers, lovers.*

"You look shocked. It *is* shocking. And you don't know the half of it. I've known Alec almost all my life. I loved everything about him. He wasn't serious, like Conor and I, who were always taking too much responsibility on our shoulders, worrying about doing the right thing. Alec was daring, and fun and, boy—did I love that about him. One night, hero worship turned into something else. We were sixteen."

Geena didn't move. Her expression didn't change. She could have been talking about the weather.

Cherish couldn't take her eyes off her.

"I don't blame him," she said. "But I knew Conor would. So when I found out I was pregnant, I told Alec. Only Alec. He begged me not to tell Conor, begged me to get an abortion. I think he would have done anything to get me to agree to get rid of the baby. At first, he tried being nice. He cajoled. He painted lovely pictures of our future together, how he would marry me and we would show Conor that we could make it on our own, that Alec could take care of me. Us against the world. Why mess it up, baby?"

Cherish shook her head. "Geena, I can't imagine—"

"When that didn't work, he tried to bully me, saying it was my fault. I should have used something. He thought I was on the pill." She shook her head. "He was good at that, reinventing history to suit himself. On the pill?" The anger was there now, and the hurt. "He damn well knew I wasn't on the pill. He knew every detail of my life. Especially what would hurt me most. Two days later, I walked in on him with my best friend."

Cherish shut her eyes. *Oh, Alec . . . monster things.*

"He wanted to hurt me." Geena said it so calmly. "Because I'd hurt him, refusing to get the abortion. That's when I finally saw Alec for who he is. Beautiful on the outside, twisted up on the inside. Nothing Conor or I could do would ever change that. When I met Marc, I thought he was the same. Charming— too good looking. I didn't want to have anything to do with him. But he didn't give up. When I fell in love, I thought, 'This is it—just like Alec.' The chase was over and now it was payday. But Marc is nothing like Alec. He didn't give up on me. Never."

The way she said it, *never.* Another accusation hurled at Cherish. "What happened to the baby?" she asked quietly.

"Eventually, I told Conor. He stood by me. I had fucked up my life"—she blinked her eyes very quickly, looking up— "I wasn't going to the Air Force Academy. Everything he'd sacrificed for, everything he'd tried to build for me . . . I'd just thrown it away. There was even a good chance they'd take me away, when the social worker found out. But Conor swore he would get me through it."

She was crying now. Not in a way that changed the calm tone of her words either. Just tears welling up, spilling over, running down her cheeks.

"I had a miscarriage," Geena said, "and that was that."

Geena had gone on to do well at school, to train on an F-15. Few women did—few had the nerve. Now Cherish knew how she'd earned those nerves.

"You never told him who the father was," Cherish said.

"And drive a stake through Conor's heart?" Geena asked. "It was something he wouldn't be able to forgive, a code of honor that Alec never should have violated. But he found out." Geena leaned forward, smiling now. "Guess when he found out. I want you to guess."

"No," Cherish said, getting the punch line right between the eyes.

"You bet your ass. The night you were getting married. Right after Conor found out they were pulling his wings, Alec decided to drop one more bomb. Can you imagine? Can you see it? Conor at his absolute lowest and Alec thinking, how can I make this work for me? He figures, Conor has you. Here's a chance to change that. He adds one more juicy piece of information to let Conor know what a royal fuckup he is. Another person he failed, like the people on that plane. So while Alec was *comforting* you, letting you cry on his shoulder, Conor was here. With me and Marc. Having it out with me."

Cherish was shaking her head. No. It wasn't possible. Alec told her about the safety board, that Conor wasn't himself. He'd made excuses for Conor. He wouldn't have . . . how could he . . .

"Conor was in this incredible rage," Geena said, her smile and her tears both gone now. "He paced up and down my living room, yelling at me like a crazy man. I'd never seen him like that. Never. Why didn't I tell him it was Alec, he wanted to know. All those years he helped Alec, he yelled. He treated him like a brother, let him live under our roof. Yelling this at the top of his lungs. As if Conor wouldn't have forgiven Alec. As if we didn't always forgive Alec."

Geena shook her head, trying to shoulder the pain of the memories. No big deal. It's in the past. "I said, Conor, calm down. That was fifteen years ago, Conor." But the words were choked up, coming out rough. "And then, he just . . . collapsed. Right there on my couch. Collapsed, crying his heart out. These big, gasping sobs. I'd never seen Conor cry. Not when they told him he might lose his eye, not when he found out about the baby. Not when one of the men in his squadron was killed on an F-4 accident. He looks up at me, and he says, 'I killed them, Geena. I killed those people.'"

Geena stared ahead, reliving the moment, bringing Cherish into it, so she, too, could live it.

"A little bit of my brother died with the people on that prototype. If you knew Conor, if you knew him even a little, you would know how it would affect him to hear he was responsible."

Of course, Cherish thought. Conor, the protector. The talented fighter pilot.

"He called you the next morning," Geena continued. "Do you remember? You didn't want to talk to him. You were too . . . hurt."

That pause—the look Geena gave her. It said it all. *Your puny little feelings were hurt . . . while my brother's world was falling apart.*

Conor's sister stood. But Cherish didn't move. She was too frozen inside.

"Alec isn't your friend," Geena said. "He isn't trying to help you. There isn't anything in him to give. It's like he's twisted. His mother took drugs when she was pregnant. Maybe it caused something to be chemically off. Maybe the synapses don't fire when it comes to his conscience. But Conor. Honey, you would have been lucky to have him."

In the echo of those words, you could hear a pin drop, allowing Geena's accusations to pound in Cherish's head like a kettledrum. *You didn't want to talk to him the next morning.*

"Before he ran into you, my brother had never backed out of a commitment in his life. You're right," Geena said. "I don't like you. The way I see it, when you were licking your wounds, Conor needed you to hunt him down and ask him, 'Why Conor? That's so unlike you, Conor. Snap out of it,

Conor!' No, Cherish," she said, using her name for the first time. "I don't think you deserve him. Not nearly."

"Okay Geena, that's enough."

Geena turned to find Conor standing at the door. Brother and sister stared at one another silently.

Something in Geena appeared to deflate. She turned to Cherish, as if she might have something more to say. But instead, she turned and walked out.

Cherish felt pummeled. *The next morning, you didn't talk to him.* As if she'd had this one shot and she blew it. As if Conor couldn't have driven over and talked to her! As if she hadn't written him every single week for the last year, silently begging him to do exactly that.

"Boy, I love that." Cherish stood, some of the freeze from Geena's spell dissipating. "I love that! It was all my fault because I didn't go after you? I was supposed to hunt you down and confront you?"

"Look, forget what Geena said—"

"Here I am, the one you left waiting at the altar, and boom. It's all *my* fault?" But even in her anger, she felt the guilt. *I could have . . . I should have.* "I wasn't good enough to fix your problems? I wasn't *magnanimous*"—her voice cracked on the single word—"enough to get beyond my broken heart."

"Geena has a way of seeing the world where I'm infallible."

But she was just warming up, because she didn't want Geena to be right. She didn't want those words haunting her for the rest of her life. *He came to you, and you failed him.* So it was all her fault? Because she'd believed Conor was capable of changing his mind about his commitment to her? Of course, she'd believed it! She'd been vulnerable. She'd been in love! *Why didn't I fight for him?*

"Well, let me be the first to clue you and your sister in," she said, venting her anger and hurt, making sure someone heard her side of the story. "You were the one who made the mistake that night, Conor. Not me!"

"Calm down. I'm not saying any different—"

"We were good together. I loved you. And you loved me. Oh, you never said it. But I saw it—I knew it here," she said, pounding on her chest.

"Look, I know I can never make up for what I did. But those weeks after the accident I just wasn't myself—"

"Don't you dare," she said, barely able to voice the words, her throat was so tight. "Don't you dare!"

"I'm trying to give you that damn apology you've wanted all these years!"

"I don't want an apology, dammit! I want you. That's all I ever wanted. And I had you. During those short weeks, you were mine, Conor. I will never believe that you didn't love me. That what you felt didn't come from your heart! Damn you. Damn you for showing me this wonderful, passionate man I couldn't live without."

"For God's sake, Cher—"

"Do you remember when you asked me to marry you?" She walked up to him, getting close. "You woke me in the middle of the night. I could see you hadn't had a wink of sleep. You looked almost feverish. You asked, could we go to this place in Beverly Hills—California's version of the quickie marriage. Did I mind? you asked. Running off, just the two of us with Alec as our witness?"

She should have questioned it, should have known. It was just a little off, that fevered request, almost as if—sensing the safety board would call—he'd needed to marry her before he heard their decision.

"Do you know how many times I've wondered what would have happened if the safety board hadn't called that day, Conor?"

"Cher—"

"Now, you're standing here, trying to tell me, oops, I wasn't myself after the crash. Well, you know what, Conor? That's the man I fell in love with. That wonderful, vulnerable man.

So don't tell me he doesn't exist, that it was all a mistake. Post-traumatic something or other. Don't tell me the real Conor Mitchell would never have asked me to marry him after knowing me only six weeks.''

She stepped right in front of him, within reach. "He's this . . . cold-hearted bastard . . ." She pounded both fists against his chest with each word " . . . who doesn't need anybody . . . especially me.''

When he reached for her, she jumped back, shaking her head. She couldn't let him touch her. "You let me into this world. And then you told me it didn't exist. And I will never forgive you for that. My fault? No Conor. I was there for you . . . and I *would* have been there for you. Forever. And I don't care what Geena says. I would have been enough.''

He looked pained by everything she'd said, but he said nothing, standing there so stoically. It made her even angrier.

"I hate you, Conor.'' This, barely whispered. "I hate you. Because, until I have what you let me savor for six short weeks, I'm going to dream about it. I'm going to wish for it. And no one but that man will ever be good enough. That's what you've done to me, Conor. You've ruined me. You can hate Alec for taking advantage of Geena, a bunch of hormone-driven kids. You can flog yourself for being human and making a mistake flying that prototype. You can try to use those things to wipe away every good thing you've ever done in your life and say you don't deserve to be happy. Why even try? But when you decided to bail out on us, it wasn't just you who got hurt.''

This time, he didn't try to stop her when she walked out.

SEVERE CLEAR

Countdown: 21 days; 19 hours; 35 minutes

Chapter Nineteen

All right, Cherish thought. So Geena and her brother had a point. Cherish hadn't known that much about Conor Mitchell when she'd fallen in love with him.

But those were just facts. And Cherish knew where she could find facts.

She started at the Huntington Beach Public Library.

She considered it purely a tactical move. Power through knowledge. She needed to even the scales between them, make up for the advantage she'd given Conor in her letters the past year. And there were Geena's accusations doing an aria inside her. *You made a bad choice, letting him walk away. You didn't fight for him!*

Suddenly the "what ifs" in Cherish's head changed. It wasn't so much a question of the safety board's bad timing, but hers. *What would have happened if you'd hashed it out with him the next day?*

But she wasn't one to run away from the question. She wanted answers. And whether Geena was right or wrong about that night so long ago, the truth was, Cherish hadn't known Conor well enough to challenge the obvious—that he'd changed his mind about marrying her. She'd stamped it a common case of cold feet and walked away, licking her wounds.

So the morning after Armageddon at Conor's, she'd come to the library, past the brick quad and through the glass doors, hoping that, if knowing "facts" about a person could give insight into the soul, she would find her treasures here, digging as deep as she needed into those data files.

By the time she was ready to leave, she'd photocopied and scribbled enough information to fill a folder.

The local papers in particular loved Conor, running story after story in the human interest sections. By lunch, she knew even the silly things, like his favorite color was blue, his favorite meal, Geena's lasagna. These were the tidbits the newspapers paraded out in warm and cozy interviews that catalogued his life. Local-boy-done-good stories. Good Conor Copy.

He'd heroically changed his life; *what a guy!* Through no fault of his own, he'd been orphaned at the age of eight, his parents dying in a pileup coming down the highway from Big Bear Lake. He and his then two-year-old sister had fallen through the cracks of the overworked foster care system. At first, they'd been juggled back and forth between their aging grandmother and their father's youngest sister, a twenty-year-old struggling to achieve her beautician's license. Both had been overwhelmed by the instant family.

Next came the foster homes, a run of bad luck for brother and sister—*we changed our mind, we wanted infants, our adoption came through!* They'd ended up in a state-run home, an institution usually reserved for troublemakers and difficult-to-place cases.

But Conor never let it discourage him; *what a man!* He'd socked away an astonishing $12,000 before he finished high school, all from after-school jobs. It impressed the court enough that he'd been granted his emancipation at seventeen. Shortly thereafter, he was given guardianship of his sister and friend, Alec Porter. Both Alec and Geena had been only twelve at the time.

Selflessly, he passed on his scholarship to the University of California at Irvine to become a full-time parent. Only when his sister and Alec earned berths at the Air Force Academy did he attend UC Irvine, majoring in engineering. Later, he'd entered the Air Force and flight school.

He wanted to be an astronaut. He photographed like a model; *what a hero!* The all-American boy with the all-American dream.

The astronaut thing explained a lot—his stint as a test pilot, the doctorate in composite materials from Stanford, the body that could model underwear for Calvin Klein ads. The Astronaut Corps was an elite group. Basically, you decided to be an astronaut around age nine and started working toward your goal. Conor was a little old when he'd entered the Air Force, so he'd had to work harder than most. From where Cherish was looking, he might have made it . . . until the crash. Once the safety board determined to convene an FEB, those dreams vanished.

When her aching back reminded her that she hadn't moved in hours, Cherish scooted out, bleary-eyed from the microfiche. She carried in hand Conor's thick file.

After that, she did what any sensible woman in her situation would do.

She went to see her mother.

These days, Gladys Malone wore her hair short and dyed a flattering copper brown. Gone was the characteristic braid tucked in a knot at the base of her neck, a style that Cherish realized had made her mother appear ten years older than her actual age. Cherish hated to admit it, but emancipation from

Dad had done her mother a world of good. She looked like another mother altogether. A happy one, it seemed.

They were in the kitchen, Gladys pouring tea, wearing a T-shirt she'd tucked into jeans, the words, *Jung Did It In His Dreams,* stamped across her chest. Her mother lived in a one-bedroom condo overlooking the water in Belmont Shore, a happening place with theaters and restaurants nearby. These days, Gladys preferred going out for Thai or Indian food.

But her mother still smelled of White Shoulders and she still loved to cook, simple traits that Cherish found incredibly comforting at the moment. Right now, the kitchen smelled of baking wonders. Gladys had made scones for their tea.

"Your father called," her mother said. "He's worried that you haven't gone to church with him for the last two Sundays."

Cherish thought about where she'd been Sunday morning. With Chuck and Lori, coming up with strategies for the meeting Monday at Reck's Newport office. And things weren't getting any less complicated, either.

"Maybe you should call him." Her mother put a tray of scones into the lower oven, then wiped her hands on a dishrag. "Mike told him about Ben."

Cherish swallowed the piece of scone she'd almost choked on. "Wow." Ben was her brother's significant other. "Is Daddy still alive?"

Taking the seat across from Cherish, her mother picked up her cup of tea and smiled. "Barely."

"When did he tell Dad?" Even though Mike had been talking about "coming out" to their father, Cherish was a little surprised he hadn't discussed it with her first. But then, she wasn't exactly available these days.

"He told him last night." Her mother reached over and gave her hand a squeeze. "Your father will be fine. It's you I'm worried about and not that old goat." She smiled at Cherish's grimace. *Old goat?* "Tell Mommy what's the matter."

Cherish tapped her fingers against the eggshell cup. Wouldn't it be nice if she could pour it all out for her mother to make better? But there were so many things she couldn't talk about: *I'm afraid someone might try to kill me ... my company's planes could be the target of a terrorist group—or possibly Alec is responsible.*

The wing fragment—the flight data. Those little gems would remain buried. Instead, she focused on the personal, forgetting the XC-23 WingMaster to bring under the microscope a different crash.

"Mom. Do you remember Conor?" she asked.

Her mother sat up straighter. If she was surprised by the question, she didn't show it. "Why, yes, Cherish. I believe I do remember him. Quite well, actually." This, followed by a significant look. "It's not as if you've had a lot of boyfriends, darling."

Cherish reached for her briefcase and brought out the file. She pushed aside her tea cup to make room for the folder brimming with papers. "Yeah, well. I did a little research on him."

Her mother looked down at the one-inch-thick folder. "I see."

"Apparently, he was in the news a lot."

Her mother folded her hands on the table. Here was a woman who had accepted her son's homosexuality without batting a lash, had held her daughter through nightmares about fiery crashes, and quietly left her husband of more than thirty years the day she thought her family could get along nicely without her, thank you very much. *It's my turn now.*

"And?" her mother asked. Clearly, the situation needed a little more explanation.

"Those weeks after the crash, when we decided to get married, I didn't really know a lot about him." She waved at the pile of papers. "There was apparently a lot to the equation that I missed."

Her mother's brows furrowed, two little lines facing each

other like partners in a square dance. "If I remember correctly, the two of you were fairly inseparable."

They had, in fact, spent nearly every free minute together. Like Geena, her father had taken offense to the relationship, particularly its exclusivity, nodding and saying, "I told you so," when Conor had dumped her. Only her mother had been genuinely distressed.

Gladys cleared her throat. "What exactly did the two of you talk about all that time you were together?"

"Talk?" Cherish looked up. She stared down at the file. She felt herself blush. "We didn't do a lot of that. Talking, I mean."

And there, so succinctly, was the problem. Conor and his pheromones. *Again, Cher.*

Her mother cleared her throat. "It is very important to be compatible in that way," she said, blowing on her tea, reading the silence correctly. "But what does your file say?"

Cherish drew little circles on the top of the folder with her fingertips, then placed her palm flat on the top, as if she might be able to keep the facts from jumping out. "I think it says I might have made a mistake."

Her mother stood and brought out her reading glasses. Quietly, she opened the file on the table before her. Fifteen minutes later, she took the glasses off and folded them on the table. "Is it too late?" she asked.

"That depends. I would have to forgive him . . . and trust him." And then, seeing how utterly futile this all was, "And, of course, he would have to ask me to marry him again. I don't think he's going to do that, Mother." She frowned, thinking about how she'd felt when it had all fallen apart. "And I'm not sure I want him to."

"You must have scared him very much, my darling."

"Scared him? I would have done anything for him."

"But dear"—her mother leaned forward, taking her hand— "you must see how incredibly confusing it must have been for him. He loses his parents and has his life turned upside down.

He must have spent his entire life fighting to get everything under strict control. Saving money, joining the military, planning goals that would take a lifetime of commitment to achieve. Can't you see it, darling? Why he would want to fly into space? He's looking for his parents. A little boy who's worked his whole life to reach the heavens.''

Apparently, her mother was still heavily into those therapy courses at the local counseling center.

"And it looks like he succeeded admirably," Gladys continued. "Until the accident. Cherish, three people died that day. And then you swept into his life. You, with your wonderful energy, your daring to love without question''—her mother shook her head—"the one thing your father admired enough not to snuff out."

Gladys looked away, gathered herself together. Obviously, she didn't want to bring her own bitter experience into the picture.

"He asked you to marry him after knowing you barely six weeks," her mother said. "It must have been frightening to have his life be out of control again."

Cherish frowned. Because what her mother was saying made sense. For Cherish, the hurricane of emotions that followed the crash didn't seem abnormal. Her love for Conor had been the release she needed. She didn't want control over what she felt for him. She'd just ridden the wind of it, finding solace with the man she loved. But Conor—certainly, it would be different for him.

Crumbling the last of her scone on her plate, Cherish frowned again. "You're still going to your counseling classes, aren't you, Mom?"

Her mother smiled. "I'll be certified to start talking to patients in a few months. You could be my first."

Cherish closed her eyes. She was so incredibly tired. "Oh, Mommy."

Her mother took her hand and pulled Cherish over to her

side of the table, wrapping her daughter in her arms. Cherish stood there in silence, letting her mother's cool hands run up and down her back, comforting her.

"It just hurts so much," Cherish whispered. "That he may not love me."

"Cherish. Do you know what I think? I think you should run away from home. No, I'm being honest. Do you know where fear of flying comes from? You don't feel grounded. You don't trust yourself. That's your father at work, with all his nay-saying, trying to cram you into a nice, safe world he could trust. If you had felt a bit more secure with yourself, you might have fought for Conor." She turned Cherish's face to hers. "You might fight for him now."

"You make it sound so easy."

But Cherish hadn't just woken up one day and said, "Gee, I can't get on a plane." She had lived through an incredible trauma. No matter how much her mother and the slew of psychologists she'd sent Cherish to see wanted to put it into psychological terms, the fact was, she was just plain scared to crash and burn again.

"Okay, Mom," Cherish said, pulling away. "If you hang out your shingle, maybe I'll try the therapy thing again."

"Cherish." Her mother shook her head sadly. "It hurts my heart to see you like this."

But after a kiss and a pocketed scone, she left her mother's house—in Lori's words—to face the beast. Following the ribbon of highway that hugged the shoreline, the clouds gathering over the ocean, their fierce pewter color heralding a potential storm, her thoughts returned to Conor. Would he be waiting for her outside her door? Had he even tried to find her after the things she'd said last night? At work, she'd called in sick, checking her messages . . . only to ignore the lot. She felt as if there was this ticking clock inside her. *Hurry up! Solve the problem!* A different kind of bomb ready to explode into more regrets.

When she pulled into her driveway fifteen minutes later, Conor wasn't parked outside as she'd half expected. The Toyota 4Runner was nowhere in sight. She didn't know if she was disappointed or relieved—or just too numb to feel much of anything.

Inside, she dropped her briefcase on the coffee table. She headed for the kitchen and grabbed a bottle of Evian water from the fridge, not even bothering to glance at the pool table. Too many memories there. The answering machine blinked steadily in the dusky light coming through the window shades. Taking a sip from the bottle, she pressed play.

Michael called three times. "Need to talk to you, Sis." During the last message, she could hear Ben, his lover, yelling in the background, "Big news! Call us back!"

Oh, boy. Dad would be a mess.

There was Thomas. "I think you need to call Dad—but call me or Mike before you do anything."

Lori was the fifth message. "You're absolutely right. I am giving up this happy hour thing. By the way, shoot me. I had sex with Gary. Where are you!"

The last message was Conor.

"Meet me at the airfield. Four o'clock."

She had seen Alec like this many times, but it still frightened her.

Allison folded her legs under her, watching from the chair in the corner of Alec's motel room. She could hear the surf tumbling outside, keeping cadence with Alec's pacing across the carpeted floor.

"The Conman's letting her call the shots, leaving her to them, easy pickings. I don't get it. What the hell is he doing, letting her out of his sight? I told him they would kill her, Allison. I told him!" His steps ate up the cramped space, making him turn back and forth. "If there was something in this world I thought was solid, that I could rely on . . . Damn you, Conman.''

He was smoking, fast and furious. He swept his hand through his hair, the motion almost a slash through the air. Manic, like his pacing.

''It's falling apart,'' he whispered to himself.

She realized he was in his own little world. For Alec, Allison wasn't there anymore. She was no longer important.

''I can't keep it together. Sydney—the papers. I don't even have Eric's goddamn papers.''

''I told you I could get them. You need to be patient, Alec. I don't want to get caught.''

He stopped, turning to look at her. He narrowed his eyes against the smoke, peering at her in a way that made her want to squirm. Alec always had incredible energy. Now it was turned inward, giving him a harsh quality she didn't often see because he tended to be playful, even about life-and-death matters.

He blew out the smoke, suddenly still. A predator catching sight of her. ''I don't have time for patience, Allison.''

''It wouldn't help you if I got caught,'' she repeated, her voice softer now.

''I need those papers.''

''I can get them.''

In two steps, he was on her. He tossed the cigarette and grabbed her arms, pulling her up and out of the chair. ''Are you sure? Are you absolutely certain?''

''For you, yes. Anything for you, Alec. You know that.'' And then, because she was frightened. ''But I can't get caught. You understand that, don't you? It's better for both of us. I need to wait for the right opportunity.''

He let her go, not quite pushing her back into the chair, just letting her fall there. She tucked her legs underneath her again, biting her thumbnail, watching him.

''You came to me,'' he said. *''You* told me you could get

those papers. Remember? I never asked you for a goddamn thing until you offered.''

"I know."

"It's falling apart. Too many balls up in the air. I'm making mistakes.''

"No, no you're not. You've been brilliant, Alec. No one else could have done it.''

Self-doubt was the worse part. He had to believe—in himself, in his plans. Everything hinged on that solid belief. And Allison always did her best to bolster him, using all her talents to help him.

She did that now, running to him. She held on to him, tight. And when he pushed her away, she came at him again, holding on, whispering of love and belief and everything that was in her heart.

He collapsed to his knees, clinging to her. "I can't fuck this up. Do you understand? They'll kill her. I can't fuck up.''

"I'll get the papers. Soon. I can take a few chances.'' She crooned the words, because this was her job. Her reason for being. To become everything this man needed. To help him. It was too soon for the papers, but he seemed so desperate. Forces closing in on him. On them both.

"Those papers, Allison. Eric's papers.''

"Shh. They're yours, my love. I'll get them for you. You'll win, Alec. You'll beat them all.''

Chapter Twenty

Conor was flying straight up, into the sun. Like a rocket.

The g-forces kicked his head back. He glanced at the altimeter and horizon, adjusted the back pressure on the stick.

A light flashed inside his head, disorienting him. For an instant, he was back in those fly-by-wire fighters, edging up to the sun where the high g-levels could mess with your head, causing gray outs.

Another flash, like lightning. Suddenly, it wasn't the same sky—no clouds out over the West. It was the perfect conditions of another day. Severe clear.

He blinked. He almost reached for his oxygen mask, but realized where he was. The Marchetti trainer just off the coast, safely within the dense air of 7,000 feet. *Shake it off, Conman.* He looked out the window to see that, yes indeed, the weather was clouding. He inched the stick back.

Flash! Alec talking to him, smiling that Alec-knows-best smile.

Flash! The red warning light. *Losing altitude!*

The Marchetti eased up and over the top of the loop, canopy-side down. Weightless. Then falling, falling . . .

The ground came racing up . . . but this was no longer a controlled aerobatics maneuver, rather a memory. Screams were coming from aft of the cockpit. The prototype was losing cabin pressure. Alec was yelling: *right engine flame out!* The plane sliced to the right, yawing out of control. *We're going to stall!* Conor pulled back hard on the yoke; he kicked in right rudder. *She's going on us,* Alec screamed.

An incredible explosion, the sound, deafening. Suddenly, the plane dropped and rolled to the left. Conor fought the controls. *Shit!* The plane pitched out of control.

Alec shouting—*turn the goddamn thing off, it's going to kill us!* Conor pushed forward on the yoke, cut back power, holding on . . . holding on . . .

Isn't it true, Colonel, that if you had simply let go of the controls, let the computer take over . . .

Alec's face, twisted in fear—*turn it off; the damn thing is going to kill us!*

You reviewed the flight data. This was clear PIO, wasn't it Colonel Mitchell?

Geena's sixteen-year-old face—*Don't make me tell you who the father is, Conor. Don't make me tell you.*

The screaming pulse of the Marchetti's warning system cut through the visions in his head. Conor blinked, coming back to the present. "Shit!" He cut the power.

The Marchetti stalled.

He jammed the yoke forward, knowing he was in trouble. The altimeter was winding like a backwards clock. *7,000 feet; 6,000.* He was speeding to earth like a bullet. *5,000.* He eased the yoke back, pulling the nose up, feeling his stomach stay behind. *4,000.* The horizon inched up over the windshield. *3,000.* Hanging on to the yoke for all he was worth, he added full power.

Earth below, sky above, straight and level flight.

He studied the altimeter—*2,500 feet*—breathing hard. When he thought he could, he gave his call sign to the tower and headed home. He felt cold and hot at the same time—just like that day. *Isn't it true, Colonel . . . pilot induced oscillation.* He shook his head, blinking rapidly.

Twenty minutes later, he taxied right up to the hangar for the air school. Even after he pulled up, he stayed at the controls, calming his breathing, slowing it down. *One-one-thousand, two-one-thousand, . . .*

The wild blue yonder had always been his haven, the only place where he could block out the world. There, in the severe clear blue, he could forget about those deaths, Henry and Eric, the reporter. He could clear out the image of Cherish crying in his living room. *We were good together.*

In the sky, a pilot needed to focus on the business of flying. *Wind two seven zero at ten. Traffic, three o'clock high.*

Focus or you're dead.

A loud knocking made him jerk around in his seat. It was Marc, smiling . . . then not smiling.

His brother-in-law motioned for Conor to open the canopy. "Hey Conman. You okay?" More knocking on the canopy.

We were good together, Conor. . . .

I killed those people. Henry and Eric . . . the reporter.

"Conor?"

Pilot Induced Death!

Conor scrubbed his face with his hands. He realized he was sweating. He was sitting there, staring into space, right in front of the hangar. He didn't know how long Marc had been knocking on the canopy.

"Conor!" Marc yelled, banging now.

"I'm okay." He opened the canopy and grabbed the sides of the Marchetti, prepared to swing out. But the truth was, he was far from all right.

He couldn't run away anymore. Just like Cherish, his nightmare had followed him. Right up into heaven.

* * *

After thirty-five minutes of cooling her jets in Conor's office, Cherish must have dozed off. She nearly fell out of her chair when he barged in, the door slamming behind him.

He looked good and pissed. Gone was his oh-so-cool, I-laugh-in-the-face-of-death, poker face of a test pilot. Something had gotten under his craw.

Her immediate response was to comfort. *Are you all right, Conor?* But she choked off the words, thinking they sounded too much like the Cherish of old, she of the Florence Nightingale tendencies. *Geez, if I don't watch myself . . .*

She would be putty in his hands, despite everything she'd said last night.

"You know, of course," she told him, "that I have better things to do than wait around for you."

She knew she looked a mess. She was wearing jeans, a tie-dyed cotton shirt, no makeup. The moisture at the beach had given her curls the green light. Just do your thing, girls!

Luckily, Conor didn't look any better. He hadn't shaved. His face appeared drawn—Harrison Ford after he'd been crawling around the bowels of Air Force One. She'd give odds he hadn't slept a wink last night.

"It's four-thirty-five," she added, going for the jump-start when his glazed look continued. "Your message said four o'clock."

His eyes focused on her for the first time. But if she was waiting for the *thanks for coming so quickly . . .*

"I went to the lab early," he said. "I was hoping to run a couple of tests on that wing fragment. In the middle of setting up for the MTS machine, the phone rang. I was told there was an emergency with one of the kids. My sister was waiting for me in my office."

She knew Conor's office was in the next building over from the lab where he worked, familiar with the campus at UCI where he taught part-time. It would have been a good trek. She could imagine the whole thing. Conor, sleepless and wired. He hears "emergency" and "kids" in the same sentence. He was probably out the door and sprinting before whoever was on the other end hung up.

"Of course, Geena wasn't there," he said. "When I called home, she was just getting the twins ready for school. By the time I got back to the lab, the wing fragment was gone."

She closed her eyes. "Not to be pessimistic, but let me take a guess. You weren't able to determine anything about the material?"

"I did a little preliminary stuff, looked under the microscope and such. It didn't look like anything I'd seen before, so I cut the dog bone sample out, strain-gauged it. The sample disappeared before I ran the tensile test."

The tensile test would have been the initial test to discover the strength and stiffness of any material. You cut a flat piece of the material, thin in the middle with flared ends like a dog bone. A measuring device called a strain gauge is attached to the middle to measure what happens when you pull the thing apart on an MTS machine. From this, you get a stress-strain curve plotted on a graph. Based on the slope of that curve, you determine the stiffness of the material tested; the stress level it breaks at tells you strength. It was a fundamental test. Without it, there wouldn't be anything to work with.

"There's something there, Cher. Something they don't want us to find. And now, they know we're looking for it."

She covered her face with her hand. "Please define 'they.' "

"Russell Reck. And Kinnard. I don't think Reck could pull this off without Kinnard."

"And Alec?"

"Who knows? Maybe he found something and he needs our help to uncover it—maybe he's in on it. Or maybe it's all unconnected, the terrorist bomb, Alec, Reck Enterprises. Maybe now, someone just wants to find a scapegoat and Alec is the easy mark. My guess is, we find out what that material is and go from there.''

There was nothing subtle about her emotions at the moment. Confusion, fear, the sudden shock of *this is wrong!* The avalanche of doubts that followed made it worse. *What material could have withstood those forces they'd seen on the flight data? How did they get it on the wings? How is Alec involved?* It seemed impossible to make sense of anything. She was jamming the wrong puzzle piece into the slot.

"I called you at work." His voice sounded impossibly even. "I drove around your block a couple of times. I even scoped out the parking lot at Marquis. I don't care what you think about me personally anymore, Cher. You have to understand—"

"What?" she asked, seeing all those words she'd spent the morning hunting up parade through her mind. *What a guy . . . what a hero!* The man who didn't love her. "Are you trying to tell me we're joined at the hip until you figure out I'm safe?"

She thought again about the Sartre play, *No Exit.*

Welcome to my vision of hell . . .

She stood, biting her thumbnail, pacing in front of his desk. Because things might not be good between her and Conor, but he was still the only person she could trust right now.

"What about the FBI?" she asked, still pacing. "Agent Lebredo? We could go to him with what we have—"

"You don't get it, do you, sweetheart?" She heard emotion now. Plenty of it. "Whatever is going on, the government is in on it. Maybe it's just Kinnard working on his own. But how far is his reach? He heads up one of the most influential offices in technological development. Not to mention his buddies at the CIA. Until we know what we're dealing with—until we have something solid—we're on our own."

She dropped down into the chair, overwhelmed by the vision he'd set out. Government agents running around, covering up mystery materials on experimental planes. She thought back to an article she'd read recently. An F-117 Stealth Fighter had fallen out of the sky into a neighborhood during an air show. The government had warned everyone not to take "souvenir" pieces of the plane's outer skin and sprayed the neighborhood with special chemicals to keep the fragments from flying away, all because the plane was coated with a special radar absorbing material that was classified.

"We have to go to Russia, Cher."

Cherish looked up. She'd been lost in thought. Now, she blinked at him, confused. "Could you say that in English?"

"That's where we'll find Joystick."

She held up her hand. "Wait. Quick rewind. Joystick, Russia, wing fragment. And the connection is?"

"I was on the Internet today, after I got tired of playing hide-and-seek looking for you. It still exists, Joystick. Eric's Russians took it over."

He pulled out a drawer to his right, and dragged out a set of papers from his desk. He stood, walking over, dropping the lot on her lap.

"The Russians must have bought the name back from Reck after he sold the company off in parts. If we want to figure out what that material is, we need to go to the source, to the people who helped create it. And I think these are the guys."

She stared at the papers and its list of Russian names. It all seemed so unreal. *Unobtainium.*

She shook her head. "Even if Reck has some strange synthetic metal on the wing, how can we prove it now? Someone stole the fragment."

He reached into his pocket and pulled out a slice of the wing skin. It was about half the size of the original piece. She could see the sheered end where he'd cut it. Two inches in diameter, it was large enough for molecular analysis, if you had the right equipment.

"The first thing I did was cut it with a diamond saw. I had the other half with me when I got the call." And then, "I've already contacted Bolkonsky, she runs Joystick now. I didn't say exactly what was going on, just that I had something they might want to look at. When I mentioned Eric and Reck Enterprises, she got real interested.''

"Well," she said, amazed that her voice sounded so calm. "I guess you can't just pop it in the mail." She rose shakily to her feet. Because she knew what was coming next. "I suppose it would be a good idea for you to go to Russia. I mean, if they developed the material and it shows up on the WingMaster, that could mean something. I really would like to go." She was walking to the door. "It's too bad you'll have to go without me."

He grabbed her hand. "I can't do that, Cher."

She could feel herself get hot. She stared at the door. *No Exit.*

He leaned down, whispering in her ear, "You can try, Cher. I'll be right there, beside you."

She didn't look at him, just stared at the door. "I can't fly anymore, Conor. You know that."

"Bullshit."

The next thing she knew, he'd hoisted her up and over his shoulder. She was a sack of potatoes, hanging upside down, his hand clamped over the back of her knees to keep her still.

She was so numb, she didn't even protest. Instead, she asked rather mildly, "What do you think you're doing?"

"This is ridiculous. Alec said someone was trying to kill you. And I'm starting to see his point. Until I know it's safe, I can't let you out of my sight. That means we're both getting on that plane."

He opened the door and walked into the main office, past Geena and Marc, both of whom sat back to watch as he lugged her outside. She wasn't fighting him. It didn't even seem possible that this was happening.

"I know about the nightmares, Cher. I know you're scared. But if I leave you here and you turn up dead . . . you think about that. See if it doesn't motivate you a little to get on that plane.''

He was walking toward the tarmac. She could see them on the flight line, the planes ready for takeoff, waiting like good soldiers. At first, it was like being in a cartoon. There was no sense of reality. She was upside down on a man's shoulder, bouncing along with his long steps.

But the planes were getting closer. She couldn't feel Conor's shoulder digging into her hip anymore. Her vision seemed to center there, on one plane in particular, until it became an enormous looming beast.

He put her down. She was a rag doll, transfixed by the sight of that plane. Conor was talking to her, then shaking her. But she couldn't hear him. She could only see the plane, the beast.

The shaking started then, under her feet like an earthquake. She couldn't find her equilibrium. She would have fallen if Conor hadn't grabbed her.

He looked at her strangely. She pushed him away and staggered back, the weakness in her legs, her knees. But he grabbed her again. He was still saying something. She could see his lips moving even though she couldn't make out the words.

She shook her head. She realized it wasn't Conor talking. She was the one speaking, the words coming out too fast, too soft. She was repeating the same thing, over and over—*I can't get on the plane. I can't get on the plane*—until it became a single word, like a child learning the alphabet, not making a distinction between the letters. *LMNO . . .*

Conor let her walk away. She could see from his expression that he finally understood. *LMNO!*

She kept walking backward, stumbling, then righting herself, getting farther from Conor and his beast. *I can't get on the plane.*

And then, she was running.

* * *

Conor watched Cherish almost fall to the ground, then turn and run away. The expression on her face, her voice, reedy and breathy like that—he'd seen it before. When a pilot loses it, that's the way they looked, how they talked, a soft mumbling only they could understand.

To him, flying was like breathing. Even after his near miss today, with the memories of the crash botching up a simple loop, he wasn't frightened. It only made him angry.

He thought it would be easy. Get her up in the Marchetti. *You see. Cher? Nothing to it.*

Instead, he'd watched her become a zombie. It was as if she was back on the plane after the crash, sitting beside the decapitated body of the reporter, not even able to unbuckle the safety harness and save her ass as the cabin became a volcano ready to blow.

He realized for the first time that Geena and Marc had followed him out. They had come up behind him, were standing to either side of him. Geena touched his hand.

"Let her go," she said.

He looked down at his sister, about to say something. But Geena wasn't looking at him. She was watching Cherish with a puzzled expression.

"Maybe I've been too hard on your weather girl." She said it under her breath. When she looked back at Conor, she told him, "Let her go, Conor. She can't go far. And this time, I think she'll be back. Be ready for her then." She squeezed his hand. "And be careful."

Allison continued to float, the feeling of comfort getting stronger and stronger as she rose toward the light. It was energy. Pure energy.

Something waited there. Someone. She reached out her hand, extending her fingers to try and make contact. And then she felt it, that iridescent touch, suffusing through her. Love.

Tears come to her eyes. Allison had never felt such love. It was something that she didn't ever want to lose.

She could feel herself change under that touch from beyond. Evolve. She was Allison, and yet, she was something more. She had found some hidden sense inside her, a part of her that she'd never known she possessed. As if she now manipulated a part of her brain that had been dormant.

"Show me," she whispered, knowing there was more.

When it came, the beauty of it was almost too much. The future lay out before her. She was a part of that future. An instrument. She felt the others there inside her, knew that they felt her, too. An aura surrounded them, spotlighting them, so that they would always know each other.

But she wanted more than the dream. She needed more than the memory of the touch from beyond, waiting for the day it would return, as they had been promised it would.

Only then would it happen. When the others returned, that love would be a part of her life forever.

"No. Don't leave me. Don't leave," she murmured as the light floated away, disappearing like the stars. "Don't leave."

Allison opened her eyes.

She was still in Alec's motel room. It was night. She could hear the surf pounding outside. This close to the water, the sheets felt moist from the humidity. She stood, walking to the window. She parted the curtains and peered outside, watching the surf glow under the spotlight from the motel.

Alec was such a beautiful man. An exciting man. Once, he would have been everything she wanted in her little-girl dreams. Once.

She sighed and returned to the bed, sitting there cross-legged. She picked up the phone, dialed, then waited patiently.

A voice picked up on the other end. "Dean, please. It's Allison."

She pulled out Alec's cigarettes, lining them up on the bedside table like pickup sticks as she waited. Alec had frightened her today, enough that she knew what she had to do.

"Dean?" she said when she heard the familiar voice. "I need the papers now. It can't wait any longer."

She flopped back against the pillow. She could still smell Alec's cologne. It made her smile.

"Nevertheless," she said very firmly into the mouthpiece, "it can't wait any longer. Have them ready for me in an hour."

She hung up and dressed to go out.

Chapter Twenty-One

Cherish sat back in her chair, taking a sip of the Diet Coke she'd bought downstairs from the vending machine. After she'd left Conor at the airport, she'd gone directly to Marquis. It was the one place where he wouldn't be able to shanghai her. Or, at least, he would have to get through security to do it.

Conor, as it turned out, had settled for calling her every half hour, instructing her, as if she was a child, that she should stay precisely where she was, in the relative safety of the plant's secure facility. When she was ready, she was to call him for a "pick up" so that they might discuss their "options."

The last few times, she'd merely picked up the phone and said, "I'm still here," into the receiver before hanging up. She hoped it was still Conor calling.

She was taking life one hour at a time. She hadn't a clue what she would do when she left work tonight . . . or perhaps, it was more precise to say, she hadn't decided where to hide. She hadn't called Mike or her father—for once, leaving them to work out their own crisis. For the moment, she chose to focus only on the menial: press releases, inter-office memos, filing. Catch-up work.

She glanced at her watch. It was almost ten o'clock. She sat back and stretched her neck, knowing she couldn't stay holed up in her office forever. Not that she was getting much done at the moment. The last hour, Eric had dominated her thoughts.

Eric Ballas had been on a personal crusade to oust the government from the private sector in aerospace. Now, Conor was suggesting it was all tied together. Eric's research . . . the Wing-Master prototype . . . the strange composite on the wings. And Cherish was the only one who had worked on both programs—albeit in a very different capacity. Someone who could tie that composite material on Reck's plane back to Eric's research.

She turned the Diet Coke can in her hands, frowning. Certainly, a synthetic metal was a potential gold mine, like plastics a few decades back. Easily adapted to the civil sector, it could eventually replace anything, revolutionizing aerospace, car manufacturing, even shipbuilding.

And computers. The high-tech fibers were only a molecule in diameter. Because they could conduct electricity like a superconductor, they could be used to make "nanowires" for very small computers using very little power. If people thought electronic devices were small now, nanotube filaments could make the current stuff look downright bulky.

Cherish placed the Diet Coke on her desk, a million scenarios and motives flashing through her head. Eric had tried so hard to beat the system. Maybe someone hadn't wanted him to succeed.

She sighed, sitting up, saying to herself, "Well, girl. If Conor thinks you're a threat to someone, maybe it's time you start acting like one."

Making a decision, she pulled the keyboard toward her before she could chicken out. She typed in the old file name and pushed enter.

The computer alerted her when her file came up. But instead

of the Ballas file, the screen flashed: Getting curious, little girl?

She sat there, dazed. *Little girl*. Alec.

She took a deep breath, letting her pulse settle down to just below cardiac arrest levels. Somehow, he'd managed to hack into her computer system. She remembered Alec's ruse with the fire alarm. He didn't seem to have any trouble beating security around here.

"He must have programmed a response to Eric's name." Because she'd used *Ballas* to bring up the file.

Almost cautiously, she typed in the word: Yes.

The message came back: Thank God.

The screen went blank. A round circle appeared dead center. Simple geometric lines blossomed into view, giving the circle eyes and a mouth, like a happy face. The circle turned in profile, reminiscent of Pac-Man. It began chomping its way across the screen, turning each time it reached the end of the screen to retrace its steps. Back and forth, back and forth, chomping madly.

The screen went blank. And then:

Where, oh, where has your little file gone? Oh, where, oh, where could it be?

"You're playing games, Alec." A game that could cost someone their life. If Alec was involved in the WingMaster bombing, it already had.

She typed: Where?

After a while, the response came up: Not here? Curiouser and curiouser.

She thought she understood. She did a quick search of the file directory.

It was gone. All of it. Anything to do with the fullerene project she'd worked on for Eric Ballas had been deleted.

She frowned. That, in itself, wasn't suspicious. The system's administrator could very well have purged the inactive files, making room for others. But it was unusual.

She stood, remembering that she'd come across a hard copy in an old folder in her files. She thought for a moment, trying to remember exactly which filing cabinet, then pulled out a drawer to search through it.

Twenty minutes later, she had gone through every single drawer. The file was no where to be found.

And yet, it had been there as little as a week ago. The day the second prototype had crashed, she remembered coming across it when she'd been looking for Lori's press release.

Cherish grabbed her purse and strapped it on like a backpack. Quickly now, jogging most of the way, she headed for building 22. Everyone had left for the day; the plant was basically deserted. She didn't know if she was getting paranoid, but she looked around a bit, having the eerie sense that someone might be watching her. The night had clouded over, the moist air hinting of rain. A full moon hid behind the opaque cloud cover. *All just a little too atmospheric for my taste.* By the time she reached the building, it had started to sprinkle.

She used her card key to get inside the building. Marquis kept a hard copy of research files going as far back as the last five years. It was company policy. And Cherish had a passkey that accessed all the facilities on the plant, including the archives.

She stopped, thinking she heard an odd scraping sound, listening for the sound to repeat itself. Perhaps because she'd been thinking about Eric, or perhaps because she was ready to believe anything these days, she recalled the Millennium Society.

"Maybe that's what we're overlooking," she muttered. "Aliens are behind this. It's Roswell all over again."

She kept walking, slowly now, listening for any other odd noises, knowing that she was getting jumpy. "Great time to think about aliens, Cherish. Right here in this nice abandoned hallway, on your way to the basement archives."

She rode the elevator down. Luckily, no pesky extraterrestrial made an appearance as she pushed her card key into the combination lock at the door. She punched in four numbers and was gratified to hear a sharp *slap, click.*

She turned on the overhead fluorescent lights. The archives reminded her of a research library, gray metal filing cabinets lined up in rows, taking up the square footage of half the building. The filing cabinets were six feet tall, each bearing the name and date of a particular research project.

It took her a good while to find what she was looking for. But when she did, the evidence spoke for itself. These files, too, had been purged.

She heard the familiar *snap, click* of the door opening behind her. This time, there was no mistaking it, that hushed scraping sound. Hard-soled shoes on the linoleum floor.

Someone was in the archives with her.

"Hello?" she called out. She stepped out from behind the row of file cabinets. "Is anyone in here?"

The lights snapped off. Cherish stopped, sucking in a breath. Instinctively, she took a couple of steps back. The room was almost pitch-black. Only the "Exit" sign above the door gave off a weak green glow.

The scraping echoed loudly across the empty room. Whoever was inside was now coming toward her. And they didn't feel the need to hide anymore.

She took off down the corridor behind her, her hands feeling her way past the filing cabinets as her eyes adjusted to the dark. She switched back down the next alley of cabinets, plunging ahead, taking the opposite direction. *Up ahead. Something there!*

She almost careened into a large figure looming at the mouth of the passageway. In a single motion, she snatched her backpack off and swung it, hard. She was gratified to hear a deep, *umpf!* from whoever had been standing there as she veered around him.

She stumbled down the next row of filing cabinets, turned,

then headed back to the door. Reaching it, she grabbed the knob, turned.

Locked!

Behind her, she heard a strange click. A sputtering sound erupted. Out of the corner of her eye, she caught a glimpse of a light flaring.

Instinctively, she dropped to the floor, her cheek slamming against the linoleum. Holding her breath, her hands shaking, she reached up to feel along the dark wall right in front of her. There was a spot just above her head. She put her finger on it. A hole.

A bullet hole.

She scrambled to her feet, ducking back into the black maze of the archive cabinets. Someone was openly chasing her now. Small blasts sounded, each distinct and frightening. She skipped around the next file cabinet, then turned to bolt down another corridor, trying to run as silently as she could.

Too close!

She raced ahead, disregarding any sound she might make now, but keeping low. She opened drawers, pulled out files, hoping whoever was chasing her might trip over the opened drawers or slip on the papers. She wove her way toward a back door that connected the archives with the only other room in the basement, hoping whoever pursued her didn't know about the exit. That door might be open. If she could get to it.

Out of nowhere, someone grabbed her, pulling her backward. A hand clamped over her mouth, then pushed her up against a file cabinet.

"You've been a very busy girl tonight," Alec's voice whispered into her ear. "But you have bad timing. Be very quiet now."

She tried to catch her breath, stop her chest from heaving for air. She told herself Alec was here. She wasn't alone anymore. But she had to do as he said. She had to be very quiet.

Two men passed, so close she could have touched them. In

the dark, they didn't see her or Alec standing up against the cabinets.

Alec hunched down, pulling her along with him into the corridor the men had just vacated. He doubled back, heading for the front door. She didn't know if he realized it was locked from the outside and couldn't risk telling him. But he seemed to know what he was doing. At the door, he pulled a card out of his pocket, slipped it into the crevice where the door fit against the jamb. By the light of the "Exit" sign, she saw him smile before he pulled the door open.

A stream of pale yellow glow leaked into the room. The emergency lighting from the hall. Suddenly, two men in dark clothes ran out from the stacks. One raised something in his hand—

Alec grabbed her, pushing her out into the hall, putting himself between her and their assailants. She saw another burst of light, heard a sputtering sound.

"Go!"

She and Alec darted into the hallway. He punched the elevator button, running past, still heading for the stairs. Cherish kept with him, her belief in him complete. There was no room for doubt.

Shouts, down the hall behind them!

They flew up the stairs. Hand in hand, they raced for the emergency exit. Alec pushed the door open, lunging outside. Miraculously, her car waited, parked there. Somehow, Alec had managed to start her car and get it past security.

He rounded the car and jumped into the passenger side as Cherish fell into the driver's side. "I thought we'd need a quick getaway," he said by way of explanation. He collapsed against the seat. "Drive."

She peeled out. There was a road for cars inside the plant complex, and she took it now, winding her way to the front gate. When she reached the bright lights of the security gate, she took her first clear breath.

She flashed her credentials to the guard, a man oblivious to gunfire and hoodlums on his watch. And with Alec in the car beside her, she wasn't about to blow the whistle.

The guard smiled and waved her through.

Alec was breathing hard, slumped to one side. "They were following you," he said. "I was following them. That little experiment with the piece of the wing skin." He smiled, shaking his head. "Not good."

"Who are they, Alec? Do they work for Russell Reck or Joseph Kinnard?"

"I don't know. Not for sure. A year ago, I discovered something when I was investigating the crash. I was trying to help Conor. He was taking it so badly, the stuff about pilot error. I stumbled onto the truth. They've been hunting me ever since."

She was trying to listen and concentrate on driving at the same time. She veered down the dirt road outside the parking lot, following the fields used for crops. "The truth? What truth? You're talking about the first-phase prototype? The crash that killed Eric?"

"It wasn't Conor's fault. There was no pilot error. Someone brought it down, just like the second-phase prototype two weeks ago. And the final model if Reck pushes the test flight." Incredibly, he smiled, his white teeth shining in the muted moonlight. "It's going to blow like the Fourth of July."

"Ohmigod. Is it Russell Reck?"

"We're going to find out, aren't we? Pull over."

They hadn't gone far, just over the dirt field behind the plant. She turned to Alec, about to protest, when she saw his shoulder.

"You're shot!"

He jumped out, slamming the door in her face as she reached for him, leaning into it so she couldn't open it from inside the car. He motioned for her to lower the window. She rolled it down, about to protest, remembering how he'd jumped in front of her. He must have realized that man had a gun, that the bullet would hit her.

He grabbed her chin, keeping her there, inside the car. "You, me, and Conor. We're going to redeem ourselves." He kissed her, leaning in through the window. "I would have never left you if my life didn't depend on it. I wasn't going to give up on us, not like Conor. I would have gotten you to love me." He slapped his hand on the top of the roof. "Get out of here. *Now!*"

And then he was gone.

Cherish drove, her hands shaking. She kept looking in the rearview mirror, wondering where they were, the men who had shot Alec. It started to rain in earnest now, the drops coming down in heavy plops against the windshield. Surely they were following her. But she didn't see anyone.

Crazy thoughts ricocheted through her head. She remembered her conversation with Geena. *You don't know Alec. There's nothing in him to give. His mother took drugs—synapses don't fire when it comes to a conscience.*

But he'd taken a bullet for her.

She kept driving, trying to make heads or tails of her thoughts. *Not pilot error—not Conor's fault.* She didn't know where to go, or where she was driving. And then suddenly, she did.

Half an hour later, she'd parked in Conor's driveway. She knocked on the door, then pounded her fist against it. She was wet, incredibly scared, and when Conor opened the door, she had never been so happy to see anyone in her life.

"Okay. You're right," she told him. "Someone is trying to kill me."

And then, for some strange reason she couldn't fathom, the floor came rushing up, right at her.

Chapter Twenty-Two

Sydney struggled with the key, holding a bag carrying takeout from the Yankee Tavern, a seared tuna salad she didn't feel like eating. She opened the door, coming in through the garage into the butler's pantry, dropping the umbrella for the maid to deal with in the morning. She walked into the kitchen and slapped her purse on the counter, then stuffed the tuna salad into the Sub-Zero refrigerator and grabbed the wine bottle there. Kicking off her shoes, she poured herself a glass of chardonnay, in too foul of a mood to eat. Russell had phoned. *Don't expect me for dinner.* Again.

She walked into the front room, thinking she'd just get into a hot bath and drink her wine, forget about the dreadful night ahead . . . until she saw him.

James, the repairman from her security company, waited for her in the living room.

He had helped himself to one of Russell's prized cigars, was seated in her husband's favorite chair, leaning back like a lord. Hair wet, clothes wet, he'd just come in from the rain.

"Come in, Sydney." He smiled and blew a smoke ring. "Looks like your hubby's working late again."

"How did you get in here?" She remembered a news show she'd seen once about serial killers. The reporter said they could be very charming.

"I set an override code into your security system without telling you." He grinned the perfect little boy smile. "Oops."

He stood and walked drunkenly toward her. Had he been drinking? But she noticed his face appeared very pale and pinched, as if he were in pain.

And then she saw the blood, seeping through his shirt at the shoulder. He wasn't drunk; he was hurt.

"What happened to you?" She could barely get out the words.

"Oh, this?" He glanced down at his shoulder. He puffed on the cigar, leaning hard against the wall. "A damsel in distress, I'm afraid."

"You should see a doctor. You should go to the emergency room."

He came closer, watching her with that smile, the smile she'd found so sexy before. "They have a bad habit of reporting gunshot wounds," he said.

She could smell the cigar perfuming the room. His face was chalky white, showing a light spray of freckles across his nose. When he stumbled toward her, she had to catch him.

She hoisted his good arm around her shoulder and helped him back into Russell's chair, almost falling into it with him. Still holding his arm, she stared at him. He wasn't wearing contacts anymore and she could see his eyes were a very dark brown, leaving almost no distinction between the iris and the pupil. He wasn't smiling anymore, either, just breathing in shallow short bursts, like a hurt animal.

"I must be crazy," she said more to herself. To James, she said, "You stay here."

She came back with a first aid kit and a bowl of water.

"For fuck's sake," he said. "It's Florence Nightingale."

She ignored him, instead, getting down to the business of cleaning his wound. Once she had his shirt off his shoulder, she could see the bullet had only grazed the skin, but it had left a deep gouge of a wound. She put the fingertip towel over the bloody skin, holding it there with enough pressure to stop the bleeding.

"I was wrong about you, Sydney," he whispered, the words fluttering her hair at her temple. "Why was I wrong? Most women find me irresistible."

She hesitated, then admitted, "I was attracted."

"Ah. But you refrained?"

"I take my marriage vows very seriously."

"Really? What a shame your husband doesn't."

She heard him suck in a breath when she pushed a little too hard on the towel.

"He's with her now, I bet," he said, ignoring the pain. "Getting his brains fucked out while you sit here all alone, chaste and loyal."

She was amazed that his words could hurt her. She knew the truth. And still . . .

She tried to forget Russell—tried to focus on getting this man out of her house. *Five minutes of pressure ought to do it.*

"I bet she's great in bed," he said, his head lolling back. "I'm great in bed, did you know that, Sydney?" With his other hand, he raised her chin so that she looked up at him. He gave her a cocky grin. "Are you sure I can't change your mind, baby?"

She pushed his hand away, glanced at the clock. *One more minute.* "There's nothing sexy about a man who breaks into my house and threatens me." She pulled off the towel, saw that the bleeding had ebbed. She took out a package with an antiseptic pad.

He grabbed her hand before she could clean the wound with

the antiseptic. "You have me all wrong, Sydney, really you do. You think I'm the bad guy. You *live* with the bad guy."

She raised her chin. "Do you want me to clean this or not?"

"He was always after you, wasn't he?" he whispered. "He planned your seduction so carefully. Because he saw something he wanted. His partner's wife."

She didn't pull away. She was very certain she'd never told this man about Henry.

"Why should Henry have such a smart and pretty wife?" he continued. "Why should Henry have someone better than I do? Those were the questions going through the bastard's head when he came after you, ruining your marriage so he could have you, then throwing you away when he got bored. You were scammed, Sydney. But once you cheated on Henry, you were his. You were part of the conspiracy."

She closed her eyes. Conspiracy. How curious that he should pick that word. Because that's how it had felt. A conspiracy. After Henry died, leaving her a widow—leaving her free to marry Russell—she had felt a little felonious in her intent.

"Now how about those vows?" he whispered. "Can I tempt you just a little?"

She pushed his hand away. She covered the wound with a bandage, then looked him straight in the eyes. "I hate to disappoint you. But at the moment, I find you quite repulsive. How do you know all these things, and what do you want?"

He shook his head. "I had such plans for you, Sydney. For us. It saddens me greatly that I have to give up those plans. But now, I need you to do something for me. You tell Russell that if anything happens to Cherish Malone, all bets are off. It's over." He looked serious for the first time. "You do that for me, and I promise. I'll leave you alone."

He stood, suddenly looking strong again. Taking the cigar with him, he ambled over to the door, looking cocky rather than injured. "I like you, Sydney," he said, his hand on the doorknob. "I like you a lot. You remind me of myself. Someone under the thumb of another, a person you're supposed to trust, but who hurts you, again and again. And you're powerless to do anything about it. I wanted to help you.''

She stared at the door after he closed it behind him. She felt a little paralyzed with her relief. Nothing like this had ever happened to her. A man following her, sneaking into her house. And who was Cherish Malone? Was that the woman in the photographs the private investigator had taken? Had Russell somehow stumbled upon James's girl?

You tell Russell that if anything happens to Cherish Malone, all bets are off. It's over.

Somehow, that didn't sound like two rival bucks after the same doe.

Sydney frowned, remembering the day James had shown up at her door in his security uniform. It had been quite an elaborate ruse to put an override code into the security system. Why would he do that? Certainly, not to show up later for an uninvited chat with her.

Sydney scrambled to her feet. She ran from the room, careening up the stairs. She made it into their bedroom, breathing hard, and threw back the impressionist painting over the fireplace. It opened onto a small safe. She dialed the combination, then searched through the papers inside.

Everything was there. The money Russ kept for emergencies, his papers, her jewelry. Nothing had been taken.

But something had been placed inside.

She wouldn't have seen it at first. A small card toward the back. She picked it up. On it, he'd written:

I like smart women.

She turned the card over. On the back, there was a telephone number and a pin number for a pager.

Sydney collapsed against the fireplace, holding the tiny card in both hands. Something was going on. And she didn't trust James or whoever he was to tell her the truth.

She should speak to Russell. Let him know what had happened. She should give him the strange message and show him the card.

I like you, Sydney. . . . You remind me of myself. Someone under the thumb of another, a person you're supposed to trust, but who hurts you, again and again. And you're powerless to do anything about it.

She stared at the card, those words going round and round inside her head. *Someone under the thumb of another . . .*

Supposed to trust . . .

Hurts you, again and again.

Slowly, she rose. She walked over to the bed in the middle of the room. To either side, there were matching antique French nightstands with marble tops.

She slipped the card into the drawer on her side of the bed, beneath a paperback novel—where Russell would never find it.

Chapter Twenty-Three

Cherish woke to the sound of Conor opening the hotel room door, loaded down with more packages than Santa Claus. Before she could ask about his sudden bout of consumer frenzy—a condition with which she was not unfamiliar—he unloaded like a dump truck and dropped on the bed facing her.

"How are you feeling?" he asked.

"Like my life suddenly flashed before my eyes."

She sat up in bed. She was still wearing her clothes from yesterday, the jeans a little worse for wear from the rain. They hadn't talked much last night, mainly because Cherish had been in a state of functional shock. Maybe, still was.

"What's with all the stuff?" She pushed her bangs out of her eyes. "Did I miss the sale of the century?"

"I did some shopping. And Marc came down, bringing a few things. You were still asleep. I thought you could use the rest. Hang on a minute, there's more downstairs. I didn't want a bellboy to bring it up."

Cherish watched him step out of the room. She slumped

back against the pillows, the night rushing back at her. After she'd done Conor the honor of swooning at his feet, she'd given him the scoop—the missing files, Alec and the men shooting at them. The one thing she hadn't discussed was Alec's incredible revelation: Conor hadn't caused the crash that ended his flying career. There was something almost too delicate about the disclosure. Perhaps it was bad rationalization, but she knew neither she nor Conor had been up for the discussion last night.

So when Conor had suggested it was time to get out of Dodge, she'd agreed without going into the full details about her encounter with Alec. With Marc and—amazingly— Geena's help, they were reasonably sure they'd ditched who- ever might have been watching the house. Marc had taken them to the airport; from there, they'd rented a car. Conor had driven them to the seaport of San Pedro where they were now, staying in a hotel near the harbor.

By the time Conor brought up the final load, Cherish had washed her face and was riffling through some of the packages. She found an odd mix of sturdy clothes, toiletries, and first aid supplies. And surprisingly, a lot of Cup-a-Soup.

Cherish shook her head, thinking Conor had spent a bundle. "What is all this stuff?" She opened a shopping bag and pulled out a backpack.

"You need clothes don't you? I thought it wouldn't be smart to go back to your place, not with someone shooting at you. I bought Geena's stuff for years so I figured I could go it alone."

She held up a lacy bra in her size. "So much for the feminine mystique."

"Do you want a Diet Coke?" He tossed her a soda. She caught the can in both hands. "I'll get us some ice."

She shook her head, pulling the tab. "Don't bother. The can is cold." She stared at all the packages, shaking her head. "I'm glad at least one of us is thinking."

He came back from the bathroom with two cups filled to the brim with ice. He poured some of her Diet Coke into both cups and handed her one. "We need glasses for a proper toast." He raised his. "To a clean getaway."

She had to smile, amazed that he could still keep his sense of humor. She tapped her plastic cup to his and took a sip. "Right. And just where exactly are we getting away to?"

He crunched some ice. "I found us a safe house. We'll be there in about two days."

She put her cup down on the nightstand and walked over to one of two chairs upholstered in neon orange bracketing a small table. She sat down and shivered. "I hope Alec is all right."

"So you're worried about Alec?"

The way he said it, she could tell he wasn't happy about the prospect.

"Conor. Last night, Alec took a bullet for me. For all I know, he could be seriously hurt."

"I couldn't be so lucky." Conor picked up her drink where she'd left it on the nightstand and brought it over to her. "Look, it's our butts hanging out there now. I think it's time we talk about those options."

She took a sip then put the cup on the table, standing. She walked over to the bed where the packages had been strewn across the covers, her arms wrapped tightly around her stomach. Options. Suddenly, she just wanted to jump in the shower and disappear under a spray of hot water.

Conor brought her the cup still filled to the top with Diet Coke. "Come on, take that look off your face. I'm not the Big Bad Wolf." He handed her the cup. "Here. I have another toast."

He came to stand incredibly close. Cherish stared at the plastic cup instead of Conor. Why was it that, despite everything that had happened, this man could still take her breath away?

"Maybe we should clear up a few things first. About us." He tapped his cup against hers. "I'm sorry."

She looked at him guardedly. "Be more specific."

"About everything. This is a real apology, Cher. From the

heart. And since we're stuck together through this mess, how about easing up on the hostilities?''

He had a point. ''I'm really stuck with you?'' she asked.

He tipped her cup to her mouth. ''Drink up. Otherwise, my apology doesn't count.''

She took a swallow, still frozen up inside, thinking about Alec and what he'd said. There was just no easy way to tell Conor. If the accident wasn't his fault, if indeed it wasn't pilot error that had brought down the first prototype, then the last eighteen months of their lives had been a complete lie.

''Okay, but I have to tell you something first.'' She licked her lips nervously. ''Look, I don't even know how to start, so I'm just going to say it. Okay?''

He put his finger over her mouth. ''I don't want any revelations, Cher. Whatever it is, it will keep. For once, I want to forget the past and concentrate on the future. Our future.''

He stepped closer, his arm coming around her waist, confusing her with his gentleness. ''I want to start over, Cher. Together, this time. Do you think we can do that? Do you think we have a chance?''

He kissed her, oh, so sweetly, it took her breath away. It was nothing like the past week, no give or take, just a lot of give on his part. When she opened her eyes, she could only stare at his chest, letting him hold her, thinking she must be hallucinating this moment. The tenderness.

She remembered what her mother had told her after reading the file from the library. *Is it too late?*

''Cher, my love. I've been so unfair to you.'' He angled her face up to his. ''And somehow, I don't think you'll ever forgive me.''

She wasn't prepared for this. She hadn't seen this side of him before. My love? Had he ever called her that? And now, he was smiling playfully, his beautiful mouth, his dreamy eyes, the scar on his cheek giving character—his crooked grin stealing the breath from her lungs.

He sighed. "We have to get going. I don't know how safe we are staying in one place this long." He tipped the cup she was holding between them to her mouth. "To be continued. Okay?"

"Okay," she said, mesmerized by him.

"Bottoms up."

As she drank the Diet Coke, he told her, "I don't think anything has ever scared me as much as last night. When you passed out, I realized how important you are to me." He played with her hand holding the cup, warming her fingers on the outside while the ice inside cooled her palms. "I need you, that's pretty scary to admit right now. After everything."

She was having trouble catching her breath. This was what she'd dreamed of hearing from him. She felt like pinching herself.

"The other night, what Geena said . . . it's more complicated than Alec and the safety board, Cher. I've never depended on anyone in my life. It's always been the other way around for me. I was the one they needed. Geena, Alec. And then you came along, and that all changed. Maybe, after the safety board called and I knew my career was over, I just didn't see what I was bringing to the plate anymore."

She shook her head. "I don't buy that, Conor. It was me. I needed you. Not some test pilot jockey or a hero who saved my life. I fell in love with *you*. That's all I wanted you to bring to the plate."

"Then I was a jerk. And I'm sorry."

She thought about what her mother had said. How difficult it must have been for him, the little boy who'd lived his life trying to find the security that had been stripped from him one fateful day, trying to reach his parents in the heavens.

"I want you to forgive me, Cher," he said. "And it's crazy, because you don't even know half the things you need to forgive."

The way he said it, it was so genuine. Finally, he was there for her. Just like she'd always dreamed.

"Will you?" he asked. "Will you forgive me, Cher?"

She nodded, because there wasn't enough breath in her lungs to speak.

He tapped his cup against hers. "To our future."

He drained his cup, his eyes never leaving hers.

She took another sip. He reached over, shaking his head, saying, "All of it." His gaze still held hers, that Svengali stare. "Make it count, my love."

She drained the cup, under his spell. She'd never seen him this charming. That was Alec, the charmer. But she liked it. Liked that it was for her. "What do we do now?"

He watched her for the longest time. And then, "We're going to Russia, Cher."

She frowned. "How are we going to do that?" Could you sail there by ship? How long did that sort of thing take? The final prototype was set to fly in less than three weeks.

He pulled a set of plane tickets out of his back pocket. "Marc bought them for us. I have about ten thousand in cash. Enough to get us there and back."

She took a step away from him. She was shaking her head. Because things weren't quite making sense. "We talked about this already. I can't get on a plane."

The thought alone made her knees weak—that, or she had suddenly lost control over her motor skills. She stumbled back onto the bed.

He sat down beside her. "If I thought there was any other way . . . but I can't leave you here. And I have to go. I have to take that sample to Eric's Russians. I need you there with me, Cher—to link Eric's work to that wing fragment—to keep you safe."

Her mind was starting to cloud up with fear. "I *can't* get on a plane. If I could, don't you think I would have done it by now? I am director of public relations for an aircraft company, for goodness' sake. Getting Lori to take over all my traveling has been a nightmare. I've tried hypnotherapy, meditation, visualization.'' Her tongue was starting to feel thick, making it difficult to talk.

"Nevertheless, you are going with me."

Suddenly, very clearly, she saw a pair of suitcases half hidden in the corner by the bed. There was a large package behind her . . . she reached back, her arm feeling as if it belonged to someone else. She pulled the tissue aside to expose a parka.

"You bought me a parka." She wasn't confused anymore.

"We're going to Siberia," he said. "It gets cold there. Even in late spring."

Her vision began to blur. She stared at the empty cup still in her hand, then looked at Conor. "What have you done to me, Conor?"

All those beautiful toasts, making her think he loved her. *Drink, my love.*

"Geena takes medicine for migraines, headaches the regular pills can't touch. On a bad day, she takes two. They knock her out for the night. I had her call the pharmacist; he told her she could safely double the dose. I put four in your cup with the ice while I was in the bathroom. I made sure I gave you the cup with the pills crushed inside."

She fell back against the pillows, unable to sit up anymore. Panic setting in. His voice didn't sound right. It was as if his words were coming from the other side of a long tunnel.

"I'm so sorry, Cher."

He was going to put her on a plane against her will.

"I have an old friend from the Air Force. He flies for one of the airlines now. I told him about your fear of flying and that we had important work to do in Moscow. I explained how you would be heavily sedated. He's clearing it with the cabin crew to get you on board. The head flight attendant will be expecting us."

"My passport? Visas?" But the words sounded jumbled in her head. *My ratchet? Weesas?*

"Marc found your passport in your nightstand. Most of the morning, I was waiting for the visas. They're forgeries. Good and expensive. The rest is being taken care of on the other end. By Joystick."

It took several hours to fly a transatlantic flight. No matter how strong the pills, she would wake up midflight. But even as the terror started to rise up inside her, the drug blanketed over it.

"Conor, please . . . don't do this to me. I won't . . . forgive you . . . not this time. I swear . . . I won't."

"I know," he said, looking down at her as she passed out.

Conor pulled her feet up on the bed, settling her there. His heart was going a mile a minute. He glanced at his watch, seeing how much time they had before the flight. He'd never been so scared in his life.

"God, please don't let me have killed her."

And then he started to pack.

The pager on the bedside went off. Alec sat up, using his good arm to reach for it. When he'd gotten back last night, Allison had fixed him up a sling. He brought the pager close, so he could read the number. He smiled.

"It's her," he told Allison. "It's Sydney."

"Of course," Allison told him.

What woman could resist Alec Porter when he set his mind to it?

Russell paced across the tumbled marble floor of his office. The morning paper lay on his desk, folded open to the story about the break-in at Marquis Aircraft.

"Do you think you could have been a little more obvious?" he asked Joseph. "Shooting the damn plant down?"

But Joseph Kinnard remained stoic, standing in front of the floor-to-ceiling windows, staring down at Newport Harbor below. The final prototype would arrive at Edwards next week. It was set for its first test flight at the end of the month, just a few weeks away. If they met the flight schedule, they would get the next installment of money for the program from Congress, a healthy half-a-billion dollars. It was vital that the final prototype fly—and Kinnard had his people playing shoot'em up in the press, putting them all at risk.

"Joseph, listen to me," Russell said, trying to keep the anger out of his voice. "Is it really necessary to take these risks? It's Porter you want. Where the hell is he?" Jesus. All Russell needed was to have last night's shooting linked to Reck Enterprises.

"So you think Ms. Malone isn't a threat to us?" Joseph nodded, as if he agreed. "Yes, I remember you saying something similar after the first-phase prototype crashed. I believe the term you used was, 'a zero.' She didn't count."

Dressed impeccably, Joseph turned to look at Russell with those cold, colorless eyes. He nodded his head to Leo Sharps seated in the leather guest chair in front of Russell's desk. "Why don't you tell him, Leo?"

"Tell me what, for God's sake?" But Russell didn't like it, this little conspiracy among the ranks. Leo Sharps, idiot that he was, still worked for Reck Enterprises. Russ still signed his goddamn paycheck, didn't he? Christ. He should have gotten rid of the fool years ago. And now, the way Leo watched Kinnard, looking for clues, even his loyalty was in question. But Leo knew where all the bodies were buried. That knowledge alone had been the man's insurance for years.

Leo Sharps gave Russell a look that asked, *how much do you want to know?* "The Malone woman stole a piece of the wing from the hangar at Edwards. She gave it to her boyfriend to run tests. Luckily, we got the heads-up from Joseph's people. One of my men was able to get the piece back before Mitchell tested it. But now . . .''

Leo Sharps shook his head, looking over at Joseph, wearing that nice, oily smile that made Russell want to rip the toupee right off the man's shiny fat head.

"They're going to Russia," Joseph Kinnard said. "Mitchell and the woman. To Siberia, I presume."

"My guys saw Mitchell's brother-in-law buy the tickets," Sharps added. "Two of them." He crossed one leg over the other, the picture of complete confidence. "I have a couple of boys on them now."

Russell dropped into his chair, completely nonplused. *Russia?* "They're going to find Joystick."

"Oh, yes," Joseph said. "To speak with Ekaterina Bolkonsky. Another woman you underestimated."

Russ looked up, about to protest. After Eric's death, Joseph and his people had equal say on the follow-up. Now, Kinnard was dropping it all on Russell's lap? *Another woman you underestimated.*

Shit. What did it matter whose fault it was? Russell sure as hell didn't care. Not anymore. He just wanted the problem fixed.

"What are we going to do?" he asked.

Leo Sharps gave him a toothy smile. "Hey. It's the fucking Wild West out there. Between the Russian Mafia and the high level of crime, a couple of dead American tourists isn't going to mean a damn thing."

Chapter Twenty-Four

Cherish was being sucked down to the earth, racing, racing, knowing the impact would kill her.

She woke up with a start, her eyes wide, her heart pumping wildly. She was sitting in her chair, fingers clawed into the armrest. Only, this time, when she woke, the nightmare didn't end.

She was on a plane.

She was flying.

"Oh, God. Ohmigodohmigodohmigod."

"Don't panic, Cher. You're going to be okay."

She turned to Conor seated beside her in the aisle seat, boxing her in. They were in the coach section of a McDonnell Douglas DC-10, she recognized the plane's layout immediately.

"I am not going to be okay," she told him. And then louder, "I am *not* going to be okay!"

He covered her mouth with his hand. "It's a direct flight to Paris. We're almost there."

She reached for her seat belt. "I've got to get out of here."

He grabbed her hand. "Stay in your seat."

She elbowed him in the gut and flipped off the seat belt. Before he could stop her, she loped over him, reaching the aisle.

She could feel the plane beneath her, that familiar vibration that she would have sworn she would never feel again. She walked down the aisle, holding on to the seat backs like an accident victim in rehab. She could see people staring at her. *Who's the crazy woman in the aisle?*

A jolt, like a hiccup. The plane began to vibrate under her feet.

Turbulence.

"Cher?"

She turned. Conor was standing in the aisle right behind her, holding his hand out to her like someone trying to soothe a wild animal. "You're going to be fine, Cher. Just get back to your seat."

She heard the soft chime of the seat-belt sign flashing on. From the ceiling, video screens hung like small television sets every fifth row or so, showing a film, the screens bringing an eerie light to the cabin. Only, Cher was lost in the images in her head. The plane falling. The reporter from *Aviation Weekly*. The terror in his eyes as the plane bucked and buckled. *We're going to die!*

The captain's voice came on over the intercom, telling everyone that they were experiencing a little turbulence. Nothing to worry about. Just remain seated until the seat-belt sign turns off.

Nothing to worry about.

"Cher." Conor took a few steps toward her.

Behind him, the flight attendant looked concerned. "Sir? You're going to have to return to your seat."

"Just take my hand, Cher," he said, holding his hand toward her.

She stumbled backward, shaking her head. She was still

groggy from the pills. The turbulence made the plan shuddered under her feet. "I have to get out of here."

"There's no going back, now, Cher. You know that. We both know it. So, dammit, let me help you get through this."

"I can't be here!"

"Take my hand, Cher."

She turned, stumbled, then raced ahead. She reached the aft bulkhead at the tail section where the bathrooms were located. "Get me out of here. I can't do this." She grappled with the handle of the lavatory. Somehow, she needed to open a door, any door. Go somewhere. "I can't be here!"

The plane dipped beneath her. She stumbled into the bathroom and shut the door, leaning against it. Inside the metal cocoon of the lavatory, she felt instantly better. But she still couldn't breathe.

She was going to pass out.

The door pulled open behind her, making her fall backward. Conor crowded her back inside, closing the door behind him, locking it. There was a mirror on her left and directly in front of her, over the toilet. The bathroom was set against the hull, so the roof partially domed over her. She could see everything reflected in the mirror before her, Conor standing directly behind her, trying to take her in his arms.

She turned, putting all her energy into fighting him. She tried to imagine that she wasn't in hell. There wasn't this little stainless steel sink with instructions in three languages or paper towels falling out of the dispenser at her knees and littering the floor. She wasn't *flying!* She should just focus on hitting Conor, and it would all go away.

"You did this to me, you bastard! How could you do this to me!"

He grabbed her hands and pulled them around her back, pushing her up against the sink, keeping her there braced between him and the counter. There was barely room for the two of them.

"How could you do this to me?" This, barely a whisper.

"I swear I didn't have a choice, Cher. I know how bad this is for you. But it's there. Waiting for us. The answers. And you have to help me get them."

"How could you do this to me?" She was taking deep breaths, sucking the air into her lungs. She could see her face in the mirror behind him, her expression looking so wild. A mental case. "How could you do this to me?"

"Listen to me. You're hyperventilating—"

"How could you do this to me!"

"Shhh." He released her and held her face in his hands. He kissed her. "Please, love. Don't. Please."

She grabbed onto the counter behind her. She closed her eyes. "I can't breathe, Conor, help me. I can't breathe."

"Open your eyes, Cher." He was still holding her face. "Look into my eyes."

She did as he said. "I can't breathe." The words were a bare squeak.

"Just do what I do, Cher. You take a breath. See," he said, demonstrating.

"Now, let it out. Let it all out. Just empty your lungs. Breathe in through your nose and out through your mouth. Try not to take in more air than you breathe out."

She did as he instructed. The turbulence had stopped. To her left, the red square panel turned off its light with a soft chime, letting them know in both French and English that they no longer needed to return to their seats.

"How could you do this to me." She kept breathing in and out, using the rhythm of his lungs to try to stave off the terror ready to erupt inside her.

"I had to get you to Moscow. I didn't know any other way to do it."

"I don't want to go to Moscow."

He kissed her again. "Yes. I know. I know, my love."

"Don't call me that! You don't mean it." She felt tears

coming to her eyes. She didn't want to cry. She didn't even feel like crying. She wanted to get out of here. She wanted *not* to be here, in the sky, ready to fall down and crash and die. "It was all a ploy. You wanted me to drink those pills."

He pushed the toilet seat down and pulled her onto his lap as he sat down. Holding her, he buried his face in her hair. She could feel the air vent to her left hitting her arm, could hear the engine noise mingling with its soft hiss, telling her, *yes, indeed Cherish, you're flying!*

"I hate you," she whispered, holding on to him, clinging to him. "I don't think I have ever hated you until now. I know I wrote all those letters, telling you that I did. I know I said it before. But what I feel now is so much more intense. This is hate, Conor."

"I can see that."

"Those things you said to me in the hotel, so that I would drink the Diet Coke. I hate you, Conor. I hate you. I hate you. I hate you."

She just kept saying it over and over. She didn't know how much time went by. Only that he was rocking her on his lap. After a while, the flight attendant knocked on the door.

"Is everything all right?"

"Just give us a minute," Conor called back.

The plane began to buck again, the turbulence hitting it hard this time. She could see the room swaying. She stopped breathing. *We're going to crash!* The plane was in a spin. Debris crashing through the cabin. *We're breaking up!*

"Stop it, Cher." He was holding her face again, making her look into his eyes. "The seat-belt sign isn't even on. You're imagining the turbulence. It's not there."

"Oh, please, make it stop." She was crying in earnest now, holding on to him. "Please, please, please, make it stop!"

"Listen to me. Just listen. You need to be brave. We both need to be brave. I was a coward. I have always been a coward when it comes to you. But you're brave."

She was shaking her head.

"You are very brave, Cher. And you're going to help me be brave."

"No. I'm not. I'm a coward. I can't be brave."

"You can. You most certainly can. You're being so brave now. I'm going to try to be brave, too. All those things I said to you in the hotel. I meant every word. It wasn't a ploy. It was me allowing myself to say what I feel . . . what I'm afraid to feel. You are my love and you don't know how it scares me to admit that to you. That's just one of the things that scares me. I'm going to tell you all of them, okay? You're going to listen to every single one. And you're going to help me stop being a coward."

She was trying to understand what he was saying, focusing on his eyes, using them like a drowning victim uses a lifesaver, following the pattern of his breathing. *In through your nose, out through your mouth.*

"Okay." She focused on her breathing. In through her nose. Out through her mouth. "Okay."

"I'm afraid of spiders. No, seriously. They scare the shit out of me. Geena always gets rid of them for me. Especially the big fat hairy ones. Marc thinks it's a hoot."

"Something else."

"I don't like to swim. That whole body immersion thing gives me the creeps."

"You're making this up."

"Honest. I never swim if I don't have to. Only in training. And I only take showers. No baths. And I was scared every time I got into the stirrups of one of the experimental planes for a test flight. I was scared that this time, the rocket would blow up under me. But I did it over and over, and I just got used to it. Being afraid. But you know what really frightened me? Something I couldn't get used to, something I ran away from instead of facing? I was scared of being that man you loved. The one who let you take care of him during the investigation. I was scared of needing you. And I was scared to admit that I could fall in love so quickly. If it was fast, how could it be real? How could I trust it?''

She nodded, trying to listen. Breathing. ''More.''

''Only, a year goes by, and it's not going away or getting better, this hunger I feel for you. I start looking for your press conferences on television, hoping to get a glimpse of you. I'm scouring the paper for quotes from you. I'm looking forward to my Thursday letter—even though I'm dreading it, because I *am* looking forward to it. I'm calling out your name when I try to make love to a woman I don't even know—somebody I tried to have sex with because it's been so long, I think there's something wrong with me.''

She was trying to concentrate on what he was saying. *I'm not here. We're back in the hotel. He's talking to me there. Saying these wonderful things there, in that nice safe hotel room.*

''But the only thing wrong with me, Cher, is that I want you. It's that simple. Not some other woman. Only, I threw you away and it's too late for regrets so I convince myself I'm okay with it. That we were all wrong for each other anyway. But I keep your letters, all of them, in a drawer, by my bed. And I reread them, laughing at the jokes, worried about the dark parts, reading them over so many times, I have whole passages memorized. You said that no one would be good enough for you now. That you wanted the man I was for those few short weeks. Well, he scares the shit out of me. Because I never wanted to need anyone. And that man needs you.''

He was hugging her. There was no hesitation or anger. It had to do with meeting some need deep inside their souls, Conor giving her the air in his mouth, the oxygen she couldn't find without him. She, doing the same for him.

He was the air in the cabin. He was her courage.

She pulled back. She sniffed back her tears. ''I don't think you've ever said so much at one time.''

"Maybe that scares me, too. God, Cher, I knew who I was before I met you. And then, suddenly, the accident, the safety board, wanting to get married and chuck it all. I just didn't know myself anymore."

The light behind them chimed on. *Retournez à votre siege.* There came a knocking at the door. "You must both return to your seats. We're beginning our descent into Paris."

He held her face up to his. "Are you ready?" And when she didn't answer. "Be brave for me."

She leaned her forehead against his. But at that moment, she didn't know how to be brave.

"Did you bring any more pills?" she asked.

"I brought the whole bottle."

She took a deep breath, standing, grabbing onto the sink and Conor. "Thank God."

Sydney spotted James sitting in the corner booth. He'd told her they'd meet at Ruby's Diner, a restaurant clinging to the end of the pier at Huntington Beach, the surfing capital of the world. The restaurant's round structure hovered over the water like a life preserver. Big picture windows looked out over the horizon while waiters and waitresses dressed in a style reminiscent of a fifties soda fountain delivered food on plastic trays.

She took off her sunglasses and slid into the bench seat across from James.

"I'm glad you called," he said. "Try the onion rings. They're great here."

She pushed the menu aside. "I'll pass." She saw that he was using his hand without any sign of pain. "Your shoulder is better?"

Again that patented grin. "I heal fast."

"I called because I wanted you to know that I didn't give Russell your message about your friend. I'm not on board for your little agenda. And I think it's a mistake, tipping your hand." She could see she'd surprised him. "If Russell knows who you are, what you want, he'll put a hole the size of Kansas into your little arrangement. My husband can be very tenacious when he wants."

"You got my attention."

"You said something about a change of plans. Well, I want to go on with the first one. What did you have in mind? Get me jealous. I divorce Russell and take all his money?"

He popped an onion ring in his mouth, eating with a grin, his eyes lit up like the Fourth of July. "That was part of it."

The air between them fairly crackled with his sensuality. The sultry look, the cocky smile. Poor boy, he'd turned it up to high. "You can forget the part where I fall madly in love with you to mend my broken heart," she added.

He had the audacity to broaden his grin. "Ah shucks, Sydney. That was the best part—"

"Save it!" She was so damn sick of this. Men using her. And she, playing their eternal victim, shedding her endless tears. She'd married Henry because she thought she loved him, but now she wondered if it was the sense of power surrounding him that she loved, the security he provided. And Russell and that damned monstrosity of a house he'd had her pour her life's blood into the last year. How many tears had she shed over Russell?

Well, she was all dried up inside. There would be no more tears for Sydney.

"I don't want the lover boy act, James. I want the plan. I want to know what you're doing to my husband." She leaned back, the anger like an animal inside her. "And I want to help."

James watched her with some speculation. He appeared suddenly older. She'd always thought he was in his twenties. Now she wondered if he wasn't closer to her own age. "Why are you really here?" he asked.

She thought about her answer. *How do I get him to confide*

in me? She settled for the truth. "What you said, about powerful people hurting you. I think that's the first time I saw genuine emotion."

He smiled. "I do like you, Sydney."

"What was it, James?" she asked, her voice coaxing now. Because she needed to know. "What did you want from me?"

He leaned forward, focusing on her and only her. The contacts he surely wore made his eyes a sharp lime green. "Listen very carefully, baby. What if I were to tell you that Russell killed your first husband?"

She felt as if he'd slapped her. It wasn't what she'd expected. He couldn't be serious. She almost grabbed her purse and stood, leaving him to play his ridiculous games on someone else. But something made her stay. *I have to know the truth!* "Henry died in a crash of an experimental plane."

He shook his head, watching her as if he felt sorry for her. "Russell wanted you, Sydney. Whatever the cost. I happen to know that he needed that prototype to crash. But part of the scenario was to have representatives from each company on board. Russell could have chosen anyone. He chose your husband, his partner. Maybe he convinced himself it had to be someone high up in his organization, and Russell's butt wasn't going on that plane. But I think he was killing two birds with one stone. Henry's death got Reck Enterprises through the suspicion of the crash—and it got Russell the girl he wanted for himself, not to mention sole control over his company through you."

"You're lying. Henry was never any threat to Russell. He did whatever Russ wanted. And Russ already had me. We were having an affair. Why would he kill Henry? He had no reason. No motive."

"Am I lying? It's not like you were filing for divorce from Henry any day soon—that would have been messy for the company."

She was shaking her head. What he suggested, it was too horrible.

"Sydney, baby. You live with old Russ. You sleep with him. You know him, inside and out. Tell me it doesn't have a ring of truth? Tell me you weren't the good little trophy to your Henry until Russell came at you, day after day, getting in your face. Until he had what he wanted?"

She sat perfectly still, cutting it all off inside her. The dread, the fear. Because she knew it *was* possible. She told herself she felt nothing. Not shock, not panic, not even a drop of sadness. She was a rock, unable to feel. Except for Henry. Yes, for Henry, she did feel something. She felt shame.

"What do you want me to do?" she asked quietly.

"I have access to some pretty incredible places, but I can't find it, the evidence I need to prove that Russell Reck is a murderer. But you, Sydney." He smiled. "You're his wife. You know the intimate workings of his mind. Where would he hide his secrets—where did he make a mistake? You're a very smart woman. How about it, Sydney? Want to take a look around?"

She had come here ready to listen about subterfuge and revenge. *Powerful people hurting you.* But what he'd told her. It was worse than anything she could have imagined.

Sydney Shanks Reck stood. She didn't say a word. She simply put on her sunglasses and walked away.

Chapter Twenty-Five

The hotel room was spacious, reminiscent of a bygone era. Only if you looked closely would you see the worn edges of the upholstered settee, the fading wallpaper on the walls. Like Russia itself, the room had adapted. There was a mini bar next to the armoire and British toiletries in the bathroom.

Cherish splashed water on her face, then used a towel that would have served as an excellent dish towel back home. She caught sight of herself in the bathroom mirror. "Girl," she told herself, "you could frighten small children."

They'd arrived from Paris earlier that day. Conor could breathe easier now; he'd gotten his money's worth from his forged visas. He'd already faxed Ekaterina Bolkonsky, stationed somewhere in the Arctic North near a trading outpost called Vanavara. The guidebook Conor brought along said there was great rock climbing just south of the train stop, near Krasnojarsk. *Rock climbing in Siberia?*

They were taking the Trans-Siberian Railway in two days. Conor promised no more planes—until their return to Los Angeles, of course. She had ten of Geena's pills left.

Cherish stepped out of the bathroom to find Conor in a chair facing the coffee table, eating a *pirozhki,* Russian fast food he'd bought from a street vendor. It looked like a giant dumpling stuffed with potato. Several packages wrapped in newsprint sat on the table before him, along with a few bottles of water.

"Do you want something to eat?" he asked.

She shook her head and walked over to the window. They had a splendid view of Red Square. Lit up like Sleeping Beauty's castle at Disneyland, with its onion-shaped turrets appearing so colorful and otherworldly, St. Basil's Cathedral reminded her of an amusement park attraction.

"You go ahead," she said, letting the curtain fall back into place. "I don't feel much like eating."

She should hate him—she'd told him that she did. She leaned back against the windowsill, watching him for a minute. Maybe she didn't have enough energy to hate right now. Maybe, in the morning, she could hate him.

He put down the pirozhki and opened one of the bottles. "At least have something to drink," he said, holding out the water.

She stared at the mineral water.

"Still suspicious?" he asked.

"Let's call it healthy distrust." She walked over and dropped into the antique, oval-back chair across the coffee table from him. "I don't want to give you the wrong impression, Conor. I have not forgiven you. It is not in my character to forgive and forget."

Which wasn't true. She had the nauseating ability to do just that.

"I am still incredibly angry," she continued. "And I don't care how sweet you were with all your confessions on the plane."

Another lie. It had made all the difference in the world.

"I am waiting until I am strong enough. Then, I plan to beat the stuffing out of you. And if I can't, I'll get my brothers to do it for me."

"Which brother?" he asked. "The gay one or the short one?"

She knew he was trying to be obnoxious. He'd gotten along rather well with both Mike and Thomas. "How politically incorrect of you."

"What can they do to me now?"

He wasn't talking about her brothers. He meant the government. With the general discharge, he'd lost his military standing.

She thought again about what Alec had told her concerning the crash—*it wasn't Conor's fault.* She sighed, feeling as if that was a lifetime ago.

She looked across the room, disbelieving that she was here, carrying the weight of their history to Moscow. Running for her life with the man who had once saved it, then left her waiting at the altar to break her heart. Was still breaking it.

Changing her mind about the drink, she took the water he'd offered and drank straight from the bottle. It was carbonated and tasted salty. "Wow. How did they sneak this out of the chemistry set?" She put the bottle down. "Now what?"

He leaned back, balancing the chair with its claw-and-ball feet on two legs. "We could get drunk on vodka. Get into the spirit of the trip."

"I'm still groggy from the pills, but thanks."

She watched as he finished a second pirozhki, this one, stuffed with rice. He stood and stretched. The still-sane part of her realized he couldn't possibly be as attractive as she found him. His features were too irregular, the square mouth too wide, the nose, too angular. The scar, well . . . it was a scar, for goodness' sake. By definition, it disfigured. Only her hormones made her think it accented the beauty of his hazel eyes.

Face it, the man had drugged her, shanghaied her . . . these things alone should make him ugly.

And yet, through some trick of the eye, or maybe some mysterious chemistry that only Conor seemed to ignite inside her, none of that mattered as she watched where his muscles stretched the fabric of his cambric shirt and the denim hugged his thighs.

"Why don't you take the bed?" Grabbing a small tasseled pillow off the bed on the way, he ambled over to an oversized chair with a matching ottoman. "Get some sleep."

"I just spent the last sixteen hours dead asleep courtesy of Geena's little magic pills. I'm not tired."

He slouched into the chair, putting his feet on the tufted ottoman. "It's going to be a long day tomorrow."

Tomorrow.

She watched him lounge back in the chair. He closed his eyes, looking as if he was actually going to sleep.

To her, the silence in the room seemed deafening. Her life was now on overdrive. She had given Conor complete control over their fate. And here he was slipping away into dreamland where she couldn't follow.

On the plane, he'd talked for hours. He'd bared his soul, soothing her into surviving those horrible moments when she'd been awake enough for the terror to sink in. He'd spoken about his childhood . . . shared memories of his parents, his voice falling into an easy cadence that seemed to lull her into some semblance of normalcy. He'd talked about the bad years with incredible candor. How he and Geena had played musical chairs with foster homes—meeting Alec at the state-run facility where they'd all finally landed.

And the miscarriage. For Conor, that had been the worst. Geena had really wanted the baby. It was the first time he realized how their parents' deaths had affected his sister. He remembered his parents, but Geena, she'd been two years old when they died in that car crash. She'd never had a real family. For her, getting married and raising children, it was the end all and be all of her existence.

That's why she'd been so hot to see Conor settle down. "She figured now that she'd attained this blissful state with Marc, I needed the same." That's what he'd told Cherish on the plane, one of their many conversations as he held her head against his shoulder, trying to comfort her. He'd shut the window blind tight, so she couldn't see out, could stare at his chest and pretend they were someplace else. "And she has this asinine guilt thing stuck in her head," he said, explaining so much. "Geena thinks she's responsible for my bachelor state. As if, somehow, I used up all my energy for hearth and home during those years I was struggling to raise her. Just because I took care of her and Alec."

Cherish remembered it all—each word, every pregnant pause. Held on to each like a treasure.

And she remembered his quietly spoken confession to her in the bathroom on the plane: *Only, a year goes by, and it's not going away or getting better, this hunger I feel for you . . . I read your letters so many times, I have whole passages memorized.*

Now, he sat with his arms crossed over his chest, his eyes closed, breathing deeply. Leaving her so very alone.

"I liked it better when you talked," she said.

She walked toward him, seeing him lazily open his eyes. She'd taken enough of the pills to keep an even keel during the flight. It made everything that happened between them on the plane seem too dreamlike. Made her want to test that intimacy here to see if it might be real.

"Do you remember the day we first made love?" she asked, still coming closer, asking the one question she hadn't dared voice before now. "Right in the entry at my house. I'd stopped calling you that week because I could see I was getting on your nerves. Then, out of the blue, you're at my door, kissing me."

"You finally got the message," he said, watching her closely now. "I didn't want your thank-you-for-saving-my-life or your hero worship. Not until I earned it. Not unless the safety board cleared me.''

She searched his eyes. "Then why did you come?''

"I couldn't stay away.'' He spoke with complete candor; he looked at her with such longing. Just like on the plane. "I missed the phone calls ... the damn cookies. I missed you, Cher.''

She took his feet off the ottoman and pushed it aside. She knelt there before him, spreading his knees apart so that she could move closer to him. Hold him. *I missed you, Cher.*

She remembered how happy she'd been those weeks after the crash when Conor had been hers to touch, to hold. In those days, she could explore the warmth of his skin with her fingertips, discover the different textures of his body. He had been this wonderful mystery to unravel. A man's body.

Now, she let her hands travel up his thighs, her palms pressing against the denim. He was a large man, and she was so very small, even her hands flat against the muscles of his legs didn't reach across, thumb to pinkie.

He didn't touch her, didn't move. But he watched her, suddenly alert. She pulled his shirt out of his jeans. She unbuttoned the shirt and sighed softly as she reached to touch his chest.

She spread her hands over his chest. It was covered with dark hair, showing glimpses of the bronzed skin beneath. She had always loved the color of his skin. All those marauding Turks from the Ottoman Empire.

"Are you sure about this, Cher?''

"Only if you talk.'' She pressed up on her knees to reach for him, kissing one of his nipples. "You have to talk.''

His hands were in her hair, letting it slip through his fingers with incredible gentleness, then digging almost painfully into her scalp. They stood together and took their clothes off slowly, until they were both naked. Conor picked her up and carried her, then lowered her onto bed, the motion itself filled with anticipation as he followed her there.

"I can't stand the silence," she told him. "Not anymore."

He covered her with his body. She could feel his erection nudging against her thigh. "And what am I supposed to say?"

She smiled. "I leave it to your ample imagination."

His hands spread her legs and lingered there, on the inside of her thighs where the skin seemed more sensitive, as if the nerve centers were somehow closer to the surface. A place that seldom felt such a touch. He had calluses. On his palms, on his fingertips. They were rough hands.

"In my dreams," he told her, "I do this with you all the time." She was so ready for him as he entered her, a smooth, easy motion. "We come together like this." He kissed her shoulder. "And I don't feel alone anymore."

The rhythm of it was beautiful, sweet, like a dance. She closed her eyes, her legs coming up around his hips, her hands caressing his back, holding him closer. Closer still.

"And I call your name." He brought his mouth to her ear. "My Cher. Over and over. *Ma chère. Ma chère.*"

She kept her eyes closed. "In French like that?"

"Yes." And then, in English. "Because you are so very dear to me." To show that he knew what it meant.

"On the plane," she said, opening her eyes. "You called me 'my love.' "

"Yes, Cher. Always."

His hands eased under her, cupping her buttocks to lift her as he sat up, bringing her onto his lap so she faced him. Her legs still around him, Conor remained deep inside her as her breasts pressed against his chest.

"Why can't it always be like this?" she asked, resting her cheek on his shoulder.

"Shh." His hand came up to frame her face, his thumbs on her cheeks softly stroking. "Quiet now. It's my turn to talk."

He opened his mouth over hers, kissing her. If a man could steal your breath with a kiss, that man was Conor. He could make his touch both gentle and fierce, letting you know with his infinitely soft touch that he possessed you. You wouldn't forget him. No one else would kiss you like this. No one else had his mouth, his taste, his patience.

"In my dreams," he said against her mouth, brushing his lips across hers in another kiss. "I remember that your eyes are the color of the sky and they look incredibly dark when you climax. Like smoke. I remember the first time. How surprised you were ... how happy. How you cried in my arms afterward and told me it had never happened before."

His hands lowered to her breasts, stroking the curve of them, lazily coming up to brush his thumbs across her nipples and watch them raise to that touch. "And I think about how your breasts feel in my hands. How they fit so perfectly." He choreographed his words to movement, cupping her breasts, then tipping her back to kiss each nipple until he took one in his mouth, sucking gently.

His mouth was soft and warm, making her shiver with the pleasure of it. He was incredibly deep inside her. She could feel the orgasm building with the sweet pressure of his mouth and the seduction of his words.

"I remember how you taste," he whispered in her ear.

He lay her on the bed once more. He parted her legs, then lowered his mouth to her, kissing her there, where he'd just filled her so wonderfully. "I can never forget anything about you," he said, still kissing her with his mouth and his tongue, making her die with the pleasure of it.

Her eyes open, her hands fluttered over his back as she came then, pulsing with the rhythm of his kiss. She hovered there, in that blissful state, letting it wash over her while she felt his hands still on her, then his fingers inside her, so that he too could feel the magic of it.

He rose up over her before it died away, those faint flutters of her orgasm, not saying anything, just brushing her hair from her face. She could feel tears filling her eyes as he entered her once more. He leaned close, his mouth kissing her neck just below her ear as he whispered, "Again, Cher."

This time, she clung to him, hugging her arms around him, holding him so tight. She wanted to shout: *Please don't take this away from me, Conor. Don't hurt me again.* But she bit her lips against the words, just taking him inside her, keeping him a part of her for as long as he would let her.

"God, I missed you," he said.

He made it perfect, coming with her, staying inside her so that they both felt her pulsing around him long after their breaths had calmed and his lovely words melted into silence. When he rolled to his side, he spooned her back against him, one hand on her hip, the other on her breast.

"Those weeks after the accident, you kept me sane," she told him, breaking the silence. "But you walked away from this." She turned to look at him. "Wasn't it special enough? What did you want that was missing?"

He took a curl of hair and turned it around his finger. "They called me late in the day. The safety board. They were recommending a determination of pilot error. That meant they would convene an FEB hearing. They would pull my wings. Maybe you're right. Maybe I didn't think I deserved you."

"I would have been selfish and tried to grab for as much happiness as I could," she said fiercely. "I wouldn't have thought for a second that, gee, I better walk away, leave you for someone more special. I would have just kept you there with me and thought: *lucky me.*"

He smiled, stroking her hair, his thumb following the curve of her ear. "Is that right?"

She let her head rest on the pillow next to his, facing him. Alec had told her the crash wasn't Conor's fault and she believed him. Until now, she hadn't known how to break the truth to Conor.

Yet here, in the quiet of this strange place, the words sounded loudly in her head, pushing out of her mouth until she whispered, "Did you ever think that maybe it wasn't your fault?"

He frowned, his fingers tangling in her hair, then dropping away altogether.

"What if you discovered the safety board was wrong." She said the words in a single breath, rushing on. "That it wasn't your fault, after all."

She saw an odd flicker of pain behind his eyes. She realized then how much she'd come to know him these last two weeks. She could read his mood in the troubled look he gave her.

"Alec told me he'd done some investigating right after the crash," she said. "He did it for you, because he knew how painful it was for you to believe that crash was your fault. He said he discovered something that made them want to kill him. That's why he's been on the run the last year, why he's running now."

She could see that he wanted to know more, but at the same time, he was afraid. Finally, he asked, "What did he tell you?"

"It wasn't pilot error, Conor." She took his hand in hers, believing this moment would be no more different for him than any plane trip she might be forced to take. "It wasn't your fault."

He rolled to the side of the bed and sat up. His shoulders rounded, the muscles of his back shifting until his shoulder blades stuck out. He rested his hands on his thighs.

"They investigated the crash," he said. "It was determined pilot error."

She came up behind him, kneeling on the bed. She wanted to hug him, and before she could think better of it, she did. "And they were going to blame the second crash on Marquis's wing design before they found out it was a bomb. It could have been something like that. Maybe someone needed to hide the truth . . . to let you, the pilot, take the blame and save the program."

But he was shaking his head. "The safety board determined

it was Pilot Induced Oscillation. Do you know what that means? A pilot can overcompensate, maybe give a little too much rudder to correct what he sees as a roll or a slip. He overdoes it, you see? Gives the wrong command, screwing with the computer. The plane swerves in the opposite direction, taking an even harder swing to compensate. Suddenly, he's panicking, forcing the plane in the other direction. Pretty soon, the plane is moving like a pendulum out of control, or a car fishtailing on ice.''

"You didn't do that," she said firmly.

"You don't know what it's like to fly those planes. It's difficult to remember things afterward. It happens so fast. You question your memory. I thought . . . I thought . . ." He shook his head, then pushed his hand through his hair. "The plane, it wasn't responding to the correct commands. It did the opposite of what it was supposed to do. I told them it was the computer. But the software checked out. Afterward, when they convened the FEB, they *showed* me the flight data. I tried to figure it out, to make it fit with what I remembered. And I couldn't.''

He turned to look at her, his eyes, incredibly dark. "It was all there, Cher. PIO, all the way. And I had to admit I was wrong.''

He tucked her into his embrace, anchoring her to him. She could feel his breath on her skin, his heart beating softly against her. After a long while, she reached down and held his hand in hers.

She realized he didn't believe her, that he still blamed himself. *PIO, all the way.* She wondered what would happen if he could forgive himself. What it might mean to them both if he could let himself be happy again.

She woke up when a hand clamped hard over her mouth, keeping her from crying out.

In the dim light coming from the window, she saw Conor standing over the bed. He was dressed, pointing to the door. Someone was slowly moving the handle.

She dressed in her underwear—the only thing within easy reach—quickly, quietly, while Conor shaped the blankets over the pillows to make it appear as if they were still in bed. They ducked into a darkened corner next to the armoire just as the door inched open.

She felt the touch of cold steel on her leg and looked down. In the glow of moonlight streaking through a crack in the curtains, she saw Conor carried a gun. He held it with the ease of practice.

A dark figure stepped inside, a hunched shadow that merged then separated with the black slab of the door to slip cautiously past a table with a vase. Cherish caught her breath, begging her body for complete silence. No heartbeat, no pulse. *No sound!* The black lump of shadow crept closer to one of the upholstered chairs, picked up the small tasseled pillow Conor had left there.

He aimed for the bed. Two shots, fired straight through the pillow, almost soundless. Feathers flew into the air, catching the moonlight like dust motes.

Cherish jerked back with each shot, the motion, involuntary. Conor tugged her back behind him, running forward, keeping low. The man moved then, stepping toward the bed. He threw the covers aside just as Conor came up behind him.

Conor grabbed the man's hand and forced him to empty the gun's cartridge into the bed, four shots in rapid succession. As Cherish watched, the two shadows became one struggling hump. She heard a soft oath followed by the clatter of metal hitting metal as Conor's gun dropped to the floor. Conor stepped back and turned in a perfect roundhouse kick. The assailant's gun flew across the room.

The man pulled a knife from his boot. Cherish could see

Conor's gun now, a few feet away, near the table with the vase. The two men circled. The assailant lunged.

They rolled across the ground, bear-hugging, first Conor on top and then the other. But the man froze when he felt a gun barrel pressed into his neck.

"Up," Cherish whispered, the gun pushing up the man's chin so he would be forced to stand. She reached behind her and turned on the lights. She was holding Conor's gun on a pimpled, white-faced man who smelled of garlic, his blond hair hanging in greasy hanks to his leather-covered shoulders. Conor stayed crouched on one knee, trying to catch his breath. He was watching her with a strange expression. Possibly shock.

"One of my brothers taught me to shoot." She gave Conor a meaningful look. "The gay one."

In a sweep of her hand, she brought the vase she'd been holding behind her back down on the man's head. He crumpled to the ground.

"But I much prefer to shoot targets than people," she said.

She checked the pistol. She snapped on the safety. While Conor stayed frozen, still watching her.

She *tched* softly. "There's something about a woman in her underwear holding a gun, right, flyboy?" She tossed him the gun. "Just don't call me babe."

He shook his head and tucked the gun into his waistband at the small of his back. "I'll try to remember."

"Tell me there aren't any more like him waiting downstairs for us," she said, helping Conor roll their assailant over on his back.

"Ever heard of the phrase 'cheaper by the dozen?' "

They used the belts from the terry-cloth robes in the bathroom to tie him up, then propped the man up against the bed. Conor checked his pockets and pulled out the thug's wallet. He flipped through it and took out a thick roll of bills, all hundreds. "Dollars from the good old U.S.A. for a job well done. Looks like somebody doesn't want to get his hands dirty, hiring Russian hit men.''

"Russell Reck."

He pocketed the money, giving her a nod. "Let's get out of here. Before his friends check up on him."

She stared at him. "You're taking the money?"

"Hell, yeah."

Conor gave her just enough time to dress and grab her backpack. They ran down the hall, but stopped at the top of the stairs. The hotel was pre-Soviet, its lobby, turn-of-the-century elegant, marble pillared, and gilded. Down by the entrance, they could see three men dressed like Hollywood's version of the Mafia, all wearing fur hats and mufflers tucked into their trench coats. One looked at his wristwatch, talking to his buddies.

"The friends," she said.

"When our guy doesn't show," Conor said, "they'll come to take a look."

"This is a public place. They won't dare hurt us out here."

He gave her a look.

"What?" she hissed.

"You wouldn't have lasted a day without me."

"Lest you forget, I wouldn't have been here without you. How do you say camera in Russian?"

"Why?"

She gave him the same look. "Are you going to quiz me now?"

"Try photo. It's universal."

She ran down the steps before he could stop her. Trying to make as much noise as possible, she reached into her backpack and brought out a camera, the disposable kind. She walked straight up to a lingering bellhop snoozing by registration, Conor forced to follow.

Using a lot of pantomime, she managed to coax the man

into taking their picture outside on the steps. Dirty snow covered the ground. It felt close to freezing.

"Not bad," Conor whispered, smiling as the bellhop snapped the shot. When he handed her back the camera, Conor said, "Now, I suggest we run like hell."

They raced down the street, followed by shouts. When they reached a Metro entrance, Conor pulled her past a flank of gypsies huddled there and scramble down the dimly lit stairwell. Together, they bounded down escalators steep enough to cause vertigo. At the turnstiles, he popped a green jeton into the coin slot and pushed her through, following closely.

"That way," he said, grabbing her hand again.

The sound of their footsteps bounced eerily off the arced ceilings and mosaic walls. There were just a few souls in the Metro at this hour, mostly street people looking for warmth who hadn't been cleared out by the local police. No crowds for camouflage, just long empty spaces. It wasn't long before the rapid fire of their pursuit echoed down the abandoned corridor.

They reached the tracks just as the doors to the carriages were closing. Conor threw himself between the breach, the doors opening again when they met resistance. Trying to catch their breaths, they both watched from the windows as the car pulled away from the terminal and the three men slid to a stop at the edge of the tracks.

Cherish fell into one of the seats, the cold air catching in her chest. "Great. Only the clothes on my back again. Where did you get the gun?"

Conor stood over her, his eyes already studying the map inside the car. The gun was tucked into the waistband of his jeans, now covered by his parka. "You can buy just about anything in the Russian black market."

She shivered. She could see her breath fogging in front of her. "It's real. Someone is trying to kill us."

"I'm sorry, Cher."

He took her hand, holding it tight. She was getting good at

this, reading his expressions. And Conor was worried, worried that he'd taken her out of the frying pan and into the fire. She wasn't sure he was wrong, but somehow his hand holding hers made all the difference.

"Okay, flyboy. What's next?" she asked.

He stared ahead. "Plan B."

Chapter Twenty-Six

"Help me," Cherish swatted a feather from the chicken lovingly cuddled in the arms of a woman seated across from her in the train compartment. "I'm stuck in a Marx Brothers's movie."

After a sleepless night at a riverside hotel of dubious repute (were those prostitutes in the lobby?), she and Conor had boarded the Rossya, a train that departed Moscow daily for the port of Vladivostok at nearly the opposite end of the world. It would take three and a half days and five time zones to reach their destination, a desolate spot in the very heart of Siberia. After twenty hours of alternately tossing and turning in her berth, staring out into an endless snow-covered forest, Cherish had made the grave error of wandering into the corridor. *Babushka* bait.

The woman had forced Cherish back into the berth as soon as Cherish opened the compartment door. She was an elderly grandmother with a handkerchief tied securely under her beefy chin, but spry enough to hustle an unsuspecting Cherish back into the compartment to display her wares.

From what Cherish could gather, the woman and her chicken were trying to barter. The babushka had some dubious-looking meat wrapped in newsprint, sausage rolls, and fish eggs that looked good enough to catch some fine mountain trout, but which she was passing off as beluga.

Conor remained impervious to the woman's wheeling and dealing. With a shrug and a shake of his head—and a steady finger pointed at Cherish—he'd managed to make the woman someone else's problem. Now, he sat slouched against the corner where the bench seat jutted against the wall of the vibrating train. He'd crossed his arms over his chest, his eyes firmly shut.

The woman continued to harangue Cherish in Russian, the smell of ninety-proof something perfuming the air in steamy wafts. But Cherish knew Conor was listening to every word. Every so often, his lips twitched. He was trying not to smile.

Finally, with a bribe of two bottles of their coveted beer and ten dollars, Cherish managed to oust their guest, closing the door to the compartment behind her.

"Trans-Siberian Railway." She dropped back onto the bench seat that had served as her bed the night before and let her head fall back against the cushion. "Somehow, I imagined things a little more glamorous. Compartments worthy of the czars."

What they'd gotten was functional but sterile. She could imagine these babies being pumped out, one at a time, from some East German factory in days gone by. She'd heard once to avoid anything with a manufacturing date at month's end. Production quotas.

With a sigh, she pulled the sleeves of her sweater over her palms, holding them tucked under her fingertips as she crossed her arms. Lumpy wet snow sleeted past the window pane, making it impossible to see anything but the arthritic shadow-forms of pines and birches. She had thermal underwear on under thick cords and she was still cold.

She lifted the turtleneck up over her mouth, curling her toes inside her hiking boots and their wool socks. Conor had managed to retrieve most of their things from the hotel yesterday by the simple ruse of a disguise. He'd bought a Soviet general's uniform, complete with medals, for twenty-five dollars in the *Arbat,* the outdoor market. A few hours later, success.

Which was a good thing. They'd needed their passports. And soon after settling into their berth, they'd been told by a kindly attendant that there was precisely one day's supply of food on board. Cherish glanced at the empty cup with the train's insignia on the handle. She'd left it sitting on the collapsible table under the window, the dregs of her Cup-a-Soup cooling at the bottom. Now she knew the reason for Conor's booty of the stuff in San Pedro. The only thing available in abundance on the train was hot water, supplied by an enormous samovar at the end of each car. She tried to imagine what a steady diet of beer and Cup-a-Soup could do to a person's insides.

She swung her legs up onto the seat, but it was impossible to get comfortable. She was, in a word, hungry. She was, in another word, cold. But most of all, she was scared, wondering what the future held for them at the end of the line.

With her foot, she reached across the compartment and gave Conor's leg a good shove. "You know. I'm really sick of being the entertainment here."

She had for all intents and purposes been talking to herself since dawn cracked over the horizon. After their lovemaking last night, the loquacious Conor had made an exit, stage left. At first, she'd assumed he'd been too focused on the job of getting them on the train. But once on board, the silence had taken root, sprouting with suffocating vigor, as if the blanketing quiet of the forest had entered the berth itself. For Cherish, the endless expanse of white had had the opposite effect. She wanted to talk, to connect. Hers had been a monologue—Conor, generously contributing the occasional grunt. A deep man, that Conor.

"You know what?" she said. "I think I'm going to be real quiet now." She huddled back against the seat cushion, plumping up the parka she'd been using as a pillow. "In fact, I'm going to just sit here and listen. Because I feel certain that, if I am very patient, you will have something to say before the next millennium."

Conor smiled. "Want to hear a joke?" He didn't even bother to crack open an eye.

"Maybe I should guide this a little," she said.

"What do you call a blonde who dyes her hair brown?"

She pressed her lips together. "Don't go there, Conor."

"Artificial intelligence. Here's another one. Two blondes come across a set of tracks. They start to argue. Are they rabbit tracks or bear tracks?"

She stuck her fingers in her ear. She started to hum, "God Bless America." Loudly.

"They were still arguing when the train ran them over."

She stood, veering for the door. The babushka was better than this.

Somehow, he was out of his seat and standing next to her before she reached the door, a movement so swift, it hadn't registered in her peripheral vision. His hand manacled her wrist, keeping her from reaching for the handle. He looked very serious. "We stick together, remember?"

"This blonde has to go to the little girl's room." She glanced down at his hand. "Do you mind?"

In some more sensible part of her brain, she acknowledged she was acting out of anger. For her, when they'd made love . . . well, to put it bluntly, the earth had moved. It didn't seem right that he could once more become Conor the Cold.

When he let go, she slid open the compartment door and told him from the corridor, "Send out the cavalry if I don't come back in ten minutes."

The corridor was crowded with people, some staring out into the primal forest that appeared to have devoured all signs of life—a few sharing a bottle of sticky, sweet Georgian wine, speaking in hushed voices. The natives wore fur hats and leggings over their jogging suits and pajamas, the standard train apparel for those in-the-know. Down the corridor, a line formed in front of the samovar for hot water. She felt her stomach growl and thought longingly about her Cup-a-Soup as she sidled past. What the heck, maybe chicken noodle next time?

After she checked the bathroom, she was about to mangle through a pantomime to the attendant that they were out of those nifty little sheets of *Pravda* in the little girl's room when she saw him.

Like the men in the hotel lobby last night, he looked like a reject from a Francis Ford Coppala movie. His dark wool coat flapping against his knees, he wore a fur cap slung low over a Neanderthal brow. He had an enormous mustache streaked with gray. He was watching her as the attendant explained she was on her own with the toilet paper. Whether intentionally or not, he blocked her way back to Conor.

She started in the opposite direction, toward the doors separating the two cars, forgetting nature's call, hoping she was wrong. Just being paranoid.

Unfortunately, he followed her.

Reaching the doors, she pried them open, struggling against the weight of the pneumatic pistons keeping them closed. She passed through, the doors automatically shutting behind her. Coal dust from the boilers flew up into her face with a slice of cold air, choking her with black dust. The floor beneath her felt like a carnival ride, bouncing with the tossing motion of the train, threatening to slam her against the flimsy accordion walls that connected the cars. The frozen steel of the handle nearly burned off her skin as she grappled to open the next set of doors. She couldn't catch her breath, but took off running as soon as she wriggled past, into the next car.

He caught her at the dining car. She struggled, trying desperately to get away. He shouted at her in Russian. Just over his shoulder, she saw Conor. Another man stood right behind him, a clone of her thug, his hand inside his dark wool coat suspiciously held against Conor's side. The staff was watching, but a few barked commands from the man holding her sent them speedily about their business. She'd read somewhere that the Russian Mafia ran the country.

She stopped struggling, looking up at the man who held her, trying to understand what he was saying.

"English," she said, wondering what would come next.

He reached into his coat. She forgot to breathe. *This is it,* she thought, meeting Conor's gaze over the man's shoulder, waiting for the gun to fire.

Instead, the man flashed a picture ID. "My name is Viktor Petroff," he said in perfect but heavily-accented English. "I am with the government of the Irkutsk Oblast. You and your companion are under arrest for the illegal transfer of sensitive technology."

"I'm telling you for the last time, I am not a spy."

Cherish fell back against the slats of the wooden chair, tired. After two days of traveling under house arrest with Viktor and the gang, they had arrived at Tayshet station where a car had been waiting in the dim light of the dawn. Heading north on a highway surrounded by the taiga forest, Viktor and company drove them to the city of Bratsk, a place you shouldn't miss if you liked really big dams. The hydroelectric station there stood as a testament to Soviet ingenuity. A kilometer long, the monstrosity carried a road and the BAM railway running across its back and accounted for the flank of factories belching thick clouds of poison into the air.

They stopped at one of the small settlements on the shore of the "Bratsk Sea," the artificial lake, a by-product of construction for the hydroelectric plant. There, they were ushered inside a primitive building that looked like an innocent bungalow. A few steps revealed the institutional air of a jail, perhaps the equivalent of the local police department. There was even a drunk tank housing one boisterous resident.

Wherever they were, Viktor had enough clout to make the digs his own. He interrogated her for the next hour in a very cold room where she sat on a very hard chair, bringing back hazy memories of *Gulag Archipelago*.

"At six-thirty in the evening, your companion sent a fax to Ekaterina Bolkonsky. We know that this woman is conducting experiments of a sensitive nature. There are rules about the international sale of technology."

Viktor's weather-worn face and rheumy blue eyes fixed on hers. Amazing how the man could remain this intense about his questions. He'd been repeating himself for the last hour.

She glanced around the office, bare except for two chairs, a very functional table and a desk, and a lamp that kept threatening to wink out. Whatever heating the building used, it was on the fritz. The few souls she'd come across wore coats, mufflers, and fur caps. She reasoned Viktor cultivated the enormous mustache on his upper lip for warmth. As he waited for her to answer, the thing had a habit of twitching, as if it were alive. A couple of times, she'd felt like swatting it.

"I am very familiar with the laws governing the transfer of technology," she said tiredly. "I am not here to purchase anything."

"Then you will please be so kind as to tell me what you are doing in Siberia?"

She looked at him deadpan. "Rock climbing."

The mustache twitched. "Ms. Malone. I am not a man who enjoys humor."

"What a shame. I just came across a couple of excellent jokes on the train. Really, you'd be in stitches."

Sour-faced Viktor with his hound-dog eyes did indeed look as if he needed a sense of humor. But she'd been sitting too long, wondering how Conor was getting along with Viktor's sour-faced clone. She was losing her patience, getting uppity.

The grooves around Viktor's mustache deepened. "I will take you back to your companion now."

With a loud sigh, she followed him into the hall, watching her step on the uneven floor and cracked tiles. The offices were Spartan, the bathroom, with which she was already acquainted, a mere hole in the ground. She imagined the last time it had been cleaned was when Gorbachev was president.

She wrapped her arms around her middle, holding the parka tight. It was incredibly cold and she wondered vaguely if they'd used some of the furniture for firewood. Apparently, the thaw came late in Siberia. Her breath was a steamy gush of white in front of her as she walked. She tried to remember what she'd read about the gulag.

Viktor took her into a room stocked with the familiar-style dilapidated desk and table surrounded by chairs. Conor sat in one, his arms crossed over his chest. He hadn't shaved since they'd left Moscow and there were dark circles under his eyes. At that moment, she'd never seen a man look so good.

"They didn't want to hear your jokes," she told him.

"Surprise, surprise."

"Upon your arrest, we contacted Dr. Bolkonsky," Viktor said, hovering at the door and signaling his clone to follow him out. His breath plumed like smoke as he spoke. "She has been waiting in town for your arrival. We will see what she has to say about your presence here."

When they were alone, Cherish took one look at Conor and ran to him, dropping into his lap, curling her body around his. He was incredibly warm beneath his parka. She thought perhaps his body temperature ran hotter than most people's. She'd noticed that about him before, when they'd slept together. Her own little space heater.

"Okay," she whispered. "I thought I was frightened before. But I wasn't. Not really. *Now,* I'm frightened."

He pushed back the hood of her jacket and brushed his hand through her hair. They hadn't been able to touch each other like this since their arrest and it already felt foreign and tenuous. "At least these guys aren't shooting at us."

"What do you think is going on?"

He sighed, his arms coming around her and the bulky parka. There was very little light in the room. Just a bare bulb overhead. No windows. "I get the impression Viktor here has something against Bolkonsky and Joystick. Apparently, we're just what the doctor ordered. A pair of American spies."

"His cup runneth over."

She rested her head on his shoulder. On the train, she'd slept in spurts and starts. Every time she'd dozed off, her nightmare had been waiting for her. The falling plane—that image of Eric speaking to her, giving the same cryptic message she could never remember once she woke up. And Alec. She'd thought about him a lot, worried that whatever threat she and Conor were running from might have already found him.

"I keep thinking about Alec," she said, focusing on that one fear. When she felt Conor stiffen through the layers of their jackets, she whispered, "Don't. Just listen a minute. Every day, I believe in him a little more."

She looked into Conor's eyes, seeing that he didn't share her optimism.

She tried to sell it. "If what he said is true, that he somehow stumbled across some plot or conspiracy. Well, he could be in even greater danger than we are."

"If you want to worry, think about our sorry—"

She pressed her hand to his mouth, because he'd spoken the words so savagely, not bothering to hide his true feelings. "You were so close," His mouth felt warm under her fingertips. She moved her hand to touch his scar. "Now, you hate him. Because of Geena." When he didn't answer, she added, "She said you couldn't forgive that kind of betrayal."

"Could you?"

"You would be surprised what I would forgive," she said. And then she kissed him full on the mouth.

When she pulled back, he didn't say anything, just watched her. He looked so incredibly tired with his dark circles. Even the scar seemed more visible, as if it too weighed on him more heavily these days.

The door opened. Both Cherish and Conor stood as Sour Face II stepped into the room. "You will follow me now, please."

She glanced at Conor. He gave her a nod. Walking side by side, they stepped into the corridor, their footsteps echoing down the hall. Halfway down the hall, Conor took her hand.

It shouldn't have surprised her. But it did. *We'll be okay,* that touch seemed to say. *I'll keep you safe.*

They were led inside yet another office. Sour Face Viktor sat behind an enormous desk, one far more substantial than the others she'd seen. A woman stood in the corner with her back to them. She turned as they entered.

She wore a white jumpsuit with a fur-lined collar that would probably keep her toasty in subzero weather, the woman inside, no bigger than a minute. She had a bold streak of white in her hair near her face. Everywhere else, it hung in inky black to her shoulders, making her eyes appear very gray, very sharp.

She came over to Conor and gave him a hug, kissing him on both cheeks and saying something that sounded like *Gesundheit!* while embracing him. Before Cherish could rally up a modicum of jealousy, the woman did the same to her.

"It is good to see you again," she said in flawless English. "I was telling this idiot here that he has arrested my houseguests."

"You have papers for them?" Viktor snapped.

She opened a thick wad of papers. "I have full government sanction from the governor of Irkutsk as well as from Moscow for Dr. Mitchell and his assistant to work for my company."

Viktor looked over the papers, then grimaced as he folded them once again, the mustache twitching spasmodically. He picked up the phone and—presumably verifying the papers' validity—ended up barking most of his conversation into the mouthpiece. He hung up and handed the wad of papers back to the woman. "One day, I will catch you, Ekaterina Bolkonsky."

She smiled and said in a perfect imitation of an American, "In your dreams, Viktor."

Outside, three motorcycles with sidecars waited. A man poured gas from a gallon tank into one, while another motioned them closer. They all wore the same white jumpsuits. The woman called Ekaterina climbed aboard one motorcycle, speaking amicably to the taller of the two men, the one not pouring the gas. He straddled the second motor bike while Ekaterina directed Cherish and Conor to mount up into the sidecars.

"This is Misha Zelinskaya," she said, indicating the taller blond, "and Georgy Siyagin." The man holding the gas tank nodded, his huge smile buried deep within a dark beard. "Georgy will wait for your gear, if there is anything left after Viktor's rats scavenge through it. My husband is waiting for us at the laboratory. He knows I can take care of Viktor alone." She muttered something in Russian, her tone conveying something like, *that scum of the earth!*

She smiled ruefully at Cherish. "Truly, only the titles of the bureaucrats have changed, not the faces."

"How did you do that back there?" Cherish asked, climbing into the sidecar attached to Ekaterina's cycle. "How did you get those papers?"

"This is nothing." She put on a pair of ski goggles and handed another pair to Cherish. She turned over the engine. "If Eric Ballas was alive," she shouted over the noise, "you would have had diplomatic papers and a car with a driver waiting for you, beluga and Georgian champagne in the back-seat. Hold on. It will be a long trip."

Before Cherish could comment, Ekaterina gunned the engine and sped toward the forest ahead.

* * *

Russell concentrated on his brush strokes. The Chanel nail polish was a delicious sherbet orange. He'd had his secretary buy it on a whim, telling her it was for Sydney. He'd just known Allison would love it.

He sat back, admiring his handiwork. Allison wiggled her toes, the nails shining like perfect little gems.

"You look good enough to eat," he told her, his gaze traveling up the line of her leg up to her pubis. She'd let him shave it into the shape of a heart.

"Do the other one now," she said, extending the foot with the unpainted toenails regally.

But he put the nail polish down, staring at the perfect arch of her foot, thinking he'd finish up later. Much later. He massaged the pad of her foot right beneath the big toe. She kept her eyes on him in that perfect laser-blue stare of hers.

"That feels good," she told him.

"Does it?" He pulled her to him, then put her toe in his mouth and sucked gently. Allison closed her eyes.

It was an inopportune moment for the phone to ring.

"Don't get it," Allison said, coming up to him, wrapping her legs securely around his hips.

He thought about just blowing it off. But when the phone kept ringing, he suspected who was on the other end. Knew he had to answer.

"Yes?" he said, practically barking the word into the phone.

It was Leo Sharps. Apparently, Russell didn't rank enough to get the call directly from Kinnard. Leo was passing on the bad news.

Russell turned away from Allison, swearing into the phone. "What the fuck do you mean we lost them?" Russell said. He closed his eyes, feeling a sharp pain in his chest. "I *know* it's a fucking big country. Jesus Christ! They're probably halfway to Joystick by now!"

He listened, trying to calm his breathing. If he wasn't careful, he'd have a heart attack right here in this goddamn hotel room. He even imagined it, Sydney's face when they told her he'd died in bed with his mistress.

"Dammit, Leo. That launch is just over a week away—" But he forced himself to listen. Kinnard had a plan. He had men working on it. Some covert operations guys from defense intelligence. Mitchell and the Malone woman wouldn't get away. Not again. "Keep me informed."

He slammed the phone into the cradle. He felt as if his brain was going to explode, his head hurt so badly. Maybe he had an aneurysm. Christ. It sure felt like it.

"What is it?" Allison asked, cuddling up to him.

"We can't miss that launch," Reck said, talking to himself. But he shook it off, sitting back against the pillows. "Well, now it's in that spook's hands," he said referring to Kinnard.

For Joseph Kinnard, this was what life was all about. Dogma. Politics. Power. Making sure the United States economy and military stayed on top—keeping the U.S.A. the number one superpower. And Joseph wanted to be the man who got the credit, the guy the generals came to for their cutting-edge technology.

But Russell, he just wanted the Pegasus Satellite. He'd settle for being King of the Hill in communications.

"Is there a problem with your launch?" Allison had turned away, was finishing her toenails by herself. He'd told her a little about what was going on the last week, though she rarely showed any interest in anything but keeping him happy.

"It's going to be fine," he said, reassuring himself as much as her. "We're having some problems with terrorists," he said, giving her Kinnard's scenario.

He and Kinnard had talked it over, what they would do about Mitchell and the PR woman if they reached Joystick. Joseph thought he could make it look like they were in on it with Porter—part of his group, Marduk. Hadn't they survived that crash together, spending a lot of time in each other's company afterwards? And if Mitchell and the woman couldn't talk to defend themselves . . . so much the better.

Well, Joseph would handle it. This was right up his alley.

"We've tracked down the terrorists," he told Allison, taking the polish from her and setting it on the table. He reached for her, ready to take care of business. "It's a simple matter of keeping our eyes open. Nothing to it." That's what Leo had said just now on the phone. "If they try to enter the country again, we'll be ready for them."

FLAT SPIN

Countdown: 10 days; 9 hours; 45 minutes

Chapter Twenty-Seven

By late evening, the caravan of motorcycles reached Ust-Lensky, a nature reserve covering thousands of kilometers of tundra, including the still-frozen mouth of the Mother Lena River. Ekaterina woke Cherish early the next morning to board a specially outfitted hovercraft where they zipped along the frozen Angara River and snow-covered permafrost for yet another day. Cherish was beginning to realize that Eric's Russians had no rinky-dink operation here. The group stopped at Vanavara, an outpost near the Bolkonskys' lab where they spent the night. The next morning, they boarded snowmobiles, making for the lab.

The Bolkonsky laboratory reminded Cherish of an army barrack, but was in fact a state-of-the-art modular building, complete with telephone satellite dish, solar power cells, and a set of generators that could power a small village. It sat upon the permafrost ground on wooden pilings, able to withstand the unforgiving weather of the region. Shortly after their arrival, Ekaterina's husband had shepherded them out to visit what he referred to as ground zero. Ekaterina had wanted to spend time with their daughter, whom she was still breast-feeding, confiding to Cherish that, while she could hand express, there was nothing like the baby to "clean you out." The phrase gave Cherish a rather alarming image—baby as human vacuum cleaner.

Now she and Conor stood looking out over a great bowl of white. A week after they'd left Moscow, they had finally reached the site of the Great Siberian Blast Mystery.

The area had reforested, new growth poking up through the snow. But old growth still spiked up here and there, the dead and broken trunks a testament to the force that had pounded the earth here a near century ago. Cherish had read somewhere that a study of the rings on trees showed a marked step up in growth rates after the 1908 blast, evidence that the explosion had been atomic in nature.

Maybe a spaceship heading in to check out the unusually diverse water life found in Lake Baikal nearby? That had been the hypothesis Misha advocated. The native Muscovite was a great proponent of the "aliens crashed here" theory for the Tunguska Blast, regaling Cherish with evidence gathered by experts over the years.

There was, of course, the photograph by Kulik taken during his expedition in 1927. Hadn't that same pattern of upright but leafless trees been found in Hiroshima? And the fall pattern of the trees. Its elliptical shape, mapped out by experts such as Zigel and Krinov, could be explained only if the object careening to earth contained a material capable of exploding from a protective shell. Like a spacecraft, for instance.

Staring at the desolate landscape, Cherish felt as if she was in the middle of an *X-Files* episode. Alien abductees, synthetic metals, hit men taking potshots—all that was missing was a government conspiracy. Scratch that. Joseph Kinnard fit the bill rather nicely, thank you.

Valeri Bolkonsky, Ekaterina's husband, had brought them

up to a ridge overlooking the blast site. An almost preternatural silence hung in the air, making the sight a bit surreal.

Standing beside her, Valeri Bolkonsky shuffled his boots in the snow. After two days with the dynamic Ekaterina Bolkonsky, Valeri had been a bit of a surprise. Quietly shy, bald, and rounding in the middle, he made a contrast to the sleek and attractive woman he'd married. But it only took the sight of his warm reception and Ekaterina's passionate kiss in return to make Cherish envious.

What would it be like to have someone waiting for you like that? Someone willing to follow you to the ends of the earth, to this wild and dismal place?

Catching her staring at him, Valeri smiled. "Katya comes here often to gather samples," he told her, using his wife's nickname. "It was part of our work for Eric. But I prefer the warmth of the lab. Come," Valeri said, smiling. "Katya will tell you more."

But Cherish didn't follow immediately. She stood, rooted in the snow, feeling tense and tired at the same time. In the summer, Misha had told her this area would be a swamp, a breeding ground for mosquitoes and midges. It appeared that, even during its brief months of warmth, Tunguska was an inhospitable place. To Cherish, it felt completely foreign, like something out of a science fiction movie. Another world altogether.

She stomped her boots, feeling her toes come to life, thinking about those theories of Misha's.

"What is it?" Conor asked, coming up beside her.

She shivered, and not from cold. "Nothing. Let's go."

Ekaterina first came across her theory on carbon nanotube filaments while studying early soil samples from Tunguska. The work of such scientists as Yavnel, Krinov, and Florensky, led her to believe that there was indeed extraterrestrial material to be found buried in the permafrost of the tundra. She differed from other scientists in that she didn't much care *how* the stuff got there—ice comet or spaceship. To her it was a tool, a vehicle to use in her quest to study a revolutionary material. She'd been analyzing Tunguska soil ever since.

"Eric discovered my research," she told them over strong tea and shortbread imported in tins from Great Britain. "He was very interested in the field of synthetic metals and thought I might be . . ." she seemed to grapple for the right words ". . . on to something. He was working with Dean White then." She frowned. "Dean claimed to have access to old KGB files. These papers supposedly contained analysis of an alien spacecraft. I tried to ignore that aspect of Eric's work. At the time, I was interested only in discovering clues here, on earth."

"That's how you found the nanotubes?" Conor asked.

She nodded. "Buried in the permafrost are radioactive clumps of soil. Valeri analyzes them using the scanning electron microscope." She swiveled the chair around, did a little searching, then pulled out a heavy binder. She dropped the binder on the desk in front of Cherish and Conor, flipped through page after page of Polaroids.

Cherish frowned, staring at the photographs that resembled X rays of bath bubbles, fuzzy circular lines bunched together.

Katya turned the binder around so Conor and Cherish could see. "This is what Valeri found for me."

Conor reached out and touched the photographs almost reverently. "Nanotube filaments."

"Fullerenes," Katya said, giving the more precise name. "It is like diamonds, yes? The strongest fiber in the world. Only, on a molecular level. If we could find a way to replicate and mass produce these filaments . . ."

"You would have a very advanced composite. A synthetic metal," Conor said.

"Years ago, I managed a joint program between Joystick

and Marquis,'' Cherish said. ''At the time, Eric had only the whiskers, not the filaments.''

Ekaterina slid back into her chair, crossing her arms. ''It's as far as we got with our research. We couldn't grow the filaments. We needed more samples for analysis.'' She nibbled on a cookie, shaking her head. ''But it's difficult to find the soil samples containing the naturally occurring fullerenes. I have covered all areas within a hundred kilometers.'' She shrugged. ''According to my analysis, there should be a great deal more of these, but it is rare when I come across any at all. Perhaps it is the tundra, the permafrost in particular seems to soak things up like a sponge in summer. The material barely exists now. I was becoming desperate for enough samples to continue my work.''

''We were beginning to lose hope,'' Valeri said, standing to put his arm around his wife. ''Until Alec Porter sent us the formula he discovered at Reck Enterprises.''

Cherish caught her breath. In her head this voice was screaming: *Back up a minute! Alec? At Reck Enterprises?* She tried to swallow the cookie she was chewing, but her mouth was too dry. She struggled to form the words.

''You're working with Alec Porter?'' Beside her, Conor sat down slowly.

Valeri and Katya stared at each other as if confused by the question. Valeri said something to Katya in Russian. Cherish waited, waited for any possible explanation . . . half afraid that she already knew what it was.

''But I thought you knew,'' Katya said. ''It was Alec who told us to expect you. This was months ago.'' Again, Valeri spoke quietly in Russian to his wife. ''This is why I was able to get the paperwork I showed that pig, Petroff, so quickly,'' she told them, as if translating. ''Alec Porter informed us that you would be contacting me. That you would come—that you would deliver a piece of the composite for us to analyze.''

Cherish started coughing, then managed to swallow the bit

of cookie before she choked. Alec had told the Bolkonskys months ago that Conor and Cherish would arrive here? Would bring a piece of the wing skin. *Months ago.* As in, before the accident.

"Maybe you better tell us what else he said," Conor said.

Katya nodded. "He sent us the formula for reproducing the nanotube filaments. Reck Enterprises used much of my research—Mr. Russell Reck makes Viktor Petroff look like a nice guy. Alec thinks it is Russell Reck who had Eric killed. So I did not feel so bad, stealing back my own research, although they were able to devise a formula to grow the nanotube filaments and I was not. Alec said you would bring a piece of the composite. The proof we need to show Russell Reck killed Eric. He wanted Eric's formula."

Again, she glanced at her husband. At his nod, she leaned forward, staring earnestly at Conor and Cherish. "You did bring it, did you not? A piece of the composite from the prototype? The XC-23 WingMaster?"

Cherish sat drinking vodka. It was the good stuff, she'd been told by the Evenki nanny. Stolichnaya, still factory sealed so they knew no one had replaced the contents with the equivalent of rubbing alcohol.

Dimitri, that was the nanny's name, had been speaking in broken English and pantomime, his foot rocking the wooden cradle on the floor with the sleeping angel, Erika, inside. Amazing, Cherish thought, taking another sip of the vodka. The baby favored her father, but somehow, on the little girl, those same features managed to look adorable.

"Imagine the brain power you're carrying in your DNA," she told Erika, taking another sip from the glass.

The Evenki grunted as if he understood. He was tall, dressed in a short jacket and pants made of reindeer skin, the only animal that seemed to thrive here in the tundra. The tattoo on his forehead resembled a small wreath, making him look aboriginal and distinctly foreign from the rest of the crew here.

He said he was a shaman. He had read her palm. She didn't try too hard to understand, but he seemed encouraged by what he saw there. Given her current situation, she figured he might not be too good at this fortune-telling business.

She took another drink. Alec had known months ago that she and Conor would arrive here with a piece of the wing fragment.

Katya had told them the whole story, her husband urging her to compare notes. Apparently, Valeri trusted Alec about as much as Conor did, while Katya perceived him as a necessary evil if she wanted justice for Eric.

Katya explained how Alec had contacted her through the Internet, then arrived here, in Siberia a year ago to explain he'd been the copilot on the plane that crashed, killing Eric. He claimed the death was no accident. Since then, he'd been working closely with Katya and her husband to get the evidence they needed to prove it.

"He's very talented," Katya told them. "Particularly with computers."

Oh, yes, Cherish thought.

He'd been able to hack into Reck's protected program—how, Cherish wouldn't even hazard to guess. Eventually, Alec had delivered the data showing that Reck Enterprises had used Eric's research to develop a synthetic metal, the material that Conor believed was on the wing fragment from the XC-23 WingMaster.

You could see that Katya was ready to believe the worst about The Wrecker, a man who'd pirated Eric's company under the guise of "helping out," only to sell the company off in pieces when the publicity died down. His first move had been to cancel the Russian contract, paying off the hefty five-million-dollar termination clause.

"I asked him why?" Katya had said. "We were doing good

work here. More than paying our way, so to speak. But he smiled and said that Eric's company was worthless. Worthless,'' she said, spitting out the word. ''I asked, if the company is not worth anything to him, I would buy the name. I offered him fifty dollars. He was happy to sell.''

Cherish could hear the anger in Katya's voice, a proud woman having to endure The Wrecker patronizing her. ''After that, we continued Eric's work as best as we could. With only the five of us,'' she said, including everyone in the room. ''Even Dimitri,'' she said, nodding toward the baby's nanny, ''has learned how to use the sputter coater to prepare samples for analysis.''

''I think I know why he bought you out,'' Conor had said. But rather than explain, he asked, ''Could you show me the transmission you received from Alec? The one from Reck Enterprises?''

That had been hours ago. Since then, Cherish had hit the vodka with the nanny.

Cherish shook her head, still thinking about all she'd learned. A conspiracy to kill Eric and confiscate his research? Alec planning for months to prove Reck's guilt? A crash that virtually ruined their lives, leaving Alec on the run, Conor living under the guilt of those deaths, and Cherish . . .

She frowned, staring at the glass of vodka. How *had* the crash left her?

Alone, she decided, draining the glass. If someone had caused the crash that nearly took her life, in the end, the accident had left her very much alone.

She felt a hand on her shoulder. She looked up into Conor's face. He'd shaved since coming to the Bolkonsky lab. They'd both taken time to clean up. She realized now how dear he had become to her. And how much it would hurt to lose him again.

She closed her eyes, shook her head to clear away her depressing thoughts. Maybe the vodka was making her maudlin.

''What did you find?'' she asked.

He crouched down beside her, looking at the cradle gently rocked back and forth by the Evenki's foot. "I don't know how he did it." He shook his head. "It's incredible to think about. The connections he must have, the strings he pulled—"

"What did you find?" she asked again.

"It's a black project." His gaze on hers remained steady, showing his confidence. "It has to be. They buried it in the contract for the XC-23 WingMaster. I've worked on these kinds of programs before; I'm familiar with some of the procedures involved. The stuff Alec e-mailed Katya from Reck Enterprises, it has all the earmarks of a black program."

He stood, heaving a sigh that said he felt overwhelmed. Making her feel the same. "That's why Reck had to get rid of Joystick's contract with the Bolkonskys," he said. "He had to keep it all in-house—keep tight control." He shook his head again, as if he couldn't quite believe it. "It's amazing. He gets all the money he needs, all hidden from Congress, no one the wiser."

Cherish thought about the implications. A black program worth billions—guaranteeing the military control of an incredible new technology. Technology that would be lost to the commercial world for years, with only Reck Enterprises and its government contracts to benefit from it.

And Russell Reck had killed to get it.

Katya stepped forward, her hand on Cherish. "We cannot be sure until we run an analysis on the scanner. But I think it makes sense, what Conor says about this black program." She looked up at Valeri. "Tomorrow, we will get an early start. Cherish can work with Valeri. If the truth is in that wing fragment, my husband will find it."

Chapter Twenty-Eight

The modular building housing the Joystick laboratory had three bedrooms, all upstairs. Misha and Georgy had good-naturedly turned over their room to Conor and Cherish, bunking down with Dimitri. It was clear that, whatever Alec had related about Cherish's relationship with Conor, Katya assumed they were sleeping together.

Which they were. Maybe she had drunk too much vodka—maybe she hadn't drunk enough. Whatever the reason, the silence of the last week, the distance between them since that incredible night in Moscow, it didn't seem to matter. She needed to be naked with Conor, needed his skin against her, heating her up. Needed his lovemaking to rid her of the cold that had dug so deep inside her, it made her question everything.

Afterward, they lay together, Cherish spooned against him, Conor stroking her shoulder with his fingertips. Back and forth.

He whispered, "What's wrong?"

She turned to him. "You mean other than the obvious?" They were after all, running for their lives, trying to uncover a composite that could revolutionize almost every industry imaginable, still wondering how Alec was involved. *He told Katya months ago to expect us.*

"You look kind of spacey," he told her.

"Spacey?" She folded one arm under her head, staring at the ceiling. It was very white, steeped at a sharp angle, the wall behind her significantly taller than the one she faced. "Funny you should use that word."

He smiled. When she reached out to trace the curve of it with her finger, he kissed her hand. "You're right. But are you feeling okay?"

"I'm not sick, if that's what you mean." She huddled down into the covers. The two of them could barely fit on the cot. There were two beds in the room, but they had squished together into one. She hoped it didn't collapse under them in the middle of the night.

"Let's go back to your word," she said. "Spacey." She turned on her side, facing him again. "I was thinking about the Millennium Society."

"What about them?"

"It's just so weird, how it all connects up. I mean, here we are in the middle of Siberia, just an hour by snowmobile from one of the greatest mysteries of our time—the Tunguska Blast. It just so happens that some people believe an alien spacecraft crashed here. Eric teams up with a Russian woman analyzing samples of extraterrestrial material she digs up near the blast site—Eric, who happens to be best buds with the guru of alien abductees, Dean White."

"That's not so strange. Eric was looking for a composite material beyond our technology. Dean promised some secret Russian papers to analyze a spacecraft that might contain such a material. Ekaterina is looking for the same thing—extraterrestrial fragments that can lead to developing a synthetic metal. It makes sense that Eric would seek them both out, Katya and Dean."

"Yes, but then Eric dies. Katya and Alec think Russell Reck killed him by sabotaging the plane." She frowned. "Then who is the terrorist? The one who blew up the second-phase prototype? And why did Dean White get the demand note?"

"It could be Alec. He ties it all together. You heard what Katya said. He knew months ago we were coming here, bringing her a piece of the wing."

"Actually, she said Alec told her months ago that we would deliver a piece of the composite from the XC-23. That doesn't mean he knew the plane would crash, does it? There are any number of ways we could have gotten a fragment to bring to her once we knew what we were looking for."

"But if Alec is the terrorist, everything falls into place, doesn't it?" he said, challenging her.

Sitting up, Cherish leaned against the wall behind her and tucked the covers up to her chin. "Would Alec bomb a plane?" She shook her head, shivering. "I hope it's something else— anything else. Some other explanation to glue it together." She shivered again, this time dropping the covers to brush her hands up and down her arms, using the friction to get warm.

He sat up beside her. "Hey? What is it?"

"This place. It's so strange here. So white and cold and vast. It almost . . ."

"Almost what?"

She frowned, her brows pinched together. "It almost makes you think something strange *did* happen here. Almost makes you believe."

"In aliens?" He sounded shocked.

She let her head fall back against the wall. "I do sound nutty."

But Conor pulled her into his arms and kissed the top of her head. "Never."

They remained silent, each lost in thought. After a while, she huddled closer to him.

Very quietly, she said, "You didn't do it."

If Conor heard her, he didn't respond.

She was beginning to believe that, whatever Alec's involvement, he had told the truth about Conor. Pilot error hadn't been the cause of the crash that had killed Eric Ballas. And if the composite on the wing turned out to be part of Eric's research with his Russians—something they were sure to determine tomorrow with the scanning electron microscope—then Russell Reck had the best motive in the world to kill.

"You don't want to talk about it, do you?" she asked, trying to prompt him. Because she did want to talk.

"No."

"All right." She licked her lips, taking the bull by the horns. "I'll talk about us, then." And when he didn't answer, "As in you and me and what is going to happen to that combination when we leave the great tundra?"

He didn't pull away, exactly. In fact, he kept his arm around her, caressing the shell of her ear with his hand. But he wouldn't meet her gaze. And he didn't answer.

"Against my better judgment," she said, "I will now admit that I am in love with you."

There. She'd revealed the awful truth. To herself and Conor. And now the ball was in his court.

Conor sighed. Suddenly, he pulled her down on the bed, holding her fiercely. But he didn't say anything.

"You're not going to say it, are you?" she asked quietly.

"Maybe this isn't the best time to talk. Everything is so mixed up right now."

She peeled away from him, pushing him until he released her. "Look. I know how difficult it is to change it all inside your head. The last year—it wasn't about what you thought. You didn't cause that first prototype to crash and you didn't kill those people. But you let it change you because you let self-doubt creep in and take over."

Conor looked so incredibly vulnerable, laying there, watching her. It made her want to give in, to hug him and say: *It's all right, Conor. You don't have to say the words. I'll just sit here and wait and hope this time we get it right.* But she bit her lip instead, forcing herself to keep quiet, not to fill in his silence.

She kept remembering Geena's warning. *If you really love him, you'll fight for him.*

Well, dammit. She was ready to fight.

"I'm not like you, Cher," he said at last. "I don't just *know* things. There's no impulse that turns a lightbulb on inside my head and says, here it is. The truth." Now, he sounded angry. "You have to give me more time."

But she wasn't going to answer his anger in kind. "It's natural to be scared, Conor," she kept her voice low. "It's a big step to say you love someone. Do you think I wasn't scared when you asked me to marry you? I was just more frightened of living without you." She knew she was rambling. She felt a little desperate.

"Is that what this is about?" he asked, still angry, the emotion building on itself. "You want another marriage proposal? It wasn't enough that I let you down once?"

"Maybe our timing was just off. Maybe we needed another try to get it right. Now you've had this entire year to realize I was the one that got away," she said, voicing her own thoughts about him. "Maybe now, if you searched your heart, you would know it would work. That it's what you want."

"And we're going to decide that now. Tonight? In the middle of all this? Jesus, Cher. Why do you have to push now?"

"Because there's nowhere to hide here. For once, you just have to talk through your doubts with me."

"You want me to talk when I'm good and angry? So I can say something I might regret?"

"Dear lord, what a concept."

"Look," he said, with that finality that let her know she'd finally hit bedrock, "You want me to talk? I'll talk. I once knew I was doing the best for my sister—then Alec gets her

pregnant. On my watch. Do you understand? And then there's
Alec, a kid I practically raised. I thought all he needed was a
chance. Now, he's blowing up planes. Because this might be
adding up to little green men to you—but me. I see it clear.
Alec wanted that money. His two million plus."

So now you're questioning everything, she thought, *even
your feelings for me.* Because, in the past—when Conor had
been wrong—the consequences had hurt him and the people
he loved. And now, he was afraid to make another mistake.

"You did the best you could for Geena," she said, trying
to shift some of that guilt he'd shouldered. "She made the
mistake, not you. People make mistakes, Conor. No matter how
much you want to protect them. And maybe Alec isn't the bad
guy. If this was about money, why not just blackmail Reck
with the information? No." She shook her head. "There's more
to this. You and I both know it."

"Like little green men?"

"Don't patronize me."

"Okay, so you think this is just about my self-doubt rather
than good old common sense? Let's talk about that. Here's
what I once thought I knew, Cher. After the crash, I thought I
knew I didn't kill those people. Then, six weeks later, I thought
I *knew* that I had. For a year, I was responsible. *My* fault," he
said, pounding on the word. "And now, I think I just need to
think, dammit. So back off."

She kept quiet, in her heart feeling so fiercely for him, hurting
so fiercely for herself.

He pushed his hand through his hair. He flipped back the
covers and got out of bed. But she grabbed his hand, not letting
him go.

"Don't," she said. "Don't."

He closed his eyes, then rolled back onto the bed to hold
her. "I don't want to be wrong again, Cher," he whispered.
"I don't want to hurt you."

"I know," she whispered, turning so he wouldn't see her face. Swallowing the words she couldn't allow herself to say.

But she thought them. They rang inside her head, over and over. The truth was, that for a few short weeks, he had known that he loved her. And now, he didn't.

Maybe her father was right. You couldn't risk some things. She should walk away now. Before her heart broke completely. Bird in hand.

Sometime in the middle of the night, Conor woke her. He made such sweet love to her, there in the dark. And then he held her, breathing softly beside her until he whispered, "Okay. Okay."

Just that. Those two words.

For some reason she couldn't figure out, it made her feel better.

When Sydney married Henry Shanks, her late husband had only one cardinal rule.

"Sydney," he'd told her, "I am not a young man." Henry was in fact twenty-three years her senior. "One day, I'm not going to be here and you are. So you need to know everything, and I mean everything, about taking care of yourself when you're on your own."

For Henry, that had meant leading her through the complicated tangle of his finances. Henry had no family to speak of. He'd never been married, had no children. He wanted Sydney to know about the secret accounts that he kept for emergencies. Life insurance policies, government bonds, his will, and the codicils . . . everything that bore his name.

He'd kept it all on computer and taught her how to access the files. He had a few tricks, things he'd learned from Russell.

She and Henry had been together nearly five years. The

transition after his death, at least financially, had been a smooth one.

But after she'd married Russell, access to those records had all stopped.

"Why would you have to worry about that sort of thing, Sydney?" Russell had asked when she'd mentioned her arrangement with Henry. "I have people I pay good money to take care of my finances. If anything happens to me, they have their instructions."

She'd been a little hurt. She'd felt cut off. But then, Russell had a passel of children and two ex-wives. She could see why he would be a little reticent.

So with her marriage to Russell, Sydney had gone happily and blindly from assistant curator at the Norton Simon Museum and equal partner with her husband to trophy wife and home decorator. She had been so blind.

After her talk with James at Ruby's Diner, Sydney had opened her eyes. She thought long and hard about what she should do. That night, she sat down at Russell's desk in his home office and turned on his computer. She felt quite comfortable there. When she'd worked at the Norton Simon, the collection had been completely computerized. Sydney had been in charge of updating the filing system.

And she remembered everything Henry had taught her. The little tricks he in turn had learned from his dear friend and partner, Russell Reck.

Sydney spent five days in Russell's office. Always cleaning up before Russell came home, getting rid of anything that might make him suspicious. During those five days, she also visited Reck Enterprises, had a few chats with Russell's assistant, as well as his personal secretary. Russell was very busy with the XC-23. The final-phase prototype was due to fly in a week. Most days, she had the run of the place.

And, thanks to Henry, she knew where to look.

Now, after nearly a week's worth of searching, she locked

herself in her bedroom and spread the evidence across the colossal canopied bed Russell didn't like.

She lit a cigarette and leaned back against the bank of pillows. When she finished the cigarette, she lit another. Then another.

If there was a heaven, surely Henry was there now. She hoped he could see her—she prayed he could forgive her.

And if there was a hell, Sydney Shanks Reck planned to do her damnedest to make certain Russell got there.

Chapter Twenty-Nine

She was talking to Eric, again. Henry Shanks, too, listened as Cherish sat across the aisle, watching Eric's lips move—almost catching the words. But she didn't quite understand. She leaned forward in her seat, asking him to repeat what he'd said, listening intently.

But there was this muffled sound in her ears. Noise from the engine? She couldn't seem to hear anything, like maybe she needed to swallow to clear her ears. She watched his lips, again trying to pick up a word here or there. Put it together. And then:

"He thinks he's won"—Eric's voice blared over the engine noise, as if someone had just tuned into the station or turned up the volume—"frying my ass like bacon on that plane. But the joke's on Reck." Eric could barely contain his laughter, now. Henry, too, was smiling. In on it. "The damn things are disintegrating!"

Cherish sat upright in the cot, completely awake.

"What is it." Conor sat up beside her. "You were tossing

and turning.'' His arms came around her. ''Were you dreaming about the crash again?''

She sat for a minute, trying to catch her breath. She felt as if she had just traveled through some sort of vortex, coming to splash down here, on the bed. ''No. Not the crash. The plane didn't crash this time.''

She huddled against him, the images still sharp in her mind. Eric and Henry, so vital. So alive. She closed her eyes, slowing her breathing.

When she opened her eyes again, Conor still cradled her against him. But he'd leaned up against the wall, getting comfortable. She glanced at the digital clock on the pine nightstand between the beds. Six in the morning. She felt exhausted. Her body was probably too confused by the time change to know the difference anyway. Morning, afternoon, evening. They were all beginning to blend.

''You're awake,'' he said, sensing her movement. ''I thought you'd drifted off again.''

''No.'' She was frowning, thinking about her dream. ''This is such a strange place.''

''And that's about the fifth time you've said it since we got here.'' He pulled her down into bed again, situating her alongside him on the narrow cot. ''Go to sleep, Cher. Katya or one of the guys will come get us when it's time.''

''Yeah. When it's time.''

But she didn't go back to sleep.

She stared at the empty cot across the room, thinking. How many times had she had the same nightmare, never to remember Eric's words? Not even a hint of them. A hundred times maybe? More since they'd gotten on that train to Siberia.

She curled her toes against Conor's feet, feeling the rhythmic rise and fall of his chest behind her. But only Eric was in her head. The way he'd smiled and said, *the joke's on him!* Henry Shanks beside him, looking as if he were part of it.

And for the first time, she remembered every single word.

* * *

Allison watched Alec unfold the papers. His hands were shaking.

He sat down on the bed, grinning from ear to ear. And then he fell back with a whoop, throwing his arms in the air, still holding tight to the KGB documents. She had to smile at his eagerness.

He sat up, took her into his arms. "I love you, Allison. I love you." He kissed her feverishly. "Do you believe me this time?"

She kissed him back. "Yes, Alec. Yes."

He pulled away, dropping back on the bed. "Do you know what I can do with this? Do you have any idea how much money it's worth?"

She frowned. "Of course," she said, hesitating. "But that's not what the society wants," she reminded him.

He gave her a look, then took her into his arms, beginning to do all the things she loved so much, with his mouth, with his hands. "Is that all you ever think about? Your precious Millennium Society? Your guru, Dean?"

"Yes," she said, kissing him back. "You know that."

He pulled away, and brushed his hands up and down her back. "Do you love me, Allison? Do you really love me? More than anything?"

She looked at him, confused. "Alec, you always knew what I wanted. Justice. For Eric. For your friends. You want that, too. Don't you?"

She waited, seeing that speculation in his eyes, frightened by it.

"What about your friends, Alec?" she whispered, reminding him. "They're in a lot of trouble." She smiled, trying to cover up. "You want to help them? Conor and Cherish? You do, don't you?"

He was watching her through slitted eyes, his hands still

brushing up and down her back. But then he sighed and pulled away. "Yup. That's me. Alec to the rescue." He smiled, folding an arm under his head as he lay back on the bed. "But wouldn't it be great? You and me and half-a-billion dollars?"

She gave him a sober look. "It was never about the money."

He laughed. "I know, baby. How I know." He held up the papers. "Don't worry, Allison. You won't regret giving these to me."

"You're absolutely right," she said, meaning it. "I won't."

He glanced at the clock. "You better hurry or you'll be late."

She nodded, letting him kiss her, then showing him out. But after he left, she leaned against the door, so disappointed, it hurt. She'd tried. This last year, she had really tried.

She walked over to the phone, punched in the number. When a man picked up on the other end, she said, "You were right."

Alec, the great pretender.

Conor steadied Cher's hand before she dropped her cup. She'd almost spilled hot tea on her lap.

"Careful," he told her.

They were seated at the table in the kitchen unit of the modular building, right next to the laboratory. He'd been watching Cherish for the last ten minutes. Worried.

When she didn't say anything about the tea, he waved his hand in front of her eyes. She blinked up at him, giving him her attention for the first time.

"You almost spilled your tea."

"Oh." She stared at the cup. "Oh." She put it on the table.

He watched her frown, staring at the cup as if it was a crystal ball. Disappearing inside her head again.

She'd been like that all morning. Not paying the least attention to anything.

Which wasn't like her. Not after last night. The way Conor

saw it, they'd finally had it out between them. Cherish had pushed and pushed, until he'd started to listen. So why was she off by herself in la-la land, acting as if they'd never had this incredible meeting of the minds?

He wondered if he'd misunderstood what had happened between them. Maybe she hadn't seen things in quite the same light. But even now, thinking it over, he felt certain she'd understood.

After she'd fallen asleep, he'd stayed awake hearing her arguments in his head. *Maybe our timing was just off . . . maybe now, if you searched your heart, you would know?* He'd lain there, in the dark, thinking about the importance of timing. His parents coming down that road from Big Bear, him and Cher, that prototype crashing.

In the heat of argument, he'd told Cherish not to push, that he couldn't just *know* things. He had to take his time and think. But the fact was, he *did* know things—in his gut. Or he had. Before the crash.

His flying had always been something he just knew and didn't challenge. He'd always had these great instincts. It's what made him such a good test pilot; what had gotten him so far, so fast, despite the advanced age of thirty-one when he'd entered test pilot school.

And last night, for the first time, Cherish had put it into words for him: Alec, the crash, the safety board—they'd made him question the instincts he'd come to rely on all his life.

Oh, yeah. These days, he doubted himself plenty.

So, after Cherish had drifted off, he'd done as she'd asked. He'd lain alongside her and allowed himself to just *know* something in his gut again. He wasn't surprised when the knowledge hit. He loved Cher. More than anything. And he wouldn't let her down again. No way.

After that realization, a sort of calm had settled over him, so much so that he'd woken Cher from a sound sleep to make love to her and tell her, "Okay." Letting her know he had it straight now. ''Okay.'' That he needed her and he wouldn't ever walk away again.

He'd thought she'd understood.

Just then, Katya peeked into the kitchen unit from the lab. ''Valeri has found something,'' she said quickly, breathlessly, then slipped away.

Conor watched Cher, waiting. Earlier, she'd been working with Valeri, looking over the volumes of data, comparing it with the work she'd done for Eric. She'd been taking a break when he'd found her here, staring into space.

He looped a strand of hair over her ear and watched her jump at his touch.

''What is it, Cher?''

But she only frowned, saying something under her breath. It sounded like, *he's going to fry my ass on this plane.*

He placed both hands on her shoulders. ''What are you talking about?''

She blinked, then shook her head. ''Never mind. I was just remembering something I dreamed last night. I'm sorry. Did you want something?''

''Katya was just here. She said Valeri found something.''

Immediately, she perked up. Coming to her feet, she said, ''Let's take a look.''

In the main room, they found Valeri at the screen to the electron microscope. He explained how he'd used the MTS machine to establish the composite's molecular binding, showing how the innovative bonding Reck's team had come up with kept the carbon nanotubes in ropes long enough to make the underlying composite sturdy. The whole setup was straight out of the formula Alec had e-mailed, though it was clearly diluted within a sandwich of more customary carbon composite material. Aside from the composite's unique shine, which Conor and Cher had both noted, you really had to scan the stuff to see the difference.

Here was the truth Conor had been waiting for. If a composite using nanotube filaments was on that wing, his suspicions were correct: A black program was in place, run under the guise of the XC-23 WingMaster. It was the only explanation that fit.

And it put everything in question. Reck's motive, Alec's actions, and certainly Conor's own guilt over the first crash.

The thing was, it didn't seem to matter so much anymore. Or maybe he'd already made peace with his past. Maybe that's what last night had been about, facing his demons, letting his gut take over again. And his instincts told him he'd been right all along. Something out of his control had caused the plane's computer to ignore his commands.

"Do you see here, Conor—" Valeri tapped at the screen, getting his attention. "This in particular shows—"

"What if it's disintegrating?" Cher blurted out.

They all turned to look at her. She'd spoken quite loudly, interrupting Valeri.

The Russian scientist turned, frowning to show he didn't understand. "What would be disintegrating?"

"The filaments, the fullerenes," Cher continued, insisting. "Could they somehow be deteriorating?"

Valeri shook his head. "Not according to the formula Alec sent. This material—"

"No wait." Katya raced over to another computer, one at the back of the lab. Bent over the keyboard, she sent her fingers flying over the keys. Slowly, they all came to join her.

She said something in Russian to Valeri, who immediately looked at the screen as she scrolled down page after page, stopping every now and then to point to a particular diagram or calculation.

"What is it?" Conor asked, not sure what was going on.

Katya turned to look up at them while Valeri continued scrolling through the material on the computer screen. Her eyes appeared very bright, her smile wide, showing her excitement.

"I told you earlier that there should have been more of the carbon nanotubes here at the fall site. For five years, I have kept meticulous records on exactly where I have found this material." She grabbed Cher's hand, squeezing it. "It's brilliant—and so simple, of course I would miss it. The permafrost isn't soaking up the filaments. That's not why I haven't found the samples my calculations show should be here. The nanotubes themselves. They must be disintegrating!"

The scientists at Joystick worked steadily, everyone remaining incredibly focused. But it was the Bolkonskys working with Conor and Cherish that made the real difference. Overnight, they confirmed it. The material Reck had put on the wings, the underlying composite made of nanotube filaments, it was deteriorating.

Cherish proved no slouch as a structural engineer. Despite anything her father might say about her skills, she knew she was right. Under certain stresses, possibly from high-g maneuvers of the plane, the material would weaken to the point that it would break. The most likely point for that to happen was the wing.

Cher sat back, taking it all in. The knowledge that Alec had been trying to bring into the light. She looked at Katya and her husband, turned to see if Conor understood.

"Alec must have known," she said. "That's why he tried to get them to stop flying the prototype by claiming there was a bomb on board. But really, he figured out the composite was breaking up."

Katya held her daughter, Erika, on her lap, bouncing the baby up and down on her knee as she listened to Cherish. Valeri, too, seemed lost in thought. But Conor's face was an impassive mask—until he turned and left the room, heading for the kitchen unit.

Cherish just sat there blinking, surprised by his silent exit. Valeri, too, let out a soft murmur in Russian, as if to say: *What was that all about?* Only Katya clicked her tongue, seeming to understand. "You go to him," she told Cherish. She looked at her husband. "Alec, he does this to men."

Cherish thought she understood.

In the kitchen unit, Conor sat at the table, staring ahead with a mulish expression. Cherish pulled up a chair next to his and sat down.

"Still holding out hope that Alec is some sort of hero in this." He didn't look at her as he said it.

But Cherish wasn't daunted by the harshness in his voice or his stony expression. She picked up his large hand, cradling it in hers. Last night, after he'd made love to her, his simple words of *okay*. Well, maybe she was reading too much into it, but things just seemed different between them after that. She felt as if they were somehow more *connected*.

"It makes absolute sense," she told him. "More sense than Alec blowing up planes. Conor, he told me he found something—maybe this is it. So he starts thinking, gee, wasn't it convenient for Reck's company that Eric died and Reck Enterprises got all Joystick's research? Alec contacts Katya, seeing a motive. She helps him figure out the rest."

But Conor only shook his head. "Then explain the two-million dollars he demanded in the note. *That's* what Alec really wants. He was even cute about it, spelling out his name with the numbers. 2532. On a telephone, that spells Alec."

"By exposing Reck—bringing us into it—didn't Alec ruin his chances of ever seeing that money?" she argued, insisting now. "He isn't a terrorist. Reck is the bad guy here. And we have to stop him. The Wrecker will fly that plane—he thinks it's safe, because he can check for a bomb. Well, he can't check for this and it's up to us to tell him so. That final prototype, it probably has twice as much of the fullerene composite as the one that crashed. It's a bomb ready to blow."

He sighed, dropping his head. After a minute he nodded. "You're right. Somebody has to stop that plane from going up. But you stay here. With Katya and Valeri." For the first time, his expression softened. "I'll come get you when it's safe."

Cherish gave him a sad expression. *Men never learn, do they?*

"Conor," she said, leaning forward, turning his head so she had his complete attention. "That man took everything away from me—from us. He put these nightmares in my head. Do you think I can just sit here and let you do the knight-in-shining-armor act? Maybe get killed while trying? I'm not sending you there alone. No way. And you're going to need me, whether you want to admit it or not."

"What about the plane trip back to Los Angeles? Your fear of flying?"

She smiled, because she was already shaking inside just thinking about it. "Heck. Don't I have ten of Geena's pills left?"

Russell wasn't taking his dismissal very well.

He was pacing the room, roaring like a tiger. What did she mean, it was over? No fucking way! He was Russell Reck. And Allison, who the fuck was she, he thought, pacing the hotel room as she sat quietly on the bed. She was nothing. A kid—nothing!

"I'd like to leave now, Russell."

She spoke in a quiet but authoritative voice. It stopped him, how quietly she could say it. She was leaving him. She really thought she could do that.

"Allison." He came up to her, grabbing her, giving her a good shake. "What the hell has gotten into you?"

"I made it perfectly clear this wasn't permanent," she said in that damn calm voice. "I was never out to become the next Mrs. Russell Reck."

And didn't it bug the shit out of him that he'd been ready to make the offer? Christ. The last few weeks of hell, only Allison had been there for him. She'd never asked anything of him—only giving, never taking. Now, when he needed her most, she thought she could just bail out on him?

His hands tightened around her arms. He wanted to ring her slim ballerina's neck.

"You're hurting me."

His hands came up, reaching around the cords of her lovely throat. He could see the fear in her face now. Well, she should be scared. She couldn't do this to him.

She reached up and grabbed his wrists. He knew he was squeezing too tight.

"You're . . . hurting . . . me."

"Yes, I am, aren't I?" He spoke in a curiously detached voice. "Just like you're hurting me, Allison. You can't leave me now," he said, surprised that he would say it. "I can't let you. Not now." Not when he needed her so much. Allison made him feel good. She was the only one who could make him forget, even for a little while, the shit he was in. She was his solace . . . his future. Like the Pegasus Satellite. The grand prize after all his sacrifices.

Suddenly, she punched her hands up on the outside of his arms, breaking his hold. He didn't know how she did it. Something they taught these damn women in self-defense classes? He massaged his wrists, where she'd hit him.

"Are you threatening me?" she asked.

He felt as if he was hyperventilating. That sharp pain was back in his chest. Jesus, she really meant it. It was over.

"Allison, please," he begged her. He was fucking begging her! But he couldn't help it. He needed Allison. "This is a bad time for me." She knew that. She knew damn well what was going on. He'd never hidden anything from her. In fact, he'd been damn indiscreet, letting her hear his conversations with

Kinnard. "I'm under a lot of pressure. Please, Allison. You're the only one who can get me through this."

She watched him with her electric blue eyes. She was almost insubstantial, weighing no more than a hundred pounds. Tiny. Maybe under five feet, even. And she was looking at him with complete contempt.

"Go home to your wife, Russell," she told him, slinging her handbag over her shoulder. "If she'll have you. You can't threaten me. You don't have that power."

He watched her leave, still a bit disbelieving, expecting her to come back and tell him it was a mistake. He sat down, shaking. He couldn't believe it. He just couldn't fucking believe it.

Right then, the phone rang.

"Now what!" he said, knowing who it was. He'd told Sharps to call only in an emergency. He'd thought he would be making love to Allison right now, putting it all behind him for a few blessed hours.

But after he answered the phone, Sharps's information changed all that. At the moment, he had bigger problems than Allison.

"All right. I'll meet you both at the office."

He hung up, his hands shaking. He felt like crying. Shit. Everything was falling apart. And Allison had left him. Him!

The image of Sydney came into his head. Beautiful, forgiving Sydney. How could he have forgotten her? What kind of spell had Allison cast over him?

Well, maybe it wasn't too late. Maybe if he groveled enough, he could set things straight with Syd again. Hadn't she stayed with him so far? Forgiving the women, forgiving everything.

Shit! How could he have been so stupid as to choose Allison over Sydney?

His hands still trembling, Russell called the front desk and asked to be connected to the florist. He sent two dozen hothouse roses to the house with a note that read: *Forgive me*.

He stood, breathing a little easier. Good old Sydney. She'd been there through thick and thin. And the Allisons of the world, well, hell. They were young kids with hot bodies. He could get himself one of those anytime. Anytime.

PERFECT TIMING

Countdown: 1 day; 12 hours; 23 minutes

Chapter Thirty

The return trip was a thousand times worse than anything she could have ever imagined.

Cherish hadn't been able to take Geena's magic pills, after all. Nothing so simple. At the time, she'd told Conor that she needed to make the trip without the crutch. Brave little Cherish. He said he was proud of her. He hugged her and kissed her on the forehead; he gave her an "atta girl" thumbs-up.

By the second leg of the trip, he was begging her to take the pills. He was, in fact, holding the bottle out to her with a pleading look, whispering sweet, seductive promises. *These will knock you out, Cher. You don't have to go through this.* And left unspoken. *Neither of us do.*

But they did. Oh, boy, did they ever.

The whole trip, Cherish didn't falter. By golly, she didn't even have a drink.

When they finally landed in Los Angeles, she was a mess. She wasn't superwoman anymore, ready to take on The Wrecker. She was a marshmallow, pummeled by her demons in the air, walking shakily through customs, unable to even pick up her carry-on. She'd turned down the wheelchair only through sheer force of pride. She had a pounding headache and felt distinctly ill.

Leaving customs, they had another surprise. Special Agent Lebredo waited for them, along with two other agents.

Lebredo took them into custody, telling them rather solemnly that they were under arrest for suspicion of terrorist activities. At that point, it shouldn't have surprised anyone that, for the second time in her life, Cherish fainted. Unfortunately, stress had nothing to do with her condition. If only.

Later, revived and sitting on the ground at LAX, the cuffs off for the moment, she thought about the irony—the complications. Their timing had been off a year and a half ago, but it had been perfect in Moscow that night in the hotel without birth control.

She was pregnant.

"They're with Lebredo at LAX," Kinnard said, sitting across from Russell, completely relaxed. "How very unfortunate that they made contact with Joystick. We'll have to do something about that, I suppose. Even in Siberia, that damned woman could be trouble."

Russell felt a chill go through him. Never in a million years would he have thought that Eric's loser Russians could ever come back to haunt him. It was a rinky-dink operation buried in the tundra for God's sake.

"Mitchell and the woman are making all sorts of wild accusations to Lebredo," Kinnard continued.

"Like?"

"They claim there is an unauthorized black program under which the second- and final-phase prototypes of the XC-23 have been reinforced using a special composite. A synthetic metal."

Russell closed his eyes, witnessing the death of his dream. This was it. The end. He'd bet everything on the Pegasus, and he'd needed that composite to make it a reality. Now, it was over. Jesus, he'd probably go to jail. For how long depended on how much they uncovered.

Kinnard surprised him by laughing. "Look at you, Russell. Already wetting your pants. Stop worrying about Mitchell and his little blonde bitch. They're taken care of." He leaned forward, suddenly very serious. "What concerns me is their suggestion that the composite is deteriorating."

Russell stared at Joseph, wondering what the hell was going on. He shook his head. "There's no way," he said, completely confident. "We ran every possible stress test. That plane is good to go. But the test pilot and the girl. What do you plan to do about them?"

Kinnard lit a cigar. "Well, it looks like I was right about their involvement with the terrorist, Alec Porter. That crash of the first-phase prototype—" He shook his head sadly, letting Russell fill in the blanks. "They must have gone off the deep end after that. The three of them were working together. They didn't want our project to succeed—the very plane that cost both men, the men Miss Malone loved, their commissions. And it looks like they were willing to die to stop the XC-23 WingMaster."

Russell frowned. "How exactly will that happen?"

Leaving his seat, Joseph strolled around the office. He stopped in front of the windows and faced Russell. "There will be a bomb on board that plane, all right." He took a puff of the cigar, contemplating. "It will be beautiful. No technical problems, so the program won't suffer. We'll get the next installment of money and our terrorists will be dead and buried."

"And Porter?"

"He wants his two million—he's made that clear enough.

Maybe it's time we give it to him. And a bullet between the eyes to go with it.''

Russell shook his head, amazed at Kinnard's temerity. "You would really blow up a half-billion-dollar prototype to kill Mitchell and the girl?''

"Pest control." He stared at the tip of his cigar. "Sometimes it can get expensive.''

Conor held Cherish as she slumped forward, her head between her knees. He could hear her suck in a breath then moan softly. She looked like death warmed over.

Jesus. He should never have let her get on that plane without Geena's pills. But Cherish had been adamant. And, at first, he'd agreed, proud that she could get a grip on her fears. At first.

Then the nightmare had started. Cherish at takeoff, her brow beaded in sweat, her hands clawing the armrest, her skin, a waxy white. Cherish, waking from fitful bouts of sleep, screaming. When she wasn't hiding in the bathroom, she would bury her face in his chest, mumbling over and over: *I'm not here. I'm not here. Please, don't let me be here.* He'd tried to help her, even coached her through some relaxation exercises— something about a light filling her body—but nothing worked.

And now, seeing the aftereffects, Cher crumbling in a dead faint at his feet, even now struggling to keep it together, he wished he'd been more insistent about those pills.

Lebredo sat across the desk from them, his jacket off but his smart burgundy tie still in place. He held his hands steepled before him. "You expect me to believe there's some sort of government conspiracy involving the XC-23 program?" he asked quietly.

They were tucked away in one of the airport offices, still at LAX, Cherish feeling too poorly to be taken elsewhere for questioning. That's when Conor had decided to roll the dice and trust the FBI agent, believing that—if what Conor feared was true—they didn't have much time. To that end, he'd explained about the WingMaster program and the composite fragment they'd analyzed at Joystick, hoping Lebredo would at least listen.

Now, Lebredo tapped a pencil against the notepad on the desk's blotter before him. Despite taking copious notes, he wasn't buying Conor's story.

"What I expect," Conor said, his attention split between convincing Lebredo and helping Cher, "is that you will at least look into what I'm telling you." The way Conor figured it, getting picked up by the FBI didn't bode well for their future. It took clout to get the FBI involved in their arrest. That meant Kinnard was involved—and he had the power to make Conor and Cherish disappear.

Cherish lifted her head, the effort it took etched in the lines around her mouth and eyes. "Look, it doesn't make sense. Why would I want to blow up my company's plane? For the last eighteen months, I've worked my tush off as the head of public relations for Marquis Aircraft. You call Chuck Odell or Lori Sweeny at Marquis. I'm no terrorist. Or has Joseph Kinnard managed to dig up a personality profile on me to show that I have terrorist tendencies, too?"

Lebredo gave nothing away, watching them with those enigmatic dark eyes. But he'd kept the handcuffs off, and he didn't seem in any hurry to hustle them out the door, all of which Conor took as a good sign.

"Remember that night I ran into you at the hangar?" Cherish asked, sitting up with enough strength that Conor eased up on his hovering. "I took a piece of the wing skin for Conor to analyze then. That's how we made the connection between Eric's research and the crash."

"When Eric Ballas died, Reck Enterprises took over his company, then sold it off," Conor said, stepping in for her. "Now, eighteen months later, the composite on the wing of the XC-23 WingMaster turns out to be based on Ballas's research. Only, the subcontractor in charge of the wing design, Marquis Aircraft, they have no knowledge about this revolutionary material. On paper, it doesn't even exist as part of the government's program with the prime contractor. Come on, Lebredo,'' he urged. ''You know how these black projects work. It's the only explanation.''

Lebredo smiled for the first time, showing even, white teeth. ''Oh, I think I can come up with something even better. Washed up Air Force test pilot seeks revenge after the crash of an experimental plane that destroyed his career. His girlfriend happens to work on the very program that builds the next generation of the same plane.''

''An inside job,'' Conor said, finishing the scenario. He walked over to the desk, pointed to the reams of material he and Katya had prepared to convince Reck to ground the prototype. ''Have your experts take a look.'' He leaned over the desk, both hands braced there. ''Contact the Bolkonskys. Or better yet.'' He picked up the phone, holding it out for Lebredo. ''Start making a few calls, ask some questions. Make sure you mention the XC-23 WingMaster and Kinnard—suggest something fishy might be going on. That you want to investigate. If you're one of the good guys, my guess is you'll get shut down so hard and so fast, you won't know what hit you. Something is very wrong here. You know it; I know it,'' Conor said, pushing, seeing just a touch of speculation in Lebredo's expression.

Whatever response Lebredo might have given was interrupted by a knock on the door. One of the other agents, a younger man with short-cropped sandy brown hair and acne scars pitting his face, motioned for Lebredo. ''We got trouble, Luis,'' he told him.

At that moment, the door opened wide. A woman in a smart navy blue pantsuit and hair slicked severely back stepped into the room, followed by a bruiser of a man in an ill-fitting suit whose height managed to tower over Conor's own six feet some. The woman thrust official-looking papers into Lebredo's hand.

"Wait a minute." Lebredo frowned, scanning through the documents. "Wait one minute, here. I run this investigation and I haven't received any notice of a transfer." He slapped the papers with his hand. "What the hell is this?"

"Your notice," the woman said, taking the papers back and folding them once more. She took out a pair of handcuffs. "This isn't your problem anymore. We're taking custody—"

"You just hold it right there," Lebredo said, stepping in front of the woman before she could reach Cherish. "No one leaves this office until I know exactly what's going on."

But it didn't take long before Lebredo received the confirmation he needed. Conor watched the agent's growing frustration as call after call gave him the same answer: *don't question orders, do as you're told.* Conor kept his gaze steady on Lebredo, making eye contact every time the man slammed down the phone. But it wasn't until he saw Lebredo's look of resignation that Conor made his move.

He ran for the door, careful to veer away from the other agents and toward Lebredo, who stopped him. Cherish did her share by dropping to the ground, moaning, creating a diversion for the others in the room. Conor grabbed the diskette he'd kept in the back pocket of his jeans, a back-up of the material on the desk, and jammed it into the agent's hand. Dollars to doughnuts, the hard copy on the desk would disappear within the hour. "Keep the diskette," he whispered. "It contains all the data. Keep asking questions."

Conor felt himself yanked away from Lebredo. The blond giant rammed Conor's hands painfully up and behind him as he cuffed him. Conor kept his eyes on Lebredo, smiling now. "You look pretty surprised, Luis," he said, using the agent's first name. "Like maybe you don't know what's going on anymore."

The giant dragged Conor out, Cherish trailing behind him. Conor turned to shout, "Hey, Lebredo. You just got my vote of confidence. Don't waste it!"

But once he stumbled into the hall and the two agents hustled them along the corridor, Conor had the sudden sick feeling that he and Cherish had just run out of time.

The woman told Cherish she was being taken to a safe house. She claimed anti-government forces had gotten wind of her and Conor's attempt to stop terrorists from blowing up the prototype. Until these men were brought to justice, she and Conor would never be safe.

Of course, it was a lie. There were no "anti-government forces" waiting in the wings—Reck and Kinnard were her biggest worries right now. But she hadn't been given a choice.

Now, Cherish waited alone in the tiny room of a run-down house that was buried in the foothills, Conor lost to her. She was lying in bed, her knees up, her hand on her stomach. With a guard at the door, the future didn't look so rosy. She felt dog sick.

"So this is what it's like to be pregnant?" The worst case of seasickness she'd ever experienced.

By the time they'd reached Moscow by train, she'd been two days late on her period. And Cherish, her cycle was an atomic clock—to the hour even. Eighteen years as a fertile woman, she'd never been late. And she could do the math.

Still, she'd been determined to get home before the test flight. So she'd boarded the plane but refused Geena's pills, just to be safe. It wasn't until the fainting spell at the airport that she'd been absolutely sure. She was pregnant.

Nursing lukewarm 7-Up, Cherish nibbled on the edge of a cracker, thinking she was going to be one of those lucky women whose morning sickness began the day they missed their first period. She'd arrived at the safe house two nights ago, and each day she'd felt worse. But if Broomhilda, the agent in charge, noticed anything was wrong, she didn't let on and Cherish wasn't about to spell it out.

Who were these people? Part of some special covert operation? Were they from one of the alphabet agencies? Defense intelligence, maybe? Certainly, Kinnard, undersecretary of defense for research and acquisition, might have an agent or two at his disposal. And if Conor was right about Eric's composite, there was plenty at stake.

Even now, just thinking about it frightened Cherish. Her government—or powerful forces within it—were introducing black projects into white government contracts? How far could that go? In particular, she thought of TWA flight 800. A lot of people once thought a missile had hit the plane. Now, evidence seemed to point in a different direction. But the possibility that civilians could be exposed to the testing of experimental materials under the secrecy of a black program—could be killed while their government used them as Guinea pigs—well, it didn't seem such a stretch right at the moment.

"And I'm just lying here like a beached whale," she said, popping another cracker. It didn't help that she was worried about Conor.

They had landed in LAX on Sunday. She hadn't seen Conor since then, though she guessed he, too, was being held somewhere in the house. It was Tuesday morning, the day the prototype was set to fly if Reck ignored their warning. Long before dawn, Broomhilda had knocked on her door, telling Cherish to dress. She had been waiting for the last half hour thinking, *what next?*

Cherish spent another anxious half hour waiting before Broomhilda showed up at her door and signaled for her to get out of bed. This time, Cherish was rushed into a black Cadillac that was waiting, the motor running, on the cracked-concrete driveway. To her relief, she found Conor inside.

"Boy, am I glad to see you," she told him.

"How are you, Cher?" He looked as tired as she felt. He hadn't shaved, so he had that *Miami Vice* look about him, only his scar hiked it up to just above thug level. She cuddled up to him, rubbing her cheek against the roughness of his face, feeling just a little more alive with the touch.

She sighed. "If these are the good guys, why are we handcuffed?"

"These aren't the good guys."

"I was afraid you would say that."

Wherever they were taking Cherish and Conor, it was a long car ride. They didn't talk, very aware of the driver and the man beside him. At one point, she even drifted off into sleep, she was that tired.

When she woke, she couldn't tell how much time had passed, but the sun still hovered on the horizon. She looked up at Conor, saw him smile and whisper, "good morning." She realized she hadn't told him about the baby—hadn't wanted to until she was certain. And now . . . she leaned back into the crook of his arm as he kissed her forehead. Oh, for the days when her biggest problem was if Conor planned to make an honest woman of her.

"Do you think they're going to kill us?" she asked, so only Conor would hear.

"Hush." He kissed her on the mouth. "You just talk too much, Cher."

He smiled as he said it. And it was such a lovely smile. If she didn't feel like puking her guts out, she was absolutely certain that smile would have given her confidence.

An hour later, they ended up at Edwards Air Force Base, arriving while it was still early morning. Whoever the people driving the car were, they had complete authorization. They were waved through, no questions asked.

Their big surprise was the XC-23 WingMaster. It was going to fly, all right. Apparently, with Conor and Cherish on board.

They were hustled onto the prototype by the agents. Cuffed

back to back, they sat on top of a large crate held down by sturdy netting. One of the men shepherding them had looped their handcuffs together, then used a chain and a sturdy lock to secure both sets of handcuffs to the fuselage frame protruding through the jet's acoustical insulation. Cherish had only one thought: *No way out*.

They were situated toward the tail end of the plane's cargo hold, behind a wall of instrument racks housing the data acquisitions equipment, the racks bolted to the floor. Interestingly enough, there was no test engineer to man the equipment—a detail Russell Reck or Kinnard must have taken care of. The pilot and crew in the cockpit would never know Conor and Cherish were on board.

Just the same, they tried shouting, pounding on the hull with their feet. No one responded. Conor even managed to send one of his shoes flying into the bulkhead separating the cargo hold and the cabin. Nothing. Soon enough, the engine noise was such that no one could hear them.

Fifteen minutes later, Conor was furiously trying to pick the lock on the handcuffs using a bobby pin.

"I guess this only works in the movies, huh?" Cherish asked, swallowing the bile backing up her throat.

But Conor kept at the bobby pin. Having discovered the pin under a chair cushion in his room at the safe house, he'd smuggled it on board inside his shoe. There was just enough give to the chain linking the cuffs to the fuselage that he had the bobby pin in hand now, was trying feverishly to free them.

"You doing okay there, Cher?"

She had her eyes tightly closed. "Oh, yeah. I'm just peachy." She was already hyperventilating, feeling clammy, the vibrations beneath them heralding what lay ahead. The motion told her the plane was taking the flight line.

"Just hold on for me, Cher," he said, working the bobby pin for all he was worth.

She sucked air in through her nose, out through her mouth.

It was supposed to relax her. It wasn't working. "How optimistic are you feeling right now?"

"It's not a high point," he told her. "I figure they get us on board. If the plane blows up—we're a couple of rogue terrorists that slipped through security."

Blows up. "Conor. Stop a minute." She tried to keep her gorge from rising again. She really did. "I am going to be sick."

He let her pull him backward as she leaned over the crate and puked delicately to the side. She scooted back into place on top of the crate, her back against Conor's. Right now, with nausea from the pregnancy and the adrenaline rush in her veins, blowing up didn't sound so bad.

"Jesus, Cher. It's just getting worse and worse."

He meant her fear of flying. She still hadn't told him about the baby.

"Yeah. If we live through this, I promise—I'll see someone. Really."

Suddenly, he was frantically working at the cuffs, using the bobby pin . . . while Cherish tried to keep it together. Several times, he manipulated the bobby pin into a new angle, tried again.

At one point, she could hear him grunt with his efforts. She felt like puking again, but knew it wasn't a good time— something was happening. Or at least, he was making a lot of noise, which she thought might bode well. She tried taking deep breaths. Conor had arched up against her, prying the bobby pin into the lock.

"Cher," he said, "I think I got—"

With a pinging sound, the bent bobby pin flew out of his grip, arcing through the air like a home run. It landed on the floor of the cargo hold several feet away.

"Shit!" he yelled. *"Shit!"*

She swallowed, seeing their last hope disappear. "It's okay, Conor." By the motion on the plane, she could tell they were lifting off. "It's okay. Oh, God. It's okay. It's okay. Okay, okay. Okayokayokay—"

"Listen to me," he said firmly. "We are not going to die. Do you understand? I will think of something. I'll get us out of here, Cher. I swear!"

"Okayokayokayokay." The pitch of her voice had risen to a tiny squeak.

"What about those visualization exercises you did on the plane?" On the flight from Moscow, he'd talked her through her relaxation exercise, trying to keep her calm. "The white light filling you with warmth? Remember that?" He sat up on his knees, was shucking off his other shoe. "We can do that now. We can try." She thought she could hear him taking his shoelace out. "Here. Give me your foot a minute."

"Oh, Lord." She, too, sat up on her knees, helped Conor ease off one of her shoes, then the other. She squeezed her eyes shut, nausea disappearing into a wave of sheer panic as the plane picked up speed. "Oh, Lord!"

"Just work with me here. Close your eyes and listen to me," he said, taking both her shoelaces out as well. "I have an idea. I'm going to talk you through the accident. Only, this time, we're going to give it a happy ending."

"Oh, Lord help me."

"Close your eyes, Cher."

"My eyes are closed." She swallowed. "I don't know if I can do this."

"Visualize, Cher. Think about the plane. Think about it flying real smooth, going easy."

"Oh, Lord. Okay. Smooth end easy. Oh, God!"

"That's it, sweetheart. Visualize smooth and easy."

"Smooth. So smooth. Smooth like ice cream. And silk. Smoooooth."

She said the word as if she could taste it. Conor closed his eyes with her. He wouldn't admit it to Cher, but this time, he thought they were cooked.

He hadn't a clue how to get them off this plane alive. And he pretty much figured that—whether or not the composite held up—one way or the other, someone would make damn sure this plane didn't land. It was the only reason Reck would let the prototype fly after analyzing the materials Lebredo had surely passed on to him. Two terrorists taken care of. End of threat to Reck's program.

But he saw no sense in spelling it out to Cher right now. Working behind his back, the shoes on the crate between them, he tied their shoelaces together to make a long rope, then knotted the end to one of Cher's tennis shoes, which was considerably lighter than his.

"Okay, so we're flying along." He didn't want her suffering more than she had to and he knew how bad it could get for Cher on a plane. "You're talking to Eric." He threw the shoe, holding onto the laces like a fishing line. But it barely cleared the crate, getting nowhere near the pin. "Everything is going great. Then the turbulence hits," he said, keeping with the visualization as he reeled the shoe in for another try. For a minute there, he thought he'd had the damn cuffs open using the pin. He needed that pin back, dammit.

"Oh, God. The turbulence!"

He realized his mistake. Quickly, he added, "Only, this time, the turbulence stops right away."

"No. No, it's not stopping! It's shaking the plane so hard."

"It's stopping, Cher. Imagine it smooth again."

"I can't. I can't. I can't breathe." She grabbed onto his hand. "The plane is shaking. It's spinning out of control! Henry smashed against the bulkhead. The reporter! Oh my God, his head is gone! Conor, his head is gone!"

"Okay, you're out of the plane," Conor yelled, raising his voice above hers, knowing those nightmares in her head because he'd lived through them, had seen the headless body strapped in the seat next to her when he'd pulled her out of that smoke-filled cabin. With all his heart, he needed to rescue Cher again—

now, at this moment—even if all he could do was get her through her fears.

"All right, Cher," he said. "You're right. It's all gone to shit and the damn thing has broken into pieces." He would take her through the bad part quickly, then move her on to a safe landing. "The worst has happened and you're spinning down to earth."

"I'm spinning down to earth!"

"Only, suddenly, you're not falling anymore. Do you understand?" He was making it up as he went along, thinking that, if he could just get her through the crash and on the ground again, she would be all right. "You're not falling, Cher. No . . . you're floating. That's it. You're floating gently to the ground."

"I'm spinning down to earth!"

"No! No, you're not listening to me. You're floating. Floating." He could feel the plane straightening out from its fast climb. He threw the shoe again. This time it landed closer to the pin, giving him hope. He reeled it in for another try. "You're floating in a beautiful blue sky, Cher. And that sky, my God. It's so clear and blue, it hurts your eyes."

"I'm spinning down to earth!"

"No, Cher. You're floating."

"I'm spinning down to earth!"

"Dammit, Cher—float, don't spin!"

"Float. Okay, float. I have to float."

"That's right, sweetheart. You're floating."

"Float. Don't spin. Float."

But in her head, Cherish was still spinning out of control. She tried to do what Conor said. She focused on the words, the way he said it. Float. It would be a beautiful thing to just float right now. *For the baby,* she thought suddenly. Yes, for the baby growing inside her. She needed to float for the baby.

"And there's nothing but clear blue sky around you," he told her.

"Blue." She licked her lips. "Lots of blue." Blue, like a boy. *My baby and I are floating in blue.*

"And there are these large fluffy white clouds. They're all around you . . . like . . . forests of cotton candy."

"Fluffy clouds." She was taking deep breaths, exhaling completely, careful not to hyperventilate. "Fluffy and white. Lots of blue. I'm going to have a baby, Conor," she told him. "And it's going to be a boy. Because I see lots of blue."

"That's right," Conor said, happy to hear even a thread of something positive in her voice. He threw the shoe, this time, leaning forward to improve his range of motion. But the chain kept him braced to the fuselage. Once again, the shoe didn't land near the pin.

Conor stopped a minute, trying not to panic. *Focus!* "We're going to get through this together, Cher," he said, trying to make her believe it. Trying to make himself believe it. "And then we're going to get married and have lots of babies."

"Blue. Lots of blue."

And then, quite suddenly, for the first time, she did see it. That endless blue sky Conor had been describing. In fact, she *was* floating, just like he told her, floating with her happy, chubby little baby in her arms.

"Lots of beautiful blue all around us."

Conor could hear her calming down. Even her breathing had changed. He could actually feel the difference, her back curving up against his wasn't tensed like before.

"Give me some slack here on the cuffs," he told her. "I'm going for that bobby pin." He threw the shoe again. For the first time, it landed right on the pin. *Thank you, God.* "Just keep thinking beautiful sky . . . lots of clouds." He pulled ever-so-gently, dragging the pin closer to the crate where he might be able to reach it with his foot. He realized that the plane didn't seem to be executing any maneuvers, which was good. If it happened before he got the damn pin, they were completely screwed.

"Oh, Conor!" she said, excited now. "There's this big white light," she added, surprising him. "It's shining right at me, Conor. It's making me warm."

Big white light? He hadn't gotten to that part of the exercise yet. "But you're still floating, right?" He eased the bobby pin closer.

"Wow, I have this incredible sense of euphoria. The light, it's just so comforting."

Conor didn't say anything this time. If she was losing it, at least she was losing it in a nice happy way. He almost had the pin close enough. *Just a little farther now.* But at the last minute, the shoe stumbled over the pin, leaving it behind. Conor closed his eyes, trying not to lose it himself. He leaned forward again. Turning, aiming, he swung his shoulders and tossed the shoe. *Bingo!* "Okay, tell me about the light."

"I've never seen anything like it," she said, her voice full of awe. "It's like those near-death experiences. That tunnel of light they always talk about. Are we dead?"

Not yet. Once again, he dragged the pin a fraction of an inch closer. He was sweating so much, he had to blink to clear his vision. "No, sweetheart. We are very much alive. Tell me more about the light."

"I feel such love, Conor. It's incredible. And I'm not scared. Close your eyes. Maybe you can see the light, too."

He wasn't closing his eyes; he was inching the pin toward the crate. "I have my eyes closed."

"That light is bringing me back to earth," she said, the elation reflected in her voice. "I'm not crashing down like in my dream. I'm floating lightly, gently, to the ground."

It was going to take a hell of a lot more than a big white light for him to feel better right now. The shoe had once again skipped over the pin, leaving it too far away to reach with his foot. He grit his teeth in frustration. God help him, he didn't want to die—didn't want to watch Cher die.

But Cherish wasn't planning on dying. Not today. She was

floating down to earth, her baby in her arms, the light blinding her with its incredible sense of goodness and love.

"Wow," she said under her breath when her imaginary self landed safely, the baby cooing up at her. "That was incredible. Just incredible."

Slowly, the light faded. She realized she was on board the plane, sitting on a crate, her hands still handcuffed and chained to the fuselage. And she wasn't afraid.

"Conor?"

"Yeah, Cher?"

She smiled. "I'm not afraid anymore."

"I'm glad, sweetheart. Really."

"We're not going to die, are we?"

He didn't answer right away. Then, "Not if I can get this damned bobby pin."

Behind her, Conor had slid his body half off the crate, extending his foot out toward the bobby pin . . . but he couldn't quite reach it. Cherish felt her anxiety rise up fresh and new inside her at the sight of the pin just out of reach. *We can't die. Please don't let us die.*

"That would be pretty rotten," she said to herself, speaking out loud, trying to keep the fear out of her voice. "We just found each other again—we should get a happy ending this time. You never even told me you loved me."

She felt Conor collapse on the crate beside her, panting, then stretching again to reach for the bobby pin. "Yes . . . I . . . did." He fairly ground out the words.

Cherish looked up, staring at the ceiling, unable to watch Conor trying so valiantly to reach that pin, only to have it remain an inch out of his reach. She licked her lips, trying to think of something else, anything other than dying. "Trust me, Conor. I would have remembered if you had told me you loved me."

"That first night, upstairs in the Bolkonsky compound." He crawled back onto the crate, leaning up against her, catching his breath. From the corner of her eye, she could see he was getting ready to throw the shoe again. "I told you then, after we made love."

"Okay?" she asked, realizing what he was referring to. "Okay means I love you?" She watched as he threw the shoe, willing it to fall past the pin so he could drag it closer, but he missed.

"Come on, Cher. You knew what I meant that night. Okay, you were right about everything. Okay, I love you. Okay, I can't live without you. Okay, I was miserable for more than a year trying to get over you. All that stuff."

"Oh, yeah. I forgot. We have that ESP thing going. Geez. Even Demi Moore got 'ditto' in *Ghost*."

He flung the shoe. Miraculously, this time it landed on the pin. Conor carefully dragged it toward them, closer and closer to the crate.

"God, I hope this is doing something," he said.

But she wouldn't answer his doubts with her own. They'd cheated death before. *Just one more time, God.*

She could feel the plane vibrating beneath her feet and buttocks. "Conor?" she asked. "This is going to work, isn't it?"

Suddenly, the plane hiccuped, then dipped beneath them, slamming Cherish back against Conor. They both watched as the bobby pin clattered across the cargo hold, falling to the farthest end of the plane, completely out of reach.

Conor closed his eyes. "It's not looking too good right now, Cher."

"Oh, God. Tell me we're going to make it!"

Right then, the cargo door slammed opened.

"Christ, I hope so," a man's voice said from the door. Cherish turned to see the WingMaster pilot walk around the instrument racks and kneel down to fit a tiny key or a lock pick into the cuffs. "But then again, you do seem to be the kiss of death on these planes, little girl."

It was Alec.

Chapter Thirty-One

"All right, boys." Cher spoke from the flight engineer's seat in the cockpit. "What do you want me to do? Serve coffee?"

Despite her brave words, Conor noticed she'd dug her fingers into the armrests of the seat. Still, other than looking a little green around the gills, he thought she was feeling better. This wasn't the woman who had nearly fallen apart in hysterics on the way home from Moscow. In fact, it was the first time he'd seen her on a plane without the whites of her eyes showing all around her pupils.

He handed her a thick book. "Look up radio frequencies. Talk to anyone willing to listen. I have a feeling Reck doesn't want our story to get out."

Shoes on, hands lightly on the yoke, Conor took a quick glance at the instrument panel, checking altitude and speed.

"Like old times, huh?" Alec said, sitting in the copilot's seat beside him.

"What are you doing here, Alec?" Conor asked, honestly surprised. "You're the last person I'd expect to save my butt right now."

"Just goes to show how you can misjudge people."

Conor shook his head, looking at their heading. 190 degrees. "Save it. I don't know what's in it for you, but once this is over, I'm sure as hell going to find out."

Alec grinned. "Just as I said," he repeated, "like old times."

"Not hardly," Conor answered.

Alec had told them he'd cold-cocked the pilot, then took the man's place and joined the flight crew on board. Wearing the pilot's uniform, he hadn't had any trouble getting past security and, once he was on board, no one had argued with the Glock he carried. He'd tied the flight crew up in the cabin, leaving them there. After he'd set the autopilot on a smooth course into the LA basin, he'd gone back to the cargo hold for Conor and Cherish.

"Now that you're through making us travel the world over for clues," Conor asked, "are you going to wait until the composites on this thing give way before you fill me in? Come on, Alec. I'm not looking for any repeat performances."

"You didn't crash the first-phase prototype, Conor," he said, completely serious for once. "You were right all along. It was the onboard computer. Reck's people programmed the software to do the opposite of whatever you told the plane. At a given command, the whole thing went nuts on us. The telemetry would read like a PIO. I discovered what happened a few weeks after the safety board came down with their recommendation against you—but someone took a few potshots at me. I thought it was in my best interest to disappear . . . if I wanted to stay alive, that is."

"What about the composites on the wing for this prototype? Are we going down in a blaze of glory?"

"Not according to my analysis," Alec told him. "If you don't do anything cute, like put it into a five-g dive, we should be okay." He grinned. "But there is one problem."

"And that would be?"

Alec glanced at Cherish. She was trying to reach someone on

the different frequencies. Alec leaned in close, so she wouldn't overhear. "There's a bomb on board," he told Conor in *sotto voce*. "It could be set to altitude or time, so we can't land until we know the trigger mechanism. The trick is, I can't find the damn thing. And believe me, I've tried."

Conor jumped out of the pilot's chair, not even bothering to take the time to get worried. He headed back to the cargo hold, Alec close at his heels. If Reck or Kinnard had planned to blow them sky-high, they wouldn't want to leave any clues for the investigators afterward. Someone had to be damn sure that, whatever pieces the investigators found, they'd be incinerated beyond recognition. Which meant two things: There was a lot of fuel on board, and he and Cher had been sitting right on top of the trigger.

He found it quickly enough. Inside the crate where he and Cherish had been manacled next to the fuselage wall.

"What is it?" Cherish stepped in from the cabin. "What are you guys doing back here? What's going on?"

Working together, Alec and Conor had managed to pry off the top of the crate. The bomb lay nestled inside a mountain of sawdust. They were looking down at a small digital readout display. Conor estimated about thirty pounds of plastic explosives lay under the mechanism.

"It's a bomb?" Cherish asked, stepping up behind Conor to look down inside the crate. She'd sounded almost conversational, as if she'd asked, *it's a jack-in-the-box?*

And then, dropping to her knees beside Conor, "IT'S A BOMB!"

Conor looked at Alec across the crate. "I sure as hell don't know what to do right now, unless it's push this thing out the hatch and cross my fingers."

"I wouldn't move it," Alec said, his eyes on the mechanism. "Not unless it's your deepest desire to blow yourself into a million tiny pieces."

Alec got up and headed back into the cabin. When he

returned, he had a small tool kit, the kind that unrolled with a screwdriver, hammer, and pliers inside canvas pockets. Cherish was pacing back and forth, talking to herself, mumbling something about a "bomb" and "those bastards" and "wringing Reck's scrawny neck." Conor just hoped she'd get the chance. He stared at the numbers, watching them count down. They had less than five minutes to go.

Alec carefully unscrewed the casing, taking his time. Checking things out every step of the way, he looked as if he knew what he was doing. He didn't slow down until he had the whole thing dismantled inside its nest of sawdust.

He'd exposed three wires. Alec put the clippers around the red one, but didn't cut. For the first time, he hesitated. He seemed to be thinking it over. Then slowly, he took the clippers away. He put them around the white wire, but just as quickly, changed his mind, going back to the red one.

Conor glanced at the digital readout. They were down to less than a minute.

But Alec wasn't cutting. He was staring at the wires, perspiration beading on his forehead, the time ticking down on the digital display.

"Cut it!" Cher said, standing over him. "Why isn't he cutting it?"

To Conor, Alec didn't look so confident anymore. Like maybe he just realized he'd done something wrong. For an instant, Alec let the cutters nearly pull free of the red wire, appearing as if he was going back to the white wire. But then he pushed the clippers back onto the red one.

"Cut it, Alec. Cut it!" Cherish shouted.

Ten seconds remained on the readout.

Alec looked up. Conor had never seen that expression on his face. A look of absolute dread. Alec turned to Cherish. He wasn't cutting.

Eight seconds.

Still staring at Cherish, Alec said, "Dear God in heaven."

Six seconds.

"What?" Cherish screamed, frantic now. "What is it? What's wrong?"

Five, four . . .

That's it, Conor thought. *We're toast.*

Incredibly, a grin split Alec's face.

"Gotcha," he said softly.

He cut the wire.

The clock stopped.

Two seconds remained frozen on the digital display.

Cherish fell to her knees, her legs collapsing under her. She rolled onto her back and half curled into a fetal position. "You are sick. You're a sick man." She took a couple of gulps of air. "I'm stuck on a plane with a lunatic."

But Conor held Alec's gaze. "No," Conor said. "Nothing so special. Just an asshole."

Alec kept his grin. "I couldn't resist."

Conor pivoted away, sick to death of Alec and his games. Instead, he turned his attention to Cherish, stepping over to help her. "Did you get through to anyone on the radio?" he asked.

"LAX." She rose slowly. "They want to know your flight plan. I tried to explain our situation; they took me for a loony. They want to speak to a sane person." She was on her hands and knees, her head still hanging. "That would be you, Conor."

Conor gave her a hand up. They would be coming in over the mountains into the LA basin now. But when the three of them reached the cockpit, they had another surprise. Two of them actually. F-15 fighter jets. One on each wing of the prototype.

" . . . will land immediately," the radio blared into his ears when Conor put on the headset. "You have confiscated government property. You will return to Edwards Air Force Base and follow us in for landing or we will be forced to shoot down the plane. Repeat. You will land this plane immediately or we will be forced to shoot you down."

Before Conor could respond, Alec stopped him from activating the mike. "If you follow these guys in, we're dead. Kinnard is behind everything and he has his own operatives to clean up loose ends like us."

Conor shook off Alec's hand. "I've made their acquaintance." Activating his mike, he spoke into the radio, "This is Lieutenant-Colonel Mitchell," he said, using his old military rank. "We have a special situation on board. We have just dismantled a bomb—"

"We know about the bomb, Mitchell."

The voice coming through the headset didn't belong to the F-15 pilot, but Conor recognized it just the same. Joseph Kinnard.

"We know you brought the mechanism on board the Wing-Master," Kinnard added.

"He's on the damn F-15," Alec said. He whistled. "Christ. That's pretty ballsy for an old guy."

"It's time to give up," Kinnard said. "We know all about you and Miss Malone's connection to the Marduk group. With or without your cooperation, we're bringing you both in."

"What about the flight crew on board," Conor radioed back. "Are you willing to shoot them down as well?"

"Hostages won't help you, Mitchell. Those are military men, just as you were once. They know what they signed on for." And then, "Come on, Mitchell. The two of you are up there all alone. Do you really want her to die with you on that plane?"

"This is LAX approach," the radio crackled in his headset before Conor could respond. "You are entering a sector of heavy air traffic. You have private plane traffic taking off from El Monte and a 747 at your nine o'clock position, descending through 3,000. Please, increase altitude to 5,000 feet and increase air speed to 180 knots, heading two seven zero. Do you copy that?"

Conor stared at the instruments, then glanced at the two F-

15 jets. He thought about what to do, quickly going through the options. There weren't many. "Negative, approach," he responded. "This is Air Force XC-23. I am flying a military prototype. We have an emergency involving national security on board. We will maintain our present altitude, speed, and direction until we speak to Special Agent Luis Lebredo of the FBI. Did you copy that, approach? Agent Luis Lebredo. Please contact the FBI immediately."

He saw Cherish raise her brows. He continued, this time speaking to the F-15 pilots and Kinnard, "Do you get the picture, gentlemen? To put it bluntly, I'm hanging my ass here, slow and low, right smack over the LA basin. You can take your shot . . . if you want to have this prototype raining down on a couple of hundred of our taxpayers. At the moment, I suggest everyone just back off." To Alec and Cherish, he said, "Hang on. We're going off autopilot."

"Giddy-up," Alec said.

Cherish leaned down over the controls. She looked out at the F-15 jets, watching them slow down. The prototype looked like a great lumbering ox next to the slim lines of the fighters. The F-15 Eagles weren't built for slow speeds like the cargo prototype. To stay with Conor, they had to travel in circles.

The prototype was down to half the fighters' minimum rate of speed. Right outside the window, Cherish watched the jets circling like hornets to keep pace with Conor. "How long before we cross the basin?" she asked.

"We have thirty minutes to play with," he said, concentrating on the instrument panel.

She nodded, taking up the flight engineer's headset. "Move aside, boys," she told both men. "This is a job for a professional. Los Angeles approach," she said into the radio, "this is Cherish Malone, director of public relations for Marquis Aircraft. I am currently on board a military prototype whose wings contain an experimental composite material that is disintegrating. I repeat, the material is disintegrating. Five weeks ago, a prototype of the same make crashed at Edwards—just check your headlines, gentlemen. The cause for that crash was not, I repeat, *not* a bomb. If you have any problem believing this story, contact Special Agent Lebredo. He can verify how dangerous the situation is up here.''

''Not bad,'' Conor said.

''That's what I thought,'' she said. ''But somehow it carries more weight with two F-15 jets on your tail. Do you think Lebredo will back us?''

It was what Conor was betting on, their last chance. ''If he's even half the agent he appears to be, he'll have checked out the operation in Siberia. Maybe he can't find evidence to nail Kinnard right off the bat, but I gave him enough to at least make him suspicious. And the man looked plenty miffed when those operatives showed up and took custody. A lot of these alphabet agencies are real touchy about their jurisdiction.''

''I'm calculating that we have approximately twenty minutes of fuel left at our current rate of speed, kids,'' Alec said, his eyes on the fuel gauge.

The radio came to life again. ''Listen to me.'' It was Kinnard. ''We've been on to your operation for weeks now, Mitchell. That's why we were ready for you when you entered the country from Russia. You and I both know, if it comes to it, we'll be forced to blow you out of the sky—''

''Put a sock in it, Kinnard,'' Cherish said, cutting him off, ''I'm talking to someone important here. LA approach,'' she said, not missing a beat. ''Can you locate Agent Lebredo for us?''

''We're patching him through now on his cell phone.''

They waited. The cockpit felt tense, as if they were holding their collective breath. Suddenly, Lebredo's voice blared through the headsets, ''How the hell did you two get up there?'' He sounded out of breath.

''Agent Lebredo,'' Cherish said. ''You can't imagine how happy I am to hear your voice. About our situation—''

"I'm familiar with your situation," he said, cutting her off. "I've been looking for both of you. So have half the agents out here. We believe you can provide critical testimony vital to this country's national security."

"I hope to God this guy's the cavalry, Conman," Alec said, looking out the window at the F-15 banking in front of them. "We're running out of time here."

Cherish glanced at Conor. "Does he mean what I think he means?" she asked, referring to Lebredo.

"Can you land this thing or not?" Lebredo asked, not elaborating on who Cherish and Conor would be testifying against. But it had to be Kinnard.

Conor took over, speaking into the headset. "That all depends on where you want me to bring this bird down."

"El Toro," Lebredo said. "We'll be ready for you there. By the way, I've been talking to a friend of yours. Valerie."

"He means Va*le*ri," Cherish said, using the correct pronunciation. "He believes us."

"Maybe," Conor said.

"Well, well. Will you look at that," Alec said.

Right then, both F-15 jets turned, barreling past in the opposite direction. Conor reached down to dial in the new heading. "Let's hope that's a good sign."

They increased their airspeed and altitude until they reached a cruising speed of 180 knots, heading for El Toro. For the next ten minutes, a tense quiet filled the cockpit; each was lost in their own thoughts. Eventually, Conor looked over at Alec.

Alec gave him a thumbs-up. "We're going to beat this bastard, Conman. You see if we don't."

But Conor wasn't so sure. There was a lot out of their control right now. He reached behind him for Cherish, squeezed her hand. "How are you doing?"

"Me?" she asked, sitting in the flight engineer's seat. "Heck, this isn't even exciting after what we've been through," she said, lying through her teeth.

"That's my Cher."

He didn't release her hand. He had no idea what waited for them at the end of the line. Lebredo was the only insurance they had. It would be much harder for Kinnard to take care of his messy "loose ends" when they had an FBI agent waiting for them to land. But at best, it was flimsy insurance.

Conor stared ahead, thinking about that. Worried. He tried to concentrate on the instruments, honing in on El Toro ahead. Tried to keep focused. *First you land, then you deal with Kinnard.* He changed the radio frequency for El Toro, decreased altitude.

A light flashed inside his head, right behind his eyes. He blinked, trying to get his focus back.

Another flash. He shook his head, feeling his pulse racing, his heart jump-starting in his chest, just as it had that day over a year ago. *Shake it off.* He glanced over at Alec, seeing if he'd noticed anything wrong.

Flash! Alec talking to him, smiling that Alec-knows-best smile.

Flash! The red warning light. *Losing altitude!*

Conor closed his eyes and buried the heels of his palms against them. He thought he could hear Cher asking him what was wrong . . .

The ground came racing up—the horizon spun like a top. *Screams, coming from the cabin.* He covered his ears with his hands, but he could hear Alec yelling: *Right engine flame out!*

The plane sliced to the right, yawing out of control. *We're going to stall!* Conor remembered pulling back hard on the yoke; kicking in right rudder.

Alec shouting—*turn the goddamn thing off, it's going to kill us!*

Isn't it true, Colonel, that if you had simply let go of the controls, let the computer take over . . .

Alec's face, twisted in fear—*turn it off; the damn thing is going to kill us!*

"Conor!"

He opened his eyes. Cher was right there with him, her severe-clear blue eyes furrowed in concern, her soft hands cupped around his face.

"Are you okay?" she asked. She stroked his face as if feeling for a fever. "You don't look so good, honey."

"Conman?" Alec asked.

He turned to Alec. The images in his head changed. Like a film when it's about to break, the frames slowed down so that you could catch sight of each picture in distinct bites.

Alec, less than an hour ago, sitting there, cool as can be. *I found out later that Reck's people fixed the onboard computer . . . made it look like a PIO.*

Alec, the day of the crash, screaming, *turn it off—the damn thing is going to kill us!*

He'd meant the computer. He'd wanted Conor to turn off the onboard computer.

"Hey, Conman. You okay?" Alec asked. "Cherish is right. You *don't* look so good, guy. You want me to take her in?"

"No," Conor said.

A year and a half ago, up in the air—right before they had pancaked in, killing three people and almost dying themselves—Alec had begged him to turn off the computer.

Suddenly, a loud creaking filled the cockpit, sweeping over them in a groaning crescendo. All three glanced around, searching for the source of the noise. Under his breath, Alec said, "Oh, shit."

Crack!

"The right aileron!" Alec yelled.

The plane yawed to the right erratically, then pitched into a free fall. For an instant, Conor thought he'd lapsed into another vision, but the yoke he grabbed was all too real, the plane's violent slice across the sky was happening now. They'd lost all directional controls.

Just ahead, low on the horizon, he could see the parallel

lines of the runways beckon, the flight line at El Toro. Working the throttles with his right hand, Conor eased back the lever controlling the right engine, adding power, using thrust differential on the engines to keep her aiming for the runway. When the left wing dropped, Conor powered up the left engine, switching back and forth between the two engines, trying to keep the wobbly bird straight and level in the air. But the plane responded like a car on ice, sliding left, then right, the banking turns too wide, almost fishtailing, making him overcompensate, feeling out of control.

Conor fought the yoke. No response. *Shit!* Going to the engines again, he reduced power in discreet increments, sinking the bird toward the runway. He kept on the power settings, adjusting the engines to bring her in. But they were gathering speed, dropping too fast.

"You said the composites would hold up!" he shouted at Alec.

"I miscalculated. El Toro approach," Alec shouted into his headset. "We've lost control surfaces. Using thrust differential to control. We need to make an emergency landing. Repeat. We need clearance for an emergency landing!"

Another *bang,* followed by a sickening roar, pulsed through the cabin like a great beast howling. *We're breaking up . . .* Conor's head kicked back. *Wham!* Something hit the back of his skull, making him see stars. *We can't recover!*

No, he thought. Not again, dammit!

He squeezed the throttles in a white-knuckle grip, struggling with the power settings . . . *sonofabitch doesn't want to listen . . .* he had to keep her straight and level . . . *only three thousand feet from dying . . .* in his mind, he could see Cherish hanging on, but he forced his attention on the instruments . . . if he let go, even for an instant, they would fall into a spin, cartwheel across the runway, and the show was over.

He kept fighting her, praying nothing else would break off, hearing the creaking of the wings . . . *the ground's coming up too fast* ... Alec screamed over and over, *Emergency! Emergency, Right aileron gone!* ... it was a bronco bust and the beast wouldn't say die ... Conor adjusted to left engine— then the right ... *decrease power for landing* ... the runway was a mere twenty degrees below the horizon ... *coming in, coming in!* ... the runway careened toward them like a bull's-eye ... *just a few feet more* ... just a little more ... a little more ... Cut power!

Bam! The wheels bounced off the runway, slamming them back into their seats. *Bam!*

Reverse thrusters! Conor punched the brakes ... the wailing scream of grinding metal rolled over them in wave after shrieking wave. The right wing dug into the runway, ripping off. Losing the front wheel, the nose executed a belly flop onto the concrete, the fuselage steaming down the centerline, sparks flying. The big bird yawed to the right, slid off the runway into the weed-choked ground.

"Hold on!" he screamed.

The back wheels buckled beneath them, sucked into the dirt. The plane slid, lurching forward, bouncing in teeth-shattering jolts. Debris crashed through the cockpit. *Boom . . boom . . . boom!* All three were tossed forward, then whipped back into their seats as the plane came to an abrupt halt.

"Get the hell out!" Conor yelled. Seeing Cher hesitate, he commanded Alec, "Get her out of here!"

Conor stripped off the safety harness and raced into the cabin. He found the flight engineer and copilot tied up in the last two seats. The flight engineer was unconscious, bleeding at the temple. Conor knelt down, began working the knots on the rope. "I'll get you out of here, guys," he said, trying to sound reassuring.

Incredibly, just beside him, Cherish dropped down in front of the copilot. She reached for the rope strapping the man to his seat.

"What the hell are you doing here!" Conor yelled.

"Trying to help you." She kept at the ropes, struggling with the knots, ignoring him.

"There's more than six thousand pounds of fuel on board!" Conor shouted at her. "I can do this without your help. Swear to God, Cher. Get out!"

But she wasn't listening, still working the knots. He thought he heard her say under her breath, "I'm not afraid."

The flight engineer moaned, regaining consciousness. The copilot burst free of his ropes, then helped Conor pick up the flight engineer, the man groaning as he flopped his arms around their shoulders. Together, Conor and the copilot carried the flight engineer between them, Cherish leading the way down the aisle.

Outside, they could hear sirens on the field. By the time they climbed down, fire crews were already pouring an ocean of white foam on the plane. The four of them hobbled across the airfield, taking the injured flight engineer onto the grass a safe distance away. They hailed the ambulance, Cherish jumping up and down, waving her arms in the air. Two medics hopped out of the emergency vehicle and ran toward them.

Kaboom! The late morning lit up in an explosion of orange. A wave of heat burst over them, stinging their eyes, almost burning in its force. Men shouted in warning, shifting the direction of the foam. Another blast echoed across the field. Fire like molten lava spewed into the sky.

Cherish, back-lit by the fire, turned to Conor. "I wasn't afraid," she told him.

Conor grabbed Cherish, holding her so tight. "Dear God, Cher." He couldn't hold her tight enough. "Dear God." He kissed her, again and again. "I was, sweetheart. Dear God, I was."

Chapter Thirty-Two

Sydney picked up the phone on the second ring. "Hello?" The word came out breathy, anxious. She'd been waiting all day for this call.

At first, it surprised her to hear a woman's voice on the line and not Alec's. But after she hung up, she smiled, thinking, *it's Alec.* Of course, there was a woman involved.

Sydney sat back in the Chippendale love seat she'd bought for her husband, in a room that she'd decorated to please him. She smiled, rising from the upholstered seat, feeling very good and very ready.

It was time.

Two hours later, she heard a key opening the front door. *Russell, coming home.* She wondered if she imagined that frantic cadence to his breathing. She knew they'd arrested Joseph Kinnard—the voice on the phone had told her that much. Soon, they would come looking for Russell.

She heard something drop. Papers? A long string of expletives followed. She smiled, imagining him laden with his treasures, all the things he would need to exonerate himself. The first place he'd go would be his office. She planned to beat him there.

When Russell stepped into his office, Sydney was already seated behind his desk. On top of the burled wood, she'd set out discreet, organized piles of documents, each representing a paper trail exposing his crimes. Sydney held her hands on her lap, waiting.

"Syd! Shit. You scared me." She could see his eyes almost darting around the room. He wasn't even looking at her. She was as invisible as the wallpaper behind her. He would be thinking frantically of where he'd left everything, how long it would take him to gather it. He already had his hands full of accordion folders. These he dropped on one of the guest chairs.

"Look, Syd. Honey. This isn't a good time—"

He stopped. He was looking at the piles on his desk, frowning. "What the hell—"

That's when she pulled out the gun. "Sit down, Russell."

She saw his eyes widen. Now, she wasn't invisible. Now, she had his complete attention.

He did as she said, dropping into the other guest chair. "Syd, what in the world—"

"It's all there, Russell. Financial records, tax forms, your personal diary. A nice trail of bread crumbs showing how you convinced Henry that his poor little wife needed extra financial protection. And he did everything you told him to do because it all made such sense—putting it all in my name, buying the extra shares. Nothing obvious, like an insurance policy. Henry wouldn't have known we were having an affair—wouldn't think that, in two weeks, he would be dead and you would get it all. But you knew."

He was shaking his head. "God, Syd. What are you talking about?"

"And the Pegasus Satellite. You tied up everything this company owns in that project. And why would you do that?

Did you perhaps know something no one else was aware of? Something involving''—still keeping her eyes on Russ, she picked up sheets from his personal diary—''a black project? A special composite that only you could develop and test, while none of your competitors even knew what to look for because it was hidden right there, before their eyes, buried in a very public program, the XC-23 WingMaster?''

''I did it for you, Syd.'' He spoke softly, sounding so honest, almost torn. ''It was our future, the Pegasus. And you were never going to leave Henry. You would have lost interest in me, stayed with him out of a sense of obligation. He was talking about kids, Sydney. What was I supposed to do? Let you get pregnant? You would never have left him then. You would have cut me off. I panicked, Syd. I admit it.''

''You're an animal, Russell,'' she said, hearing his appalling rationalizations. What had Alec said? Two birds with one stone? Because Russell was right. If she'd become pregnant, she would have put a stop to their affair—and she would have stayed with Henry.

''You cheated on me, Russell. That, I could have forgiven,'' she told him quite calmly. ''You wouldn't give me children. Even that, I could have lived with. But you killed Henry. And I don't believe it was for us, Russell. Despite the lack of backbone I have shown these last years, I am not that naive. Not anymore.''

She held up the gun propped by her other hand, ready to fire, bracing herself against the recoil.

''My God, Syd. What are you doing!''

''The FBI is on its way.'' For the first time, she smiled. ''And while you're in jail or prison or some federal penitentiary for the rich and powerful,'' she added, ''I plan to clean you out of every dime, every art object, every home—everything you've managed to shelter against your other wives who were foolish enough to sign your damned prenups. I'm going to leave you, the powerful Russell Reck—The Wrecker—completely alone, growing old and feeble, without a penny to your name. And I hope, that with that image in my head, I can finally get on with my life. I didn't save Henry, but at least I stopped you from destroying anyone else.''

He was shaking his head, looking truly frightened.

''But if you move even an inch, Russell dearest, I'll just have to settle for the sight of you lying in that chair with a bullet between your eyes.''

Conor found Alec waiting in one of the hangars, smoking in a far corner, ignoring the danger posed by the fuel drums nearby. He dropped the cigarette to the concrete and crushed it under his shoe. ''So what does this FBI agent of yours have to say?''

''That Kinnard is history. Unauthorized use of government funds, a pile of regulations he's ignored, misuse of defense intelligence. Apparently, the executive branch doesn't like learning about these covert operations after the fact. The president has the attorney general on it. Lebredo was trying to find us, the key witnesses, before he tipped his hand to Kinnard and closed down the XC-23 program.''

''Great,'' Alec said, looking relieved. ''So everything is taken care of? We're free to go, right? I mean, of course, we'll need to testify about what we know. And hell, they'll probably reinstate us now that they know the crash wasn't pilot error—''

''How did you fix the computer?''

''What?'' Alec stepped forward, still smiling. ''What are you talking about, Conman? What computer?''

''The software for the onboard computer. For the first-phase prototype.''

Alec's eyes registered something, a hesitation, before he said, ''Hey, that wasn't me. That was Reck's people. I told you. Kinnard and his black ops—''

''Did you work for Kinnard? Were you one of his opera-

tives?'' And then, before Alec could protest again, he added,
''I remembered, Alec. Right before we landed. I went through
the first crash again in my head, the one we walked away from
a year and half ago. And I remembered how, when we were
going down, you kept shouting, 'turn the damn thing off. It's
going to kill us.' ''

Alec didn't answer. His eyes narrowed, and then he grinned.
''I should have told you to throw the paddle switch on the
yoke. But I panicked. You didn't know I was talking about the
computer.''

''You switched out the software on the WingMaster for the
bugged one?''

Alec nodded. ''Right before the test flight. Kinnard recruited
me years ago, buddy. Apparently, I had the right personality
profile. Always getting into trouble, looking for it. But a damn
good pilot.''

''And a genius with computers. Your specialty.''

''But they double-crossed me, Conman. They thought I was
getting greedy.'' He shook his head, raking his hand through
that short, bleached hair Conor would never get used to seeing
on him. ''I just got so damn sick of it all. I wanted out.'' He
focused on Conor as if trying to make him understand. ''So I
told them I would change out the bugged software for the two
million. The way I saw it, the military didn't pay shit, and I
didn't want to freelance for Kinnard anymore. I guess I pushed
him a little too hard.'' He took another step toward Conor,
holding out his hand as if pleading with him. ''Listen to me,
Conor. They told me the software would make the plane look
bad—only that. Then the contract would be canceled. Believe
me, I had no idea they were trying to crash the damn thing.
You know that's true. I wasn't trying to get us killed, man.''

''But it was all right to ruin my career? That was an accept-
able cost for your blood money?''

Alec had the decency to look away. ''I felt . . . bad about

that. Shit, Conman, I wanted out of Kinnard's organization. I was desperate."

"And when you walked away from the crash, they came after you. They had to. You knew too much. There really was someone trying to kill you. That's why you started traveling, never staying too long in one place."

"The loose end. That's me. I was trying to figure out a way to fix it for us," Alec said, and the way he spoke, Conor wondered if he'd actually deluded himself into believing it. "And then this woman, Allison, she finds me. She says she's from the Millennium Society. Eric was a sort of mentor to her. She told me she knew it was all fixed, the crash, that Reck wanted Joystick's research on the fullerenes. She wanted to avenge Eric's death. So we started working together."

"Joseph Kinnard wanted Eric dead."

He nodded. "Eric was going to cut off the government. With his Russians and his Millennium pal, Dean White, he was going it alone. That's what killed him. Kinnard thought Eric might actually pull it off."

"How far up does this go?"

He shook his head. "Who knows? Far enough."

"Monster things, Alec? Isn't that what you said to me?"

Hearing Cherish's voice, both men turned to face the hangar door. Cherish stepped inside, walking toward them, her short curls disheveled, soot on her cheek. "Damn you, Alec. I believed in you! How could you do that to us? To me and Conor. We were your friends. If you would have asked us . . . explained . . ." She shook her head, the pain she felt so clearly coming through in her expressive voice. "I would have given my life for you. And Conor. My God, he *has*—he's sacrificed so much for you. Over and over. But all this time, you were using us. So that we could make it safe for you?"

"I was trying to expose the bad guys," Alec argued. "Get Kinnard and Reck out of the game. They would have killed you, Cherish. You were the only connection between the two programs, you see? You worked with Eric on those fullerenes. You would always be a danger to them, someone who could put it together.''

"No way. You didn't do any of this for me," she said adamantly, looking regal and impervious as she stepped closer. "This was all about you, Alec. Getting us to do your dirty work, making *us* take the chances. Then, when it's safe, you walk away with . . . what was it? Two million and some? You were hoping to get the money. But even if they paid you, you knew you weren't safe until Conor and I exposed the operation."

He shook his head, his eyes narrowing. Conor watched as Alec reached back, his hand easing under his jacket. *Shit!*

Before Conor could stop him, Alec pulled out his gun and trained it on Cher. "I did it for us, Cherish," he told her, backing away. "I love you. I *need* you. Can't you see that, little girl? I came back for you. This was the only way."

"Think about what you're doing, Alec," Conor said, circling toward him, holding his hands out to show he wasn't armed. "You don't really want to hurt Cherish. You love her, remember?"

But Alec wasn't listening to Conor. He was focused only on Cherish, on convincing her. "It was always Conor you wanted," he said. "This guilt-ridden ass, who couldn't even take the goods when you threw yourself at him! But I came back for you. He didn't want you and I risked everything for your love!" He was completely focused on her, a half smile on his face. "You remember that night, don't you? The night Conor didn't show up? Because, I sure as hell can't forget it."

"Things have changed," she said.

"Oh sure, but only because I threw the two of you together. Nothing changed before that, did it?" He skirted around Conor, still moving toward the hangar doors. Only Cherish moved with him, keeping between him and the doors. "Is that what you want, little girl?" he asked, jogging his head back at Conor.

"Some idiot who can't even make up his mind unless someone pushes you in his face? Or do you want a man who would risk it all to get you back?"

"I think I'll take the idiot," she said.

Even Alec had to laugh. "Whatever." But then he shook his head, as if he didn't understand. "I could have left you on that plane today. I had everything I needed—but I came back for you. I didn't let you die up there. I love you, little girl." There was real emotion in his voice. "And he will *never* love you the way I do."

But she only shook her head. "How can you love me, Alec? You don't know how to love."

He stopped, looking as if she'd slapped him. At that precise moment, Conor made his move.

He launched himself straight at Alec, seizing the hand holding the gun. With his foot, he swept Alec's feet out from under him. But Alec reached out and grabbed Conor at the last minute, bringing Conor down with him.

Both men fought for control of the gun, wrestling each other. Cherish searched the hangar for a weapon, any weapon. A stick or a heavy tool. Anything. Seeing a crowbar, she raced over to grab it off the floor. But before she could even pick it up, she watched, horrified, as Alec swung his hand back.

"Alec! No!" she screamed.

Catching Conor off guard, Alec struck him with the butt of the gun across the face, hitting the scar dead-on. Cherish heard a dreadful *crack,* then watched as Conor crumpled to the ground.

Alec stood over him, panting. When Conor groaned, pushing up with his hands, Alec pistol-whipped Conor again, hard across the back of his head. Conor dropped to the concrete. This time, he didn't move.

Alec turned the Glock on Cherish. He wiped away a dribble of blood from the corner of his mouth using his free hand. "Okay," he said, still panting from the effort of fighting Conor. "So the guy in the white hat wins again. *Ciao,* little girl. I hope you realize someday what I did for you, getting on that plane.''

But instead of letting him pass, Cherish turned and grabbed the crowbar from the floor. She held it braced in both hands, standing her ground. "I'm not letting you leave," she said, moving with him, keeping between him and the door. "You'll have to shoot me first, Alec."

Alec frowned. "Get out of my way, Cherish."

"No, Alec. I am not letting you get away with this. Not this time. No way. This time, you're taking responsibility."

She wasn't afraid. Even witnessing Alec's vicious attack on Conor, she didn't believe Alec would hurt her. Not the man who had taken a bullet for her, who had boarded a plane he knew was sabotaged.

"What are you going to do to me, Alec?" she asked, walking toward him, still holding the crowbar, having the satisfaction of watching him take several steps back, away from her. She nodded at the gun. "Are you really going to shoot me? You said you loved me."

"Let him go," Conor groaned the words. He was struggling to get up, shaking his head as if disoriented. "He's not worth it, Cher."

"Are you going to shoot me, Alec?"

"Cher!" Conor yelled, trying to warn her.

"Damn you," Alec said. "Couldn't you have let me be just a little good?"

He pulled the trigger.

She heard the sound of the bullet, felt it echo across the empty hangar. The sound wasn't even loud—the gun had a silencer—only a sharp *pop*. It was incredible how the pain came so much after the sound. It took her time to let it register, to even realize what had happened.

He shot me. Alec had shot her.

Almost as if she was watching a movie, she saw herself fall to her knees, then drop the crowbar. She collapsed to the cold concrete, her cheek pressing against the floor. She must have passed out, because, when she opened her eyes, Alec was standing over her.

"Maybe you're right, little girl," he said. "Maybe he is the better man."

She could hear him running, the echo of his footsteps sounding as if it were coming from beyond a long tunnel. The pain in her shoulder was excruciating. She blinked up at the steel girders of the hangar ceiling. *He shot me.*

But then, Conor's face came into view. He looked so worried, checking her over, not saying a word. He was kneeling beside her, gently pulling down the sleeve of her shirt to examine the bullet wound.

"He shot me." She was breathing fast and hard, almost panting. "I can't believe he shot me." She stared at Conor as if to ask, how could this happen? It didn't make sense to her. "Right in the exact place where he took a bullet for me."

Conor had taken off his shirt. She could see the side of his face swelling grotesquely where Alec had struck him with the gun. She wanted to reach up and soothe the hurt, but she couldn't move her arm.

"On that plane," she said, blinking hard, trying to keep her focus, "he risked everything to save us. He knew there was a bomb on board. Why do that then shoot me?"

Conor folded his shirt and wrapped it around the bullet wound, applying pressure there. "He was willing to take risks, Cher. But just now, you cornered him. You weren't giving him a choice."

She kept breathing fast because she couldn't seem to get enough air in her lungs. And the pain. It hurt so much. "He's going to get away."

"Yup." Conor stood, then reached down and picked her up. He carried her toward the hangar door, cradling her against his chest. "The bullet only grazed the skin, but you're bleeding pretty bad."

She stared at him. She couldn't even raise her arms to loop them around his neck. "I didn't think I was wrong about him."

"Well, you were, damn it."

"Conor? Am I wrong about you?"

He sighed, looking at her with those clear hazel eyes she loved so much. "No," he said. "You're not wrong about me, Cher. You never were."

Chapter Thirty-Three

Alec stood at the corner, behind the gas station, leaning against the stucco wall. Barstow was almost bearable this time of year. Just a hot dry wind. In a backpack at his feet, he'd packed most of his belongings, including his laptop. He held his head tipped back, eyes closed, enjoying the warmth of the sun. He'd been waiting half an hour. She was late.

He wondered how Cherish and Conor were doing. No doubt, he'd married her by now. There weren't any misgivings in Conor's eyes the last time Alec had seen them together. No way. And Cherish. Well, she was just what he'd always thought she was. Cherish the Strong. Cherish the Beautiful. So pure, the bastards hadn't beaten her. His Valkyrie of Good—too good for him, as it turned out.

God, he'd hated shooting her.

Right then, a Mercedes convertible came up the drive of the gas station, blaring its horn. At the wheel, a redhead with sunglasses and scarf, Jacki-O style, waved at him. She pulled up right alongside him. He hopped inside and she peeled off.

Alec leaned back against the plush leather. He took off his hat and pushed his hand through his hair, dyed back to its original color black. He wasn't fooling anyone anymore. Time to hightail it out of town. Which he'd been about to do when he got her page.

He glanced over at Sydney. She looked good. Real good, in fact. Happy. "You surprised me, you know. Paging me like that."

"Is that so?" she said. "Well, it's good to see that people can still surprise you."

"Hell, yeah." He tipped his hat down against the sun. Allison, for example. For a year, she'd acted as if she couldn't live or breathe two feet away from him. Then suddenly, she vanishes. She'd left a note at his motel room.

You did the right thing helping your friends, Alec. But it wasn't enough for me.

Funny, he'd never thought she'd been with him because he'd been doing "the right thing." But then again, he'd gotten revenge for her dear old Eric. Maybe she'd fooled him. Maybe that's what she'd been after all along.

"So why'd you do it?" he asked Sydney. "Why'd you ask me along?"

When he'd called her, she'd told him she was divorcing Reck and leaving town. She was heading for parts unknown. She needed a traveling companion. Was he interested?

"What you said to me that night you broke in," she told him, keeping her eyes on the road ahead, her red hair streaming forward with the wind. "That I reminded you of yourself. Someone under the thumb of another, a person you're supposed to trust, but who hurts you, again and again. And you're powerless to do anything about it." She looked over at him. "I think those words changed my life."

She really was a beautiful woman, Alec thought, watching her. And there was this strength to her now, like maybe, having defeated Reck, she could go on, reach some potential The Wrecker had kept her from achieving.

He reached over, his hand on her shoulder. "Maybe it's not too late for us, huh, Sydney?"

She glanced at him and frowned. Suddenly, she started to laugh. "Oh, Alec. This isn't about sex."

He pulled his hand away, raising his brows in question. "Yeah? Then fill me in."

"I want a bodyguard," she told him. "I want adventure. Before I married Henry, my specialty was pre-Columbian artifacts. I used to procure them for the museum. I'm on a mission to make a name for myself as a premier art dealer. I figure you'd be a good person to have along in a pinch, someone who knows his way around dangerous places."

"That's me. 007."

She smiled. "It might be good for you, Alec. To be with someone who doesn't find you the least attractive. It might build character."

He grinned, shaking his head, then reached into his backpack, suddenly needing to hold those KGB papers in his hands, his golden goose. He wanted to look them over knowing he already held his gold mine. *Fuck character.*

"That's right, Sydney. You go along and build my character." From the bottom pocket, he took out the Russian documents—the ones Dean White had kept so secret—files containing an analysis of an alien spacecraft. He wondered how much he could get for these babies. Forget the two million, he thought, opening the envelope. *Think tens of millions.*

But when he unfolded the papers, they were perfectly blank, except for a short note written in Allison's handwriting at the bottom of the first page.

There is in you the capacity to change. I will always believe that.

She'd tricked him. Allison had given him the Russian papers, and then, she'd stolen them back.

For a moment, he sat stunned. There wouldn't be any money now. Not from Reck and Kinnard—not for the Russian documents on the UFO.

"What is it?" Sydney asked. She glanced at the papers. "Bad news?"

But he shook his head. Because, the more he thought about it, the more it made him want to laugh. *Shit. She tricked me. Me.* And then, he did laugh. "Nothing, Sydney. Just another woman trying to improve my character."

He threw the papers into the air, letting them drift into the wind, away from the convertible. He slouched down in the seat, pulling the brim of his hat down lower, still laughing.

He said, "Punch it, Sydney. We got places to go, baby."

"Yes, Dean. I sent the papers along to Joystick."

Allison was leaning over, painting her toenails gold while talking on the phone. "Yes, you were right about Alec. I suppose I was emotionally involved. I thought . . ."

She sighed, thinking about the last year. It was a little sad, really. How it had turned out. But men like Russell and Alec, they simply didn't understand. They didn't have any power over her.

For Allison, there would always be one single love.

"Well, it doesn't matter," she said, putting the nail polish away. "Alec served his purpose. We have the right people working on the composite now. And once they find how to replicate the material, we'll be ready."

Ready to face the future and those who would come for them. There were people like Russell Reck and Joseph Kinnard who would try to take that technology away and keep it for their own purposes. But the Millennium Society would stand guard. Synthetic metals were for all of mankind . . . the key to interplanetary space travel.

She lay back on the bed, smiling. "Oh, Dean. What a glorious future it will be."

Cherish stared at the dirty socks on the carpet, the bedspread pulled halfway across the bed, puddling on Conor's side.

"Oh, yeah," she said. "I remember now." She'd raised her voice so Conor could hear her in the kitchen. "You're a slob."

She picked up the socks, holding them at arm's length, taking them with her into the kitchen. She was going to have a little chat with her man.

But when she stepped into the kitchen, she found Conor in his jeans, his chest and feet bare. He was staring at a simple sheet of paper, the document propped up against the sugar bowl. His reinstatement papers.

"But you're so cute and you're great in bed, so I'll adapt," she said, throwing the socks over her shoulder.

"What was that?" he asked, looking up for the first time.

"Nothing," she said, coming to sit on his lap, putting her arms around his neck. The bruise on his cheek had faded, but it still made her wince to look at it. Her shoulder was a little sore, but otherwise, she was completely healed. "What do you think about life now, Lieutenant-Colonel Mitchell?" she asked.

He put his arms around her waist. "I think life's good."

She nuzzled against him. It *was* good. Very good. Lebredo was helping out in the attorney general's investigation to prosecute both Reck and Kinnard. A surefire chance for promotion, he'd called it. And thanks to the evidence she and Conor had been able to put together, the prosecution began to look more damaging than mere misappropriation of funds for Kinnard's black programs. He and Russell Reck had committed murder, pure and simple.

Lebredo had turned out to be a real bulldog. He wasn't going to stop until he uncovered everything about Kinnard's black operations and who was running them. It made her feel creepy to think her government could be using her and others as Guinea pigs, infusing top-secret research into white programs.

"You know, Cher," Conor said. "When you talked about that white light on the plane. What was that about—that light?"

He asked the question in an overly casual voice. She could see something was bothering him. She frowned, thinking it had been rather weird, that light on the plane. She'd chalked it up to her relaxation exercise, but honestly, she'd never been able to repeat the experience. And then, there was the strange dream about Eric telling her the fullerenes where disintegrating. What about that?

She shook her head. "I don't know. Why?" She looked at him suspiciously. "Did you see it?"

He shook his head. "Not a light, no." He glanced over her shoulder, thinking about it, like maybe he had something more to say. And then he admitted, "But I did have these flashes." He frowned. "When I was trying to land at El Toro, parts of the past just flashed in my head, getting mixed up with the present. It's how I figured out Alec was one of Kinnard's operatives. I remembered something he said right before the crash of the first prototype. I realized he'd known all along the onboard computer had been rigged."

"My mother would say it's our subconscious at work."

And why not? she thought. Cherish was an engineer; it wasn't beyond the pale that she would have figured out the composite was deteriorating, then simply dreamed up that conversation with Eric. After all, there was no way Eric could have *known* the material was faulty or that Reck planned to steal it from him. Not then, anyway. Not on the plane. Those couldn't have been his real words to her from across the aisle.

She smiled, trying to reassure Conor. "You probably knew all along that Alec was responsible. You just buried it in your subconscious and these flashes were just how it came out because you were under pressure and the situations were so similar. I should ask my mother, really."

They both looked at each other.

"Then again," she said. "Maybe not."

"Atta girl." He pulled up a piece of paper from the table and showed it to her. It wasn't the reinstatement document he'd been staring at, but a fax. "Joystick sent this. Katya claims someone sent her the Russian papers, after all. She's pretty excited. She wants me to help her work on it."

"You're going to Siberia?"

He shook his head. "Nope. From here, at the University. It will be a sort of cooperative effort. I think I'll do it, too. In fact, it sounds pretty exciting."

"More exciting than being a test pilot?" she asked.

He put the fax back on the table and reached around her with both hands. "Well, maybe it's not space travel, but yeah. I think discovering a synthetic metal that could revolutionize the world is pretty damn exciting."

"Good answer," she said, hugging him back. She rested her cheek on his shoulder. "Because, I was thinking, if you're never going to get around to asking me to marry you again, I could just—"

Suddenly, it was there. Right under her nose. A little box he'd pulled off the table. *Ta dah!*

Funny, how she hadn't noticed it before. In fact, it was kind of cute, how he'd lined up the fax, the reinstatement papers, and the tiny box.

"Tiffany's," she said, recognizing the distinctive pale blue. "I'm impressed."

"You're supposed to be."

She opened the box. Inside was a wide gold band, the edges rounded for a comfortable fit. A round, brilliant-cut diamond, possibly more than a carat, was set in the gold. "Not as good as the one Pablo gave me," she said, trying not to cry, she was so happy. "But it will do."

"Geena helped me pick it out."

She smiled, putting on the ring. She thought she'd detected a meltdown in Geena's attitude. She held out her hand, admiring the diamond. She fiddled with it a little, giving him time. But Conor wasn't catching on.

"Okay, Conor," she said. "I'm waiting for the words. And here's a hint. It doesn't involve anything close to, 'okay' "

Conor picked up on cue. "This is where I'm supposed to

say something romantic like, you're the structure and I'm the composite. Let's make something beautiful together?''

The ring was really catching the early morning light. It was absolutely gorgeous. ''Well. Maybe you could work on that a little.''

She hadn't told him about the baby. Well, she *had* told him— on the plane, when she'd seen that light. But Conor had been pretty distracted at the time.

At the hospital, while they'd tended to her bullet wound, she'd asked for one of those nifty urine tests. Bingo. So, the last week, after Conor had moved in, she'd given notice at Marquis, admitting at last that it had never been in her heart to become an engineer. She'd just followed along with her father and brothers. Actually, she didn't know what she wanted to do with the rest of her life. And, it was rather exciting.

But she really ought to tell Conor about the baby. She thought he would be pleased. Heck, he wasn't getting any younger. It was time to get a move on.

Turning the ring on her finger, she felt something a little rough. She frowned, taking it off. Holding it up, she peeked inside the rim.

He kissed her neck, whispering, ''And here I thought the ring would say it all.''

She could just make out some fancy writing. She squinted, taking a closer look. Sure enough. Inscribed inside were two words: *Perfect Timing*.

When she read it, she smiled. ''Oh, yes.''

She hugged him, so happy it actually hurt. Life was good. Life was real good. ''Conor. Darling,'' she whispered, having her own little surprise. ''Let me tell you about the concept of perfect timing. Really, you're going to love this. . . .''

ROMANCE FROM FERN MICHAELS

DEAR EMILY   (0-8217-4952-8, $5.99)

WISH LIST   (0-8217-5228-6, $6.99)

AND IN HARDCOVER:

VEGAS RICH   (1-57566-057-1, $25.00)